Siblings of War

Chanochi Zaks

Producer & International Distributor
eBookPro Publishing
www.ebook-pro.com

Siblings of War: A Captivating Family Survival WW2 Novel Based on a True Story
Chanochi Zaks

Translation: Seree Zohar
Contact: chanochizaks@gmail.com

ISBN 9798878746755

This book is dedicated to

Our grandmother Yoheved and grandfather Hanokh Zaks

And our parents:
Yisrael & Haiya Zaks (Beniek & Haicha)
Volf & Hannah Zaks (Vilek & Hanka)
Miriam & Joseph Mondry (Manya & Yossek)
Yossef & Tzilla Zaks (Tzilla & Yossek)
Batya & Yehuda Levi (Basha & Labek)
Tonia & Avraham Zaks (Tonya & Romek)

May their names and memories be blessed forever

SIBLINGS OF WAR

A Captivating Family Survival WW2 Novel
Based on a True Story

CHANOCHI ZAKS

CONTENTS

GERMANY
Bremen
Bergen – Belsen
Hannover
Berlin
Langenstien
Leipzig
Ludwigsdo
Dresden
Görlitz
Buchenwald
Frankfurt an Main
Praha
Nurnberg
Stuttgart

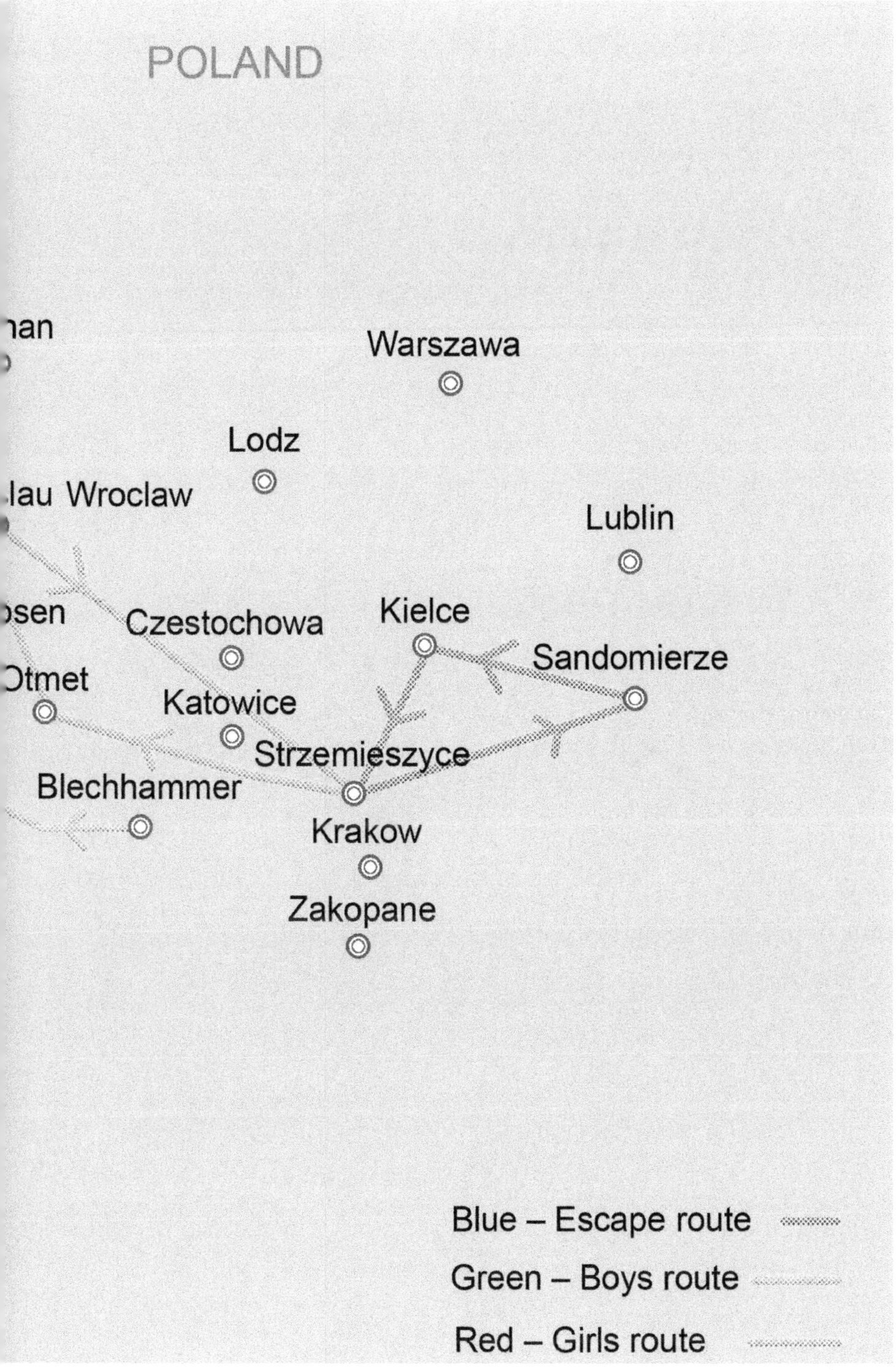

POLAND
ıan
Warszawa
Lodz
ılau Wroclaw
Lublin
ısen
Czestochowa
Kielce
Sandomierze
Otmet
Katowice
Strzemieszyce
Blechhammer
Krakow
Zakopane
Blue – Escape route
Green – Boys route
Red – Girls route

FACT: STRANGER THAN FICTION

What you're about to read is the remarkable and unbelievable story of the Zaks family. All the events here actually took place. But this is no biography. This is a literary novel in which I've occasionally allowed my imagination to lead me along hidden paths.

My late mother would say, "If the Zaks family had been accepted into the Convent of Silence, they'd have excelled there." There's no better description of the family than my mother's. The Zaks were never big on talking, which made composing the narrative so much more difficult. Only in their later years were we, the younger generation, able to eke out a little more detail from them about their life events.

There is also no better description of the plight of the Zaks family, like that of so many others, than the titles used for two sequential chapters, derived from the book of Job 10:21-22: *[21] … a land of darkness and the shadow of death; [22] …a land […] without any order, and where the light is as darkness.*

Needing to fill in the blanks that the abyss of disremembering and their tendency to silence had made necessary, I gave my imagination a certain degree of freedom, but being so familiar with the people involved, I made sure to preserve these heroes' spirits and characters.

This book is the Zaks family narrative, and from it our children and grandchildren can learn and pass this knowledge on to future generations. And that's why the protagonists' names are true. Every family member in every generation can identify with the story, finding their mother or mother, grandfather or grandmother, in it.

Yes, the events described here which occurred during the Holocaust are disturbing, but the people directly involved were infused with belief and shaped an optimistic, hopeful story. Our grandfather Hanokh, a precious man, endowed us with his heritage: stay together always! The singular meaning is, "Never break apart from each other," and those are the wishes the family aimed to fulfill. It didn't always work out, but they worked hard at achieving that goal, of remaining united until the longed-for liberation.

This is a story of a stunning win which begins with tremendous sacrifice for his brothers' and sister's sakes, and ends with *Aliyah*, the word used to describe immigration by Jews specifically to Israel, where they establish wonderful families and help build the country.

The Zaks tribe, numbering 115 in May 2020, are the offspring of our dear *Saba* (grandfather) Hanokh and *Savta* (grandmother) Yoheved, heads of our lineage.

Hanokh (or Chanochi in its current Anglicized spelling)

THE BINDNG OF YITZHAK

Four siblings stood in the forest, surrounded by tall trees and a thick hedge. They stood on a path they knew well and had walked often enough, but they'd never gone as far as they did this time, getting further and further into the forest.

Suddenly Yisrael noticed that Yitzhak wasn't with them.

"Where is he? Did anyone see where he went?" he anxiously asked.

Yisrael, Volf, Yossef and Avraham looked around, looked at each other, and began shouting together. "Yitzhak, Yitzhak!" To no avail. No one answered. A disturbing silence filled the air. "Where could he have disappeared to?" Volf asked in a shaky voice. "Let's look for him," Yisrael, the oldest, suggested. "Maybe he's at the lake?"

Every so often the brothers would play on the lake's shore. "But why would he go there alone? We were here together in the forest. What happened to him?" the brothers' questions tumbled over each other. Shaking, pale, the younger brothers' eyes filled with tears.

Yitzhak had disappeared.

They were lost for answers and had no idea what they could do other than continue calling out his name. The call of a wild animal came from the forest. They moved closer to each other, looking in the direction of the sound. At some distance they saw two shining green eyes locked on them. Trembling, they froze in their place as the eyes slowly drew closer. Fear paralyzed them.

They were so gripped by fear that they forgot about Yitzhak. Would they now disappear too, like their brother?

A wolf stood there. In their despairing imagination, it seemed far larger than it actually was. This wasn't the first time they'd seen wolves in the forest, but they'd always seen them in a pack. They would always quickly pass the pack and had never really feared them. This time was different. A lone wolf, particularly large, its underbelly covered in gray fur, its back gleaming white, not the usual brown. The white fur shone, accentuating its green eyes, sparkling, piercing their souls. The wolf growled again.

The same thought raced through all their minds: had the wolf devoured their brother? The scary beast simply gazed straight at them, as though understanding their question, locking its green eyes on them. They, in turn, were frozen in their despair, unable to move. It growled again, this time stronger and longer. Could it be a cry for help? Did it want to scare them? The wolf took a step towards them, a long howl coming from its throat. That broke the invisible chain binding their legs. Instantly they began racing home, startled by the great beast.

Five brothers had set out for the forest.

Four returned home.

Yitzhak was gone.

Their father Hanokh was waiting for them. They said a quick hello and went to their rooms, praying that he wouldn't ask, that they wouldn't need to tell. He followed them. "Where's Yitzhak?" he asked. They said nothing. "Miriam, Batya," Hanokh called out to the sisters, asking again, "Yitzhak? Where's Yitzhak? Why isn't he here with you?" His voice broke. "Where's my little boy?" he shouted again and again, directing his question to Yisrael, the firstborn. "Where is he? What's happened to him?"

The brothers looked down when Yisrael answered, his voice a whisper, barely audible. "Yitzhak disappeared in the forest. We were playing and next thing, he wasn't there. He must've gone somewhere else. We searched everywhere but couldn't find anything. And then a wolf appeared."

"Wolf?" Hanokh screamed. "Where did the wolf come from?"

Yisrael muttered. "He was just... there. We heard him growling and got frightened. We stood there holding on to each other and didn't know what to do. The wolf kept staring at us as though it knew something, as though it understood we were searching for Yitzhak, as though showing us that it knew what had happened to Yitzhak. But then it howled really, really loudly and we got so scared we raced home without Yitzhak."

Their father gazed at them, tears falling from his eyes as he said sternly, "You never come home without Yitzhak. Is that clear? Go back, now, before it's dark, and take your sisters with you. Six of you is a decent search party. I'm not healthy enough, I can't go with you, but all of you, go now, right away, to the forest and don't dare come home without Yitzhak. Is that clear? Yisrael, you're the oldest, and you're in charge. Look for Yitzhak until you find him."

The six of them set out, fear filling their eyes. They walked quickly, staying close to each other, trembling from the cold and fear. Yisrael instructed, "Let's go back to where we saw the wolf and then continue from there. Maybe we need to go towards the lake, or look along the paths. It's just not possible that Yitzhak would not stay on a path."

They reached the place where they'd last seen their brother and had also encountered the wolf, and stood there helplessly on a path that led deeper into the forest and which they'd never taken before. "Let's call his name really loudly," Yisrael suggested, "and shouting out his name will also help us stop being so afraid. Maybe the wolf will be scared of us instead. We need to stay in sight of one another, and not split up so that no one else disappears, G-d forbid. That would be an even worse catastrophe. Shout loudly. That's the main thing. Yitzhak's surely thinking we're out looking for him. If we shout, and then I'll signal when to stop, we'll also be able to hear if Yitzhak is shouting back. Maybe he fell and is hurt. Maybe he broke a leg, or fainted somewhere... We'll alternate between shouting and silence."

"Yitzhak... Yitzhak..." they called, over and over. Not even an echo returned.

Then they stood in silence at Yisrael's signal. Nothing but more silence.

The forest's silence enveloped them. Their shouts began pointing to some terrible thing having occurred.

Two shining eyes gazed at them from the forest.

"Look," Volf said to Avraham, "the wolf is back."

Once again, the wolf showed itself, its fur a shade of pale gray, its leg muscles powerful, its head very large, its teeth sharp, revealed each time it threw its head back to howl. Shining, its green eyes roused the siblings' fear, yet the message they conveyed was not clear. Six siblings moved closer, clutching each other, gazing at the wolf. It howled briefly and shook its head as though beckoning them to follow. It took a step back, shaking its head again. This time they saw it clearly but couldn't believe their eyes. The girls stood still in fear.

"I understand it," said Volf, "it's saying we should follow it."

"What do you mean, you 'understand' it?" Yisrael asked skeptically.

His brother answered. "I'm also 'wolf,' that's my name. 'Volf.' And it's a well-known saying," he added, purposely playing on the renowned proverb, 'that a wolf is humane to a fellow-wolf. '"

After briefly discussing this with each other, Yisrael and Volf, the two oldest, decided to follow the wolf and instructed the two youngest brothers, Yossef and Avraham, and their two sisters to follow, but at a safe distance. Yisrael emphasized, "Don't get too close but there's no doubt the wolf's trying to tell us something."

The wolf headed off deeper into the forest in a direction that was unclear to the siblings. It stopped, howled briefly, and shook its head again. Their fear began to dissipate. Volf whispered. "It wants us to come. Let's keep following. He'll find Yitzhak for us." The wolf increased its pace; with the six of them following. They wondered about shouting for Yitzhak again but Yisrael instructed them to stay silent. "We mustn't scare the wolf," he warned. "It's a predator and could become dangerous if scared." And so, they walked, faster and faster, until they reached a small, familiar lake. The wolf howled long and loudly, then disappeared as quickly as it had appeared

Yitzhak's body floated in the lake. Shocked into silence, the siblings wondered how it had happened. Yitzhak was dead; a wild wolf had led them to the body. How did it know what they were searching for? Was it their protective shield? In silence they gazed at the body. Yisrael was the first to come to his senses. "We need to take him home," he said.

They dragged their brother's body from the icy waters. They weren't sure if the tremendous weight was due to Yitzhak's wet clothes, or the burden of his death on their hearts. They all felt responsible for this death; they would never be free of their guilt. Five boys had set out together, but Yitzhak hadn't come back alive. Now four boys and their two sisters carried his corpse.

The closer they got to home, the heavier the weight became.

And the wolf, so scary, and of such unusually colored fur: where had it come from? Had it really guided them or had they just imagined the idea of it leading them to Yitzhak? They had no answers, nor did they have the strength to carry Yitzhak all the way home to their father. They had reached their street in their town of Strzemieszyce. The house was not far off. But they were afraid: what would their father say? On the other hand, they also felt that they'd obeyed his wishes: they'd brought Yitzhak home even though they had failed terribly in bringing him back alive. Although they could feel their strength dissipating quickly, they continued until they were home.

Hanokh peered at them. Their mother Yoheved broke into heart-piercing sobs. Hanokh instructed them to take Yitzhak into their bedroom. They did, laying the body on their father's bed. Their father, who suffered from a heart condition, studied them, his sons and daughters, before speaking in a quiet tone that did not conceal his fury. "This is our Binding of Isaac. But we did not manage to keep him alive, as Avraham our Forefather did. Our forefather did not harm the lad, placing all his faith in G-d. I am asking you: believe in G-d, but never, ever leave one of you behind. Ever! Then G-d will be with us."

They stood together in silence, six siblings, their father and mother, gazing at Yitzhak.

A wolf's howl came from somewhere. But they weren't at all sure whether their imagination was playing tricks on them or whether the large wolf with light gray fur was out there, in the forest.

ESCAPADES

Friday, September 1st, 1939, was a terrible day. War was declared although it didn't really surprise anyone. The flow of refugees grew thicker and longer. Streets in the southwest Polish town of Strzemieszyce filled with people fleeing. The Zaks family sat in their home, gazing through the windows at the human flood moving down the street. Roaring deafeningly, Warplanes flying above weren't bombing but definitely scared the family. The younger family members crouched in fear. The older ones, watching, tried to estimate the Warplanes' destination.

The street was crowded. The Zakses knew most of the people passing through: family, friends, including many from adjacent towns. A mass of people was heading east.

With worried faces, the family sat around the large dining table in the kitchen. It had seen happier times when the large, cohesive family had sat together on Friday nights celebrating the *Shabbat*, or Sabbath meal, or on Jewish festivals. Despite the despondent mood and fear of the future, Hanokh and Yoheved had kept to their custom, the family seated together for this Shabbat meal, too. The braided challah breads were baking in the oven as they did every Friday. Food simmered in pots on the stove, filling their home with wonderful aromas. The chicken soup had come to a boil, enticing the familiar senses of the waiting family. But unlike other Shabbat evenings, no one had an appetite. The house was filled with the scent of home-made cooking but outside there was the smell of war. And the Zakses: what did they do? Feeling hopeless, they sat staring at each other as though an answer would present itself.

For a year now Yisrael, the oldest son, and his wife Haiya had been living in the adjacent town of Sławków. "We're going to flee too," Yisrael said. "Haiya and I have already decided: we're going east. I suggest we all go together. During the war's early days things will be a total mess. No one will have any idea of what's going on. That's precisely the best time to find somewhere new. We'll go with the crowd. The longer we wait, the worse things will get for us. I suggest we set out on Saturday night, once the Shabbat is over. We have enough cash; we have belongings. We can organize quickly. We'll get by along the way with the money we have, but we have to go right away because in a few days' time, the overcrowding on the routes will be much, much worse. Together with another few people from Sławków we've already bought a wagon and two horses from a villager. True, I don't have too much experience as a wagoneer but I'm sure we can get pretty far with horses and a wagon. We'll be picking them up tomorrow."

His twenty-four-year-old brother Volf and fifteen-year-old Avraham nodded in agreement as they turned to look at their father, waiting to hear what he'd say. He spoke in his slow, quiet but firm tone. "I'm not fleeing. My home is my fortress. I won't feel safe on the roads. In this town people know me. I'm not a healthy man, and I won't be able to do a long tough trip. I'm not telling you what to do but remember my wishes: stay together. Don't forget your dear brother Yossef in the Polish army. He will surely come home at some point, and someone needs to be here. Mother and I will stay at home."

Miriam, now nineteen, and Batya, aged sixteen, hesitated for a moment or two before making their decision. Her voice trembling, Miriam spoke up. "I'm staying home to help Mama and Papa."

Batya continued. "Papa needs me. Someone with a heart problem can't be left alone and Mama can't do everything on her own. He needs his medications. He needs rest. We have a large shop and it has to stay open to support us. I imagine that in a few days, things will get back to normal and we can continue selling our goods. The city's residents will stay, and they'll be needing what we have. I'm staying to manage the shop and help Papa."

Volf, who also worked in the family shop, added his thoughts. "I'm joining Avraham and Haiya. You'll do fine without me in the business. We'll try to get to a calmer place in the east, maybe Russia, and find a way to let you know where, so you can join us. Maybe we'll find a better place to live. After all, the war can't go on for too long. The first to reach a safe haven will be better off than others. We'll be the pioneers going out to look for something safer than our town before it gets worse, which I'm pretty sure it will."

Hanokh's face reddened in anger. He slammed his fist down on the table. "I've always told you it's better to stay together. I'm asking you not to leave. Together, here, we'll be a lot stronger."

Yisrael countered, keeping his tone calm and staying respectful to his father. "Papa, we have to look at the future, at this reality. We're near the border. The Germans will be here soon because the Polish army's worthless. I was in the army up until two years ago and know what goes on. The Germans are equipped with tanks and Warplanes and will beat our army in no time. In a few days there won't be an independent country, there won't be a Poland. We'll be under German rule. And add to that the fact that we're Jews… we don't have a future here. We've got to think about what will happen next, Papa."

But Yoheved stood firmly by her husband. "Papa can't walk. He wouldn't survive that kind of journey. He'd die along the way. We're staying put."

A Warplane passed overhead, rattling the windows. A deafening noise was heard. Glass shattered. The family raced to their front window. Horrified, they saw that the house across the street had disappeared. All that remained was a cloud of dust above a plume of thick black smoke, and a circle of stones much like a tombstone. The building had collapsed, smothering its residents. The blood drained from their faces: they gazed at the debris. The girls broke into tears. Hanokh coughed from the smoke entering their home's broken window, but remained steadfast. "I believe in G-d. By his will I live, and by his will I die. Either way, I'm staying here."

But Yisrael wasn't ready to give in. The shocking images only reinforced his view. "See? That's what we'll get if we stay here. Sunday morning I'm leaving with Haiya. We're going back to Sławków now to get organized and will come back here tonight. Who's joining me?" Volf and Avraham got up from their seats and went to stand with Yisrael. Sobbing, the girls stayed next to their parents.

The family had split. Hanokh clamped his lips together, forcing himself not to shout. He walked to the door, unexpectedly slamming his head against the doorpost. Red with fury, he went off to pray, wrapping himself in his tallit, the traditional prayer shawl, as though taking refuge in it. He needed to speak to G-d.

Although she understood his anger, Yoheved tried soothing Hanokh. "Just accept it, Hanokh. They're grown up and want to build their lives."

From inside the tallit wrapped around him, Hanokh answered. "But we won't be together, Yoheved. We must never separate. We have to be together. They'll see I was right. I told them that when Yitzhak died. They know they must never leave anyone behind, and nonetheless they're leaving us here. Us, and the girls. No, Yoheved, I'm not moving from here. Here I'll live and here I'll die. You'll see. They'll be back after they admit they made a mistake." Hanokh paused. "Let me pray a bit, Yoheved. Maybe that'll help me. I'm truly furious with Yisrael, who's misleading his brothers. If not for that, they'd all stay. But I can't answer as to what's the best to do. The future will answer that."

Once again Warplanes flew overhead and bombed. Another building was destroyed, going up in smoke. Yisrael whispered to Volf. "That's what will happen to us here. We've got to get out otherwise we're all gone."

Without basements or bomb shelters, all they could do was pray that the next bomb wouldn't fall on their home. Outside, the flow of people continued down the street, though faces were now showing panic and fear. Most were on foot. Very few were on horse-drawn wagons.

It was a difficult Shabbat. The house was silent. Each of the boys packed a single, small bag. Yisrael left and came back later that evening with the wagon and two horses. The Zaks family were not big on talk, but their silence can fume.

Once the Shabbat had ended, Yisrael and his father sat down in the kitchen to talk. Hanokh had come to realize that the decision had been made. He was angry but tried to keep himself in check. “Yisrael, my dear son, yes, I’m angry. But more than that, here my son Yitzhak is buried. Your brother. I can’t leave him alone there in the cemetery. You remember what I told you when you all went to search for him? Never leave anyone behind. Even though I’m angry, I understand. I know you’ll come back safely and I hope it will be very soon. Remember, my son, our home is our fortress. In the end, it’s the safest place.”

Yisrael hugged him. “Papa, we’ve got to try, because doing nothing is worse. We’re young, we’ll survive, and we’ll get some place better for us all. I’m sure of that. I’d just like to ask you for one thing, Papa: don’t be angry with us. We can’t endure your anger.”

“I can’t control my anger, son. It’s how I feel. My heart tells me you’re making a mistake, but go, and may G-d watch over you.”

Hanokh slipped his hand into his pocket and drew out an envelope thick with banknotes. He placed it in Yisrael’s hand, hugged him warmly and burst into tears. Then he moved away from his son and went to his bedroom.

On Sunday morning, September 3rd, twelve people sat on the wagon parked outside Hanokh’s and Yoheved’s home. All were from Sławków. They were only slightly familiar with one another. Yisrael, Haiya, Volf and Avraham joined them. Batya and Miriam sobbed, finding it hard to say goodbye. Yoheved and Hanokh didn’t go out into the street, but watched from a safe distance behind a window. The boys looked up at their home’s windows above the shop, studying their parents’ worn faces. A squadron of German Warplanes flew over, dropping a flurry of bombs over the town’s peripheral streets. Startled, the horses broke into a trot. The town, shrouded in smoke, was quickly left behind.

EASTBOUND WAGON

The horses galloped. They couldn't be stopped. Nor could they be controlled. The Warplane engines. The bombs. The shouts coming from behind them. The noise made the horses jittery. They raced east down the road. Yisrael put all his strength into keeping control of the reins, but the horses were not obeying.

Sixteen men and women were seated on the wagon. The passengers were having a hard time keeping in their places. They grasped the wagon, and clung to each other. Eventually, the horses started to calm down.

Haiya sat behind Yisrael. Volf and Avraham sat next Yisrael, who was clutching the reins. Haiya noticed two other women sitting close to each other: the Zonnenshine family's mother and daughter. They lived near them in Sławków. She assumed that Mr. Zonnenshine was also on the wagon. Volf, always the measured voice among the siblings, looked behind at the distancing town. He saw the smoke, and wondered whether those still there would remain unharmed. He held some reservations about fleeing but from the moment he boarded the wagon, there was no going back.

At fifteen, Avraham was a strong, healthy, young man who matured overnight. His mischievous boyhood face took on a serious air and in a matter of minutes, had become the face of a young man aware of the hardships he and his family would be facing. He trusted his older brothers, knowing he could rely on them as needed. Avraham decided to sit next to Volf, leaning against him as he remembered their father's warning: "Never leave anyone behind. Stay together at all costs." Seated in the wagon left no room for doubt. They were heading east and would get as far from the town as they could.

Volf and Avraham turned to look at the others. They were also familiar with the Zonnenshines from synagogue prayers. The mother and daughter sat quietly, their eyes darting back and forth in fear, their faces pale. They were probably thinking about the home they'd left behind. Several other unfamiliar young men were in the wagon. One was particularly well-built and aroused their curiosity. "Who is he?" Volf whispered to Avraham, "do you know him?" "No," Avraham answered. Yisrael supplied the information, whispering, "He joined us on the way between Sławków and Strzemieszyce. We did him a favor and let him join."

Meanwhile Yisrael had regained control over the horses and brought them to a gentle halt. After an hour of fast galloping, everyone was happy to stand and stretch their legs. Yisrael tied the reins to a tree. The horses happily munched on grass. He wondered where he'd find water for them: completely inexperienced in handling the animals, he felt responsible for them. As the horses rested, Yisrael decided to call the travelers together at the roadside.

"We'll drive towards Lublin, as close as we can to the Russian border. I really want us to get there as quickly as possible. We saw all the others fleeing in that direction, more or less. We should get there as fast as we can, and certainly before the Germans. We've got another three hundred kilometers or so, which will take ten days. It's going to be tough, but we'll do it, I'm sure."

Yisrael glanced around. "Do we all know each other? We should at least know each other's names. We'll be together for some of the hardest days of our lives until we reach safety." Clearly no one had any idea who the large man was. All eyes turned to him first. But he didn't look at anyone and simply said, loudly and clearly, "I came from another city, Bendin. My name is Pollack and more than that no one needs to know, it's not your business." He looked away, making it clear he was not to be questioned.

With his eyes, Yisrael signaled to his wife and brother to come closer. He put his hand into his pocket and drew out the envelope. "Papa gave me money when we left. There's a lot here and it has to keep us going for a long time. I've split it in advance into four envelopes. Look after it well. Keep it close to your body. I don't like the look of this Pollack. I've a hunch he's going to give us trouble." They hid the envelopes in their clothes and headed back to the group. Pollack watched, suspicious.

An ear-piercing noise shook the surroundings. German Warplanes made a low sweep over them. Pulling wildly, the horses managed to free themselves from the tree and set off at a gallop. The wagon bounced uncontrollably behind them. Suitcases and bags flew off in all directions. But fearing the Warplanes, everyone was face down on the ground. Terrible cries could be heard everywhere.

Avraham roared. "The horses! They've gone! With the wagon!" Yisrael grabbed Haiya, Volf and Avraham. They made an initial start after the animals, but they struggled to keep up. Breathing hard and continuing to pursue, the four eventually managed to gently approach the horses, which had meanwhile stopped by a stream and were gulping water happily. Turning their heads, the siblings saw the rest of the passengers racing after them, gathering their belongings as they went.

Despair filled the motley crowd. Clearly the journey wasn't going to be easy, and they'd barely gotten started. The travelers put their belongings back on the wagon; Yisrael took a firm grip on the reins. Janusz sat down next to him. He was the same age as the boys' father, a familiar neighbor, and suggested helping with the animals, claiming experience, and that he'd swap places with Yisrael as needed.

Seated on the wagon, the passengers were silent, their eyes glued to the floor. The horses trotted on slowly; Yisrael didn't urge them on faster, wanting to save their strength. So far, they'd made about ten kilometers. That's very slow, Yisrael noted to himself. The Germans could easily overtake us. We haven't come across any yet, he thought, nor have we come across the Polish army retreating, but trouble will come for sure and we all need to keep our strength up.

As evening fell, the group stopped at an old wooden bridge, its posts lodged in the shallow creek. The railings were so low that it was easy to jump over and into the creek. Yisrael spoke to the group.

"We'll go over the bridge and continue. I want us to keep going through the night. Try to sleep in the wagon. The routes will be less crowded later. Most of the people fleeing will be stopping for the night so we'll gain some valuable time and distance."

Pollack opposed. "I want to sleep and I don't agree to continuing. We'll stop here."

Yisrael tried calming him, convincing him; nothing worked. They crossed the bridge and prepared to sleep on the ground. Exhaustion overwhelmed them. Avraham fell asleep too, but Yisrael couldn't. He chatted with Volf and Haiya, who'd begun to have doubts. "Maybe you really should have stayed home with your sisters and parents?" she wondered aloud. "I think me being here will make things harder for you, and it'll get very tough on me too."

Convinced they'd taken the best decision, Yisrael tried to assure her. "We've only just started out. True, it's going to be tough, but we've got a goal. We'll get to a safer place and then we'll bring everyone else over. It's the best way.

Volf, deep in thought, remarked in a quiet tone, not wanting to wake anyone. "You can never know. Remember what Papa told us: never separate. Meanwhile let's go on and maybe some news will come from one of the fronts, which will give us a better idea of how the war is developing."

Lying on ground moist from the dew, Avraham thought about his childhood: his happy times in "heder" where Jewish studies were taught to mischievous little kids, and during which the rabbi laughed a lot with them. He thought about the prank that Yossef, his brother, who was the biggest mischief-maker of them all, had carried out, salting the Rabbi's soup so much that the Rabbi vomited violently, accusing his wife, and saying he'd divorce her over the terrible food. Now Yossef was serving in the Polish army. Avraham chuckled quietly and fell asleep, dreaming of his parents, especially his mother, whom he loved deeply. It occurred to him, in the dream, that he'd left her behind in the town. In the dream she hugged him close. It felt real, as though someone was enveloping his body. He forced himself awake. Pollack was rummaging through Avraham's clothing! Pollack's right hand was covering Avraham's mouth to prevent him from screaming. Clearly the big man was after Avraham's money. Putting all his strength into the move, Avraham kicked him hard in the groin. Pollack, taken by surprise, let go. Avraham rolled onto his side, Pollack on top of him. But that was enough to let Avraham shout for help.

The brothers heard Avraham's calls. In the dark they could see him fighting someone. Instantly they were on their feet and raced over to him. Pollack was lying on top of their youngest brother, pinning him down, trying to rob Avraham. Yisrael and Volf slammed into the man, pummeling him mercilessly, kicking, punching, until he pulled away. Startled, they gazed at each other: they'd never hit anyone before.

Now everyone was awake. Everyone saw the three brothers standing up for each other. Avraham stood and kicked Pollack's butt. Volf turned to the others.

"Look at that, will you? Pollack tried stealing money from us. We're banishing him from the wagon. He will *not* continue with us. That's the only way to overcome external enemies."

The travelers nodded in agreement. Yisrael suggested moving on right away. Everyone agreed. Fifteen people climbed onto the wagon. Pollack was left behind, bruised and beaten. Avraham threw Pollack's suitcase at him.

Having drunk their full and rested a while, the horses were ready to move on.

AND ANOTHER FAREWELL

Night fell upon the forest. Yisrael and his brothers decided to stop and let everyone sleep. Like other refugees, they settled down for the night in one of the public parks in the small town of Nowy Ujków. Still unharmed by German bombs, the town's residents offered people passing through handouts of food and drink. Haiya and Yisrael talked quietly. Haiya sought diplomatic words that would not hurt her husband's feelings but made it clear that she couldn't continue.

"Yisrael, you know I've always done what you wanted. I've always supported your decisions, but I don't have the strength to go on. I'm sorry. But I just can't," she said as tears fell onto her cheeks. Yisrael said nothing, trying to digest his wife's message as she stroked his hand gently. "I'm seriously considering going back home. I spoke with Mrs. Zonnenshine and her daughter yesterday and they also want to go back. We aren't capable of carrying on."

Yisrael heard. His thoughts weighed heavily on his mind. "I don't know what to say," he whispered to her, his voice trembling. "I truly believe we should continue, because really, we have no choice. I'm asking you, Haiya, just a few more kilometers and let's see how things stand. I'm hoping that luck will bring us better opportunities. I believe things will improve if we just stick to the plan."

Crying, Haiya could not be persuaded. "I'm also missing my home," she said, "our bedroom, my kitchen. My peace and quiet. If my fate is to suffer, better to suffer in a familiar place, in my own home. I can't keep up this wandering. You're determined to keep going, and I understand, but I'm not cut out for this. If you and your brothers find a place we all can be, send me a message and I'll come and we'll be reunited."

For Yisrael that was too much. He was bone-tired, and his soul was too strained, to find the words that would change her mind. In his heart he knew she'd already made her decision to return. All he could think of saying was "We'll go to sleep now, Haiya. Let's see what tomorrow brings us."

Early in the morning, an hour before sunrise, they woke up and set out. Haiya sat silently behind her husband, her eyes glued to his back as though trying to pierce his obstinate armor. Yisrael sat, determined, reins in hand. The horses trotted lazily. Here and there people walked, fleeing like them, determined to reach a safer place. It was their sixth day of flight. They had covered eighty kilometers. To Yisrael, that was very slow progress.

Another creek, a tributary of the Vistula River, had to be crossed. The creek wasn't broad at this location, and it being the end of summer, was also fairly shallow. They kept moving forward until they reached a stone bridge. The horses stopped. Janusz tried goading them on. Unsuccessfully. The horses would not move forward, despite whistles and the whip crackling in the air: Janusz was too gentle to crack the whip against the horses' flanks. He pulled and tugged, talking to them constantly. "Come, dear horse, listen to me. Come and cross the bridge with me. We need to leave this place quickly." But the horses stood their ground, their hooves lodged obstinately in the earth.

Having dozed off in the wagon, the travelers weren't even aware that the horses had stopped. Silence filled the air. As the first rays of light began to show, the horses backed up, whinnying loudly in fear, lifting the wagon, and causing the travelers to be rolled off. Only Janusz and Yisrael were able to stay in their seats, grasping the reins hard as they tried to regain control.

Volf and Avraham found themselves on the earth to the wagon's right. They gazed towards the bridge. And couldn't believe their eyes. Sparkling ahead were two green eyes. The sun's early rays caused the creatures eyes to glint.

As though hypnotized, the two brothers stared at the wolf; it stared right back at them, positioned like a sentry at the bridge's entrance and preventing the horses from moving forward. Yisrael also saw it from his seat on the wagon. Avraham and Volf stood, unable to take a step further. The wolf stared at them for a long time, then turned and hurried away, letting out a long howl before disappearing among the trees lining the creek.

"Did you see what I saw? Or am I imagining it?" Volf whispered to his oldest brother. "I saw, I saw," Yisrael answered, simultaneously enchanted and fearful. Janusz never saw a thing: he was completely focused on trying to calm the horses from whatever had riled them. The other passengers still lay on the ground, some bleeding from the impact. Others fingered their arms and legs to see just how badly they'd been hurt.

A tremendous explosion tore through the morning's silence. The sky flashed red, then filled with thick smoke. Stones hurtled through the air, landing on the people who were prone on the ground. No bridge. Gone, collapsed into the creek. The travelers looked again, in disbelief. On the opposite bank, Polish soldiers rubbed their palms in joy. Behind the veil of smoke they turned and moved east. If the Polish army was going to retreat, it was going to blow the bridges up as it went. Standing next to each other, knees quaking, Avraham, Volf and Yisrael gazed at the ruins. None doubted that they'd just been saved from certain death by horses too scared to cross because the wolf had come to guide them once again. Slowly, quietly, Volf spoke.

"It saved us. Once again, the wolf gave us a sign. It comes when needed, then disappears..."

A heart-wrenching cry brought them back to reality. The Zonnenshine women wept bitterly. "Father's dead. Father died!" Everyone ran over to Mr. Zonnenshine, who lay unmoving on the ground, his head bleeding profusely. He wasn't breathing; his wife fainted into Haiya's arms as the daughter cried. "Father's dead. Our father's dead."

Mrs. Zonnenshine came to. Haiya did her best to soothe the two women's sorrow. Others moved aside, shocked at this sudden change, asking themselves what might happen next. Should they keep pushing ahead? What should they do with the body? Yisrael suggested placing it on the wagon. "We won't leave him here on the open road. We must bury him. Let's look for the best place we can."

Carefully, together, the men raised Zonnenshine's corpse onto the wagon, covering him with a coat. His wife and daughter walked next to the wagon, arms around each other, eyes glued to the ground, legs trembling, and bodies hunched forward, as though their world had come to an end. Yisrael drove. The others walked slowly behind the two women. Yisrael brought the horses to the creek's edge, then brought them to a gentle pace along the bank. The women cried. The group had become the accompaniment to a funeral without a grave or cemetery.

And so, they walked for close to an hour until Janusz asked Avraham to halt the horses for a moment. The group was happy for this respite. "Yisrael, look. I think I see the church spire behind the hilltop," Janusz said. "Really close, I think. If there's a church, there's a cemetery. Maybe the priest will agree to let us bury Zonnenshine there. It doesn't sound logical but who knows... After all, what else could we possibly do?"

Yisrael hesitated, thinking how inappropriate it would be to bury a Jew in a Christian cemetery. But what alternative did they have? To put him in the ground in an unmarked place? No one would be able to find him in the future! He pondered, then decided, and spoke up.

"We're all suffering from the Germans: Jews, Christians, everyone. Let's go and talk to the priest and ask his permission to bury our friend here. We must find a grave for him, even if it isn't in a Jewish cemetery. There isn't any other solution."

Yisrael's brothers agreed. The rest of the group said nothing, not even the fresh widow and orphan, both of them totally exhausted and deep in mourning. All they wanted was to see their loved one buried.

Reaching the church some thirty minutes later, Yisrael and Volf asked everyone to wait while they went inside. The priest, a man of about sixty, short, and who looked much older because of the deep wrinkles on his cheeks and around his kind blue eyes, gazed at the people next to the wagon. Yisrael looked straight at him and spoke honestly.

"We're Jews. We're fleeing the German conquerors, and we've just experienced a catastrophe. One of our older people has died. For hours now his body has lain on the wagon. All we ask is your permission and generosity in allowing us to bury him here."

"Certainly, Jews. I'm at your service," the priest answered immediately. "I'll allocate you a place next to the cemetery walls, distanced and a little separate from the other graves. I understand the sensitivity. It's very unusual for a Jew to be buried in a Christian cemetery, but I promise that your friend's place of final rest will be marked and clear, and one day, you'll be able to come here and pray for his soul. Come, let us dig the grave together."

Volf and Yisrael returned to the Zonnenshine women. "We were given permission to perform the burial here. Please G-d, when the war is over, you'll come back and bring his bones for burial among our own, in a Jewish cemetery. But for now, here is much better than on the roadside, without a marker."

The women said nothing. They understood Yisrael's reasoning and nodded their agreement, sobbing silently.

The priest brought several spades. The digging began. He also brought several sheets to wrap the body in, instead of shrouds. The grave was dug adjacent to the outer wall. To their surprise the priest brought out a small Siddur, the Jewish prayer book, thumbed through it and pointed to the Kaddish, the traditional Jewish mourner's prayer. Yisrael looked at him, his eyebrows raised.

"For me, every prayer book, no matter of what religion, is holy. I have a collection in the library." The men thanked him. "We know this prayer by heart," Yisrael said, as the men in the traveling group began the Kaddish: "Yisgodol veYiskodosh shemyo rahbo…"

The grave was covered in earth, the travelers thanked the priest again, and he blessed their continued journey. "May your G-d be with you wherever you go." They left the churchyard and sat together, despondent, until eventually the weeping daughter broke the silence.

"We won't be continuing with you," she said softly. "Mother and I have decided to go home. Better we die in our own home than on these roads."

At that, the brothers glanced at Haiya. She glanced at Yisrael, who knew very well that they were about to part. She also wanted to return. Haiya and Yisrael hugged each other. Then she hugged Volf and Avraham. Each of the brothers gave Haiya some of their money for the journey. She found places to hide it in her clothing. One last hug with her husband, and she and the two mourning women turned and made their way back. Once again, the family had separated, against their father's clear wishes.

PRAYER

The women had gone. Yisrael sat pondering, although looking at him, no one would have guessed at the turmoil rampaging in his heart. Separating from his wife was unbearable. He felt as though a piece of his heart had been ripped out; he couldn't hold his brothers' gaze. Avraham and Volf hugged him, with Avraham saying quietly.

"They'll get there safely, Yisrael. Don't worry. Haiya always figures things out. Let's move on and keep looking for a better place for the family and then we'll all be together again. Now's not the time to fall into despair. We've got to keep forging ahead."

Back on the wagon, they continued east.

On the tenth day of travel, Lublin still seemed a long way off. Everyone felt how the horses were tiring, and were always hungry. Janusz halted the group frequently to let the animals rest, leading them to water. As the now more docile creatures drank, Janusz spoke quietly to Yisrael.

"You do realize, don't you, that the horses won't hold up for much longer. We may have to forego them and continue on foot." Yisrael had no idea how tired the animals were, and right then they were the last thing on his mind. He was thinking of his wife, who'd turned back just days ago. He'd never stopped thinking about his parents, or that he was the one who acted against his father's wishes. The confidence he'd felt when they left was quickly dissipating. They'd come a long way by now, and turning back was no longer an option. He knew he had to appear confident and not let his doubts influence his brothers and the other travelers.

As though his voice was part of a dream, Yisrael could hear Janusz repeating himself. "Yisrael? Are you listening?" Yisrael blinked, and in a firm voice, answered. "Sure, yes, you said something about the horses, right?" Janusz pointed at them and whispered. "I think we're going to have to leave them here. They're done. The past few days they haven't been able to trot nearly as fast as needed. They're hungry, they're exhausted, and they're becoming useless. I think we'll just have to walk from here on. What do you say?"

Yisrael studied Janusz's face as he was thinking. His plan, which had seemed so sound at the time, wasn't sufficiently thought out, he could see, and was coming apart at the seams. "I think you're right. Without the horses we'll have a few less worries. Let's unhitch them and let them roam around the creek. Then we won't have to constantly find water for them. We'll just go on without them."

The two men returned to the group. Briefly Yisrael presented this new decision. Volf and Avraham agreed right away. None of the others presented any objections. If any did think otherwise, not a word was said. With heavy hearts, they let the hungry horses go. Perhaps a farmer in the vicinity would take them in. The group set off, walking slowly until night fell and they reached the town of Sandomierz. To their surprise, several shops were open: they stocked up on bread and potatoes. Deciding to spend the night there, sleeping under the open sky, they set about making food, using containers they had with them to boil the potatoes. Seated around the bonfire, they ate, sprinkling the bread and potatoes with salt. They ate very little and quickly felt full. Nothing could beat potatoes as a way to fill their stomachs. Someone asked how far Lublin still was, and how many days it would take to get to the city. Someone else reckoned that they had about one hundred kilometers to go and if they walked at least twenty each day, they'd be there at last within the week.

Lying next to each other, the three brothers gazed at the stars. "No moon," Avraham said dreamily. "We barely saw the moon for some nights and there aren't any clouds to hide it."

Volf jumped to his feet, excited. "Don't you get it? The date? There's no moon because tonight is Rosh Hashanah." The brothers gasped: it was the Jewish New Year! "Are you sure, Volf? Yisrael, is he right? That it's Rosh Hashanah now?" Avraham asked. Yisrael quickly calculated. "We left home on September 3rd. We've been on the road for ten days. So it's the thirteenth. And there's no moon." His voice dropped to a whisper. "And so there's no doubt that the Hebrew date is indeed Rosh Hashanah."

Deeply distressed, his tears fell freely. "G-d, just look at us this Rosh Hashanah. No family. No prayers. No synagogue. No fresh challah and no fish. G-d, how tough this is. Not even a festival prayer book," Avraham said sadly. Wanting to lessen his brother's sorrow, Volf quickly chimed in. "But we do remember parts by heart. Let's pray."

Standing on the creek bank, they watched the flow of water. They knew it ran east; they turned to face that direction, covering their heads with their caps, praying to the best of their memory. What one forgot, the other recalled; so they stood, the three of them, quietly praying, each word enunciated clearly. "Thus, we wait for you, Lord our G-d, to quickly see the splendor of your might… as is written in your Torah: G-d will rule forever more."

Never before had they thought so deeply about each and every word of the prayer as they did now. Each holy word and phrase came from deep in their hearts and was said with true intent. They prayed on, their bodies trembling, their voices clear and infused with faith, until at last they reached the rousing prayer familiar to every Jew, secular or religious, its words piercing the speaker's heart.

"Let us now relate the power of this day's holiness, for it is one of awe and reverence… Even the angels will be gripped by trembling…for on the New Year each person's fate is recorded, and on the Fast of Yom Kippur it is finalized: who shall live, and who shall die…"

Tears rolled down their cheeks at the weight imbued in the prayer's words, at the thought of their parents left behind, at Haiya who took a dangerous path home, at themselves, not with their loved ones in synagogue and at home but out, alone in a field. As they reached the prayer service's closing lines their voices became louder and pleading. "Provide peace, goodness, blessing, grace, kindness, and mercy, to us and to all the nation of Israel...and hear our plea this day, Amen; receive our prayer with mercy and good will, Amen."

The rest of the group lay on the ground watching the three brothers, entranced by their prayers. Three figures standing erect, welcoming the new year and praying it will bring them all only good. But as they lay there, their hearts seemed to grow heavier, and doubts rose, and their thoughts carried them home too. Surely the synagogues would be brimming with worshippers now, surely families would be celebrating together, or had the war already begun to cull its victims in the small town they'd turned their backs on?

Even as these thoughts disrupted their peace of mind, they already felt better, the prayers raising their spirits. Perhaps speaking to G-d had helped them. In an undertone, each asked for G-d's guidance. Yisrael, Volf and Avraham returned to their places on the creek's bank and fell asleep right away, hoping that their prayers would be answered favorably.

CLOSE-UP ON THE INVASION

The new morning didn't start well. Woken by planes passing overhead, the group also noted the noise of dozens of vehicle engines on the nearby road. "Fearful days are dawning upon us," Yisrael said. He and the others realized that a convoy was on the road. They decided to get a closer look without revealing themselves. They wanted a better idea of what was happening.

Quickly covering the distance of some two hundred meters in the road's direction, they hid behind tree trunks. And were stunned by the images: heavy trucks and motorbikes bearing large swastikas passed quickly. They were particularly disturbed by the large open-ended trucks holding hundreds of straight-backed soldiers in helmets. More trucks passed. And more. After counting several dozen, they stopped tallying. They hadn't seen tanks or foot soldiers, only the motorized convoy. The color draining from their faces, they sat as though some order had been given. A realization had dawned upon them: the entire region had been taken by the fearful Nazi army. They'd heard no shots, no sounds of war, only the motorized column making its way to Lublin and the Russian border. They were surprised that the soldiers were not firing at the countless pedestrians walking on the roadside. But the military was moving east, focused only on that goal.

Yisrael felt as though his world had come crashing down. His plans had collapsed. He'd hoped to get to their destination before the conquering military, but it had shown up far sooner than he'd expected. He could feel the tears pooling in his eyes. He had let his brothers down. He had disappointed his family, who relied on him to do what he'd said he would. He had misled the others in the group. He hoped against hope that Haiya would get back safely but he was very uncertain. Yisrael wanted to be by himself, feeling a tremendous urge to scream at the heavens. Instead, he bit his lip and argued with himself in his mind: Why? Why did I set out on this journey? I've put everyone in danger: my brothers, my wife, and everyone I left behind.

Feeling his anxiety, Volf and Avraham went over to him. "We've got to go back," they said quietly to their older brother. "There's no point in going forward now." Silence, broken only by the heavy truck engines.

Only when they looked around to call the others, did they realize that they were on their own. They'd been standing a short way from the others as they discussed the situation, and now eight people had fled along the creek bank and disappeared from sight. Shock and fear had disbanded the group. At that moment, the brothers realized they were at a turning point: from now on, it was only the three of them. They'd need to rely on each other. Flinging their arms around each other, they made a tight circle. "We'll never separate, never ever again. From now on we'll stick together, like Papa asked."

Yisrael was the first to regain his composure. "Let's go back to the creek. That'll put some distance between us and this road. It's much more dangerous now because the Germans are using it. Then we can sit and think about what to do next."

They searched for a quiet, concealed place near the bank and sat down, not speaking for a long time. Their thoughts were vague, their minds more focused on the sights they'd just seen. They waited for the convoy's noise to end.

It was a while later when they heard indistinct voices and words. People were walking along the bank, fleeing, just as they were. At first the brothers thought it best to stay hidden, then changed their minds. Yisrael suggested checking who they were. The brothers stood and stepped out from their hiding place, facing an oncoming small group of people. Four of them. Clearly, they were refugees fleeing their homes; they pleaded with the brothers not to harm them.

Yisrael and his brothers drew closer. "Don't be scared," he said, "we aren't going to hurt you. We're also fleeing. Where are you from?" Yisrael asked the oldest of the four, "and where are you going?"

The man took a deep breath. His voice was unsteady. "Three days ago, the Germans went through our town and shot in every direction, massacring innocent residents." His eyes watered. "Many were injured, many were killed. We don't know exactly what happened to our families and neighbors. But we decided to flee and look for a hiding place, if there is such a thing now."

Volf had another question. "But we saw German convoys on the road, further up, moving east. We didn't see them shooting people walking down the road."

Another of the four, who'd calmed down a little, explained. "The soldiers in those trucks have just beaten the Polish army. They don't bother with random citizens. But they're followed by other units who massacre without mercy. Those are the ones you need to fear."

"And where's the Polish army?" Yisrael wondered. "What happened to them?"

The older man swallowed hard. "There is no army anymore. We were beaten. Our soldiers fled. The whole lot of them. They have taken off their uniforms and switched to civilian clothes to avoid German captivity. Without a doubt, you'll find Polish uniforms on the roadside where our soldiers dropped them as they ran. And another important thing to know: you're Jews, right? Admittedly without sidelocks and beards but just be warned: be extremely careful. They're on the lookout for Jews and they'll kill any they find. Get rid of anything that marks you as Jewish otherwise they'll kill you."

The four turned and left. "They're also Jewish," Avraham said.

The brothers returned to their hideout, having difficulty in deciding which direction to go. They were silent for a short while before Yisrael spoke up.

"We don't have any choice. We have to keep going. But we'll move at night and hide by day." Avraham gazed at his two older brothers, his face showing doubt. What he didn't say, his brother Volf did.

"But where will we be able to go from here? I think we should go home.

If the Germans are killing Jews, it's our moral duty to protect our family. So, we have to go home, and right now." Avraham and Volf stared at Yisrael, but Yisrael said nothing.

Contemplating this dilemma, he still wondered about moving east, or west, back home. Gazing at the creek which flowed quietly east, it seemed to hint at the direction they should go. The three stood still, watching the creek, when right there, staring at them from the opposite bank in the last rays of light, they saw it watching them. The wolf, eyes shining, but this time it was silent. It didn't howl. It simply turned west and walked slowly away until it disappeared from view.

Not a word needed to be said. It was clear: they had to go home.

CAPTURE

At nightfall they set off. There was no need for words. But each of the brother's talked to himself in his own mind. Yisrael berated himself: I'm the firstborn, I was always so practical; whatever was I thinking? What kind of son abandons his parents? What kind of brother abandons his sisters? Now I'm going back with the two brothers I persuaded to join me. I was wrong.

Volf, the most sensitive among them, wondered about his sisters, and whether they'd managed to look after themselves and their parents. What did we put them through? We walked away from responsibility and left them dealing with it all, alone. What a dreadful mistake we made. Fear gripped his heart. Had the Germans reached their town? Was everyone still alive? Volf, unable to bear the thought, tried ignoring it but it came up again and again.

Avraham was missing his mother. He loved her to bits, that noble woman whose face always expressed kindness. Mama managed the household placidly and confidently, and he, the baby of the family, was always not too far off. He was very mischievous, but loyal to the bottom of his heart to her, to his father, to his siblings. How could I have dared to flee the house and leave Mama to handle everything herself, to care for Papa who is ill, to take care of the girls? How? Because I wanted to be a grown-up, like my two older brothers. That's why I joined them.

Without noticing, the three had begun walking faster. Longing to be united with their family and the wish to correct their error made them move faster.

Now, having set themselves a goal, they were determined to get back home as quickly as they could. Remembering their father's command, "Stay together," they understood that the family needed them, just as they needed their family.

Shots broke the night's silence. The three dropped to the ground, lying still, so panicked that they stopped breathing. They lay there, terrified. "Everyone okay?" Yisrael asked a few moments later. Breathing properly again, the brothers calmed down a little. "Yes, I am," Volf whispered. "Me too," Avraham said softly. Then they heard people running and shouts in Polish: "Quick, quick, to the creek." In the dark the brothers could make out figures racing towards the water, wanting to cross the creek. They stopped for a second, tossed something into the water, and ran on.

The brothers continued lying where they were in utter silence. Their first thought was, rather Polish speakers than German soldiers. They never blinked. About an hour later, Avraham spoke. "Let's stay here. I'm scared to continue in the night." Yisrael tried to soothe his fear. "Don't be afraid, Avraham, it'll be all right, you're here with us. Together we're stronger. That's what Papa always says and he's right." Yisrael's reassurance did help Avraham.

What they saw when the first light of morning broke made them sick. Bodies in pools of blood lay along the creek's bank. The brothers never imagined they'd been so close to the corpses all night. Yisrael and Volf inched closer to the dead. Avraham couldn't stomach going with them and stayed at a safe distance. They could hear words. "Did you hear that? Someone over there is still alive," Volf said. They halted immediately, fear paralyzing them. The dying man raised his hands and with his last surge of strength, begged. "Help, save me." The man closed his eyes, whispering again, but nothing could be heard. Yisrael forced himself closer. "Volf, stay here and watch over Avraham."

Yisrael bent over the man to hear better. "The Germans are shooting everyone. Hide. They're looking for Jews." Yisrael could barely catch what he was saying. "They shot us because we didn't obey their order to halt. If you don't halt, they shoot mercilessly." Every word was clearly costing the man a good deal of energy. "Polish soldiers are fleeing. They're traitors. They take off their uniforms and put on civilian clothes and hope to be saved." The man drew in a deep breath, then spat blood and spittle from his bluing lips. "Behind the trees you'll find uniforms of the soldiers who fled. They threw their guns into the creek. Cowards." He closed his eyes, a gurgle coming from his throat. "The Germans left," the man continued, "but they'll be back. Germans don't give in. They seek, find, shoot, and kill." He died, his eyes open wide to the heavens as though seeking solace.

Disturbed, the brothers distanced. They couldn't look at the shot bodies. Avraham started vomiting, crying, vomiting and crying again. Volf hugged him, and respectfully looked away. Yisrael sat down, lost for ideas. Terrible times, he thought. They didn't feel able to walk on, the sight of the bodies horrifying them, and they were too upset by the dying man's last words. Pale, legs trembling, they all stood, vomiting repeatedly. Then they went back to the bushes that offered shelter and camouflage, and tried to catch their breath and calm their souls.

How do we move on from this? The question echoed in their minds. Yisrael raised the idea of putting on the abandoned uniforms, masquerading as Polish soldiers. "Maybe that way, in uniform, we'll have a better chance of getting away," he whispered, as though fearful that the Germans might hear him. "At least we wouldn't need to hide from the Poles. The Germans are our main worry, and we'll have to hide from them anyway. What do you think?"

Volf agreed. Avraham raised certain doubts. "Look at me, Yisrael. I'm way too short and young. No one would believe I'm a soldier." Yisrael placed a steady hand on his shoulder. "Let's try. I'm sure that in uniform you'll look a bit older. We have to try. It'll be easier to move around as soldiers."

They found the uniforms among the trees and quickly changed, rolling their clothes up into the bottom of the bundle they were carrying. At once they became soldierly, the uniforms infusing them with greater confidence. Their military appearance raised their hopes. Even Avraham felt more mature, straightening up to his full height.

They set off in daylight, at first hesitantly but as their confidence grew, outfitted in their uniforms, they increased their speed. They decided to stay close to the creek, avoiding contact with other civilians or soldiers.

For three days they walked, and every time they stopped at one or another village, they listened to German radio announcements blaring through the local bathhouse windows. That's how they learned that the Germans had actually conquered the whole country. Poles still fought around Warsaw, but were nothing more than small pockets of resistance.

The brothers walked back along paths, keeping away from roads being used by freely-moving German units. Their confidence grew the closer they got to Strzemieszyce.

But their luck in hiding from the Germans didn't hold out. "Halt, or we shoot," they heard the shout in German a short distance away. They stood dead still, their knees folding. "It's the end of us," Volf whispered. Avraham couldn't hold his tears back. Yisrael turned very slowly towards the voice. Five German military police advanced; weapons pointed at the brothers. The Germans asked no questions, did not search them, but stood facing them and indicating, with their rifles, that the three should approach. Slowly the three moved forward. "Schnell, schnell," one German hurried them along, keeping their weapons aimed at the brothers the whole time.

They never had time to wonder about their actions or their decision to change out of their clothes and into uniforms. Exhausted, they reached the road where a German military truck was parked. "Get on," the Germans signaled with their rifles.

The canvas-covered truck set off. Next to them were several more Poles, but they were not permitted to talk among each other. Two German soldiers sat at the far end; rifles pointed at the captives. The van drove on; the canvas prevented everyone from seeing where. Sitting close, the brothers held each other's sweating hands, but none dared speak.

The truck stopped without warning, jerking everyone out of their thoughts. How long had they been traveling? No one knew. Noise and stench welcomed them when the canvas flaps were untied. Soldiers shouted German commands which not everyone understood. From a distance, shouts in Polish could be heard. The two languages crashed into each other. Other trucks were parked in the large parking lot; men in Polish military uniforms were getting off.

Everyone was told to walk in the direction of the terrible smell. Avraham vomited. Some tried blocking their noses with their sleeves. But the closer they came, the more they realized it was impossible to overcome the smell.

"Halt!" the German commander ordered when the convoy had reached a large structure from which the stench emanated. Inside the building, a deafening sound could be heard. The doors opened. The captives were rushed inside. Yisrael, Volf and Avraham looked around, realizing they were in an old stable. The stench came from horse manure that was no longer there. The crowding was terrible, body shoved against body. Yisrael and Volf kept a tight grip on Avraham, preventing him from getting lost among the others. Every few minutes more captives were stuffed inside.

In German, soldiers announced. "Everyone. Quiet. Not a word. You talk, you die." To demonstrate that they meant what they said, they shot two captives closest to the door. The two crumpled onto the ground in pools of blood. Silence filled the stable. Hundreds of captive soldiers and a smattering of imposters stood shivering in fear. There was nowhere to move in the packed, stinking stable. They stood like that for two hours. When night fell, it was a blanketing darkness. The doors opened again. Loaves of bread were thrown in. And pandemonium broke loose.

Captives trampled each other, punched each other, but only a few managed to rip a fistful of bread from the loaves. Yisrael, Volf and Avraham were not among them. They didn't budge from where they stood. They were not hungry and at that moment, felt no need to fight for food. They stood shoulder to shoulder, keeping together. The stable filled with shouts. German soldiers appeared again and demanded silence. When the captives did not obey, the Germans opened fire. Several people crumpled to the ground, some still holding bits of bread. Others quickly leaned forward, snatching it from them. The brothers counted themselves fortunate to be far from the skirmishes near the doors, far from the shots.

The captives stood that way until morning. Some collapsed onto the ground, still covered in horse manure and urine. The brothers kept a tight grip on their bundles: everything they owned was in there, except the money they'd now hidden in the uniforms. The doors flew open: German soldiers announced that they would now conduct identification procedures, that they knew there were imposter soldiers, but nothing was said about what would happen to the imposters.

Captives were brought outside in groups of tens, questioned by Germans with a Polish interpreter on hand. Those determined to be true Polish soldiers were put on trucks and sent away. With typical German efficiency, Jewish imposters were shot on the spot. It was not difficult to see that the brothers were not soldiers. "The only way out of this,' Yisrael whispered to his brothers, "is to convince the Germans that we're Polish and not Jewish." Questioning was brief. The interpreter's role was to chat with the captives and ascertain by their accent and fluency whether they were Jews. The brothers spoke perfect Polish, better even than that of the interpreter. Their excellent education stood them in good stead, and no outward markers indicated that they were Jewish.

"Let me speak," Yisrael whispered to his brothers.

"Ask them their names," they heard the officer say in German to the interpreter.

"Beniak, Vilek and Romek Zaks." Before the interpreter could speak, Yisrael had given their Polish names.

"Can you speak German?"

"Yes sir, officer. We all speak German. We also speak German sometimes at home."

The interpreter spoke in Polish. "What unit are you from? What are your numbers?"

Yisrael quickly weighed his options. He'd served in the Polish army up until two years ago and did have a number, but decided on admitting that they weren't really soldiers. "Sir, office," he said in Polish, "I admit that we aren't soldiers. We found these uniforms on the creek banks and decided to put them on because our own clothes were dirty and torn, and these uniforms seemed a good exchange."

The interpreter sniggered. "I knew it. You certainly don't look like soldiers. What did you think? That the kid there," he pointed at Avraham, "looks like a soldier?"

The stern-faced German did not comment but called the interpreter away, and spoke in a whisper. "Do you think they look like Jews?"

"No, absolutely not, sir," the brothers heard the Pole answer. "Their Polish is far too good. I have no doubt that they are clearly Polish."

"Check again, If they're Jewish we'll shoot them right now. No point in wasting any more time on them."

The interpreter faced them. "May we go?" Yisrael asked coolly. "We've admitted we're not soldiers. Let us go and you can continue your search for Jews, may they be damned."

The Polish interpreter said nothing. He went back to the German office. The brothers saw him take a document from the German and come back. "Drop your pants," the interpreter smiled smugly. "I want to be sure you aren't Jews. Once we check that, we'll give you the document and you can go on your way."

Volf and Avraham shook and went pale but Yisrael kept calm, whispering to the interpreter. "What do you feel about skipping the check for 100 zlotys? Let us go and you'll be free to hunt stinking Zhids. There's so many of them."

"Come with me," the Pole instructed. The three followed him off to the side, far from the German officer. Yisrael slyly passed the banknotes to him; and he gave them the document.

With relief they hurried away, blessing their good fortune. The Germans and their helpers, the Poles, seemed to lack the time to check each person thoroughly, and the bribe clinched their release. They walked quickly. Reaching a field, they quickly stepped undressed, throwing the stinking uniforms aside, and put their own clothes back on. For the first time in days, they smiled: there was a lot less risk this way. They weren't sure how effective the document they now held would be, but that's what they had: a slip of paper stamped by the Nazi military. Nonetheless, they were worried.

"Where are we, anyhow?" Avraham wondered. They had no clue. Nor did they have any idea which way was home. "There's a hill over there," Yisrael pointed. "Let's walk there, see if there are any villages nearby, and find out."

KIELCE

The brothers plodded up the hill. They were tired. And hungry. Realizing that they hadn't eaten for more than twenty-four hours only made the trek harder.

What they'd just been through had pushed hunger and thirst aside , but back on the road, their legs started hurting and their stomachs were growling. "Maybe we should stop to rest a bit?' Volf suggested.

"C'mon, Volf, just a bit more. We'll get to the top and rest there," Yisrael convinced them, "and we'll also be able to figure out where we are and if there's any food or drink we can buy nearby."

They walked on, checking how much money they had left. Not a lot, but enough to get by for a few days more. It took another hour before they reached the peak. There was no sight of the creek they'd walked along for so many days. What they saw was flat land: fields, partly worked, a smattering of trees. How different from the previous location. They realized that this region would offer them nowhere to hide.

They rested for a couple of hours on the hilltop before deciding to look for food and water. It was early afternoon and the sun was shining from the south. "We're going north," Yisrael said. They walked on. Not much later, a relatively large city came into view in the distance. Going down the hillside, they headed to the main road where countless people were making their way to or from the city. "We've got no choice. We have to go that way and find food," Avraham said. Silently his brothers nodded in agreement. They blended in among the others walking on the road, understanding from conversations around them that the city's name was Kielce.

Yisrael was pleased. He'd been there before and knew where the fairly large Jewish quarter was. "Let's stop here on the roadside," he said. "A bit of good luck." Relieved, he smiled for the first time in days. "The camp we were held in is, I reckon, about one hundred kilometers north-west of where they caught us. So, in fact, we've advanced a good way towards Strzemieszyce. We've been saved days of walking." Encouraged, they rejoined the people walking along the main route.

Farmers at roadside stalls were selling apples. It was peak apple season: a living could be had from the thousands of people walking by. The brothers stopped at a stall made of wooden crates holding bags of apples. Clearly, they'd been freshly picked. "Tell me, sir, how much is this bag?" Yisrael asked, pointing to one. "One zloty. Cheap and delicious." the man smiled, yellowed teeth showing beneath his thick mustache. "Do you have change? We only have ten and twenty zloty notes," Yisrael asked. The farmer laughed. "Listen, young man, I don't have change nor does anyone else here. Give me ten zlotys and take ten bags or one bag, same thing to me." Not wanting to be burdened with excess weight, the brothers handed ten zlotys to the farmer who beamed with pleasure at his good fortune, took one bag each and moved on.

Distancing several hundred meters more, they stopped for a break, biting into the apples with a hearty appetite. The fruit also slaked their thirst, and there was plenty left in their rucksacks. Back on the road, they walked on, their stomachs full, their spirits lifted. Some two hours later they reached the city's outskirts. Their first goal was to find bread. Luckily there was no shortage of flour here: countless residents were baking and selling loaves of bread to the refugees. Stopping at an adjoined shelter with about twenty loaves of simple white bread, Volf turned to the seller. "How much are these?" "A zloty a loaf," the man said impatiently. "Do you have change for ten zlotys?" Yisrael asked hopefully, only to be disappointed again. No change, but their need for bread was too strong. He handed the man a ten zloty note. "Give me this loaf," Yisrael said in a sad tone. The man wrapped it in newspaper and handed it over. Once again, they'd paid a fortune for a bit of food. "We've got to get some small coins," Yisrael said through gritted teeth, "or we'll run out of money very soon."

Yisrael broke the loaf into three and the brothers walked as they ate. It was now afternoon. "Let's go to the Jewish quarter. I know the way there well." As the sun set, they reached their destination. The quarter was almost dark, and only a few candles flickered behind windows. The sight seemed odd to them: Was there no electricity in this neighborhood? In every house candles were lit. Puzzled, the brothers stood wondering. At one window a curtain was pulled shut, as though wanting to hide the household from outsiders.

The brothers glanced at each other: A realization dawned on them at exactly the same time. "It's Yom Kippur tonight!" The Fast of Atonement. In their efforts to escape they'd lost all sense of time, forgetting even the Gregorian date, let alone the Jewish calendar date. Now they were surprised to realize that ten days had passed since they'd prayed together on the creek bank. Only yesterday they'd been in the Germans' hands, at risk of death, and had managed to evade the Nazi officer's order which would have exposed them as Jewish. "This is the first time in our lives that we're not in synagogue for Yom Kippur night services," Volf trembled, saying what the others were thinking. "Let's knock on the door and ask to join people in prayers."

"But we need to be cautious," Yisrael raised his reservations. "We've got documents attesting to us not being Jewish. If any official finds us in here, if we get caught here during prayers, that document is going to be worthless and we'll get killed on the spot."

Avraham intervened in support of Volf. "Praying on Yom Kippur… isn't that more important than anything else?" Yisrael's response was delivered in a tone of impatience. "Staying alive is more important. It must never be discovered that we're Jews. We're risking our lives." But Volf, contrary to his usual placid nature, challenged his older brother. "We'll never forgive ourselves if we don't pray tonight, and if police show up, we can always say that we went in to look for somewhere to sleep. We've got documents saying we're Polish Christians. So officially we aren't Jews."

Yisrael thought about that. He wasn't used to Volf being so persistent, and certainly not towards him. On one hand, he felt deeply responsible for his two brothers, wanting to protect them as much as he could. On the other hand, it was Yom Kippur, not just any regular day. It was the holiest day of the Jewish year, a day on which each person should seek forgiveness. How could they just forego saying the "Kol Nidrei" prayer, which releases people from vows and statements they had made during the year that passed? No, despite the risk, they could not forego Yom Kippur.

Standing outside the house, they could hear the prayer being recited inside. "Kol Nidrei… All vows and things we have forbidden ourselves." Trembling with awe, glancing at each other, tears rolling down their cheeks, the brothers stood silently. Inside, the voice grew stronger. "…and oaths and items we have dedicated to the Temple and vows we have issued… From this Yom Kippur until the next, may it come as a sign of good."

Yisrael, his throat choked up with emotion, turned to his brothers. "Let's knock on the door." He knocked once, then three times. The door opened no more than a slit. In the darkness a candle flickered and a short man looked out at them, concerned. Yisrael spoke to him in Yiddish. "We're Jews, we fled when the war started but now we're trying to get home. Please let us join you on this holy day. We have nowhere else to go."

The man opened the door wide. "Come, come inside, my brothers," he answered in Yiddish. "There are no synagogues left here anymore. They've all closed. It will be our privilege if you are our guests tonight and tomorrow." Volf, deeply moved, interrupted. "We heard Kol Nidrei outside. We also want to pray. The sun hasn't set yet. Please, let us join you, let's pray Kol Nidrei together. We feel a great need to ask for release from our vows."

"I am Hershel, and this is my wife Tova," the older man made the introductions. "Sadly, only the two of us remain here. Our children left for the Land of Israel some years ago with the Gordonia movement. We are here on our own." He walked over to a drawer and took out a Mahzor, the traditional Day of Atonement prayer book, and three prayer shawls. Each brother draped himself in a Tallit: and draped, they closed their eyes and prayed together:

"Kol Nidrei, all vows and things we have forbidden ourselves..."

By the time they reached the closing words, "Let our vows not be considered vows; let our self-imposed prohibitions not be considered prohibitions; let our oaths not be considered oaths," they felt uplifted, holding their prayer books, which they kissed as they cried silently. They felt as though they were in a secret house of worship, hidden from non-Jews, risking their lives to fulfill their commandments as Jews. "If only Papa could see us now," Avraham said softly, "he'd be so proud of us." Yisrael stroked his shoulder. "And how," he agreed.

Volf was still immersed in prayer, looking as though he wanted to earn every moment of grace that G-d is said to give on this special day. Raising his head a little, he smiled at his brothers for the first time in many days. "No war can take our faith from us," he said, his eyes shining with tears. "Despite the document in our pocket, we're Jews and tonight is proof." To Yisrael and Avraham, Volf manifested the spirit of Hanokh's deep belief and commitment to the Jewish way of life; and surely their father was praying devoutly, sobbing, forgiving his sons, asking G-d for forgiveness and guidance on bringing his sons home. "Soon, Papa," the boys said in their hearts. "Just a bit longer, and we'll be home. Nothing will stop us."

"We ate the meal before the Fast some thirty minutes ago and can't offer you food or drink. Yom Kippur has already begun," Hershel apologized.

"Don't worry about that," Volf reassured, "because not so long ago, we ate some apples without even realizing they'd be our meal."

Yisrael and Avraham took out the apples still left in their bags. "These are for you," Yisrael said. "Dip them in honey when the Fast is over, for a sweet year."

Tova sat them round the table. "Rest a bit," she offered, "and then shower and meanwhile I'll make up the beds in the children's room." Mentioning her children, Tova's voice broke: it reminded her of how alone she and Hershel were.

One by one the brothers showered, removing the stench of the stables and the grime of days of walking from their bodies, washing the sight of the dead and the smell of corpses and blood from their memories. Even though none of it had actually soiled them, they felt unclean from the events of the past few days. Their hosts' clean house made them miss their parents and siblings even more; sitting around the table made their hearts ache for their family.

For hours the brothers sat with their hosts, telling them about everything they'd been through since leaving home. Describing the events to their hosts highlighted how dangerous their journey had been. They went over details repeatedly. Yisrael spoke about his wife turning back. Tova was moved to tears, asking herself what she might have done in the same situation. Volf spoke about the wolf showing up again and again, clearly guarding them from terrible situations. Hershel had trouble believing that. "We were taught to beware of wolves," he said. Volf smiled and slowly said, "There are wolves, and there are wolves." Then Avraham described being locked up, and the terrible fear he felt. "I still hear the shots and see the dead," he said, choking back his tears. Slowly, exhaustion overcame them. Apologizing to their hosts, they asked permission to sleep. For the first time in a while, they slept on real beds, with real pillows and clean sheets.

Yisrael managed to ask the others, "What do you think? Are the terrible times over?" without expecting an answer; Volf and Avraham were already asleep, and he fell asleep right away too.

Loud knocks on the door woke them from their deep sleep in the morning. "Open up, open up," someone shouted in Yiddish. The brothers sprang out of their beds and dressed in seconds, ready to flee. Hershel, at the window, calmed them. "It's all right, they're Jewish neighbors." He opened the door and three bearded men quickly stepped inside. "Last night the Rabbi and three key figures in the community were arrested. They were easily caught, because the Nazis, may their names be forever erased, knew it was Yom Kippur. They'll let them go in return for thousands of zlotys. We're collecting from all the Jews of town. Let's hope we are able to collect enough to redeem them."

Hershel went to his bedroom, and shortly afterwards came back with a thick envelope. "That's all I can give. Take it and save them." Glancing wordlessly at each other, the brothers put their hands into their pockets and pulled out several banknotes, leaving themselves a small amount for the rest of their journey. The collectors left to carry on their mission.

"It's Yom Kippur," Yisrael said to Hershel, "but I think that we should push on nonetheless. We don't want to be a burden. There could be other raids and arrests during the day and if they come here and find us, it could bring trouble to you and Tova. We'll be all right. We've got documents stating we're not Jewish. We want to thank you so much for hosting us and for allowing us to be in your home on this special night. We will never forget praying Kol Nidrei here, together with you. But now we're going to head back to our city, Strzemieszyce."

Thanking and hugging Hershel and Tova, the brothers left, taking the main road heading west. They estimated about one hundred kilometers to get back home. Four to five days of walking. They decided to look for a wagoner to speed things up. Not long after leaving the city they saw a parked wagon that seemed large enough for all three of them. "Transport anywhere," was chalked on its side in Polish. The wagoner was a fat man with a pocked face.

"Hello, mister. Can you drive us?" Yisrael asked.

"And where would you wish to be taken?" the wagoner sniggered.

"Strzemieszyce," Yisrael said.

"That's a long way, mister," the wagoner said, smiling sneeringly, "and I'm not sure I can do that but if you offer me a good price, perhaps I can make a special effort. I understand you're in a hurry."

"And what is your price?" Although fuming inside, Yisrael made an effort to stay calm outwardly.

The wagoner drew his eyebrows together as though calculating. "The horses will need food, I will need to make the return journey, and who can know if I'll have a return passenger? No, it won't be cheap, mister."

"Let's just walk on," Yisrael said, turning to Volf and Avraham. "We came this far on foot, so we can do the rest on foot. He's trying to take advantage." The brothers nodded.

Yisrael turned to the wagoner. "We won't be needing your services, sir, but thank you anyhow and good day."

Seeing an excellent opportunity slip away from him in an instant, the wagoner spoke up. "How much can you pay, if I may ask?"

Yisrael was not falling into that trap. "First you tell us how much it would cost. If we find it too expensive, no deal. We'll leave on foot right away and not waste anymore of your time."

The wagoner sighed. "For one thousand zlotys I'll take you."

Avraham and Volf glanced at Yisrael, shaking their heads. "Thank you," Yisrael said to the wagoner, "but we'll just walk on and not disrupt your day."

The man wasn't about to give up so easily. "Nonetheless, how much could you pay? Let me see what I can do for you."

"Four hundred zlotys, final offer and no negotiations," Yisrael said.

The wagoner sighed. "All right, get on. But I want payment up front."

"Not at all," Yisrael answered firmly, "I'll give you one hundred now, another hundred in twenty kilometers from now, and another hundred after the next twenty, and the rest when we reach our destination."

"Get on then," the wagoner sighed in agreement.

They sat on the back seat, the wagoner tugged the reins, but nothing happened. "These horses won't move unless I have at least two hundred zlotys in my pocket," the wagoner said and waited for an answer. Glancing at his brothers, Yisrael caved. They pulled the notes out of their pockets, counting out the amount. The wagoner whipped the horses cruelly. The wagon took off, the brothers in higher spirits than they had been for a long time. They leaned back and let the wagoner do his work.

Some two hours later, as they drew closer to Strzemieszyce, the wagon began to slow down. The horses no longer galloped but were now moving at an easy canter. Yisrael stood up to look around. From a distance he saw a convoy at a standstill, mostly comprised of wagons, a few cars, and plenty of people on foot. "What's going on there?" Yisrael asked.

"It's a military police barricade. The Germans are checking everyone's papers. Drivers, passengers and pedestrians. I'm scared to go on."

Yisrael reassured him immediately. "You've nothing to worry about, sir. We have papers that allow us to travel. You can move on."

The wagoner was less sure. "What about we rest here a bit and I'll feed the horses, and then we'll see what's next. And it wouldn't hurt you to rest a bit too and stretch your legs," the wagoner suggested.

Taking their bags off the wagon, the brothers took the dry bread and remaining apples out, sitting down in the shade. As they relaxed, they saw the wagoner crack the whip, the horses breaking into a gallop as he turned them back towards Kielce, two hundred of their zlotys in his pocket.

WALKING HOME

Broken-hearted, Haiya left Avraham behind, walking quickly to prevent the uncertainty from changing her mind. Just minutes earlier she'd hugged Yisrael, then moved away, turning and walking quickly to join Mrs. Zonnenshine and her daughter. Haiya wanted her home, her bedroom, her bed; she missed her own, familiar four walls all the more precisely because her familiar life had collapsed.

Haiya knew the way back. She led the Zonnenshines confidently as they moved forward at a comfortably slow pace. Every so often she asked herself whether she'd made a mistake by letting them join her because they slowed her down, but immediately she banished the thought as petty, feeling ashamed because, after all, the women had been recently bereaved. Zosha was only sixteen; it was to be expected that she and her mother, Fanya, would still burst into tears each time they stopped to rest. They refused to eat from the meager portions they carried with them. "I can't eat a thing," Zosha said, I'm too choked with sorrow," as her mother stroked her head gently.

"Fanya, you must eat and get your strength back, otherwise you won't be strong enough to make it home. It's vital to eat," Haiya said softly.

"What for, Haiya?" Fanya sobbed. "There's no point to our lives. I don't have a husband, my daughter has no father, and I'm sure our house hasn't survived and has been plundered while we're away."

Haiya looked at them a little sternly. "True, you've experienced a catastrophe.

You don't have a husband but you do have a daughter. She's young and she needs you to help ensure her future survival. Zosha must believe that you and she have what to live for, and you need to think about her. It will help you both."

Fanya sighed. "Look at me," she whispered. "I'm in the seven days of mourning but not sitting at home according to our mourning customs. Instead, I'm walking. I'm not praying for my husband, who's buried of all places in a non-Jewish cemetery. In a churchyard! Who'd have thought such a thing… And instead of Zosha and me sitting in our home, being consoled by well-wishers, we're walking home into the unknown. So, eating… I can barely breathe, let alone eat."

Haiya tried soothing her. "My dear, Fanya, mourning is much more than just rituals. Mourning is in your heart. That's where it happens. You can mourn even if you aren't able to fulfill the custom of staying home for seven days. Believe in yourself and we'll find our way in this twisted world. Let's walk a bit further and get back home as fast as we can. Enough crying now. Let's eat and move on. We have a bit of dry bread to share, but better we eat that, than be so hungry we can't walk at all. We need to get back."

The three women sat down to eat, rested for an hour or so, and set off again. Every so often they came across kind people who let them ride on their wagons, moving much faster ahead while giving their sore feet and legs a welcome respite. At night they slept in village barns near the roadside, usually sneaking in under cover of dark without the owners' knowledge. When they encountered locked barns, they paid a few zlotys to stay there. Usually, those owners also provided a bit of food for the next day's journey: apples, a few vegetables, and bread of course, given as generously as a farmer felt was appropriate.

After the most peaceful sleep the women had enjoyed in the four days since leaving the group, they were woken by shouts in Polish. Three men entered. "Up, up, up right away!" they ordered. Zosha and Fanya immediately burst into tears. Haiya, although as scared as they were, and trembling in fear, knew she had to stay level-headed.

"What do you want, you hooligans!" she shouted right back.

"Give us everything you've got, right away!" a short, solidly built and heavily mustached man said, his eyes cold and cruel.

"We don't have a thing. Only the clothes we're wearing," Haiya answered firmly. "We're refugees just like you and don't have any possessions with us."

"So, what's in those bags?" his mate, a tall slim fellow, snarled.

"Some food from yesterday. You're welcome to it," she said as Fanya and Zosha cried louder.

"Leave us alone," Zosha begged. "My father died just days ago and my mother and I are alone in the world. We're just two miserable women trying to get back home. Take the food if you want and go."

Rummaging through the bags, the men found some of Haiya's money, took it gleefully and turned to leave the barn. But the youngest man suddenly turned back, eyeing Zosha, moving closer to her. "Maybe there's something more I can get from you, girl? Maybe you'll even like it, who knows…" he said, his hand reaching out towards Zosha's breasts. Zosha covered her face with her thin hands, rooted to the spot in panic. Fanya and Haiya felt paralyzed.

The roar of Warplane engines and bombs not far away broke the tension. The barn's roof flew off in the aftershock. Everyone covered their ears with their hands, the women dropping to the ground in fright, and the men crouching, as though that would provide them shelter. Fire broke out, lighting the sky. The men raced off: lust being the last thing on their minds as their eyes took in the smoke and fire. For some time longer, the women lay on the barn floor, hands over their ears, faces drained of life. When they eventually looked up, they realized they were now alone with only the clothes on their backs. Their bags had been stolen, along with their money and food.

Haiya was the first to stand up. "Well, at least we're alive," she said, encouraging Fanya and Zosha. "Let's get out of here before they come back. I hope the worst is now behind us," Haiya said, hurrying the two along, but they were too dazed to move, taking small hesitant steps as though walking in their sleep. Only the smell of smoke, which was growing stronger, and the cries of the injured, shocked them enough to make them race out of the barn.

With nothing but the clothes on their backs, they returned to the road leading to Sławków and Strzemieszyce. They reached a small village which, like so many others, had farmers lining the main street selling their goods. "Please, we have no money but we're hungry," Zosha pleaded. "Go away," one answered gruffly, "no money, no goods. Scat." Zosha's eyes filled with tears. Fanya sobbed silently, spreading her hands to her sides. "Have mercy, we're good people," she whispered. No one gave them the time of day.

"You two keep walking ahead and do not look back. I'll get us something," Haiya whispered to her companions. Not even thinking to question Haiya, Fanya and Zosha walked on. Haiya went over to a seller, an older man whose apples looked especially good. Haiya's stomach growled. "Give me one bag please," she asked, swallowing hard. The man happily held out a bag filled to the brim. Haiya pretended to be searching for money in her pocket. "Strange," she said a moment or so later, "but I can't seem to find the coins I had in here." The seller frowned and reached out to take the bag back. "Lady, give that back please. No money, no apples."

Haiya studied him sternly. "Is that what you think?" she snapped and sped off holding the bag tightly. In an instant she'd disappeared from view. She had no doubt that the older man wouldn't give chase: he couldn't risk abandoning his loaded wagon. He cursed loudly and spat on the ground. She quickly covered the two hundred or so meters to catch up with Zosha and Fanya, puffing hard not only because of the sprint but at the shock of having stolen something. Fanya's and Zosha's eyes opened wide. "Did you steal that, Haiya?" they asked. "Yes. In war, be warriors," Haiya said, shrugging.

Zosha looked at Haiya, astonished, then smiled for the first time in a long while. "My turn," she whispered to her mother and Haiya, nodding with her head towards the bread stall. She approached, said nothing, and touched a loaf fresh out of the oven. The baker had no time to get a word in edgewise. Zosha simply gazed at him with wide eyes and spoke fast. "I don't have money so I won't pay," she snatched the loaf and set off at a run, gone from his sight in no time. The other two women took off quickly too, looking behind them in case the baker wanted to chase after them, but he simply gave up.

Zosha, her mother, and Haiya met up again some minutes later and sat down to eat fresh bread and crisp apples. "How easy it is to steal," Zosha said, wiping her lips from the fruit's juice. "I'll be a thief. I'm quick on my feet. From now on there's no need for us to go hungry."

For two days they walked on, Zosha taking responsibility for stealing their food. As a teenager she had no problem approaching sellers, chatting them up a little, smiling sweetly to gain their trust and then, in a flash, snatching their wares and hightailing it out of the market. No one gave chase. No one suspected the other two women as partners in crime. The three of them kept their strength up this way. "I never imagined it was so easy to steal…" Zosha would say each time she showed up with food.

On they walked until Sławków loomed in the distance. Stopping on the roadside, they gave vent to their emotions, sobbing, erupting from the pressures of the long journey, the father and husband buried in the churchyard. They were almost home, although there was no joy in that achievement. They felt burdened by a deep sorrow on seeing their town, which now looked very different. Many homes had been blown up. Many others stood empty. Filth piled up in the street. In just two weeks since they'd left, they now felt as strangers. "This can't be our town…" they whispered to each other.

Haiya stopped. "I'm not staying here," she said firmly. "My family is in Strzemieszyce. My husband's family is there, at least. That's where I'll go. Be well, friends. Go to your home, and if anyone's in it, demand that they leave." She spoke, but didn't quite believe her own words. Silently the women embraced each other before Haiya moved on. She still had some five kilometers to Strzemieszyce, to rejoin her sisters-in-law and parents-in-law.

Evening was quickly setting in and darkening the night. Haiya's legs were hurting from so much walking. Her feet hurt even more. Her shoes were completely worn out, her clothes bedraggled and dirty, barely covering her. Her hair was as wild as a wandering gypsy's hair. Haiya hoped she'd meet someone familiar along the way. But silence was all she met as she walked into what now looked like a ghost town. She'd left a place bursting with life until the war broke out. Now the place was dead and rotting. Haiya made her way to 78 Warshevska Street. She stood outside the large structure, gaping open-mouthed. The Zaks family's street level shop was locked. She wondered if anyone was home. She wondered if they'd been banished. She moved back a little, studying the building, and eventually noticed a faint light in one of the upstairs windows. What joy!

"Anyone home?" she shouted as loudly as she could. She whispered encouragement to herself: I'm going in, no matter what. In an adjacent house, a window opened. Haiya heard a man shout: "Get inside, silly woman. We're under curfew. Do you want the Germans to drag you off to jail?"

Now Haiya understood the reason for the town's eerie silence. At the sound of shouting, a window in the Zaks family's home opened. Haiya could pick out a female form cautiously peering through the curtain. "Batya, it's me, Haiya! Open up. Quickly!" she shouted. Stunned, Batya could be heard shouting to the others inside. "Haiya's outside. She's back." From the window she called out instructions. "Come in, hurry. It's dangerous. Come, come inside…"

Haiya rushed to the door, crying, laughing and shaking with emotion. The door opened. She raced inside, almost crashing into Batya and Miriam, her two sisters-in-law. They embraced, they wept; they had no words, but they could feel their hearts thumping.

It had only been two weeks since she and Yisrael had left, but the whole world had been turned upside down. Batya whispered: "What's with our brothers? Are they alright? Alive and well?" Haiya answered immediately. "When I left, they were fine. I believe they still are."

Slowly Yoheved and Hanokh came downstairs, smiling at her warmly. "Come, my dear," Yoheved welcomed her back. "Go shower, there's still hot water here. Change your clothes. We'll put some food together and you'll tell us everything."

TRADITION

For years until the war began, Friday night's family meal at the Zakses was sacrosanct. Everyone sat around the big table, their gazes directed respectfully at Hanokh, head of the family, as he recited the prayers welcoming the Shabbat, the Queen. "And the heavens and the earth and all their hosts were completed. And G-d finished by the seventh day all His work, which He had done, and He rested on the seventh day from all His work which He had done."

The shop had always been closed well before the Shabbat would start on Fridays at dusk. Non-Jews knew Friday heralded Shabbat, as even they called it, and respected the fact that the Zaks's store would be shut by early Friday afternoon. Each member of the Zaks family had her or his fixed place around the table. And around the Shabbat table there was a well-entrenched custom: no talk of everyday affairs, of work, of the shop, not even of studies at school. Rather, the atmosphere was festive, infused with holiness, and they carefully preserved the tradition of not bringing the secular into the holy day of rest.

The aromas from meals cooked in advance for Shabbat filled the air from early on Friday afternoons. Later, at the table, each person would sip from the wine over which Hanokh had made the blessing, before quickly moving on to the main meal. From infanthood, these were the scents and rhythms they had grown up on. Now they couldn't live without them. Chicken soup: it was always part of the meal, a staple in the Zaks family, small blobs of golden fat floating on the surface, enriching the flavor, drumsticks and chicken necks lying at the bottom of the pot. Volf and Yisrael loved those necks; Avraham and Yossef preferred the drumsticks. Batya and Miriam were less keen on the chicken itself and usually wanted nothing but the actual soup, but they loved the little blobs of fat, which were Yoheved's pride and proof of the quality of her cooking. The more the fat floating on the surface, the more nourishing the soup.

Next came the main course of chicken and meat, cooked for half a day, served alongside chopped liver and plenty of challah, the traditional braided loaves. Challah held a special place of honor at the Shabbat table. Yoheved timed it to place on the table, piping hot, at the last minute. Its aroma was even more loved than that of the soup. The challah had to be fully baked before Shabbat, to prevent desecrating the laws against cooking on the day of rest proscribed in the Bible. Each family member dipped chunks of challah in the soup, the aromas of the two foods blending.

Once a month another aroma filled the home. It was particularly comforting: cholent, eaten on the day of Shabbat, Saturday. All through Friday night and half of Saturday the family had to wait patiently, sniffing at the air as the cholent thickened into a wonderful stew, the scent so enticing that people walking to synagogue on Shabbat morning would smile.

Lunchtime was when cholent was traditionally served. The huge pot was kept warm all Shabbat on a small flame; it held bits of soft meat nestled among potatoes which had cooked ever so slowly. On top of them, "kishkeh," a sausage-styled dish with a tasty filling, cooked slowly.

Everyone loved the special meals of Shabbat night and the next day. It was at one of these Shabbat dinners, in the summer of 1936, when Hanokh sat down at the head of the table as he always did, and Batya noticed that her father seemed very pale and more quiet than usual.

"Papa? Do you feel okay?" she asked. Hanokh answered briefly. "Yes, I'm fine, don't worry, my dear daughter." Unconvinced, she never took her eyes off him the entire meal. Batya noticed sweat forming on his forehead and his hand started to shake so badly that he was unable to hold the spoon firmly, and soup kept falling back into his bowl. Standing, Batya quickly went over to him. At that instant he collapsed in his chair, almost toppling over, but Batya caught him on time. Her brothers, scared now, jumped out of their chairs and hurried over to support their father. Hanokh was conscious: "My chest hurts badly. I need to lie down," he said. Fleet-footed, Avraham raced out for the doctor; the other brothers helping their father to his bed. Yoheved peeled his clothes away. Hanokh groaned, spreading out on the bed, the family worriedly surrounding him. Slowly he calmed down, his breathing stable but heavy. Lying on his back, he smiled to his family. He appeared to be overcoming the pain.

Just then the doctor entered, asking everyone to leave the room. But Batya's gaze never left the doctor. "I want to stay in the room with Papa," she said. The doctor glanced at Hanokh. "It's all right. I want her to stay." Then came a pulse check, a stethoscope check of his heart and lungs front and back, and the doctor's hand rested momentarily on Hanokh's forehead to check his temperature. The doctor opened the bedroom door, calling Yoheved and the children back in.

"It seems your father has just experienced a light heart attack," he said softly. "Nothing much can be done. I'll prescribe medication to calm him but he needs to rest as much as possible now. Watch over him and make sure he doesn't overexert himself."

It was the first time Hanokh had experienced such an event. The family geared up to assist him. Batya, at just thirteen, was determined to take on responsibility for her father's care. "Mama, you manage the house, and let me take care of Papa," she said in her insistent tone, "I can do it, trust me, I won't let him do anything physical, just like the doctor ordered."

Although it was Shabbat Eve, and although it was not their custom to plan the week's events on the day of rest, the unexpected turn of events brought the siblings together that night to sit with Yoheved at the table and divide up their responsibilities. Batya had already taken on a role, and added that she wouldn't return to school until Hanokh was back to his old self. Volf, an accountant, took on the shop's management, and Yossef agreed to handling sales and suppliers. Avraham, still young, helped wherever he was needed. Miriam, older than Batya, would help Yoheved manage the large household. Yisrael worked as a manager in the nearby city: it was decided that he'd continue his job to ensure there was at least one salary constantly coming in.

Life started getting back to normal. A few days later Hanokh expressed his wish to return to the store. The brothers opposed his idea. "It's too early, Papa," Volf tried persuading him, but Hanokh was insistent. A discussion led to a compromise: Hanokh would return to certain activities in the shop, but wouldn't get involved in the stress of management. Batya said that she'd join her brothers to ensure their father wasn't overdoing things, and to care for him. And that's how Hanokh chose a spot near the back, watching and listening from a comfortable chair, but away from the hassle of dealing with clients. The brothers and Batya worked in the store, where they sold small items of furniture, shoes, and other basic pieces of clothing; but the store's focus was on quality fabrics used for sewing suits, curtains, sofa coverings, and so on.

Batya positioned herself at the till. Although still young, she was quick-witted for her age. That left Volf free to handle the accounts in a back room, and Yossef available to handle clients and suppliers. Even before the store reopened, Hanokh guided her: "Batya my dear daughter, pay close attention to me. I'll signal what you need to do. You always read me well, and I'm sure you'll understand my intentions."

It was hard to see Hanokh in the gloomy spot which the family had chosen to shield him from everyone. When a client was ready to pay, Hanokh gazed at his daughter. Batya, in turn, understood exactly what needed to be done by his facial gestures. When he raised an eyebrow, she knew she could let that client buy on credit. When he closed his eyes and dropped his head down a little, the client could be given what was asked for. By contrast, when he moved his head ever so slightly from side to side, Batya understood that the particular client needed to pay in advance. Sometimes Hanokh smiled broadly: that signaled to Batya that she could offer the client a generous discount. And so they spoke to each other, wordlessly, with no one catching on. Batya was a quick learner: it wasn't long before she was familiar with every client. Hanokh sat in his spot in the back, one hand clutching the other in silent applause: she was skilled, smart, and had a good sense of commerce, he thought to himself, smiling proudly.

But Hanokh Zaks was not only a successful businessman. He was a true mensch; a very decent, honest man of integrity, diplomacy and caring. One day Moisheh, in his shabby clothes, came into the shop, his eyes peering around for Hanokh, finding it strange that he wasn't at the counter. Moisheh was among the town's poorest people, barely able to provide for his family. He was also a merchant, but didn't have a shop of his own. He would come into Hanokh's shop, receiving fabric on credit, going house to house selling the goods. In the evening he'd pay for the fabrics he managed to sell, and return the rest. Hanokh never stated a sum, but let Moisheh pay whatever he could.

Not seeing Hanokh anywhere, Moisheh turned to Batya. "Could you give me some bolts of cloth to sell?" he asked almost in a whisper, ashamed that he needed to ask for goods on credit from a young lass. Batya glanced at her father, and in an instant realized what needed to be done. "Go into the warehouse. There's a pile of cloth ready for you, a bit of different kinds of things. Don't worry, I'll wait here until the evening," she said casually, as though this was an everyday incident for her, and turned to attend to another client waiting to pay. Moisheh bowed his head a little, went into the back, and loaded fabrics up on his shoulders, carting them out to his wagon. On the way out he noticed Hanokh and his face filled with concern: why was Hanokh seated aside from everyone else?

Hanokh smiled. "She knows our arrangement. Don't worry. Your honor won't be disrespected in any way." Moisheh, reassured, smiled bashfully again and left town in search of buyers for the fabrics.

Batya noticed the glimmer of satisfaction in her father's eyes. He'd done something helpful for the town's poor folk, who held a special place in his heart. She remembered that as a very small child she'd been sitting on her father's lap in winter, an icy wind howling outside. Snow was falling when a woman entered the shop.

"And how are you, Mrs. Beriski? How are you managing on these especially cold winter nights?"

The woman looked down in shame. "Yes, it's very cold in the house. We have an oven but it isn't enough to keep us warm, and we get into cold beds, my children and I."

"I have something that could help," Hanokh answered. "Wait a moment. I'll be right back." Putting Batya down on her feet, he went into the back room, then came out quickly with a very thick, warm blanket that he held out to her, smiling. "Please, take this," he said softly, his eyes lighting up. "I just remembered that there was this one which I hadn't been able to sell. It seems no one wanted it. So please, if you take it, you'll be helping me clear some space in the warehouse. I think it could be good for your girls."

"But Mr. Zaks, I have no money," the woman mumbled.

Hanokh waved his hand dismissively. "It's all right. You don't need to pay. I was planning on throwing it out. At least now I can sleep soundly knowing someone's putting it to good use. Take it, please, and be well."

Thanking him warmly, Mrs. Beriski took the blanket and left with a huge smile on her face. Batya watched her father. "Were you really going to throw it away?" Hanokh laughed. "Of course not. But we must let people keep their dignity. That's much more important than a few zlotys that people can't afford, and the main thing is that at least now they'll be warm in winter. Everyone deserves to live in dignity."

Hanokh's reputation spread far and wide. People from the towns surrounding Strzemieszyce came to shop at his store because he was known for being fair. Non-Jews loved him. He treated the poor with the same respect that he treated the wealthy. And the latter knew he would never try to overcharge them.

***

Batya could tell what he was feeling when he was in pain. She knew right away whether his heart was working normally or whether he should be given medication. She became his personal nurse, and he was her singular patient. The father she loved so much.

One evening before closing time and heading back upstairs to their home, Batya spoke to her father. "Papa, one second. I need to ask you something." Hanokh glanced at his daughter. "Papa, I want to learn medicine, or at least become a qualified nurse. What do you think?"

Hanokh relaxed, smiled, stroked her hand and spoke gently. "You already know almost everything. You were born to care for others. Please G-d, of course you can learn, depending on our situation and the possibilities. But first of all, complete your studies at the gymnasium," he said, using the term common at the time for high school.

"My child," Hanokh added, "G-d gave you a great gift. You'll heal people just by looking at them. Take me, for example. I'm getting well faster just from the way you watch me, from your ability to understand. Yes, you were born for that, Batya." She smiled, pleased that he would support her choice of profession. Up until that conversation she'd begun to think that she would need to spend her whole life caring for him, and she was ready to do that, with great love, but giving his blessing to her choice made her swell with joy. Yes, Papa understood, too, that she was born to be a great doctor or nurse.

***

The war, though, meant that the shop closed down as the battles worsened, and his sons leaving worsened Hanokh's health. Only after banging his head against the door in frustration and helplessness over the circumstances that had led his sons to leave the house; and only after praying to G-d for tranquility and support, was he finally able to calm down a little.

***

Right after the boys had gone on their way, Hanokh called Yoheved and his daughters. "We're on our own. The shop's closed. The boys have left despite my opinion and wishes, despite my vision to stay together as one close-knit, united family, and despite the education I gave them." He choked on his tears as the girls watched him with growing concern, remembering how he'd given the boys money and even wished them success. Hanokh stroked Miriam's and Batya's hands gently. "The boys are in my heart, and always will be. We'll stay together and wait for them here at home, because I'm sure they'll be back once they realize there's nothing better than our family being together."

Some days later, not a week into the war yet, things quieted down a little in the street, but fear clouded the air. Every so often, German soldiers would march through the streets but kept out of the town's affairs. Hanokh considered reopening the store. "We have to get back to a routine," he said to the girls. Miriam, predominantly busy with household matters, didn't react. Batya, by contrast, had a response ready. "Not yet, Papa. I'm still very afraid. You're not healthy, and we're going through tough times. I think it's still a bit too early. After all, our merchandise doesn't go bad."

On the Friday after the boys left, Miriam and Batya set the Shabbat table. "You rest, Mama," Miriam said to Yoheved, "and let us cook." Miriam made soup, baked challah exactly the way Yoheved had taught her, and the aromas of chicken soup on the fire together with the bread rising in the oven began to fill the house. But something was missing: the aroma and ambience of a family together. The food smelled of war, of smoke, of dust raised by refugees, and tanks, and military trucks. It was a smell of absence: not so much a material shortage, since there was plenty of food on the table, but the absence of holiness which was usually present at their Shabbat Friday night meal. The table itself was in short supply of family members: it seemed meager; it spoke of lack.

Hanokh and Yoheved, dressed in their Shabbat clothes, came to the table. Yoheved barely stifled a cry. Hanokh scowled. "And where are the boys' chairs? And Haiya's?" Hanokh asked.

Yoheved, Miriam and Batya gazed at him, their eyes wide. "But Papa, they aren't here," Batya said, and paused before continuing in a sadder tone, "and we have to get used to it."

Hanokh looked at them, his anger evaporating, and the touch of a smile playing on his lips. "Tell me: is Elijah the Prophet here? He's also not in this house right now, is that not so? But every Passover on the first evening, we prepare a seat for him, and believe he'll come. We've never stopped believing that. For two thousand years we've prepared a place for him at the Passover celebration. So now, just a week after the boys have set off, shall we start believing they'll never be back? Absolutely not! Set the table again, and make sure there's room for everyone, for Avraham, for Haiya, for Volf and Yisrael, and add a chair for Yossef who's in the army. Each one of us in our set places."

Miriam and Batya were not about to argue. Immediately they shifted chairs and tableware around, and did exactly as they had done for years: places for everyone at the table. Once Hanokh was satisfied, he sat down. "Add wine glasses. They're part of our Kiddush, our blessing over the wine and Shabbat."

Yoheved made the blessings over the candles. Hanokh poured the wine. Miriam, who usually said very little, spoke up. "Admittedly, the chairs are empty but the wine makes up for it, lessens the feeling that the family isn't whole." The rest of the family glanced at the empty chairs, and together recited the blessing over the goblet of wine, as they did every Shabbat.

THE BROTHERS' JOURNEY

Yisrael, Volf and Avraham were left with a few banknotes in their pockets, stunned that they'd fallen victim to the sly wagoner who'd left them pretty much in the middle of nowhere. More than that, they were furious with themselves for not being cautious and suspicious enough. Why, they wondered, had they let the wagoner take control, especially since they'd realized the danger?

Yisrael was the first to recover. "C'mon," he said to his brothers, "let's just keep going. There's nothing else we can do. I reckon we have a bit less than a hundred kilometers to go. Five days if we keep up a good pace. We'll go on foot and from now on we won't let anyone bluff us. We'll be okay. We've got papers. They'll protect us."

Volf and Avraham nodded their agreement. None of them was going to take any more chances. They'd just plod on. With only two hundred zlotys left, they'd barely have enough for food along the way.

A few hundred meters off, a barricade was buzzing with police. They approached carefully. Yisrael spoke in an undertone. "The main thing is to stay cool. It's natural and logical to be afraid of police but anyone who looks afraid is immediately going to make them suspicious. We don't need to be scared. We've got papers."

At the barrier, Avraham, short, young, and inexperienced in the big wide world, was unable to hide a tremor. He held onto Yisrael's hand for moral support. They were facing two police officers, one German and one Polish, recruited to identify criminals and Jews. The brothers showed their documents, keeping their backs straight. The German looked the documents over. Yisrael spoke to him in fluent German.

"Sir, we've already been okayed by the German military at Kielce. As the officer sees, we've been authorized to go on our way." Yisrael knew that lower-level officers loved hearing their rank stated out loud and being spoken to with respect. The German was pleased with the tone of dignity Yisrael used, glancing repeatedly at their documents until satisfied.

"Everything is fine, you are free to go," he said, returning the papers. "Have an easy journey."

Without looking back, the boys distanced themselves from the barrier. Once they'd gone far enough not to arouse doubt, they broke into a trot, getting as far as they could as quickly as they could. Only then did they sigh with relief.

They passed through several towns, each one preceded by a military or police barrier. Many refugees left the main roads and preferred the fields as they attempted to bypass the barricades and avoid contact with officials. The three walked on the road, following Volf's logic. "We've got documents," he said, "so standing at barriers shows we have nothing to fear. And it'd look strange to get picked up going through the fields if we've got documents. That wouldn't make any sense to them."

"Nothing to fear but being Jewish," Yisrael added as the brothers broke into smiles and shrugs. As they approached the small township of Checiny, which they knew well, they were already feeling a whole lot better about things. They stood in the line briefly, their papers were checked, and very quickly they were waved on.

Going through barrier after barrier let them pick up on the latest news: the curfew, placed on villages and towns every nightfall, residents being forced to remain indoors until the next morning's sunrise. Curfews now dictated when people went to bed. Beforehand, they'd always gone out in the evenings, and they would often sleep outdoors. Now, as they approached their own town, they were charged with new energy. Sore legs or not, a spring had revitalized into their step.

The fourth day of walking brought them to Wolbrom, some thirty kilometers from Strzemieszyce. They walked into the town minutes before sunset and the start of the curfew. "Well, we know people here, so let's find somewhere to sleep," Avraham said. Yisrael considered the idea and opposed. "No," he said firmly, "we're very close to home. One more day and we've made it. So we don't want to risk anything. We have no idea what's happened to our acquaintances in this place. Maybe they fled. Maybe they were arrested. No, we shouldn't stay here. Let's get out beyond the town's borders and find somewhere to spend the night outside. I also think we should stay awake the whole night. No risks at the last second."

They walked away from the town. Not far off, they found an abandoned rickety shed on the roadside, adjacent to an apple orchard and clearly used as a packing house and storage for apples. Here and there, there were still some apples hanging off the trees, and the boys went out and picked as many as they could eat, plus a few more to take with them the next day to ward off the hunger.

"What do you think is the situation at home? Is everyone alive? Did Haiya already get home? What about Papa? Is his heart holding up?" Volf wondered aloud.

"*Ayayai*," Avraham whispered, "I miss Mama so much. I've been dreaming about her food, about the smell of her cooking."

"I'm sure they're all fine," Yisrael reassured them. "Papa's a smart guy, Batya's looking after him, and I have no doubt they're managing well."

Knowing that there wasn't too far left to go moved them deeply. Not for a moment did they shut their eyes. Volf calculated out loud. "Today's Thursday. Four days ago was Yom Kippur. So we've been on the road for almost four weeks. Tomorrow, we'll make it home. I'm dreaming of our Shabbat table. Oh, what a wonderful day it'll be to be home again. No better day than that!"

"And Papa won't forego our Shabbat meal on Friday night. No war will take that from him!" Yisrael added.

The hours ticked by slowly. They sat awake, waiting for first light. Through the treetops, they eventually noticed the sky changing hue, but because they weren't sure whether the curfew ended at sunrise or at full light, they decided to wait another half hour.

At last, the three set out at a brisk pace. The first ten kilometers were an easy stride. Then they stopped to rest briefly. They continued along the paths they knew so well. The main road was a mess, cratered by the German air force's bombing, rain filling the pits in the street. The path became muddier, but they never slowed down. On the contrary, they walked faster. For the last five kilometers, they broke into a run. People walking along the street gazed at them in wonder. "Where are you rushing off to?" they asked. What could they say? That they could feel their home's presence drawing them closer? They said nothing and ran.

Fractured along its edges but still standing, the sign announcing "Strzemieszyce" with its rusty pole was a welcome sight. Only when they'd entered their town, did they stop running. Fear crept into their hearts as they noticed destroyed homes, islands of shards and broken items everywhere; with filth piled up in the streets. "Are we home? Is this really our town?" Volf asked aloud. Avraham began to sob. "What if our house is also destroyed?" he whimpered. Volf and Yisrael hugged him. "We're also very concerned about that," Volf said softly, before slowly adding: "Until we actually get there, we're not even sure we have a house, parents, or a family." But Yisrael shook his head firmly. "Don't worry. I've got a good feeling about this. C'mon, let's get home!"

It was almost evening but the sun hadn't set yet; the curfew hadn't begun. Encouraged, they strode on, hope mingled with worry. Minutes later they were in their street, passing the synagogue, stopping, stunned. The original doors had been ripped out. In their stead, planks of wood had been nailed diagonally to block the entrance. The outer walls had lost their plaster; the plain gray brick was laid bare. Looking at the shattered windows, the brothers realized that no prayers had been held there for some time. This night, too, the synagogue would remain silent.

And in the distance, their home's high roof. "Look! It's standing!" Avraham shouted. "Yes, we've got a home," Yisrael added. "I just hope it's our family there inside," Volf said. Only minutes to go to Shabbat, and the start of the curfew. The brothers sprinted the final distance. "Cholent. It's the smell of cholent!" Volf exclaimed. "Mama's cholent!" Avraham roared, "To last for tomorrow, it'll be sitting on the fire all night… just like I dreamed of. It's our house, our family!"

Avraham was the first inside. Seconds later, Volf and Yisrael almost catapulted themselves in. They stood there, silent: at the table, set for everyone, their father stood, holding the Shabbat wine goblet, saying the prayer: "And the heavens and the earth and all their host…"

Cries of joy broke out all at once. Haiya fell into Yisrael's arms. Miriam and Batya hugged Avraham and Volf. Everyone hugged Yoheved and Hanokh. And everyone cried. With relief, with joy. Despite the war, the fear, the curfew, here they all were, reunited. How uplifted they all felt.

"Sit, sit, my children," Hanokh said. "Here are your seats, your place settings, ready and waiting. Everything in place, ready for you."

"How'd you know…?" Volf wondered aloud.

"Of course we knew," Hanokh answered. "Look! Your chairs are ready, your wine glasses are full, everything's in its place just waiting for your return."

"But…" Volf wondered, "how'd you know we'd be back today of all days?"

"Of course we knew," Hanokh answered again. "Every Shabbat Eve, everything was readied for your return, and here you are. Now, let's drink the wine as though celebrating your redemption, like the glass of wine symbolizing the redemption to come that Elijah the Prophet will announce. Come, be seated, my children, just as you are, dirty from the road but happy, and let's start the Shabbat meal together."

Ah, the scent of fresh challah, the aroma of hot chicken soup, the heat coming from the Shabbat cholent warming in the oven, made a singular message very clear to them: "We're home."

REOPENING

Having eaten heartily, the brothers described the events they'd experienced from the moment that Haiya left. Hanokh and Yoheved listened, eyes wide and mouths occasionally falling open. Miriam and Batya actually cried.

That over at last, Hanokh sighed. "My dear sons, from this moment and until the war ends, may that happen speedily, we're staying together. That's, well, that's an order and we won't stray from it. Through good and bad, we'll stay together. Nor will we forget your brother Yossef, off soldiering and at risk. Although we have no idea where he is or what's happened to him, my deepest feeling is that he'll return too."

Hanokh paused to catch his breath before continuing. "On Monday we'll reopen the shop. Germans are wandering around, casting fear wherever they go, but the sooner we restore our routine, the better it'll be for us all. For now, my dear boys, go and shower. There's a lot of work awaiting us. Tomorrow, Shabbat, will indeed be a day of rest and getting your energy back for the week ahead. On Sunday we'll all go downstairs into the store and prepare the place for reopening."

Once Yisrael had showered, he and Haiya went to their room. Volf and Avraham went to bed while Batya and Miriam cleared the table. The house looked very much like everything was back to normal, and only the sound of German boots marching down the street imposed on the family's togetherness.

Batya slipped into the boys' room for a last hug before going to bed. "You know, it's been so hard for me to fall asleep," she said to Avraham and Volf. "Every night I hear those boots slamming down on the street and I just die with fright. In my mind I see them coming in here and taking me. Every footstep I hear outside makes me jump from bed. Only when they go away, do I fall asleep for a few minutes but then I wake up again, panicked. But now that you're back, I feel better. Thank you for returning. I love you so much."

Miriam also came to wish them goodnight, quiet, easygoing, as always. She sat down on the side of Avraham's bed. "I missed you all so much," she whispered. "I was so worried. I wanted to cook for you… every Friday I baked the bread and made the soup with Mama and waited for you to come through our front door. And here, today… a miracle. Papa never gave up hope, you know, not for a second. Every Friday he insisted we set the table as though you'd all just walk right back in on time for the meal and sit down. Ever since you left, the food was nowhere near as tasty as usual, but the instant you came back, it smelled so good, it tasted so good. Please, I'm begging you, don't leave us ever again…"

"How's Papa's health?" Volf asked.

"We didn't let him do a thing," Batya said. "But irrespective of that, I'm sure from now on he'll feel a whole lot better." Batya hugged each of her brothers, wished them goodnight, and the boys fell asleep in an instant.

Strolling down the street on Shabbat morning, the brothers encountered a sad and pitiful town. Jewish shops, such as the bakery and the butcher, were shut of course, it being the holy day of rest, but there was some other strange element in the atmosphere. "There are no Jews in the street. Only non-Jews. I wonder if we shouldn't get right back home," Yisrael said. On their way back, they saw German police standing at the windows of the family store. "What do you think's going on there?" Avraham asked softly. "What do they want?"

"Is this your shop?" one of the officers asked as the brothers approached the front door. He looked like the group's commander.

"Yes," they answered simultaneously.

"And when does it open?" the German asked.

"Monday, sir," Yisrael answered.

The German pointed to a can of paint and brushes lying at the entrance. "Take those, and tomorrow you will paint a large Star of David on each display window and the door. Until you do that, you can't open up." Flashing threatening stares at the brothers, they Germans turned on their heels and went to the next store.

Upstairs, the brothers conveyed the new decree. Hanokh listened, his face severe. He thought, then spoke. "We'll do as they ask. The main thing is to reopen. Everyone knows we're Jews. We can't escape that. So we'll carry on as usual and see what happens."

Early on Sunday morning the family cleaned the store, arranged the merchandise, and were happy to discover that nothing had been damaged in the bombings other than two shattered windows. Avraham found and inserted new glass panels. The sisters cleaned shelves, Hanokh reorganized the till and the ledgers, and the brothers brought rolls of cloth from the warehouse into the store. Avraham painted the Stars of David as required. By evening, the store was ready to open its doors on Monday morning.

***

Stomping down the street woke Batya during the night. She stayed in bed, trembling. The footsteps stopped under her window. What was happening? Would they carry on? Would they try to come upstairs? She thought of waking her parents but then decided on waking the boys instead. On tiptoes she went into the room, shaking Volf and Avraham gently, putting her finger to her lips. "Sshhh…but there's the sound of boots again outside and they've stopped under my window."

Silence. They heard voices in German but couldn't make out the words. Some minutes later, they heard more heavy footsteps walking by. They held their breath. Then they heard the footsteps disappearing into the night. A sigh of relief came from each of them. "They must've come to check if we'd painted the Star of David before reopening tomorrow," Volf whispered.

***

The entire family woke up early that morning. They wanted to open shop as quickly as possible: the need for routine carried a sense of urgency. In their minds, they knew that this morning would be different from the mornings before the war when they'd opened shop after Shabbat to start the new week.

Batya settled herself down next to the till, asking her father to take his place on his mostly concealed chair. Avraham went into the warehouse to check last minute arrangements, and Yisrael and Volf stood at the entrance so that passersby would get the impression that things were indeed back to normal. An hour passed. Two. No one came in. People walking down the street glanced at the store and walked on.

It was early afternoon when Marek, considered one of the wealthiest men in the town, came in. Marek was Polish, not Jewish, and had always enjoyed excellent relations with the Zaks family. Hanokh stood, came over to him and held his hand out. Marek ignored it, refusing to shake it, to the family's shock. Marek signaled to Hanokh, the two coming closer to one another, and Marek asked to speak privately to Hanokh.

"Hanokh my friend, things are really tough. I apologize for not shaking your hand at the shop's entrance but we were being watched."

That startled Hanokh. "Watched? By whom? What's going on here? The Germans asked us to paint the Star of David on the store and we did, so what more do they want?"

"Things will get really difficult for you here. I tried talking to the police commander about the good Jews in this city. I wanted your lives here to be as normal as possible, but he's not cooperating yet." The blood left Hanokh's face. "People won't be coming to shop out of fear of the Germans. Maybe Jews will come in, but money's starting to run out. There's a policeman on the other corner checking who's coming in. There may be no choice but to dole out bribes to the Germans, as money, but perhaps also as goods. I'm your good friend, and I know you're admired in the community, among non-Jews too, but I don't know how long that will help."

"What do you suggest?" Hanokh asked, deeply concerned.

"Send some bolts of luxury cloth to my office as a gift to the German police commander. I'll make sure that curtains get sewn for him, and make sure it's known to be a gift, and we'll see how he reacts." With a nod to Hanokh he left the store. Hanokh stood there open-mouthed. No one else came into the store.

The siblings heard the conversation. As they mulled over what Marek had said, two Polish policemen and a German Nazi walked in. Looking around, they fingered various fabrics. Silence filled the store. None of the Zakses moved. Hanokh faced them, standing straight, looking them in the eye.

"And how may I help you?" he asked. The German looked at Hanokh with evident disdain, and called Avraham over from where he'd sat in a corner of the shop.

"Hoist the fabrics we want onto your shoulders." They pointed to several colorful, expensive bolts; Avraham did as asked.

"Those cost 500 zlotys, sirs," Batya said.

The Germans never bothered to glance in her direction. Instead, they prodded Avraham out into the street and ordered him to follow them. Unburdened, they walked quickly. Avraham strained himself to keep up, his head bent down from the effort, until they reached the office seized by the Germans as a center from which to manage the city.

"Put them down there and run back to the shop, stinking little Jew."

Avraham about-turned and ran back in fear. Puffing hard, he burst into the store. "That was terrible," he said to the waiting faces.

Volf and Yisrael suggested closing the store and reopening the next day. Hanokh studied them. "On no account. The store stays open until evening and we'll get them used to it being open. We're not caving in so quickly."

YOSSEF

Avraham was the first to see Yossef return from the army. He noticed him partway up the street when he went out to sweep the store's entrance. Initially he was sure his eyes were playing some kind of trick on him. A moment later he identified the familiar face, which was fast approaching.

"He's back! He's back!" Avraham burst into the store, bubbling with excitement. "I just saw Yossef. He's here…"

Moments later Yossef entered, slowly, tiredly, smiling bashfully. He was very pale. His lovely face was now covered in wrinkles. He said nothing, just stood there, melting into his family's embraces. They hugged; he was silent. He was still silent when Hanokh raised his eyes towards the heavens. "Thank G-d. You're back with us now, Yossef," he said in a voice choked with emotion.

Yossef looked at each one in turn but said nothing. Seconds later, he spoke to no one in particular. "I'm hungry, I'm exhausted, and I need to sit for a bit."

Batya quickly drew a chair up close for him. He crumpled down onto it. "I'm going up to make some food," Miriam said. "I need only a few minutes."

Volf placed his arms around Yossef, supporting him as Yossef stood, and together they went upstairs. Miriam had already set the table and had food cooking from whatever she'd found in the pantry. She reheated the leftover Shabbat soup; Yossef ate slowly, smiling at each spoonful, enjoying the flavors of home. The bowl empty, Yossef looked at Miriam, his face expressing love and appreciation.

Meanwhile Yoheved had prepared the bath, setting out clean underwear and festive clothing on the bed that had been empty for so many months in the boys' room.

Yossef's movements were slow and clumsy. He let his mother remove his shirt and undershirt. Yoheved signaled to Volf, who walked him to the bath, stripped the rest of his clothes and eased him into the steaming water. He sunk slowly down into the water, dunking low to wash the layers of dust from his hair and beard. Volf kept an eye on him from the adjacent room, at Yoheved's request. "Your brother isn't okay," she whispered to Volf; indeed, when he glanced in, he noticed Yossef closing his eyes and tears rolling down his brother's cheeks.

"What happened, Yossef? Are you alright? Can I help with something?" Volf asked, worried. Yossef gazed back at him. "It's just so good to be home," was all he said

Wrapped in a large towel, Yossef eventually left the bathroom. In the bedroom he noted the clothes his mother had laid out: a white shirt and dark blue pants, both ironed to perfection. Slowly he stroked the cloth. "So good to be home," he whispered. Hearing him, Batya went over and hugged him tightly. "So good to have you back with us. We've missed you so much. At last, we're all together again." He stood limply in her embrace. Then he gently moved her hands away, saying that he needed to sleep. He hung the shirt and pants on the back of a chair, lay down on the bed, and instantly fell into a deep sleep.

Batya stepped quietly out of the room, joining Volf and Miriam back down in the shop. Avraham and Yisrael were also there, worried about their newly returned brother. "He isn't all right. That's not our Yossef," Yisrael said, shaking his head. "I know him well," Avraham answered. "Let's give him a chance to sleep well and I'm sure when he wakes up, he'll be fine, happy, and laughing like he always did."

But like Yisrael, Yoheved was also deeply concerned. "He worries me, Hanokh. There's no doubt he's going through something very tough. Yossef isn't talking. He's not the same Yossef as before his military service."

Hanokh listened to his wife. "Yes, I also see that he's going through something. Time will heal him," he smiled, embracing his wife warmly. "He'll rest, recuperate, and get back to work in the shop. Yossef's our best salesman. Getting back into the swing of things will help heal him. We just need patience."

Later Yoheved checked on Yossef: his was a restless sleep, arms and legs fidgeting, eyes opening momentarily before immediately falling asleep again. Stroking his cheek, Yoheved whispered in his ear. "Sleep, rest, my beloved son. The main thing is that you're back. We'll take care of you." She kissed his forehead and silently left the room.

In the evening, the family closed the shop and sat down to eat together. Their joy at everyone being home at last was tinged by sorrow. "Yes, he's back, but he's not really with us yet," Yisrael said, as he glanced at the faces around the table. "A lot's going to depend on us. We need to help him as much as we can, keep a close eye on him. "Papa," he said, turning to Hanokh, "Tomorrow, let's give him some kind of job to do in the shop. He needs to do what he loves best. He was always good with clients, with sales. It's too bad we don't have a lot of shoppers right now but I'm sure you'll come up with something."

Hanokh nodded. "Don't worry, I've already got a couple of ideas. As of tomorrow, Yossef will be working with us in the store."

After dinner, Avraham and Volf went into the bedroom where Yossef was still sleeping. They sighed, wished each other goodnight and quickly fell asleep. But during the night they woke to odd sounds coming from Yossef's bed. His eyes tightly closed, he cried and was begging for his life. "Please, don't beat me, let me be. Enough, enough! Mama, save me…"

Gently they shook him awake. "Where am I? Who's here?" Yossef's voice trembled. He was curled up tight under the blanket.

"It's us. Volf and Avraham, your brothers. You're home at last. Sshhh. Everything's all right now," they whispered until he calmed down.

Yossef's body stretched out. "Yossef, what's going on? Where were you? What did they do to you?" Volf asked, fearful of the answer.

Yossef gazed at them, silent, then slowly his gaze wandered away. "I can't talk about it," he said, firmly but quietly.

Volf and Avraham never slept that entire night. They lay in their beds, silent, wondering what their brother had experienced, and their hearts ached for him. Yossef, waking early, noticed his brothers wide awake in their beds.

"Good morning," he said, "let's go down to the shop," as though nothing had happened during the night. "I want to get back to work."

They laughed, feeling that the brother they had known had never left. Making their way into the kitchen, they found their parents already there. Hanokh stood, walked over to Yossef and hugged him warmly, kissing the top of his head. "How wonderful that you're here. We really need you."

Looking at him, a huge smile lit Yossef's face. "What needs to be done, Papa?" Hanokh lightly clapped his shoulder. "Go down to the shop and take care of the display window. We couldn't get it looking right no matter how much we tried. You're the only one who does that properly. Bring whatever you need from the warehouse to set it up attractively. We need buyers and you're the one who can bring them. Go, my son, and I'll come down to the shop soon."

Yossef quickly made his way downstairs, Volf and Avraham at his heels. Yisrael, already there, wished his brothers a good morning and hugged Yossef. This time Yossef responded warmly. "It's so great that you're back with us, my brother," Yisrael whispered in Yossef's ear. Yossef smiled.

In the warehouse, he felt at home: all the things he was used to, in the places where they should be. He set to work, piling bolts of cloth onto his shoulders and stepping into the display window. Back and forth he went several times. The brothers watched, amazed, at his confident movements as Yossef arranged the window. First, he put a green cloth next to the yellow. Then a very dark blue one next to that. He loved white and used that next. Yossef positioned the white ones on cubes as though they were making their way down steps. In the warehouse, he found the male mannequin, stood it up in the window, and draped the best cloths over it. He'd never used the mannequin before. A few moments later, he rubbed his palms together, smiling. Yossef felt very pleased with the outcome.

Stepping out of the window area back into the shop, he found the whole family watching him, amazement on their faces. Batya clapped while the others joined in, applauding his work. Hanokh and Yoheved hugged him warmly. "That's a talented Yossef…" Hanokh said. The smile froze on Yossef's face and then disappeared. Yossef didn't respond to his father's remark but just remained silent. Then he gazed at his parents and whispered. "I'm tired, Papa. I need to go back to sleep." Dragging himself slowly, he went back upstairs to the bedroom.

Volf and Avraham went into the street. They were surprised to see several people gazing at the window display: recently hardly anyone had entered, and anyone passing the shop did so quickly. "Look what some well-arranged pieces of cloth can do…" Avraham whispered to Volf. "Yes," Volf agreed, "but what's the use of a really lovely window if no one buys the goods. I really hope people will start buying again, fast."

Hanokh locked the shop. The family went upstairs to their home. "Volf, go check on your brother," Yoheved asked softly. Standing in the corridor, Volf peeked into the bedroom. Yossef lay in bed, awake and restless.

Avraham entered and sat down next to Yossef, taking his hand in his own. "Yossef, where have you been? Tell me what happened to you." Yossef, his eyes closed, spoke in a low tone. "I was in Lublin, at the Russian front. They took us into captivity. They beat me over and over and over…It was their entertainment. Beating POWs. And then some weeks later, they just let me go home." He stopped speaking for some minutes before adding, his eyes still closed, "More than that, there's no need to know. I can't talk. Enough," and fell asleep.

On tiptoe, careful not to wake Yossef, Avraham left the room and told the family what Yossef had said. "What a trick of fate," Yisrael said. "He was in Russian captivity near Lublin, and we were in German captivity not far from there."

The family did the best they could for Yossef. They gave him various jobs in the shop to keep his thoughts busy with things other than his experiences. Yossef worked hard but every so often would need to sit and rest, silent, his gaze vague. Every night the nightmares returned, Volf and Avraham standing close and calming him down until he fell asleep again.

On Shabbat morning Avraham walked in holding a football. He tossed it towards Yossef. “Come out to the yard, let’s play like we used to,” he invited Yossef, who smiled broadly. They ran about, they laughed a bit, as the rest of the family watched from the windows upstairs. “Look at Yossef. He’s starting to come back to us,” Hanokh said. Volf nodded. “I’m waiting to hear the first time he tells a joke. Then we’ll know he’s really with us.” Yossef and Avraham played on; Yossef laughed a bit, but was mostly silent.

WORKING IN THE SHOP

Yossef was home for two months now. Although the shop was open every weekday, shoppers were few and far between, whoever did come in were Jews, and their money was running out. The family's income was dropping fast. Haiya had no choice but to work in the "shop", the nickname that stuck to the Többens and Schultz textile conglomerate, which had once proudly produced high-class clothing for shops across Germany, but since the war, had switched its factories over to sewing German military uniforms. On the Germans' orders, Yisrael went back to the refurbished metals factory in the nearby city where he'd worked before the war.

In the meantime, the German police officer came into the Zaks's shop almost daily, his greedy eyes roving over the goods. Every so often, he would simply set aside one of the bolts of cloth that took his fancy. No one in the Zaks family said a word. They watched him openly stealing, but stayed silent.

Winter came. December 1939 was particularly cold. Snow began falling. The German in his SS uniform came into the shop with orders for Hanokh. "Bring me all the warm fabric you have. We need it as blankets for the soldiers. Send your sons to the command center. The younger one already knows where it is. Schnell! Schnell! Hurry up. I want it done now." He spun on his heel and returned to his fixed place in the street.

Avraham, Volf and Yossef loaded cloth on their shoulders and set off for the SS offices. From the corners of their eyes, they noticed the town's residents watching them, fear mingling with disdain. Many of the people in the street never even moved out of the brothers' way to make it easier for them, forcing them to step down onto the road, then back up onto the sidewalk, and so on repeatedly, the heavy cloth becoming more burdensome as the walk lengthened. They didn't dare stop to rest.

They reached the SS command center after what felt like an endless walk, almost tripping over their own feet as they walked up the stairs leading to the heavy front door. Through its glass panes they saw German soldiers lounging around. None stood to open the door.

"Put your bolts on me," Volf said, almost collapsing under the extra weight as Avraham, both hands now free, opened the door for his brothers. Avraham was already familiar to the police officer at the reception counter: the man signaled Avraham to enter. "Follow me," he said. The three brothers did, placing the cloth where they were told before quickly leaving.

Hanokh looked utterly dejected when they returned. For some time now he'd understood that the shop wouldn't be able to provide the family with a livelihood as it had done. "My children, stay in the shop," he instructed. "I need to talk to Marek, face to face."

Despite being unwell, Hanokh walked quickly. As soon as Hanokh entered the wealthy Pole's office, Marek locked the door right away, not before casting a concerned glance at the street. Hanokh sat down slowly and said, "It won't be long before there'll be no merchandise left in the store. I'm asking you to help by meeting with the police officer and reaching an arrangement with him. I promise you that you'll only profit from it."

Marek was all ears. "I'm willing to set up a meeting with him, but it must be clear to you, my friend, that the favor won't be gratis. He'll want payment in return for letting your store stay open and allowing Poles to buy there rather than letting people take merchandise without paying. You know that the Jews' shops have been shutting one after the other, and the owners are being sent north, or to Germany... no one even knows where exactly."

"I'll pay whatever it takes," Hanokh agreed immediately, "but I need to receive an assurance that all of us, my family and myself, will be safe and protected."

Marek smiled, reassuring Hanokh. "I'll talk to the commander today, and let you know tomorrow when you can meet him."

Despite Marek's promise, worry and concern over the future gnawed at Hanokh's heart. On the way back, he walked slowly past the Jewish shops, checking their status. The grocery store was still running, but the bakery was burnt to ash. Hanokh had indeed heard that a bakery had gone up in flames two days ago, but for some reason hadn't imagined it possible that it would be his friend Yehuda's place. As he stood in front of the pile of ash and debris, a passerby stopped, spat and commented. "At last, they burnt the Jew's bakery. I heard he was also sent to some unknown place." Without giving Hanokh a glance he walked on.

Hanokh stopped at Avrum's menswear shop before stepping inside. "My friend Avrum, what happened to your beard?" Hanokh asked, startled.

His eyes welling with tears, Avrum explained. "Two thugs grabbed me in the street, tied me up, and some kid came along with scissors and chopped it off. The neighbors, may G-d punish them, just stood around watching and laughing. Someone spat on me, someone else kicked me, and I couldn't do anything but stand there, ashamed. All I wanted was for them to finish with their humiliation and let me go home." Avrum went silent before whispering to Hanokh. "It's no good here and it's only going to get worse. We have to flee. But we don't have anywhere to flee to."

The most Hanokh could do was hug him before going back to his own shop, where he refused to answer Yoheved and the children's questions about his talk with Marek.

The next day, an unfamiliar man walked into the shop, wordlessly placed an envelope on the counter, and then disappeared. Hanokh opened it, reading Marek's message: "Be at the police headquarters today at 3 p.m. I'll wait for you there." Folding the note up, Hanokh stuffed it into his pocket, telling the family about the meeting shortly before setting out.

Leaving at two forty-five, Hanokh took a beautiful piece of gift wrapped in crimson cloth with him. He walked up the command center's wide steps. "I have a meeting with the commander," Hanokh answered the police officer's inquiry, "and Mr. Marek." He was instructed to wait while the officer went inside to check. Some minutes later he came back out accompanied by another policeman. "Go in. The commander's office is at the end of the corridor." Hanokh thanked him. The second policeman walked Hanokh down to the office. "Wait here and you'll be called," he said. A bench was lined up against the wall a few steps away but Hanokh felt more at ease standing next to the door.

Minutes passed. Hanokh was still standing next to the door. Slowly Hanokh lost his perception of time. He stood silently. Once in a while, a police officer would pass him without even glancing his way. Hanokh could feel the blood draining from his head to his feet. He was afraid his heart wouldn't be able to withstand the physical exertion but still didn't dare to sit. It was 4.30 when the door finally opened and Marek signaled with his hand. "Come in."

Seated in a tall-backed chair at the desk was an SS officer. Behind him the red Nazi flag, black swastika at the center, hung down from the ceiling. On the wall hung an enlarged photo of Hitler. As he stepped into the office, a thought flashed through Hanokh's mind: What cheap cloth they've used for the flag! But quickly he rebuked himself: That's what I'm thinking about right now? A cloth merchant through and through.

Hanokh stood at the officer's desk, maintaining a respectful distance. He looked down before speaking. "My thanks to you, sir, for receiving me." The officer said nothing. Marek also said nothing. Don't let that put you off, Hanokh encouraged himself. Despite feeling physically weak, he stood tall and placed the package on the officer's desk. "Sir, in thanks for your generosity, I've brought you a token of appreciation." The officer stayed silent; Hanokh, feeling a cold sweat gather on his forehead and back, continued. "It would be my privilege to bring you additional such gifts. I trust you will agree to allowing my store to remain open for business, and allowing clients to visit it." He purposely did not stipulate Polish clients.

Some moments later the officer nodded. It seemed to Hanokh that the officer had accepted the arrangement. Raising his hand, the officer gave a quick wave towards the door. Hanokh glanced at the officer, then at Marek, who was still silent, and took several paces backwards as he spoke. "Many thanks, sir, commander," he said before turning around and leaving. Closing the door behind him, he breathed deeply, eyeing the bench in the corridor and feeling he was about to collapse. He hadn't sat for more than a couple of seconds before the door opened again and Marek came out.

"Go home now. I'll talk to you later."

Hanokh stood. "Thank you very much, my friend," he whispered.

Marek gave an impatient wave and went back inside the office.

Hanokh walked slowly home.

ESCALATION

Stepping into the shop, Hanokh called the family together. "I asked. I promised. More than that, I can't do. Let's wait and see what happens." The family ate dinner together, their chatter suppressed. That night Hanokh did not sleep well, waking several times from a feeling of terror. Each time he woke, he stared at the ceiling until he fell back asleep.

Marek came to the store early the next morning. Without offering his usual cheery greetings, he went straight over to Hanokh. "Listen, I spoke to the officer. He promised nothing bad would happen to you," he said in an undertone, "and also authorized non-Jews to buy here. But I can't promise it will continue that way. For now, though, you're protected."

Answering in a similar fashion, Hanokh asked: "How much will this cost?"

"What you brought yesterday is fine, but he'll be expecting something every week."

"Marek, I'll never forget your help," Hanokh said, moved. "Please, let me show you my appreciation with a thank-you gift. Take something for your wife. There are still plenty of lovely things here. Thank you, Marek."

Standing, Marek pointed to cloth which he knew was of extremely high quality and very expensive. "My wife would be happy with that," he laughed. Hanokh laughed too. "Yossef," he said, "take that cloth to our good friend Marek's office." The Pole smiled as he left the shop, Yossef following.

It seemed that the bribe was doing its work. During the days that followed, more people came into the shop, many of them Poles. Yossef put his skills to work handling sales. Volf sat in the inner office dealing with the accounts ledgers; Batya resumed her place at the till. Hanokh, looking more relaxed now, wandered around the shop keeping an eye on things. He felt so relieved that the pressure in his chest had almost completely dissipated.

Strzemieszyce began seeing the larger scale merchants returning, bringing new items from the big cities. Luckily, Hanokh had put some money away to pay for goods. A harsh winter is always a good time for sales of cloth; it was felt quickly in their cash flow. Non-Jews were purchasing, and the demand was increasing. But fellow Jews barely entered the shop. Moishe, the poor merchant, hadn't been seen for quite a while. One day Avraham asked the family if anyone knew where he was. "I heard he'd been forbidden from selling wares in the street, as were other Jewish sellers, and apparently he was sent to German labor camps set up in the vicinity," Volf said. Avraham nodded. "We hardly see men with beards here anymore. The Jews are disappearing from our town," he added.

But the Zaks family's shop was operating well, Hanokh making sure bribes were punctually sent out. Every Friday morning, he sent one of his sons with two nicely wrapped packages, one for the police commander and one for Marek.

Melting snow announced the spring of 1940. Trees were blossoming, their bare branches filling up with new promise, and life seemed to have returned to normal. But on a certain Friday, Avraham, making his regular visit to the police station, holding a package for the commander in his hand, was told by a policeman to wait. Surprised, Avraham stood in his place, silent, waiting for the next instruction. Some thirty minutes later it came.

"You're arrested on the station commander's orders." Handcuffing Avraham, he led the lad to a cell. Despairing, Avraham managed to ask; "But, sir, why am I being arrested?" No one bothered to answer. Sitting on the cold stone bench, a deep fear spread through him. What was this about? Papa makes sure to keep the commander happy, so...?

When Avraham didn't return to the shop, Hanokh realized something had happened. "Go to the police station and check on your brother," he told Volf, who hurried off right away. Entering the station, Volf made inquiries. "Wait here," said the policeman whom he'd asked. Fearing for Avraham, he stayed put. A different policeman came back.

"Your brother's been arrested on the police commander's orders. Go back to the shop and send your father here."

Anxiety made Volf cry as he raced back and shouted. "They've arrested Avraham, Papa! They want you at the station!"

Hanokh was gone in a second, striding quickly, feeling desperation rise inside him once again, fearing the worst. It was afternoon when Hanokh stepped inside and was immediately taken to the commander's office. Without hesitation he knocked on the door. A tall fat policeman opened it. "Yes? What do you want?" he barked at Hanokh.

"My boy's being kept here, so I've come to release him and I'd like to speak with the commander, please."

Moving aside a little, the policeman signaled. "Go in."

Again, Hanokh was face to face with the station commander.

"Listen, Jew. You want your boy? Bring me all your takings for today. Hurry up. Don't waste my time. In an hour I'm going home. If you don't want your boy to spend the weekend in the cell, you'd better hurry."

Hanokh left, walking as fast as he could, puffing hard. "Give me today's intake, and no questions!" he blurted the instant he stepped into the shop, "There's no time." Volf and Batya said nothing: Batya snatched the money from the till and placed it in her father's hand. He rushed back to the station and the waiting commander.

"Nice, Jew," he laughed. "From now on, every Friday, I want all the money in the till, in addition to the usual gift. What's money and what's cloth compared to security for you and your family, huh?" Giving Hanokh no time to respond, he waved him dismissively out.

Deeply distressed, Hanokh left. He sat on the bench to catch his breath while waiting for Avraham's release. Some minutes later, pale and shaking, Avraham stood before him. "Papa, come, quickly, let's get out of here." But in the street, Hanokh felt as though he couldn't walk a step. "Avraham, please, run to the shop and bring my valerian tablets. I don't feel too good right now." His tone was weak.

Frightened, Avraham held tightly onto his hand and gently seated his father on the steps. "Don't worry, Papa. I'll be back right away."

Batya's eyes shot him a questioning glance as he raced in without their father. "Batya, quickly, I need Papa's pills. He's feeling really bad. I left him near the station," he shouted. With nimble fingers Batya rummaged in a small bag, handed Avraham a jar of pills, and hurried out after him, Batya not far behind.

Avraham found Hanokh where he'd left him. Hanokh's hand was pressed to his chest. His breathing was labored. Avraham slipped a pill into Hanokh's mouth. "Swallow it, Papa."

Watching her father on the steps brought tears to Batya's eyes. Hanokh's eyes were shut; he was clearly concentrating on getting his breathing under control. She sat next to him, hugging him tightly, stroking his head. "Papa, the pain will go soon," she whispered. "It only takes a few minutes and the pill will start working. The pain will pass. I won't leave you, Papa. Ever. I'm here. I'll always be with you. I swear."

Minutes ticked by. Hanokh gradually calmed down, smiled, and spoke. "I'm ready to go home, children." He stood. The three of them went back, with Avraham and Batya linking their arms in their father's on each side of him, supporting their father.

CALAMITY

Friday after Friday, a policeman came to the shop to collect the weekly bribe. Gritting his teeth, Hanokh emptied the till and handed the contents over. But some weeks later Batya spoke up. "We can't carry on like this, Papa. The policeman completely cleans out the kitty. I have an idea. From now on, every Friday before he shows up, I'll remove some of the cash. Not too much, so he doesn't suspect anything, but we don't have a choice, Papa. We need to be smarter, or we'll end up with nothing."

"Do what needs to be done, my daughter," Hanokh agreed, kissing her forehead.

The next Friday, the policeman walked in. Batya opened the till and placed the money on the table. But he noticed right away that there was a smaller pile of notes. He studied her, mistrusting.

"Is that all the money?" he asked. Batya nodded. "Yes, sir, officer. It wasn't the best week. Not many shoppers came in." That didn't satisfy the man. "Move aside," he ordered in his gruff manner, "and let me check the till for myself."

Batya vacated the place, watching the policeman closely as he pushed his fingers into various nooks and crannies, searching in case something was left behind.

"For your sakes, I hope the commander will be satisfied with this," he said at last, leaving.

Batya and Hanokh sighed in relief. "You did well, my daughter," Hanokh said to her with love.

But their restrained joy was celebrated too soon. On Monday, right after opening the shop, the policeman showed up. "From now on, I'll be in the shop all day."

Hanokh said nothing. Batya smiled at the officer. "Of course, officer. You'll be our guest." The policeman leaned back in the chair behind the till.

Around midday, shouts came from the street. Rushing to the window, Hanokh and the boys saw police pinning down another Jew, beating him hard. The man lay bleeding on the ground. Eventually they seemed to be pleased with the result and left. The policeman also went to the shop's doorway, watching with curiosity. Taking advantage of the opportunity, Batya grabbed a handful of notes and stuffed them down her bra. The policeman threw her a questioning look when she walked towards the door.

"I need the bathroom," she said quietly.

He let her go. Batya hid the money in her underwear drawer and was back soon enough. Before closing the shop, the policeman insisted that the money in the till be counted. "Of course, sir," Batya said, springing the drawer open.

He counted the money, then turned to look at her. "That's it?"

"Hard times," she nodded, "as you can see."

He said nothing and left. But the next day he was back. Miriam came downstairs carrying butter biscuits she'd just baked. "For you, sir. Bon Appetit," she smiled at him. Catching a whiff, the policeman dug in, enjoying himself. No 'thank you,' of course, but he seemed pleased. As the day came to a close, he found another item when he checked the till: a small packet wrapped in paper. A piece of expensive silk was inside. Without a word he took the cloth and left, having forgotten to check the day's intake.

Every Friday one of the boys went to the station with costly pieces of cloth, sometimes buffered by cash. The policeman also received his dues in both cash and cloth. He stopped counting the till's contents. Whenever possible, Batya slipped money quickly out of the till, hiding it in her room. A thrill ran up her spine each time she did that.

Summer of 1940 passed and autumn announced its presence. At dinner one evening after his day of work, Yisrael spoke up. "We need to be really careful. Jews are disappearing from the town. I've heard they're being sent to a large labor camp not far from here, near Oświęcim. Our factory also had Jews from Dobrowa who suddenly stopped coming to work."

"And more shops owned by Jews have been shut. We're almost the only one left in town," Volf added.

***

One morning a German police officer stood at the shop's entrance. "Everyone stand aside. Don't move," he roared. Hanokh, the family and shoppers froze in their places. An unfamiliar officer strode in accompanied by two police. Without saying a word, he walked around the shop, taking in the shelves of cloth, tossing some on the ground. The family watched, fearful. Still he said nothing, but went towards the family home, the other two policemen trailing behind him. Only the women were upstairs: Yoheved, Haiya and Miriam, cooking dinner. Hanokh dashed after the officer and the policemen. Batya wanted to join him. Hanokh signaled no. "Stay here," he instructed.

Going from room to room, the officer then went into and out of the main bedroom. "I want that bed. Take it down to the truck now," he ordered the police, pointing to Yoheved's and Hanokh's mattress.

Miriam stood in front of him, unswerving. "Sir, officer, you cannot take that bed. Our father is very ill and needs that bed." The officer's gaze flooded with disdain and disgust, but also surprise, perhaps even a little admiration. Miriam stood in the doorway blocking the police from entering. She stared straight at the officer, holding his gaze. The officer wondered what to do under the circumstances, but decided to forego this time.

"Let them be," he instructed the policemen. "We'll find something better elsewhere." He turned sharply, going back downstairs followed by the police. Hanokh and the boys heard him, hurried back down, and stood like guards. At the doorway he turned again, his words poison: "You won't get away from me. I'll be back."

From that day on, every time the officer and his men came, Miriam stood in their way, blocking them courageously, steadfast, preventing them from robbing the house.

***

The police kept watch on the shop; and because they did, they made everyone feel unsafe, and so the number of shoppers grew less and less. Many feared going in. One morning Marek strolled in, signaling with his hand to Hanokh.

"Things are extremely complicated, Hanokh," he said when they'd moved to a private area. "I can't guarantee your safety because the station commander's changed. A small Gestapo unit has also arrived." He paused, glancing around before continuing. "Not only are the Jews in danger, but I am too, and my friends. You never know who could become a snitch for the sake of a bit of money. We have to be very, very careful." On his way out, Marek drew a deep breath, then sighed. "Well, that's it then, my friend. I can't come here anymore. I can't allow myself to be seen as being connected to Jews."

As the family sat down around Hanokh, it was clear to him that a new level of danger had entered their lives. Yossef spoke first, very quietly. "I suggest we flee. Shut the shop, shut the house, and leave the city. In a hurry."

Volf stared at him. "Flee? There's nowhere to go."

Hanokh sat still, silent. Lately it seemed he'd gotten a lot older, and his chest was playing up with greater frequency. Batya had begun hoarding more and more valerian pills, understanding that the day was not far off when they might be impossible to find. With the last of his strength, Hanokh stood, placing a hand on Yossef's shoulder.

"Let's get back to work," Hanokh said, his voice breaking. "There's still a chance and we must never despair. Better days will come."

TAKEOVER

The regular police officer never showed up the next day: the family didn't know whether the policeman's absence was a good or bad omen. The shop was empty: no one had entered. Yossef and Avraham kept themselves busy with cleaning and ordering the goods. Batya went upstairs to help the other women. In the afternoon the boys noticed a group of police outside. An official vehicle pulled up. Into the shop marched an angry-faced commander accompanied by policemen. The commander's uniform was decorated with medals, the buttons on his coat sparkled, and his black boots shone from careful polishing. As though reading their thoughts, the officer spoke in German.

"I am the local Gestapo officer. From today on, you are subordinate to me. Your shop is confiscated in favor of the Reich, and is no longer yours. A German expert will immediately enter and take over its management. Some of you will remain to work here, and others will be sent to serve the Nazi nation elsewhere."

The officer left, the police following him. Hanokh felt his legs buckling. He collapsed into the nearest chair. Volf, Yossef and Avraham, pale as chalk, were frozen in their places. Batya, who had just come downstairs, hurried over to Hanokh.

"Papa? Are you alright? Do you need your medication?"

He tried to overcome the stress he was feeling. "It's okay, Batya. I'll be fine. I just need to rest now and think. We'll wait for the German to come and then we'll see."

A short man with very thick fingers entered the shop. In his right hand he clutched a baton looped to his wrist. Letting the baton swing lightly back and forth, he spoke to them in German. “From now on, I’m the store manager and you will do as I say. Meanwhile, until some of you are sent to the labor camp, you will all continue working here and I will play your salaries, several zlotys, based on the daily intakes.”

He surveyed the store. “Who’s responsible for the till?” Batya raised her hand as she answered: “I am.”

“You will continue that,” his tone was assertive. “If you listen to what I say and do as I say, we will get on excellently. Clear?” The rest of the family watched him in silence.

“I am Herr Miller,” he barked. “You will call me ‘sir’ and only that, clear?” The family members nodded. No one dared speak. “You will not speak Polish among yourselves, only German. You can speak Polish with clients only when I am in the store.” They nodded.

“Who is responsible for accounts?” his impatience was evident. “Me,” Volf answered softly, unable to look at the German.

“Go bring the books immediately. I want to go over them before we continue.” Volf went, returning moments later with the notebooks, his hands shaking as he handed them over. The German placed them on the counter next to the till.

“From now on, you will write everything down in front of me, clear?” he said. Volf nodded. Miller then turned to Avraham. “You will arrange the warehouse and bring merchandise only in accordance with my instructions.” He looked at Yossef. “And you will deal with sales. I hope that more buyers will come now that the shop is no longer yours.”

“And you, Jew,” he said, facing Hanokh, “I don’t need you anymore but every morning you will open the store. If I have any questions, I will ask you. If not, you will go home. You are extraneous,” he said, turning his head away as though he’d seen some ugly insect which he, the enlightened German, was holding back from crushing.

Hanokh, his steps heavy, left the shop and climbed the stairs slowly back to their home. He halted for a moment, turned and looked back. "Extraneous," he muttered to himself, feeling the word pierce like a knife point. "I'm extraneous."

Indeed, German ownership increased the number of buyers. People no longer feared entering the store, and it began making as sizeable a turnover as it had in the good old days before the war. Miller supervised the family's work. At the end of each day, as the family watched, he opened the till, pulled out the banknotes, counted them, his tongue licking his lips, and stuffed them into his pocket.

On the first Friday after the shop's takeover, Miller called the family together. "Come here, Schnell!" he ordered. They stood, unmoving, in a row. Miller paced back and forth, tapping his baton against his left palm, saying nothing, and just shooting threatening looks at them. From his coat pocket, he drew small envelopes, giving one to each of them. "Do not open them now, only at the end of the day," he stated. No one dared challenge him. The envelopes burned in their pockets. They waited expectantly for the moment he would tell them to shut the shop. Once he decided the time had come, he gave his orders. "I'm leaving now. Shut the shop after me and leave immediately. I will be here Monday morning. Beware if any of you are late."

Volf, Yossef, Avraham and Batya stood frozen in their places for several long seconds. Batya broke the silence. "He's gone, so let's open the envelopes and see what we've been given." Avraham opened his: no more than several banknotes. "That's it?" Volf asked, despair in his voice, "that'll barely buy a few loaves of bread."

Slowly they made their way upstairs. The aromas of Friday's cooking filled their nostrils but couldn't lift their spirits. Hanokh's Kiddush prayer over the wine was recited hastily and quietly. Miriam served dinner wordlessly. Again, Batya broke the silence, saying what everyone was thinking. "We have to sneak money from the till during the day. There's no choice. Until Miller showed up, the policeman was in the store, and we did it, putting money aside. Now with Miller's hawk eyes on us it'll be a lot harder but we have to try, no matter what."

A thoughtful look came into Avraham's eyes as he turned to face Batya. "I've got an idea. I'll make a double drawer. Batya, every time you can, slip your hand in all the way back to the inner cubbyhole and slip something into it. That Miller, may his name be erased forever, can't possibly remember every amount coming in and out during the day. What makes it into the concealed drawer will help save us."

Volf smiled. "Yes, he goes out of the store into the street sometimes, he goes to the bathroom. Those are great times to take a bit of money and run home to hide it."

"And I can come downstairs every so often to bring the 'paskundyak,'" Miriam said, using the Polish term for a villain, "some fresh biscuits and drink. Then you can slip the money to me and I'll take it back upstairs. Yes, we have no choice. We've got to plan for stormy days ahead. No doubt about that."

***

Avraham waited nervously for Sunday. He rose early, went into the shop, easily undid the till drawer and using several thin pieces of wood, assembled a secret compartment which opened at the slightest push and silently sprung closed again.

Miller continued the Friday bribe, sending one or another of the boys to the police commander's office, cloth loaded on his shoulders. Since the number of shoppers had grown, the store's stock began to deplete. Volf decided to talk to Miller about it, but first jotted down his points in a notebook. When he thought the time was ripe, he approached Miller politely.

"Sir, if you don't mind, may I talk to you about the store's supplies?" The short German nodded. "Our stock has gotten much less, and we haven't bought any new stock for a long while now," Avraham continued. "While it's true that merchants do come here, we lack the funds in the till to pay them. I respectfully suggest, sir, that some of the income be directed towards buying up new stock, otherwise the shop will be forced to shut its doors, because the day is not far off when there'll be nothing to sell."

Miller studied the ledgers. "Next time a merchant arrives, call me. I want to meet each of them."

A horse-drawn wagon stopped at the shop's door the next morning. Volf asked the Krakow merchant to wait a moment and called Miller, who gave his instructions to the man: "I want all your merchandise. Unload it into the warehouse." The merchant, helped by Volf, Avraham and Yossef, brought the goods into the warehouse, which filled admirably.

The wagon empty, Miller spoke to the merchant again, in German. "I'll pay you next month."

The merchant protested. "What? Sir, you cannot take the goods without paying me." He spat on the ground. "Those filthy Jews always cheat me."

The German raised his baton and gave the merchant's back such a hard thump that the man screamed in pain.

"This shop doesn't belong to the filthy Jews. It's mine now. And if you want to be paid, those are the terms."

With no goods and no choice, the merchant swore in Polish under his breath and left.

Avraham had meanwhile been busy in the warehouse, first arranging the cloth by quality, and then by color. Miller walked in, studying him.

"Why are there so many brown fabrics?" he asked.

Avraham was taken by surprise. "Sir, that's no problem. Here are the reds," he pointed to a shelf, "here are the greens, but this shelf has only a few browns left."

"Go through that again," the German ordered. "What's on each shelf?"

"Sir. Here we keep reds, here are the greens, and here are the browns," he detailed.

Miller repeated Avraham's words, banging the baton against the cloth as he went down the shelves in order. "From now on," he said, "you will make sure to maintain that order and never change it. Clear?"

Astounded, Avraham answered. "Of course, sir. We won't change it."

As evening fell, Herr Miller closed the shop, stuffed his hand into the till, brought out the contents, and without even counting the notes, left. The family left right after him, using the stairwell shared by several apartments to go back home.

"What kept you so long in the warehouse?" Volf asked Avraham once they were all back home and behind their own closed doors. "Don't ask," Avraham answered, rolling his eyes. "I was arranging the cloth on the shelves when Miller walked in and wanted to know which color cloth was on which shelf. So I showed him, he repeated that after me, and then demanded that we never change the order."

"Tomorrow," Yossef flashed a grin, "we'll switch things around and see if he notices."

"Don't you dare!" Volf was horrified. But Yossef just kept smiling mischievously.

Early the next morning Yossef went into the warehouse and moved some bolts of red cloth to the shelf of browns, then waited calmly. Miller showed up on time, walked around the shop, then went into the warehouse. Yossef held his breath. Miller came back, saying nothing.

At lunchtime, Miriam came into the shop with food for her siblings. Miller left the shop to do some errands. Those precious minutes, free of his threatening presence, were the only time they could chat among themselves in Polish. Yossef smiled broadly.

"Listen, I know something that'll help us. Herr Miller, may he be damned, is color blind. He can't discern between green, brown and red. He never realized I'd changed things around in the warehouse. To him, brown and red are the same thing."

Avraham roared with laughter. "Now I understand why he wanted me to repeat the order, why he went over it again too, and insisted we don't move anything. Maybe we can use that to our advantage. The brown cloth's cheap. The red one's quite a bit more expensive. Let's sell the red but tell him we sold brown, and put the difference into the secret stash. We can fiddle the books easily."

For months they sold red cloth but registered it as brown. The secret stash grew. Miller, enjoying his personal takings, was more lenient when Batya asked for permission to go upstairs and care for her father several times each day, hiding the stash in her underwear. Nor was her request an excuse: Hanokh's health was deteriorating day by day, making it very difficult for him to come downstairs at all when Miller demanded to see him.

THE TOWN IS BURNING

Until the end of 1941 the shop operated without disruption. The money that was smuggled away by the family helped them survive, but supplies of groceries began running out and the Zaks family, like the town's Christian residents, were forced to buy from the black market operating in the town's back streets. Once a week one of the brothers went there to buy food from Polish farmers who came in from nearby villages.

January 1942 was wet and cold. On a certain Friday, snow fell, piling up. The family went to bed earlier than usual. Volf woke up in a panic, sweating, closed his eyes and asked himself: had he been dreaming? He remembered himself looking through the window into the empty street but instead of the familiar homes across the road, there was nothing but trees. Suddenly he saw it, walking slowly along, stopping opposite their home. Its green eyes shone like flashlights. A warning, coming from the forest. Volf watched, mesmerized. A forest in our street? Where had the houses gone? And the wolf: how did it get there? He barely had time to think of an answer when he saw the wolf turn and disappear with sad slowness into the depths of the forest.

When the wolf disappeared from Volf's line of sight, the forest began to change. Leaves dropped. Only bare branches remained. The branches turned black, as though charred. Volf watched the now bare forest, trying to understand where his wolf had gone but realized, shockingly, that it was not only the wolf that had gone. All the trees were going too, and only burnt ground remained. A cold sweat came over Volf, lying in his bed. He dressed quickly, waiting for events to unfold with no idea what they may be. The smell of burning seared itself into his nostrils.

Batya woke to the sounds of shouts and panic in the street. Peeping out from behind the curtain, she was horrified to see people marching down the street, flaming torches raised in their hands. She understood right away: they were going to set the shop alight. She shook Miriam awake. "Get up, quick, hurry!" She raced to the boys' room, surprised to find Volf, dressed, sitting on the edge of his bed, but didn't ask about it. "Let's wake them, fast!" she said, "they're going to burn the shop down."

Volf raced downstairs. Hanokh and Yoheved had woken up by now too. They were still dressing when the smell of something burning floated up to them. Rioters smashed the windows, throwing the fiery torches inside. The blaze caught on so quickly that the entire shop and warehouse were at risk.

Without a backward glance, the young rioters moved onto the next shop. Hanokh and Yoheved filled buckets of water in the house, passing them down to the boys who poured them over the burning cloth. Volf and Yisrael moved all the cloth away from the window. Smoke filling the shop forced them to open the doors for air. They were fortunate: the structure was built of stone, not wood. Other than sooty walls, no serious damage was caused to the house and shop. Yossef and Avraham threw burning bolts of cloth into the street, clearing them from the house. Volf and Yisrael poured water over the unharmed cloth: although they now carried water damage, they didn't burn. Miriam and Batya closed the warehouse doors tightly, hoping that the fire wouldn't breach them. For a full two hours, the family worked together in utter silence extinguishing the fire. The display window then shattered, giving them no choice but to leave the shop unprotected until the morning.

***

Standing in the street, they gazed around. Another two abandoned shops, owned by Jews, had been set alight. The town was burning. Leaving smoking islands of destruction behind, the rioters had fled. The family gathered in their home, and Miriam made a large pot of tea.

"There'll be even harder times yet," Yisrael said, "and we need to be ready for them. They won't leave us alone."

Hanokh studied his family's faces. "We don't have any choice," he sighed heavily. "We need the shop. We've saved up during the good years, and it'll help us through the bad. The money we're able to take from the till helps keep us alive. The shop's our elixir of life. We have to push on."

No one could sleep that night. Next morning, despite it being Shabbat, the family went down into the store, their eyes taking in its soot-blackened walls and ceilings, and the heavy smell of smoke which still hung in the air. Outside, burnt bolts of cloth lay where they'd been thrown. Avraham fumed, tears filling his eyes. "It's as though everything's burning up all around us. Not just the shop. The whole town's burning. We're also burning up inside, and we'll go up in flames soon. That's how I feel right now."

Volf hugged him. "We'll put the fire out completely, we'll clean the shop and ourselves up, and then we'll feel a whole lot better. The war's got to be over soon. We'll make it through. And we'll all be together, and stronger."

Plenty of work awaited them. They hung much of the cloth out to dry, doing their best to first air the smell of burning out. Cloth seared in the fire was taken to the back yard. Other bolts, having dried already, were put together in a large pile in the middle of the shop. They wiped the walls and shelves down with rags. Yisrael and Yossef, the tallest, stood on ladders wiping the ceiling clean. Hanokh sat in his old armchair, watching. Batya forbade him from helping: the physical effort would be too much for him. "You're too tired and too upset, Papa," she said, "just let us do the work. You need to go and rest."

Avraham tried to fix the display window but, not finding a large enough piece of glass, was left with no choice but to hammer up some planks from the yard. The broken window, with its crisscrossing planks, was a sorry and ugly reminder of that night's events.

On Sunday, the family continued their efforts at cleaning up. By the end of the day, the shop looked almost like it had beforehand. Only the odor still hung around. "This place is oddly clean and burning at the same time," Avraham said.

***

"What's going on here? What's this soot on the walls?" Miller barked the instant he stepped inside on Monday morning.

Hanokh told him. "The whole of yesterday and the day before we worked at making the shop presentable," he added with pride.

Miller never even looked at Hanokh. Instead, he directed his words at Avraham. "You. Boy. Get the window fixed today. Find new glass. And it's at your expense." Then he walked over to Volf, tapping his baton against Volf's shoulder. "You, all of you, will buy cloth to replace the burnt ones. At your expense. Tomorrow the store will open looking like it did on Friday. I want the burnt stock replaced and I don't care where you get it from. Now, shut the shop. I'm not going to sit here with that stench. We will open again once this place is clean. Hurry up. Get on with it!" he barked, turning on his heel and storming out.

Volf and Yossef went to Krakow in search of cloth. Avraham found a glazier happy to repair the window that same day for an exorbitant price. Every morning Miller came to sniff the air in the shop and stomped out in anger. It took four days until he was willing to reopen. A month's cash smuggling went down the drain. Everything they'd saved was used to replenish stocks and repair the window. But no sooner had Miller allowed the place to open than they went back to their red cloth brown cloth price swaps. The fire showed just how vital cheating on the till's intake was for the family's survival.

TO THE GHETTO

A new word horrified the family: Judenrein, a city clean of Jews. Haiya, returning from work one day, said she'd heard that Strzemieszyce would soon be declared "Judenrein." A heavy silence fell on the family seated at the table. Each thought the same thing: Even if we wanted to flee, there's nowhere to go. Nowhere was safe anymore for Jews. Weighing each word, Hanokh spoke in a quiet tone.

"The noose is tightening around our necks. We have to prepare for the worst possible scenario. Luckily for us, we've accumulated some money over the years. The safe is full, and the money will help us get through these tough times until the terrible war is over. I believe that we do still have friends among the non-Jews who we've helped in hard times, even if their ability to help us lately has been very limited." The family listened with deep respect as Hanokh, breathing with difficulty, continued. "Firstly, we need to prepare ourselves for an immediate escape. Each of us needs to prepare a bag, not too big, just enough to ensure survival. We'll try to flee, because at any moment we'll be exiled from here."

Hanokh took a sip of water, his hand shaking. Collecting his thoughts, he gazed at his family. "Secondly, as for the shop, admittedly it isn't considered ours right now, but we purchased the merchandise for a good sum of money. The merchandise IS ours. Therefore, we need to smuggle the goods to a safe place. I thought about our friend Marek. I have no doubt he won't refuse to accept the full stock and save it until the worst is over. I trust him. In any event, we have nothing to lose by doing that."

Yossef cleared his throat, a gentle signal that he wished to interrupt. "But Papa, how can we get the cloth out of the warehouse? It's extremely complex to get everything out in one go under Miller's close guard."

Hanokh gave a tired smile. "Here's what we'll do. Every Friday when you go the police station, take more than usual. On the way drop most of it off at Marek's. I'm sure Miller never checks exactly what turns up at the station. He's just thrilled that the bribe means the police won't bother him either. Tomorrow I'll go and talk to Marek, and let's hope for the best."

***

Hanokh knocked on Marek's back door. Marek quickly pulled him into a room where the curtains, closed, prevented anyone from seeing him there. "What's brought you here, Hanokh? You know we've been forbidden from meeting with Jews."

"Yes," Hanokh nodded, "I know that, my friend, and I promise I won't bother you again, but first I need to ask your help, and make an offer that will have value for you too."

"And what might that be?"

"I'll be forthright with you, Marek, just as I have been all our lives. It's clear that our time in this town is limited. We will almost certainly be taken elsewhere, which is why I wish to transfer my stock of cloth to your warehouse. If you need money, you can sell it. If things work out well for you, and for us, and we come back when the war's over, then I'd hope I can receive either the goods or a fair value for them, after you deduct a commission for yourself."

Marek pondered before answering. "I'm willing to accept your proposal, but just be aware that I can't give you a written document confirming our deal. You'll need to simply place your faith in me."

Hanokh agreed. "I do trust you, as I always have. Let's shake hands on it. That's enough," he said, holding his hand out.

Marek's handshake, unlike before the war, was barely a touch; nor did he look directly at Hanokh as he always had done in the past. "Another thing," Marek added, his voice dropping to a whisper. "Together with the goods, I want you to transfer your home to me."

Hanokh shook his head, slamming his hand down on the table. "Absolutely not, my friend," he said firmly, fixing his gaze on Marek. "Never will I hand my house over to someone who is not family. Not for all the money in the world. It's my family's and my home and that's how it will stay forever. Even if G-d decides not to bring me back, it will remain my home. It will always be the Zaks's family home!"

Marek flinched; that was not the reaction he'd expected, certain that Hanokh, in his desperation, would agree to any condition he set. He held his hand out towards Hanokh. "All right, my friend. I'll expect the cloth as soon as possible." This time the handshake was firm. Hanokh bid him good day and left.

Every Friday until the start of summer, three Zaks boys hoisted cloth onto their shoulders and set out for the police station. On the way, they diverted to Marek's warehouse, offloading the bulk of the goods. No one saw them come in through the back entrance to Marek's warehouse. The police were pleased as punch with their weekly gift. Miller was pleased as punch that the police demanded nothing more than that. The Zaks family's warehouse slowly emptied but that didn't bother Miller as long as he had cash in his pocket.

On a Friday in mid-June of 1942, right after Miller left the shop and as Yossef was about to lock the doors, he noticed a gang of youth armed with batons. "Hurry, get home as fast as you can!" he shouted to his family. No one argued. No one asked what he saw. Volf, Batya, and Avraham raced upstairs, leaving the shop empty. Hanokh locked the house door. They shook with fear, praying that the rioters wouldn't try to force their way inside. A deafening noise came from downstairs: the display window was smashed, all kinds of objects were thrown onto the shop's floor, rioters shouting "filthy Jews!" It took a half hour until the racket subsided. No one in the family spoke. No one moved. They stayed where they were, waiting for a while longer to be sure the rioters had gone.

Back in the shop they were stunned by what they saw. Their throats choked with tears. Hanokh looked around at his life's work, ruined in a matter of minutes. Clutching at his chest, he flopped down on the steps. "Here, Papa, take this," Batya was immediately at his side with medicine. The boys moved aimlessly among the shards and destruction. It felt like their life had come to an end. Hanokh put the feeling into words. "That's it. There's no more shop. We can't restore this. Let's go upstairs and prepare to leave before they come for us. Whatever will be, will be."

The family climbed the stairs with weary steps. Hanokh opened the safe concealed under the floor of his and Yoheved's bedroom. He took out money, jewelry, and gold that had been collected over the family's lifetime, and divided it up among the children. He took some for himself too, placing it in his bag. There was still a good quantity of jewelry left inside the safe.

"We'll leave it here," Hanokh said. "We can't take it all, anyhow. It was the family treasure. We can hide the safe and hope that no one finds it. When the war's over there'll be something here to help us start over. Consider it our insurance policy. Remember, children: no matter what happens, this is where we'll meet up after the war. Here. In our home."

They sat around the table, their bags on their laps, waiting for the unknown. As the sky darkened, Gestapo officers arrived, accompanied by several soldiers. Shots were fired in the air. Crying, they listened to the messages coming across loudspeakers. "Jews. Leave your homes within fifteen minutes. Anyone who does not leave will instantly be shot. One suitcase per person."

The family went down into the street, joining the town's other Jews. Each was handed a yellow band and ordered to bind it around the right arm. For no particular reason, a soldier standing nearby smashed his rifle butt against Avraham's back. The ousted Jews formed a slowly walking column. Once in a while someone tripped but quickly stood and kept going. Better that than being hit by a rifle butt. Bent over, tired, the Jews of Strzemieszyce trudged through the darkness carrying their belongings: men, women, children, and the elderly. No one dared glance back at the homes they'd just vacated, the homes they'd been born and raised in, had married in, had shared with grandparents or parents who had passed away. Silently they walked on, heads bowed. Only the yellow bands on their arms reflected a little light in the darkness.

SUFFOCATION

Exhausted, they piled into a tiny apartment in Strzemieszyce's poorest neighborhood. It had once belonged to Jews who'd been sent to extermination camps, so the grapevine said. The Zakses stared at the walls blackened by accumulated filth, at the moldy mattresses scattered across the floor. Two rooms for nine people. They felt helpless, hopeless. But they were too exhausted by now to care, and flopped onto the mattresses in their clothes, falling asleep in seconds.

Early the next morning, they woke up with a jerk. Were they reliving the nightmare? "Raus! Raus! Jews. Jews, out!" The orders in German were accompanied by kicking on the door. Sunrise had been only an hour earlier: the narrow street allocated to the Jews was weakly lit. Quickly the Zaks family assembled outside, joining the throng of Jews moving towards the end of the street, crowded, trembling, police constantly threatening to hit them with their rifle butts.

At the end of the street, the small square quickly filled. Gestapo positioned on the steps of buildings surrounded the crowd. A uniformed man took his place on a small wooden stage placed in a corner. The family instantly recognized him: the Gestapo officer who'd entered their shop. It felt like years had passed since then.

The officer looked straight ahead, above the Jews' heads, and raised his arm. The crowd hushed. The officer spoke, his voice harsh and formal. Every sentence sounded like a new decree.

"From now on, you will live only in this street. You are forbidden from moving to other parts of the town. Every Jew will wear the yellow armband at all times. A Jew caught without the armband will be instantly shot. Tomorrow morning, you will be sent to work in the Többens-Schultz factory manufacturing uniforms for the Nazi military. Your work will be remunerated with food vouchers. Working people receive vouchers. Non-working people receive nothing. At 6 a.m. tomorrow, present yourselves here and walk to the factory. Now return to your new homes."

He stepped down from the stage. In complete silence the exhausted crowd made its way back to their designated homes. The officer's words echoed in everyone's minds: anyone who doesn't work won't receive food.

Haiya, who had worked in the factory until now, reassured her siblings. 'Don't worry, I'll help you get used to it. The main thing is for the work foreman not to have any complaints about you."

Back in the apartment the siblings gathered, talked, and concluded that their parents would not go out to work because of Hanokh's health and the need for someone to keep an eye on him. "Mama will stay with Papa," Volf said. "We'll work and share our vouchers with them. Those vouchers will cover for the entire family."

On the second day that his children went to the factory, Hanokh, bored with being forced to stay cooped up in the filthy apartment, decided to go out and catch some air. He slipped the yellow band onto his arm before going down into the street. How surprising to see a Polish acquaintance waving to him in a friendly manner.

"Julian, what are you doing in the ghetto? Only Jews live here now," Hanokh wondered.

"Oh, I've come to see what I can sell," he said.

Hanokh clasped his hand. "Let's go inside, Julian, and chat a bit."

Julian smiled. "But take into account, my friend, that I don't accept food vouchers. Only cash. If you give me that, I'll help as much as I can. You know I have good contacts in the black market. I can get almost anything, but you need to decide quickly because the prices jump up every day. I can get food, medicine, but it will cost zlotys or jewelry."

Hanokh weighed the Pole's words carefully but knew he had little choice. If he and the family wanted to survive, he'd have to pay. "Agreed," he said to Julian. "Come, let's shake on it. I need you to bring basic food items in two days from now, such as flour and oil. If you can get some meat, we'll need that too."

Julian shook Hanokh's hand, sealing the agreement. "I'll bring what I can find. We'll meet in two days."

That evening, the young adults returned from the factory exhausted. "We were told that vouchers get distributed once a week," Yisrael said, his eyes half closed, his voice weak. "So we won't eat in the meantime. We'll get by on tea."

Despite being accustomed to working hard, the factory exhausted them but hunger prevented them from falling asleep. For two days they hadn't eaten. Hanokh, knowing that the black market flourished and that they could still pay in cash, prayed that Julian would indeed return. Meanwhile Yossef decided to take action. Saying nothing to his siblings about his plan, he left without the yellow band, slipping out of the ghetto deep in the night and creeping through the dark, quiet streets. Whenever he heard voices speaking German or Polish, he slipped into a dark hallway or between buildings. Slowly he approached the grocery store in their neighborhood. He knew it like the palm of his hand. Behind the shop was a narrow window, unlocked. Yossef wriggled his way inside. In the complete darkness he felt his way around, taking whatever his hands could grab: a loaf of bread, a small bottle of oil, sugar, flour, salt. He tossed the food items out through the window, listening carefully each time, before sliding back out.

On his way back into the ghetto, he couldn't hold back, and took several bites of bread but made sure to leave plenty for the family. Here and there, other figures moved stealthily through the darkness, risking death for breaking the curfew. No doubt, he thought, they were also out thieving.

By the time he got back into the ghetto, his breath came in short, sharp puffs: tension, nervousness, and fear all played their part. He waited until he was breathing normally again and shook his father gently awake. "Papa, wake up, sshhh, Papa. I've brought us some food," he said proudly. The rest of the family woke too: Yossef spread the food out before them.

Hanokh couldn't bear the idea that his son, raised on the Ten Commandments, had not only sinned against "Thou shalt not steal" but also put his life in danger. "You shouldn't have risked it," he rebuked Yossef. "No one dies from a day or two without food. We'll have food tomorrow. I arranged something with a Polish friend. Don't dare do that again."

Yossef was insulted that his father was not more admiring of his efforts, but not wanting to hurt his father's feelings, said nothing. He simply smiled at his siblings and hugged them warmly. Yoheved gathered the items up to prepare a meal.

Julian arrived the next day with two bags full of food and called Hanokh out to the corridor. No meat, but plenty of fruit, vegetables, and most importantly, beets and potatoes, excellent staples for a hungry family. He also brought sugar, flour, and oil. There was no bread, but what Yossef had brought the previous night would last them another day if they were careful.

Julian held his hand out. "One hundred zlotys, my friend, or no food."

"That's way too much, Julian" Hanokh tried bargaining. "You received so many bolts of cloth from me over the years at a fair price. We're nine people here. Be fair about it, Julian. We'll be here for a good while longer and will need a lot of help from you. But if you charge exorbitantly, we'll have to find another trader. And there are plenty around, selling."

Julian listened but was clearly unimpressed. "Listen, Hanokh, we're in a war. There's no fairness and no mercy here. Whoever has money and can pay, gets the goods. I've got food, and you don't. That's what makes the price fair. One hundred zlotys, or I'll take it all back and go on my way."

Hanokh, unable to convince the Pole to drop the price, opted for a different tactic. "Julian, how about I give you fifty, and throw in an expensive watch."

Julian thought about that. "Show it to me," he said.

Hanokh brought out a watch decorated in a gold-plated chain. The Pole fingered it, weighed it, and pondered on it for a while. "All right, I agree to the watch and seventy zlotys, no less."

"Agreed," Hanokh said, studying him intently. "When will you come again?"

"Three days from now," Julian said.

They shook hands. Hanokh paid. Once the Pole had gone, Hanokh shook his head. "My bargaining power is dissipating," he muttered, "and will get weaker yet. But I'll do whatever I can to keep the family going."

Hanokh carried the food back into the apartment. Yoheved began preparing dinner; by the time her children were home, a hot meal was ready, the first in many days.

Two days later the ghetto Jews were informed that vouchers would be handed out that evening at specially set up booths. Vouchers were brought from the Gestapo offices in Sosnowiec by a representative of the ghetto Jews.

Yisrael was sent to pick up the family's vouchers. He stood in front of the harsh-faced Gestapo officer. "Zaks family, you say?"

"Yes, sir," Yisrael answered.

The officer checked a list. "Only seven of you are working, correct?"

"Yes, sir," Yisrael muttered.

The officer counted out seven vouchers. "Take them. It'll get you two loaves of bread and another few basics. Tell the other two to go out and work otherwise you'll all end up hungry."

Only Julian can save us now, Yisrael thought, as he made his way back to the family, hunger making his stomach constantly growl.

THE VOUCHER TRAIN

According to the Nazis' instructions, the ghetto's Jewish representative would travel to Sosnowiec once a month to collect the necessary number of vouchers for weekly distribution based on each ghetto resident's workdays and according to Gestapo lists.

First the ghetto's residents were required to choose a committee, which would operate under close German supervision. Proposing himself as a committee member, Yisrael received an overwhelming majority of votes, the Zaks family being well-known for years of kindness and generosity to others. Shlomo, Hanokh's cousin, was also voted into the role of ghetto guard, having been an officer in the Polish police force. A small clinic was also opened, providing basic medicines and care to patients and the elderly. Batya decided to volunteer for the clinic, working there in her free time to ensure she could access a supply of the valerian pills so vital due to her father's deteriorating health.

Yisrael prepared for his voucher collection task. Equipped with a travel permit from the German ghetto commander and a yellow armband tied to his upper arm, he made his way to the train station. It was the first time Yisrael would be traveling by train since Poland's conquest. He hunkered down as inconspicuously as possible at the far edge of the carriage bench, keeping his eyes glued to the floor despite the travel permit. Two hours later, the train stopped at Sosnowiec. Yisrael disembarked, joining the line of representatives from other nearby towns. Each, like him, looked nervous. On a whim of the payments officer, or because of any small error on the Jewish delegate's part, the entire ghetto could miss out on food vouchers for a month.

Yisrael's responsibility was so burdensome that it left him tongue-tied. He thought about the ghetto's families: their very existence depended on food vouchers. They were depending on him. Before leaving the ghetto, and during the train ride, he repeated the figures he would need to convey to the payments officer: how many elderly, how many men, women, and children in the ghetto. He shook with fear when the Jewish representative in front of him became confused and was unable to provide the precise details requested. He heard the officer instruct the man to return to the ghetto and come back with the correct figures based on Gestapo lists.

With his legs feeling like dead weights, Yisrael's turn had arrived. He stood at attention before the fearsome German clerk. "Yes, Jew. Where are you from and how many Jews are on your list?"

Yisrael tried not to stutter or mutter. "I'm from Strzemieszyce, and we have 500 people in total, including children," he immediately responded. The answer wasn't to the clerk's liking. He smacked his palm on the desktop. "That's not enough, Jewboy," he barked at Yisrael. "I want all the figures: exactly how many women, men, children. Hurry up. If you don't have the numbers, get back to your ghetto and return when you do."

Yisrael trembled. A cold sweat broke out on his brow. "Sir, I will give you the figures," he said quickly. "Five hundred, of which 180 are men, and of those, 165 work in factories vital to the Germans."

The clerk wrote the information down and roared at Yisrael. "Hurry up, Jew. I don't have all day for you."

Yisrael continued. "Women. 240, of whom 100 work in vital factories. And 80 children under the age of thirteen in the ghetto."

The German didn't seem to be particularly impressed. He ran a comparison against the previous month's number. "Exactly the same as last month. Have none of you died yet this month? If so, we clearly haven't done good enough work on you yet there in Strzemieszyce."

Yisrael lowered his eyes and said nothing. The officer and the other clerks nearby broke into laughter. Yisrael could only pray he'd be given the vouchers which the ghetto Jews deserved. He glanced at the senior clerk.

"You sure?" the clerk asked Yisrael again.

"Yes, sir," Yisrael answered confidently.

The German opened a drawer and counted vouchers out, slipped them into an envelope, put it on the desktop and pushed it towards Yisrael. "Now scat, Jewboy, and get back to your town before evening or the Gestapo will kill you and wouldn't that be a shame on all those vouchers! Your friends, those Jewish mongrels, won't have anything to eat, will they!"

Yisrael didn't dare count the vouchers. Slipping the envelope into his bag, he clutched the satchel tight and rushed off, heading for the station almost at a run. A brief wait later, the train for Strzemieszyce rolled in. Once again, he sat in a corner of an almost empty carriage trying to stay calm, keeping the bag close to his chest. Exhausted from days of hard work, his eyes closed. How he'd have loved to catch some sleep, but his eyes flew open when he heard German voices approaching the carriage door. Two soldiers entered the carriage, sitting not far from him. Yisrael tried to shrink in his seat, trying not to be noticed. He didn't want them checking his papers, even if they were correctly signed and stamped by the ghetto commander.

"Kill him here or wait for the next station?" one asked his mate, signaling towards Yisrael. The other laughed raucously. "Let's let him sweat it out a bit more. Let him die of fear before we kill him at the next station's exit," the second chuckled. "What about we throw him out the window," the first suggested. "Neh, let's kill him at the station he gets off at, a bit before the train takes off again."

Yisrael sat there, pale, his hands shaking, his thoughts racing: should I make a dash for it while the train was moving? I could get killed in the jump. Should I make a dash for it when the train pulls into the next stop? But what if they give chase? He pondered. And decided. He'd flee at the next station in a way that would give the Nazis no time to harm him.

Although the ride to the next station took no longer than thirty minutes, to Yisrael it felt as though the train would never get there. The entire time, he sat perched tensely on the edge of the bench, his hands shaking, drops of sweat falling from his forehead into his eyes. He didn't dare wipe his face, not wanting them to know how tense he was. He was completely focused on his task: saving his own life. And then the train stopped at the station. Yisrael stayed in his place. The instant the train began to pull slowly out, he bounded out of his seat, opened the carriage door, and jumped onto the platform. The Germans were left open-mouthed. He heard them swearing, "Filthy Jew, we'll kill you," but knew he was safe.

Yisrael breathed a deep sigh of relief but his legs still shook. And then realization dawned: something was missing. His bag! In his haste to escape he left the bag of vouchers in the carriage. He was crushed. How could he go back to the ghetto without the vouchers? The Gestapo would think he stole them. That would be the end of him! At best, he'd be beaten soundly. At worst, they'll shoot him. Tears filled his eyes. He broke down and cried. The entire ghetto would be hungry because of him.

It seemed that he knew what to do even though he wasn't thinking clearly: he made his way to the station master's office. What have I got to lose? he thought, despite not feeling hopeful that the station master would want to help. Tearfully he told the man how he'd fled to save his life, causing him to forget the satchel of vouchers which the entire Strzemieszyce ghetto was waiting for, and without which they would all starve. But to Yisrael's surprise, the station master, an elderly German, listened, and spoke in a gentle, fatherly manner. "I'll try to help you, young man. Sit here. I'll call in to the next station's supervisor." Minutes later he was back. "The train hasn't arrived yet but the manager assured me that when it stops, he'll search for your bag. Now, you just sit here and try to stay calm."

Swinging between despair and hope, Yisrael smiled at him in gratitude. Thirty minutes later Yisrael heard the phone ringing in the station master's office. Lifting the receiver, he listened and smiled warmly towards Yisrael. "Everything's all right, young man. The bag's been found and they'll send it back on the next train. My shift has just ended, but don't you worry. I've asked the ticket collector to get your bag when the train pulls in, which should be about a half hour from now."

Moved, his eyes wide with astonishment, Yisrael muttered. "Station Master, sir, I am so thankful. You've saved the lives of many people."

The elderly German waved his hand and left. Yisrael stayed in his seat, fidgeting nervously. He realized that he'd miss the last train to Strzemieszyce, but hoped with all his heart that at least his satchel would turn up still holding the vouchers. He prayed: G-d, G-d, please, help me.

What seemed like an eternity later, the train rolled in. Yisrael quickly left the waiting room, heart pounding, temples throbbing, hands moist with sweat. The ticket collector stood on the platform. Yisrael was very surprised to see the station master was also there, quickly climbing into the carriage. Moments later, he came back down, the satchel in his hands.

"I just came back to make sure you got your satchel as we promised, young man," he said, placing a calming hand on Yisrael's shoulder. Yisrael gripped the bag tightly, and immediately looked inside. Thank G-d! he thought. The vouchers were there. For the first time on that long tense day, Yisrael smiled, his heart filled with appreciation for the older German's kindness.

"Thank you, sir. Thank you," he whispered, looking into the man's eyes. He didn't dare shake the German's hand, not only because he didn't know the man but because he was also afraid it might mark the German as a Jew-lover. But the station master smiled back and lightly bowed his head. "Glad to have assisted. Now go back to your town and keep a close watch on that bag!" he said to Yisrael.

Yisrael decided not to wait for the morning train, but to walk back to Strzemieszyce. He made his way swiftly through the darkness despite the risk of breaking curfew and being shot for it. Slipping away from the paved road, he took to the fields. Carefully, he approached the ghetto, praying he would encounter neither police nor criminals. For ten hours straight he walked. It was six in the morning, as curfew was lifting, when Yisrael reentered the ghetto. Walking into the family's tiny home, he learned that no one had slept at all that night.

"What happened? Where were you, Yisrael? Why have you only come back now?" Hanokh asked.

"Let me lie down and rest a bit. I'm completely wiped. Then I'll tell you about everything," Yisrael answered, collapsing into Yossef's arms.

ABDUCTION

Again and again, Julian returned laden with goods. The kitchen began to fill with anything he'd managed to smuggle into the ghetto but on his last visit, Hanokh noticed that Julian seemed upset.

"What's the matter, Julian?"

Julian sighed. "It's starting to get increasingly difficult to find food. I've got plenty of suppliers in the city but the bigger problem is getting here. The Germans are forbidding Poles to enter the ghetto. We need to meet near the fence. We'll decide on a place, day and time, and I'll do my best to come, but I can't promise I'll succeed. And things are looking like they'll get a lot worse. I'm sorry, Hanokh, but I have to ask for more money now too, because the danger is greater than ever."

Hanokh touched Julian's shoulder. "Don't worry, Julian. You'll get more. I appreciate the risk you take on our behalf." But Hanokh was thinking: what choice do I have? I'll pay whatever he asks as long as we have money. The main thing is for food to keep reaching us.

Julian gave a half-smile. "I'll come in two days' time to the fence, to the northern corner. There's a very narrow opening there that I can sneak through, luckily for us. They haven't found it yet."

At the prearranged time, Hanokh set out for Julian's new meeting place. Most of the ghetto residents had gone out to work in the factories. A few lads, matured before their time, sat chatting in undertones in the street. Smaller children, their faces thin and their bodies gaunt from hunger, poked about in the garbage. Hanokh's heart cringed: maybe I can give them something from Julian's supplies on my way back, he thought, looking straight ahead to avoid the harsh images.

He reached the fence. Julian was nowhere to be seen. Hanokh moved away a little to avoid rousing suspicion. German soldiers were also nowhere in the vicinity. Hanokh stood at the entrance to a house, watching the fence. Minutes passed slowly; he felt sure something was amiss. An hour passed. Clearly Julian hadn't made it. Hanokh turned and set off for home, disappointed. There'd be nothing on the table that night.

A shot rang out. A scream pierced the silence. Hanokh stopped dead in his tracks, bent low, and pushed up against the wall of a house. Another shot. Another cry of pain. He glanced towards the fence. Horrified, he saw Julian clutch at his heart, his face twisted in agony. Julian tried throwing the bundle of items towards the fence but no longer had enough strength. He fell in a pool of blood. A round of shots. Broken eggs. Flour spilled out. Vegetables rolling on the ground. With the last of his strength Julian gathered what he could of the food and shoved it under the fence into the ghetto. A third shot. Julian's body shuddered. And went still. His blood spread across the food.

Hanokh watched, incredulous. His hands trembled. Don't move, he warned himself. That's exactly what they want, those evil beings: to frighten anyone who tries to help. But that will only cause the helper's death. He wanted to walk away, back to the miserable place that was now his home, but another thought passed through his mind: there's food there and we need it. While still deliberating over the risk, he saw the children who'd rummaged through the trash. They sprinted to the food, collected it, even though some was covered in warm blood, it didn't put them off. They just wiped the blood on their already dirty clothes and fled for their lives.

Well, at least the food will be useful to someone in the ghetto, Hanokh thought. And what now? What do we do without Julian? The thought gnawed at him and brought on the pain. He clutched at his chest; first the left side, then the pain spread, and every breath he took felt like a knife being thrust into him. Hanokh knew he had to get back home quickly for valerian, but he was too weak to walk. In his mind, he saw Julian being shot, dying, the blood spreading onto the smuggled food. Replaying in his mind, the images made him dizzy, nauseous. He fought not to vomit. His mind went foggy. And then he collapsed on the street.

Hanokh had no idea how long he lay there before he regained consciousness. The chest pain had not disappeared but was not as strong as before. He forced himself to stand. He forced himself to take one step after another, slowly, heavily. He forced himself to push the front door open. Yoheved gave a loud gasp when she saw him. A long time had passed and she'd already begun to suspect that something untoward had happened to her husband. Hanokh sat down heavily, both hands on his chest.

"Hanokh? What happened? You're so pale," Yoheved asked.

"The Germans killed Julian. I saw it… they shot him to death, like a dog, when he tried to bring our goods into the ghetto. Now we don't have food, and who knows if there will be any." His words were direct and to the point.

Yoheved's hands came together. "Oh no!" she cried.

Hanokh leaned back on the chair, groaning. "We need to find a new smuggler and we need to be much more careful."

Coming back from the factory in the evening, the siblings noted the meager provisions on the table: a few slices of dry bread from two days earlier. "That's it. No more Julian. I watched them shoot him to death. No more extra food. For the coming days, that's what there'll be: only what our vouchers can get us. If we manage to find someone instead of Julian, things will improve. If we don't, I don't know what will happen to us," Hanokh said to his startled children. Fury and compassion filled his eyes as he gazed at them, their eyes half closed in sheer exhaustion from the never-ending labor. He knew they were hungry. Silently they nibbled their pieces of bread and went to their beds.

Hanokh remained seated at the empty table, anger bubbling up inside him. Yoheved heard him muttering to himself. Wanting to soothe him, she sat next to him, placing her hand on his. He didn't notice: the unclear muttering turned into words, Hanokh rallying himself against G-d. "What do you want?

Death? Is that what you want? I saw death today. With my own eyes. And he wasn't even a Jew. He was just a person looking for a livelihood in the war, but his livelihood brought desperately-needed aid to others. So tell me, why did he have to die like that? Like a dog in the street?"

Hanokh drew in a long deep breath, tears welling in his eyes. He looked up towards the heavens, as though that would help G-d hear better. "Is this what we deserve? Is this the meaning of 'Surely you shall seek to be just?' All my life I believed in you. All my life I believed in ethics and justice and integrity. And what do I get? Death, that's what I get. So what do you want? That overnight we become thieves? Here, look at Yossef. He's already stolen food because we were hungry. So, I was angry with him for risking his life, but that was just the excuse. I was furious that Yossef had to steal even though I educated him never to steal. What do you want from us? That we become not only thieves but murderers too? That we cause others to be killed so we don't get killed? So we can survive? What do you want from us all?"

Tears rolled down his cheeks. He didn't try to wipe them away. Yoheved stroked his arm. "Shh, shh, Hanokh, calm down. Things will be all right." He ignored her. Quietly he talked to his G-d. "War? You want war? You'll get war. We'll go to war in order to survive. If we need to steal, we'll steal. If we need to lie, we'll lie. If we're forced to kill, we'll kill. That's the new world you've created here. A world without the Ten Commandments. It's not the world I want to live in, but you force me to, so that's how I'll behave. I'll live in this world of yours for my family's sake, but I won't believe in you anymore, you hear me? From now on I will believe only in myself and my family. They will be my Ten Commandments. I'll do everything in this new terrible world you've made."

Having gone to bed hungry, the siblings had trouble falling asleep. Outside they could hear the thud of German boots. Batya froze in her bed. Miriam hugged her tightly. "They'll go in a second. Listen… they haven't stopped here," Miriam reassured her sister. Outside hard knocking was heard on the neighbor's door. From the adjacent apartment came the sound of crying. Batya peeked through the curtain: a military truck covered in a canvas tarpaulin was parked in the street. Germans were beating two men on their backs with rifle butts before throwing them into the van. Heart-rending cries came from the apartment next door; they continued through the night. No one slept.

The next morning all the young Zakses went off to work, leaving Yoheved in the house to care for Hanokh. "I have to do something. We don't have a choice," he said. "If I don't take some action now, things will quickly be terrible. We mustn't leave our future only to fate. I'll sneak out and go talk to Marek."

Yoheved was horrified. "Are you out of your mind? If the Germans catch you, they'll kill you!"

Hanokh persisted. "I'll take the armband off. I know he'll receive me. I'm going now."

Yoheved knew she'd never convince him to change his mind. "Promise me you'll come back. I couldn't live without you, you hear?"

Hanokh stroked her arm, smiling. "I promise I'll be fine," he said, slipping into his long coat. He raised the collar to hide as much of his face as he could; after all, he was very well known in town and Poles turned a tidy sum as informers. Hanokh walked quickly even though his heart pounded and his legs trembled.

Reaching the house, Hanokh knocked on the door. Marek was astonished to see him. "Hanokh? Are you crazy? To come here… to my home? You'll get us both killed!"

Hanokh spoke with urgency. "Marek, let me in. You have to help me and it'll be worthwhile for you. I have money."

Marek glanced quickly left and right to be sure no one was watching, then pushed Hanokh quickly inside. "I can't help you anymore, my friend. Life's becoming insufferable for us, too."

Hanokh got right to the point. "I'm afraid for my daughters," he explained. "Every night people are abducted from the ghetto to the camps. I'm asking you: let my daughters sleep here. Every evening I'll bring them and every morning they'll go back to the ghetto. No one will notice them, I promise you."

Marek sighed. "Hanokh, it's a huge risk. I don't think I can fulfill this request. I don't want to endanger my own family."

"I'll pay you," Hanokh said impatiently.

The Pole weighed the proposal. True, they were old friends, but the war and the German conquest had altered everything. True, money could be earned, Marek reasoned with himself, but if Jewish girls were to be found in my home, the Germans will kill them and me. Maybe even my whole family. The money isn't worth the danger.

Hanokh, despairing, watched him. "Marek, it's war. Tomorrow the Germans could take you and your family to the labor camps, whether my daughters sleep here or not. The Germans don't really like the Poles. You know that. I'm waiting to hear what you have to say. I'm not a well man, and can't help protect my girls. I have to find a way to look after them. I trust my boys to figure things out for themselves, but not the girls. You must help me."

"How much can you pay me?" Marek asked, "because my business is also starting to show signs of decline. I used to go in and out of the police commander's office freely. Plenty of under the table… but now I don't even know who the commander is."

Hanokh began to feel relief: the Pole was slowly backing off his initial refusal because it had come down to money. "One hundred zlotys a night, Marek. Until my money runs out or until this filthy war is over."

They hugged briefly and Hanokh, raising his coat collar again, quickly left. Julian's body still lay sprawled on the road. Hanokh slipped through the gap in the fence and walked home. That evening he talked to the family, telling his daughters that every night from then on, he'd smuggle them out of the ghetto to Marek's home. "The danger of slipping out of the ghetto is less than the Germans kidnapping you at night. You, my boys, will sleep in the basement. It's disgusting but we have no choice. We'll fix it as best we can. I don't want the Germans taking anyone. Discussion closed."

Late at night, Hanokh walked the girls quickly to their new hideout. They knocked lightly. His face drained of color, Marek opened immediately. "Quick, come in," he whispered, leading them down into his basement where he'd prepared two mattresses and bedding.

"I'll see you in the morning and pay you," Hanokh said, "and thank you, my friend. We'll never forget your help."

Walking at a brisk pace, Hanokh returned to the ghetto. Down in Marek's basement, the girls never slept a wink all night. Nor did the Zaks boys, down in their basement. Early in the morning, before first light, Hanokh knocked on Marek's door. The girls were ready.

"For you," Hanokh said, slipping several banknotes into Marek's palm. "Hurry, my daughters," he said, turning to Batya and Miriam, "there's no time to lose."

They sighed with relief once they were back home. Wordlessly, both parents hugged the girls tightly.

No replacement was found for Julian. Food began to dwindle in the Zaks's kitchen. And Hanokh's money was dwindling too.

NIGHT THIEVES

It had been several days since Julian was shot dead. The Zaks family was feeling the hunger, the energy waning. Avraham, knowing his father would oppose, decided not to say a word about his plan. He merely indicated to Yossef with his eyes that he wanted to chat privately.

"There's no choice but to start stealing from the grocery store again." Yossef agreed.

In the small hours of night, they woke Volf. "We're going out. We'll try to bring food from the grocer's. You stay here. If we get caught someone needs to be here to care for our parents," Avraham whispered.

Volf nodded and gripped Avraham's hand. "Best of luck."

Yossef and Avraham put their coats on, raised their collars to hide their faces, took a cloth bag, left the yellow armbands at home, and slipped away from the ghetto into the town they knew so well. They stopped frequently to make sure no one was following them. Their plan was simple: enter the shop through the warehouse window in the back. Avraham broke the window with his thickly padded elbow and cleaned the shards up with his gloved hand. It was pitch black inside. They waited briefly, allowing their eyes to adjust. Slowly they made out canned food, fruit and vegetables, and small sacks. Mostly they focused on basics, like flour and sugar, potatoes and oil.

Ready to leave, the brothers waited, listening for footsteps before slipping back out through the window and quickly walking back to the ghetto. They planned to reenter through a breach in the fence closest to their home. A group of armed guards stood there, blocking entry. Avraham and Yossef hid in the entrance of a nearby building, keeping a close watch. Truck engines could be heard inside the ghetto. "More kidnappings," Yossef whispered. But the trucks drove off and the German guards left.

Avraham and Yossef made their way quickly through the abandoned gap. From the street adjacent to theirs they could hear heartbreaking sobs. Volf waited for them at the entrance, shaking with fear. "They were here again, right next to us," he muttered to his brothers, tears glimmering on his cheeks. "I can still hear their boots thudding. I was so afraid they'd come inside, here. I'm glad you're back."

Yossef, the bag still slung over his shoulder, hugged him. "The main thing is that we've brought some food. It should last a few days, but we won't be able to keep doing this for long. Let's go inside," Yossef said softly. "We need to go back out soon to work."

The three boys went in. Hanokh and Yoheved were already awake. Hanokh gazed at Avraham and Yossef but asked nothing. He didn't want to know. In his heart, he prayed: Thank you G-d for looking after the boys. Yisrael and Haiya were also up and ready. Their fear that the Germans would come into their home was paralyzing.

"I won't bring the girls," Hanokh said. "It's safer for us to stay put. I trust them to make their own way back."

At first light, Batya and Miriam walked in, relieved to see everyone else safely at home. Another night of terror had passed them by. Another day of hard work awaited. The Zaks sons and daughters tied their yellow armbands on and left for their jobs with growing fears.

MEMORIES OF HOME

Every night the Gestapo raided the ghetto. Women screamed when their husbands were dragged away. Parents were taken, leaving children behind. The Zaks family could feel the abductions getting ever closer. The Germans might break into their home any night. They had never felt less safe. Worried, Hanokh spoke to Yisrael. "Maybe you should sleep with your brothers in the basement. It's safer there."

"No, Papa. I'll stay upstairs. Someone needs to protect you and Haiya at night. If anything happens, G-d forbid, I want to do my best to look after you. I have to take that risk."

That night, Volf, Avraham, and Yossef went down to the basement, Batya left on her own because Miriam wasn't feeling well and decided not to go to Marek's, and exhaustion made everyone fall asleep quickly. Hours later they woke up in panic. The walls were shaking. From adjacent apartments screams pierced the night. Numerous men were abducted as the Germans were increasing the quotas being sent to the camps.

The knocking on their door made it shudder on its hinges. "I'm going to open up," Miriam said. Her face was determined, her eyes shone: was that because her temperature had risen, or because of her defiance? Hanokh decided to put his faith in her, remembering how she'd stood up to the Germans wanting to confiscate her parents' bedroom. He glanced at her and nodded to signal his agreement, praying in his heart: G-d, watch over us all. Haiya and Yisrael closed themselves in their room when Miriam went to the door, opened it, and blocked the entrance with her body. She stared right into the soldier's eyes. He tried to shove her aside. She stood her ground, never flinching.

"What do you want, soldier?"

Her tone was so authoritative that the soldier took a half step backwards. "I need to check if there are men here."

Miriam shook her head, still holding his gaze. "Only my father. The others have been taken. But my father is old and ill and is useless to you." She paused, never looking away. When she spoke again, her voice was even firmer. "You can go now," she said, shutting the door in the shocked soldier's face. Miriam was fully expecting him to bang on the door again or even try to kick it down. Had Hanokh's prayer helped? Had her courage saved them? From behind their front door, Miriam could hear the soldier's footsteps fading away. He and his mates had left the building.

Hanokh and Yoheved were astounded. Tears were falling from Yoheved's eyes, and both she and Hanokh were trembling from the tension and the relief. Yoheved sobbed quietly. "My daughter, you are so brave. G-d is with you, Miriam, that is clear."

Hanokh hugged her. Yisrael and Haiya came out of their room and hugged her. "Miriam, from now on you will stay with us. We'll feel much safer with you here," Hanokh said.

In the basement tension was running high. Volf, Yossef and Avraham sat on their mattresses, dressed, as though waiting for terrible news. "That was close. Too close for comfort," Volf said. Yossef reached out to Avraham, taking hold of his hand. "C'mon, let's go get some food. We're not going to fall asleep again tonight anyhow."

Volf said nothing, his eyes just following their movements as they were getting ready, before they sneaked out to the grocery store. Silence filled the night. The boys reached the gap, eased through the fence carefully, reached the shop's back wall… and drew their breath in sharply. A new pane of glass filled the window. And several planks were nailed across it as protection.

"Damn," Avraham hissed. "Now what? Where'll we get food from?"

Yossef thought for a few moments. "Let's try the bakery, see what we can get hold of there." The walk took them past their home. They stopped, gazing at it fondly. Memories rose in their minds. Tears fell on their cheeks. "No life there anymore," Yossef whispered.

"Let's take a look in our yard," Avraham said softly.

They circled round to the back of the large building before entering. Pitch black. Enveloping silence. "But it's still our home and always will be," Yossef whispered. "We'll never give up on it. We'll come back once this madness is over."

In silence the brothers sat in the yard until, at last, Avraham spoke. "Remember when you came back from captivity and I brought a football out and we played here?"

Yossef nodded. "Do I ever remember! It's what slowly brought me back to life. It was the first time I smiled since captivity."

Avraham put a hand on his brother's shoulder. "We used to go wild here when we were little. Remember Jura? Didn't we love to give him trouble! We rolled him along in the barrel that was meant for salted fish. For a month he stank of that barrel even though his mother scrubbed him with soap. Say, Yossef, I was always curious why you always got off one stop before school? To this day I wonder about that. Why'd you do it?"

Yossef grinned. "Avraham, when you guys went to school I learned, ah, other things. I went to the girls' school. Every so often a girl would come over to talk to me. I also got to do a bit of touching, a bit of kissing, things between boys and girls. You were too little to understand. Miriam knew but she kept my secret. What a weird blessing that we Zakses know how to keep our traps shut!"

Avraham laughed quietly. "What a rascal you were, Yossef. A big rascal. You started with your mischief when we already in pre-school. I'll never forget how you poured the whole salt cellar's contents into the rabbi's soup. He went nuts! I was so afraid he'd smack his wife, he was that angry." The brothers broke into raucous laughter but stopped an instant later, remembering that they were out of the ghetto, but they weren't ready to leave yet. They wanted to eke out some more memories from their family home's walls, memories they could take with them into the murky future.

"When I look at our house I can smell Friday's soup, even now," Yossef sighed. "Can you smell it too?"

Avraham shook his head. "No, my brother. I can smell Shabbat's cholent bubbling away and my stomach growling louder and louder. Especially now, when I'm starving."

"Yeah," Yossef said. "Do you think we can feel full just from thinking about the aromas?"

Avraham sniggered. "That's all we've got now anyhow. The memories of aromas of our home. Nothing in our bag, though. You know what? I do kind of feel full. Let's get back to our basement before dawn. We still have to get ready for a workday."

Yossef was in no hurry to leave. "I want to touch those walls, because I have a feeling that we won't be coming back here."

Avraham watched him, smiling sadly. "Yossef, don't give in. We WILL come back. I can feel it. But for now, we just have to be happy with touching it, to give us another memory."

They walked over to the house, lovingly placing their palms on the wall. "Let's just go into the stairwell," Avraham suggested. They did. And looked around. And walked up the three steps to the front door and touched the *mezuzah*, the small container holding a parchment on which the prayer 'Hear, O Israel' was written. They kissed the mezuzah, their eyes welling with tears for days gone by. The mezuzah didn't seem to want to let them go.

Yossef raised a fist. "This mezuzah will stay here forever. It holds the house together. No non-Jew will uproot it, no Nazi will destroy it."

"It will watch over our house, and keep it whole and ready for when we return," Avraham added.

A faint ray of light brought them back to reality. Quickly they left the house and raced to the ghetto, where Volf was waiting for them.

THE LAND OF DARKNESS AND THE SHADOW OF DEATH

The sun had not yet risen on the morning of June 23, 1943, but it seemed to the ghetto residents that the sun would never shine on their world again. They woke up to the hell of shouts in German. "Raus, raus. Schnell," and bursts of gunfire. Everyone but Haiya, who'd worked a night shift, woke up into their last day in the ghetto. Outside the orders were barked in a mix of German, Polish, and Yiddish. The Zakses looked into the street and knew: the end had come. The ghetto would be eradicated. The Judenrein plan had reached its final stage.

"All Jews outside. Anyone staying inside the houses will be shot. All Jews, raus, raus to the train station. Jews, hurry out of your houses to the train station. Now!"

The order couldn't be clearer. The meaning couldn't be clearer either: life in this place was over. The street was a hubbub of noise and wailing. Of ear-deafening shouting. Of homes emptying of people who began walking to the station. Of lines of people. Of families keeping together. Of hundreds of Jews, weeping over their fate, sobbing over the unknown future. And of children clinging to parents, terror playing in everyone's eyes. Of babies and toddlers being carried, crying without even knowing why.

"Take the bags we prepared," Yisrael said. "Check that everything we might need to survive is in them, especially our valuables. I've got the cash. We'll split it up later."

"What about Haiya? Isn't her shift over yet?" Yossef asked. "Shouldn't we wait for her?"

Calmly Yisrael answered. "No. We have to be out or we'll be shot."

"What about Mama and Papa?" Volf asked.

Yisrael pondered on that for an instant and then answered. "I don't know yet. But first of all, we need to get out of the house so the Germans don't go in."

Hanokh's chest was hurting. His face turned pale. His legs shook so badly that he had to sit down. Yoheved put her hand on his shoulder.

"I won't leave Papa, no matter what happens," Batya said.

Avraham hugged Yoheved. "Look at Mama. She won't be able to handle this expulsion. I'll stay with her. We'll try to evade the Germans."

Yisrael studied them before voicing his decision. "Volf, you stay for now with Mama, Papa, Batya, and Avraham, and look after them. Yossef, Miriam, and I will go to the station and the Germans will see people have left the house. Otherwise, they'll go in and kill Mama and Papa."

Haiya's shift came to an end, but the German manager did not release the workers. "None of you are returning to the ghetto. You will now walk to the train station where you will join the other Jews." Haiya's face turned white. What's going on there? she wondered. How will I get to my family?

Half the Zaks family joined the throng of people making their way to the station. Nazis were already conducting initial selections, separating men from women. Miriam was forced to move away from Yisrael and Yossef. She turned back to catch sight of her brothers. They'd already disappeared. Within minutes she found herself standing among dozens of women on the station platform.

Yisrael and Yossef walked to a distant corner of the ramp, sticking close together. Weeping could be heard everywhere; the deep sorrow expressed by those cries was hard for them to bear. A Nazi indicated to the men to gather closer together.

"Boys under the age of 13, left. Men over the age of 50, left. Men aged 13 to 50, go right."

"Those bastards are weeding out people who can work and those who can't," Yisrael whispered to Yossef. "Those who can't work will be sent to Auschwitz, for extermination. Come, stay with the group of healthy men. Quickly."

"But what about Volf and Avraham? What about Batya? Where are they? And what will happen to Mama and Papa?" Yossef's voice cracked with worry.

Yisrael wrapped his arm around his brother, who'd already been through so much. "Who knows? I'm sure everything will be clear to us fairly soon. I trust our brothers and sisters to take care of themselves and our parents."

As the line advanced, they noticed their friend Samuel, a neighbor from their town, firmly gripping his ten-year-old son, who couldn't stop crying. Samuel would not let his son go to the left as the Germans required. "Don't cry," he said quietly to the boy, placing a hand over his mouth to muffle the sounds. "You'll stay with me. Papa won't let you go."

But as he spoke, a Nazi came over and yanked the child from Samuel's arms. "You, right. The boy, left," he barked.

Samuel refused to obey. "I'm going with my son," he insisted. But the child continued crying and the German broke into hearty laughter.

"No you're not. But if you insist, I'll just shoot you both. Got it, stinking Jew?" the Nazi said, gripping the child's hand firmly and throwing him down on the ground. "Move, child. You don't have a father anymore. You're on your own now. Go left or die."

For Samuel, abandoning his child was inconceivable. He strode after the boy already moving towards the left. "Moshe, Moshe…" he called out to his son. Aiming his rifle at Samuel, the Nazi pulled the trigger once. A hole ripped through Samuel's back. He fell onto the ramp, bleeding. Moshe, stunned, ran to his father.

The German fumed, "You go left, boy, or you die too." The boy stood there, absolutely petrified and paralyzed by fear and shock.

A moment later the Nazi shot again. Moshe fell onto his father's body. Yisrael and Yossef didn't dare turn around to look at the boy, shot in his head and sprawled, bleeding, over his father. In life and death, Yisrael said to himself, crying silently, they were inseparable.

***

Haiya reached the ramp with the group of shift workers, who were also separated by gender and age. She searched for her sisters-in-law. In the distance she saw a hand waving her over. "I'm here, Haiya," she barely heard Miriam over the ruckus. Pushing her way through the crowd of women, Haiya and Miriam were soon hugging each other in relief.

"Where's Mama? Batya?" Haiya asked.

"They stayed home for now. Batya's looking after Papa, with Volf and Avraham looking out for Mama. But Yisrael and Yossef are here, among the men on the other side."

***

In the ghetto apartment Hanokh's body trembled, but he insisted on going to the station. "If we're found here, it's the end of us," he said to Batya and Volf. "Let's go."

Batya and Volf exchanged glances, knowing when Hanokh's mind was made up. "Alright, Papa," Batya said softly, "but Avraham will hide with Mama in the basement. She'll be safer there."

Hanokh looked at his wife, his eyes welling with tears. "We'll meet yet, my beloved wife. But for now, I have to go. Be well."

Batya and Volf also hugged their mother, then linked their arms with Hanokh's, one of them on each side of him, and left. Avraham picked his mother up gently and carried her down to the basement. Births, the loss of her son Yitzhak, and the events in the store had caused a steady decline in her; and more recently, after being forced from her home to live in the ghetto while enduring the constant uncertainty about food and Gestapo roundups, the nerve-racking and never-ending shooting, the shouting and the screaming: all of this had taken its toll, and her health had markedly deteriorated. He lay her down on a mattress, crying softly as he whispered. "I'm with you, Mama. I won't leave you."

Slowly Batya, Volf and Hanokh walked together, but no more than a few minutes later Hanokh stopped, his breath coming in hard gasps. His legs collapsed underneath him. Batya and Volf tried, but couldn't, stand him up. "Volf, Papa is having an attack and I don't have any valerian," Batya said in a loud, worried voice. "There's a clinic nearby where I volunteer. I'm sure they've got valerian. Go, get some. Steal if you have to. Quick, Volf, before Papa dies here."

Volf knew the clinic. He ran off, praying he wouldn't run into Gestapo. A Nazi stopped him. "Halt, Jew," he commanded. "Stay in the line with everyone else. Try to flee, and you'll die."

Helpless, Volf joined the line of people walking. As soon as the soldier disappeared from view, Volf raced off towards the clinic. Bullets zipped above his head. Glancing back, he saw two Jews sprawled on the ground, shot dead. The German's rifle now aimed for Volf.

"This is your last chance. Get in line or I shoot," he said, his finger at the trigger.

Volf gritted his teeth, deciding to join the group of men. In his heart he knew he'd never see his father again. "He'll die because of me," he kept muttering to himself as he reached the station platform.

As though in a dream, he heard his name being called. "Volf, over here, come here." Yisrael and Yossef! Quickly he joined them, sobbing. "Papa needs his pills and I can't get to the clinic. He'll die because of me. I know he will." His brothers hugged him firmly.

A LAND WITHOUT ORDER, AND WHERE THE LIGHT IS AS DARKNESS

Batya sat on the ground next to her father, who lay breathing with difficulty. "Papa, it'll be okay," she whispered, stroking his head. "Volf will come back any moment and bring the medicine. Rest, Papa. Don't worry. I won't leave you." Tearfully Hanokh gazed at her. He tried to speak, he tried to move his limbs, to no avail. His strength was fading. He closed his eyes again. Batya stroked his cheek. She chatted to him, trying to keep him conscious. "Papa, stay awake with me, please. Open your eyes, Papa." But Hanokh didn't react: he'd lost consciousness. "Papa, I'm going to run and bring you the pills. I love you, my Papa."

Leaving Hanokh on the ground, his eyes shut and his breathing labored, she raced to the clinic through the now empty streets. Barely a couple of minutes later she burst inside, puffing hard from the sprint. She was surprised to see that, by contrast to the rest of the ghetto, the clinic wasn't abandoned. The head nurse sat at her desk sorting medicines.

"Give me valerian pills quickly. My father's lying unconscious and needs them urgently or he'll die," she said firmly.

The nurse shook her head. "I'm very sorry, Batya, but I can't give them to you," she said in a cold tone. "And in general, I suggest you don't even go back there. That would be better for you. The Germans must certainly have found your father by now and taken him away or killed him. Your father is no more. You need to save yourself. Do you understand that? But pills you won't be getting from me."

Batya understood very well: the nurse was going to steal the stock of pills and trade with them. Venting her fury, she slapped the nurse's cheek hard. Stunned, the nurse tried to slap back. Batya shoved with all her strength. The nurse fell back on the medicine cabinet.

"What are you planning, you evil woman? On killing my father?"

Lying on the floor, the nurse's lip bled. Batya rummaged through the medicines, collecting all the valerian she could find. The nurse grabbed Batya's leg, wanting to trip her up. Instinctively Batya kicked her in the face. Groaning, the nurse let go.

Batya sprinted back to the yard where she'd left Hanokh. Her heart thumped when, from a distance, the yard seemed empty. Where could he have gone? She stopped, nausea rising. She doubled over, vomiting acidic liquid from her empty stomach. Her veins pumped wildly. She felt dizzy. She sat down and cried. Where could her father be? It wasn't possible that he'd just walked off somewhere. Then she put a hand to her heart and whispered to herself. "I don't have a Papa anymore. The Germans probably found him and took him to the train station or killed him along the way." Tears trailed down her cheeks as she fingered the pills in her pocket. What good were they now? Deep exhaustion crept through Batya's body. I shouldn't have left Papa, a nagging thought upset her; If he was destined to die, I should have been there with him.

Her head spinning, she stood, not noticing the German soldiers approaching from behind her until she turned to find herself eye to eye with his rifle. "And where are you headed, Jew?" he barked.

Batya almost answered 'to my father'. At the last second, she kept her gut response in check, correcting herself. "Like everyone else. Where they're all going," she muttered.

The Nazi raised his weapon. "Hurry up then. To the train. That's where you're headed. Don't even think of escaping. I don't need much of a reason for this bayonet to be pushed right through you. Go on. Schnell."

Batya strode quickly, her arms slightly raised, the bayonet's point lightly pricking her back. In minutes, she had reached the hell on the train ramp. The only thing her tired mind could grasp was 'Jews of 13 and up, to the right. From 50 and up, to the left.' Head bowed, she joined the group of women on the right, not looking around at all, but muttering repeatedly. "Papa died because of me. I left him in the yard. I didn't get back to him on time. Forgive me, Papa," she sobbed. "Papa, forgive me for not saving your life. Forgive me for saying you've nothing to be afraid of. Papa, we're all afraid of this hell."

A strong embrace shook her from her thoughts. Looking up, she found herself enveloped by Miriam and Haiya. The three cried together softly. "I left Papa in the yard," Batya explained, "because he collapsed and I didn't have pills with me for him. I sent Volf to the clinic but he never came back. So I had no choice. I went to the clinic myself, and got the valerian… But when I returned to the yard, Papa wasn't where I left him. He's dead. I just know it. He died because of me, because I didn't stay with him. It's my fault."

Haiya and Miriam hugged her tightly, crying with her. Haiya was the first to speak. "Batya, it isn't your fault. You didn't kill him. The Germans' shameful behavior did. Now you have to be strong. You must. Let's do everything we can to stick together, like Papa said we should. That's his wish. Keeping it will keep us strong too."

Slowly a small open-sided truck approached the station. People on the platform stared at its cargo in silence: corpses, piled on top of each other, blood oozing from the murdered Jews onto the asphalt. Slowly the truck disappeared from view, leaving a bloody trail.

***

Avraham sat next to Yoheved, who lay on a mattress in the basement. After giving it some thought, he decided that it would not be good to stay down there. Better for her to be in one of the empty rooms despite the risk that the Nazis would return to scan the area again. "Mama, I want to take you to a different place." Without waiting for her response, he carried her to a higher floor where she'd have plenty of air. Gently he took her into the bedroom, placing her on the bed. Yoheved hugged him.

"Listen, my son, I am asking you to leave me here and escape. You're young, you're tough and strong, and you've got a good chance of surviving. I would be nothing but a burden. Flee, Avraham, save your own life."

He kissed her cheek. "I'm staying with you, Mama. Whatever happens, happens. But now I want to check what's going on outside. Rest for now. Just stay quiet, and everything will be fine."

Avraham kissed her cheek and went out of the apartment into the yard. Hearing voices in German, he quickly hid among the shrubs. Nazi soldiers were entering to check for people evading their orders. Avraham decided to reveal himself, crawling slowly across the yard. Papa! What was Papa doing there on the ground?

***

Hands and clothes bloodied, tears streaming like rivulets down his cheeks, Avraham changed his mind and quickly made sure he was well hidden. He could see Nazi boots pacing back and forth. 'Get out of here!' he urged them in his mind, I need to get back to Mama! Tense moments elapsed, and eventually the Germans moved away. Avraham raced to the house and up the stairs to where he'd left Yoheved. She wasn't there! He went from room to room, trying to convince himself she must have simply gone to another. He went to the upper level, back down to the lower level, checking the rooms again. There was no one in the apartment! "Mama! Mama! Where are you?" he whispered loudly. Nothing but silence. "I promised I'd come back, and here I am!" He went to the bedroom again and burst into sobs. "Mama! Why did I leave you alone? Why?"

Regaining his composure, he weighed the options. It would be best to join his siblings at the station. "We have to stay together," he whispered to reassure himself. "My brothers and sisters are all I have now." Leaving the building, his heart aching, he walked only a short distance before he found himself facing a Nazi rifle, and a laughing Nazi.

"Are you from this building? We sent the woman who was hiding there to Auschwitz." Seeing Avraham's eyes open wide, the Nazi continued. "Was she your mother, Jewboy? Well, you won't be seeing her again. Schnell, to the station, at a run!" he barked, shoving Avraham, walking behind him briskly to prevent his escape. There he told Avraham to join the group on the left, all young children. Just then, Limping Henshil, a Pole who traded Jews and received money for each one he ratted on to the labor camps, shouted at him.

"How old are you, filthy Jewboy?"

"Eighteen, sir," Avraham answered.

Henshil gestured with his hand. "Then get out of my eyesight to the other group."

Avraham strode to the group on the right, where he came across his uncle, Shlomo the police officer. "Avraham, where are you going?" Hearing Shlomo, Avraham stopped in his tracks. "Come here, to me, right away." Avraham did. In an undertone, Shlomo explained. "That was the train to Auschwitz. Children taken there never return. Good that Limping Henshil sent you to the group on the right. Now come with me to the second ramp. Your brothers are there. Run. Hurry."

Three sets of hands were waving in unison. Avraham made out his brothers. "I saw Papa, dead," he told them, choking on his words. "I couldn't save him. And Mama's also gone. Disappeared. They took her to Auschwitz. And I'm to blame. I should have brought her here but I didn't. It's all my fault."

Yisrael bent down a little to look right into his eyes. "Avraham, you're not to blame. Nor is Volf. None of us is to blame. The Germans are the guilty ones. They're outright murderers. We didn't kill Mama and Papa. Get that into your head. Now the most important thing is to keep Papa's wishes in mind: stay together. That's our heritage. Together we're stronger, and that way we'll manage to survive, as we always have. A close-knit family."

Yisrael slipped his hand into his coat pocket: it held the money he'd taken from the house. "Stand around me, really close so no one can see. I'm going to give each of us money, and we need to find a way to get some to the girls, too. It'll be really hard to survive without money."

Uncle Shlomo came over to make sure Avraham had found the others. Yisrael walked over to him. "Uncle, are you able to go over to the women's side?" he asked, barely moving his lips.

"Yes, of course. What do you need?"

"I want to get some money to them otherwise they don't stand a chance. Can you take it to them?"

Checking quickly around him first, Shlomo took the money. "I'll do my best," he said.

It was early afternoon. Women and men stood in the sun. They hadn't eaten, nor had had anything to drink, and were forbidden to sit. "Let's try to get closer to the line separating the women from the men," Yisrael suggested. "Maybe we'll be able to see the girls from a distance." Yossef, scanning the area, located them and pointed them out. They saw Shlomo make his way over to Haiya and hand her the banknotes. The girls huddled around Shlomo, then disappeared from view.

They also spotted their neighbor Genia clutching her eight-year-old daughter, among the women. "You're not going anywhere. You're staying with me," they heard her tell the child.

Then the voice of Genia's husband Leibel rose above the crowd's noise. "Genia, send the child to Grandma and don't argue with me about it. Send her right away." Surprised, Genia let go of the girl for a second. She was off at a run to her grandmother. The older woman and the child embraced. The child waved to her mother, smiling, and hopped onto the train with her grandmother. Genia, speechless at what had just transpired, couldn't get through the crowd to pull her daughter back out. She had no tears left. Her heart turned as cold as stone.

Never had the bright clear sky of June 23rd been as cold and black as on that day.

POSITION AVAILABLE: KAPO

It was dusk when the brothers walked through the labor camp's gates, discovering its name: Blechhammer. They were exhausted not only from the pressure of the past few days, being rounded up, standing for hours in the sun, and being jammed in a standing position, like cattle, into train carriages that transported them somewhere they'd never heard of; but also from realizing that, on a single day, they were now orphaned by the deaths of both parents. They'd had no time to mourn, to grieve, to cry, and it looked like they wouldn't be given any. But at least they had each other: four of them banding together.

Yisrael wanted to reassure his brothers. "Luckily for us we're not only here, but together, unlike others sent to Auschwitz. We've got some money, some valuables, and they'll be very useful, for sure. We're going to watch out for each other. We must never split up."

"Where do you think the girls are?" Avraham asked what each of them was privately wondering. Again, Yisrael took on the role of fathering them with logic. "No idea, Avraham, but one thing you can be sure of is that they're not in Auschwitz. Only the elderly and children were sent because they can't work. I saw the girls go to the right during the selection. So we have to wish them every strength in holding out until we meet again. We've got tough sisters, and they've also got Haiya with them. I'm sure they'll look after each other too."

***

The brothers stood on gravel-covered ground in the crowd of men. Behind them was a very small shed above which a sign was attached: Block 12. Shouts in German roared through the tense atmosphere. Uniformed Nazi soldiers, equipped with batons and whips, arrived and lined up in front of them. The crowd fell silent, disrupted only by the sound of one man falling to the ground. A German soldier whipped the man's back. Everyone watched, horrified.

A Nazi whose shoulder decorations ranked him as an officer barked out instructions. "From now on you stand in fives. If not, prepare to be whipped like this idiot Jew." In seconds, the men grouped off. The German tapped his knee with his baton, continuing loudly. "No one moves. Move only when we let you. From now on you stand at attention. Whoever falls will not rise."

Around the brothers were other men they knew from their town. The German officer was accompanied by a soldier whose weapon was at the ready. Registration began. The officer went quickly from one man to the next, wanting each one's first name and family name, checking them against a list. Every so often, someone was told to step out of line and was taken to a different structure. Yossef went pale. He was familiar with all the men taken aside and understood immediately. Ignoring the prohibition against talking, he tried to whisper to Avraham. "I know what's happening. They're separating…" He never managed to finish the sentence. The officer and soldier were now in front of him.

"Name?" the officer demanded.

"Zaks, Jozef," he answered weakly.

Checking the list, the officer raised his head, looking at Yossef. "Were you a soldier in the Polish army?"

"Yes, that's true, sir," Yossef stuttered.

"So, you're not only a Jew but also an enemy of the German military," the German officer waved Yossef aside. "POW camp for you. Leave the line immediately and go to the shack on the side of the lot."

Legs trembling, Yossef left the line, looked back, saw his brothers stunned, frozen in their place. Avraham began to cry. Volf grabbed his hand and tugged at it lightly to prevent Avraham from falling down. "Stand up straight, now!" Volf whispered firmly. "You must not show any weakness here, Avraham." Volf continued standing at attention, biting his lip. The family unity was cracking. Although tears welled in his eyes, Volf stood steadfast. Do not break. Do not break. Do not break, he told himself. We have to keep ourselves together. He watched Yossef moving away slowly, his head bowed, and whispered a message of hope. "Be strong, brother. They won't break you. We'll be together again soon." A moment later Yossef disappeared into the shack.

For hours they stood there, their sense of time blurred, until a German officer in a perfectly starched uniform appeared. He strode slowly between the rows, staring at one or another of the men. No one dared look him directly in the eye.

The officer stopped in front of Volf. "Leave the line and face everyone."

"Yes, sir," Volf said, doing what he'd been ordered.

"You'll be block manager," the officer said loudly.

"What is my role as block manager?" Volf asked.

Tapping Volf's right shoulder with his baton, the German explained. "You will manage these Jews," he smirked. "If they do not obey, hit them. I am giving you a chance, Jew, to live under better conditions here than most others. You will also get extra food."

Volf choked on the idea. Without thinking it through, he questioned the officer. "And if I refuse?"

The officer was taken by surprise. "In this place, you hit or you get hit. Decide which and decide now. Which do you prefer: to be giver or receiver?"

Volf's answer came immediately. "I prefer to be hit," he said, his voice shaking. Instantly the German's baton came down on Volf's back. Instantly the whip came down on the bleeding gash that had opened. Volf fell face down on the ground, screaming in pain. Avraham and Yisrael's hearts felt ripped to pieces. At the last second, Yisrael stopped Avraham from running to Volf.

The officer spat in disgust, tapped his own boot with the baton, and shouted at Volf. "You want to be the beaten Jew? Now you know how it feels." He scanned the lines of men, then picked out another, pointing to him with his baton.

"And how about you?" he asked the tall, broad-shouldered Jew. "Do you prefer to be beaten, or do the beating?"

The man's answer was prompt. "No, sir, I'm willing to beat them."

The officer smiled. "Good, good. You're block manager from now on, and I expect you to maintain order, make sure everyone shows up for work, and make sure they work properly. Otherwise, you yourself, Jew, will feel what it's like to be beaten. Take this," the officer said, holding the baton out. "Behind you is your dormitory. From now on you all live in Block 12. Move. Schnell! Tomorrow at 4 a.m. you go to work. At 3.45 a.m. precisely, you will all present yourselves here for morning roll call. Latecomers will answer to the block manager."

He turned to the new Kapo. "Allow me to remind you of your duty. Beat them or I'll beat you."

He stared coldly at the Kapo, then scanned the men in front of him. "You've been chosen to work here. You will work here to the end. See those chimneys and smoke? From this place there's only one way out. Via the chimneys." The officer smiled to himself with satisfaction. "You are now free to go to the block. Take this filth with you," he pointed to Volf, still lying on the ground. "He will also be here tomorrow morning at the appointed time if he doesn't want to leave via the chimneys. Work hard, Jews, or your lives will end very quickly."

Lifting their wounded brother, Avraham and Yisrael grabbed him on either side and slowly walked him to Block 12.

DARKNESS UPON THE ABYSS

Hands calloused, backs bowed, faces sooty; Yisrael, Volf, and Avraham shared a wooden bunk in Block 12. Their muscles ached. Their bodies felt crushed. Tears came easily to them all when they whispered to each other at night. "Do you realize we're now in mourning for Papa and have no idea where Mama is?" Volf said.

Avraham sighed. "Instead of respectfully fulfilling the commandments of mourning at home, we're carting buckets of coal to the furnaces. But the Germans have made sure we have clothes suited to mourning. We're all as black as coal."

Yisrael raised his head a little. "Listen, you two. We MUST be strong. No matter the odds. My hunch is that we're going to be here a long time. No one will come and bail us out. We're actually lucky we're in Blechhammer. It's a labor camp. Yes, it's annexed to Auschwitz, but its purpose is to produce synthetic fuel for the German army. So we're covered in soot. Okay. But as long as we can work, we'll survive. We need to mourn in our hearts only and not let that make us lag behind others when it comes to work. Now, stop thinking so much and go to sleep. We can't keep our strength up without enough sleep." But as he spoke, he noticed his younger brothers' eyes closing. Yes, we have to sleep, he encouraged himself. Sleep, even if insufficient, and the bit of food they were given, would allow them to carry on.

At 3.45 a.m., the block mates were out in the yard as ordered. At 4 a.m., the

Nazi blew his whistle. The men set off for their jobs, walking in rows of five. It didn't take long to reach the piles of coal and the furnaces. Filling buckets, shoving wheelbarrows, they moved coal to the furnaces all day. No one spoke. The only sounds were sighs or cries of pain. And Germans shouting at the men: Schnell! Schnell!

Always together, supporting each other, Yisrael, Volf, and Avraham made sure none of them stumbled or tripped, that no one stopped the flow of work. The men were not allowed to pause and rest: the order was to keep moving. Volf's eyes stung from soot dust. Everything he could see was tinged black. But stopping to wipe his eyes, he knew, could be fatal. Avraham managed to put his bucket down for a few seconds. That sufficed to wipe his own, and Volf's eyes. "Schnell!" shouted somewhere nearby made them quickly keep on going. Never show weakness, they reminded themselves. Getting closer to the furnaces felt as though they were stepping into a hell which burned at four hundred degrees Celsius, the temperature required to produce liquid fuel.

"How long do you think we'll hold out in this black dust?" Avraham whispered, his palms streaked by cuts, the skin thickening, making it even harder to carry the buckets. He had an idea. Pulling his sleeves down as far as they could go, he managed to cover his palms. It helped. "Do the same," he whispered to his brothers, "it prevents the handle from rubbing so hard."

Was it only a week since they'd started working here? In that time no small number of men who'd arrived with them had disappeared. The grapevine said they'd been sent to Auschwitz because they couldn't keep up with their workload.

Yisrael suggested they try to get to the wheelbarrow group, having watched and understood that pushing a wheelbarrow was far easier than carrying a loaded bucket. The next morning, right after roll call in the yard, they set out fast and first, picking up the wheelbarrows. To their surprise no one challenged them. Most of the men had already become apathetic and went wherever they were sent.

Yisrael stood before the Nazi. "Officer, sir, today we'll work with the wheelbarrows." The Nazi glanced at him, then signaled with his hand: over there.

Each brother picked up a barrow's handles and began to push it towards the furnace. The closer they got, the harder it was to breathe in the oppressive heat. Sometimes, not paying enough attention, they got too close and sparks singed their hair.

That night they agreed with each other that the barrows were indeed easier to handle, giving their palms a welcome respite. "Better a sore back than our hands filling with cuts, bleeding, and getting infected. Our hands will heal in a few days' time and our backs will just have to get used to this," they consoled each other.

***

"Schnell! Schnell!" was all they heard all day, keeping them at a trot. One after the other, they ran from the coal heap to the furnace, Yisrael first, then Volf, Avraham last. Pushing the barrow was the easy part: it was much harder to flip the coal into the furnace. That had been relatively easier with buckets: they could toss the coal right into the licking flames, keeping them at a distance from the fierce heat. But barrows needed to be brought up much closer, lifted, and poured in. The barrow didn't always empty fully first time around, either, and then the lifting had to be done again and again until not one lump of coal was left in it. Every time they got close to the furnaces, they could feel the flames scorching their faces.

The man who was before Yisrael couldn't get his barrow clean. He tried repeatedly. The supervising Nazi hit his back hard. The barrow fell from his hands and rolled into the fire. The man desperately tried to pull it, lost his balance and fell into the flames. His cries of anguish shook everyone to their core. Work stopped when the smell of live flesh burning filled the air. Seconds later the cries stopped. Yisrael, shocked, dropped his barrow's handles. The Nazi stared and smirked at Yisrael. Quickly, Yisrael picked the barrow up again and emptied it in one swift movement into the furnace. Volf came next, but couldn't withstand the terrible smell. Avraham halted for a moment, giving Volf a gentle push aside, picked up Volf's barrow, and emptied it quickly before emptying his own. The three hurried back to the coal heap.

"Don't think about what we saw," Yisrael whispered, "because nonetheless the barrows are better than the buckets. We must not despair. We will look after each other and keep going." The brothers nodded.

Despite singed hair, dirty clothes, and soot covered bodies, the boys fell asleep that night, the smell of burning flesh seared into their nostrils.

MISHA IN THE RECOVERY TENT

Batya arrived with a high temperature. She, Miriam, and Haiya had been marched into Otmot camp's fenced-off area but had no idea that they were not far from Katowice in southern Poland. In this small subcamp run on forced labor, shouts in German were all they could hear: "Stand in a straight line!"

That's how it is with Germans, the three thought: order, first and foremost. Haiya and Miriam, one on each side, kept a tight grip on Batya to make sure she didn't lose consciousness, fall down, or let anything happen to her, as they'd seen happen to another woman who was immediately shot.

Batya was deathly white. Her legs trembled from fear and weakness. Going down the lines, the German officer looked intently at each woman, occasionally signaling with his hand for a woman to go to the tent on the camp's outskirts. He reached their row, stared at Haiya who looked healthy as she stood straight and kept her eyes locked on him. Miriam also stood straight, one arm keeping her younger sister standing up. He came to Batya. "Drop your hand," he ordered Miriam, "Schnell! Schnell!" Miriam had no choice but to obey.

Batya wobbled, knowing that if she fell, it would seal her fate. She prayed. "G-d, give me the power to keep standing." Her legs trembled but somehow she found the strength, and stayed upright. The officer continued standing in front of her, interested to see how long she'd hold up for. Batya could feel herself wanting to faint. No, she wouldn't give in: with tremendous mental and physical concentration, she stayed upright. The officer moved on to the woman next to Batya. The danger had passed for now. Haiya, Miriam, and Batya breathed with relief. The officer spun around to Batya again. "You," he barked at her, "leave the row and go to the tent."

Barely able to walk, Batya left her sister and sister-in-law and made her way to the tent. Now she was alone. Inside the tent she saw twelve beds. All but the furthest one was occupied, all were women, all looked as pale and weak as she felt. Batya lay down on the last bed, wanting to forget this terrible day. Mama and Papa have probably died, she thought, and I want to die too.

A man walked into the tent, his eyes bright and kind. "I'm Misha and I'm in charge. You're here to have your medical status examined. You've been given two days to recover and you really must or you'll be sent to Auschwitz and from there, no one comes back. So get strong, and then go back to your friends in the camp. It's all up to you."

Her entire body shivering, her forehead burning, Batya lay on the bed, unable to eat the slice of bread on the bedside shelf or even sip water. An hour passed. Misha entered the tent again and went over to her. "I've brought you some food." His voice was gentle. "You have to eat. You must get stronger." She gazed at him, confused: could she be dreaming? Yes, it was Misha, who previously had scared her to death and was now coaxing her to eat. She ignored him, but Misha wasn't giving up easily. "Listen, my child. You must eat, otherwise they'll send you to Auschwitz. Here, I'll help you."

He sat next to her, placing his right arm firmly around her back to keep her upright. With his left hand, he brought a spoon of soup to her mouth. She wouldn't touch it. Misha gazed at her. His eyes were so kind. "Child, I'm asking you to please eat this soup. Eat. You don't want to be sent somewhere else. This is the best of the places… You have to get strong." His eyes never left hers. Eventually she opened her mouth. Spoon after spoon slowly went in. Misha smiled, encouraging her. "Excellent, keep going. This will give you your strength back. You mustn't appear weak. I'll be back in an hour," he said before leaving again.

The other young women were apathetic, some even unconscious. Batya lowered herself onto the bed, feeling a little better. At least the shivering had stopped. She fell asleep but was disoriented when Misha woke her sometime later. Batya sat herself up on the bed. Misha wanted to support her back as before, but Batya shook her head. "No, I can keep myself up," she said. Misha did insist on feeding her, to make sure she ate as much as possible. When she'd finished, he pulled a tiny pill from his pocket.

"I brought this from the clinic. Swallow it. It'll help you."

Deciding to trust him, she did as he asked. And fell asleep seconds later.

Misha came to check on her repeatedly during the night. In the morning he brought her two pieces of bread. Batya, feeling her strength returning and her temperature back to normal, was surprised to find she was actually hungry for some solid food. She chewed the bread eagerly. Misha watched, pleased. When she'd finished, he gave her another pill. "This will boost your energy. Tomorrow you'll be fine and you can get back to your sister and sister-in-law," his eyes smiled kindly at her.

Lying on her bed, Batya talked to herself. "Papa, where are you? I left you dying in the yard. I'm guilty of your death. I couldn't save you. Why did I leave you alone? Forgive me, Papa, I beg you. Help me. Even though I'm to blame, help me to stay alive. I want to live."

She slept, woke up, dozed off, woke up; nightmares and daydreams mingling. She saw her father stroking her head: she was a child, perched on his lap. Papa smiled, his eyes sparkling. She heard him whispering. "I'm here, my child. Don't fear. I will help you. It'll be very hard, but you'll get through it. And you're not to blame. Really you aren't. I know everything. You'll see that I do..." Tranquility seeped through her body. "Papa, just help me," she muttered. "Only your spirit can make me strong enough."

Morning came fast. It seemed Batya had at last slept well. She was the only woman left in the tent. She sat up, then eased her way off the bed and stood. This time she did not feel her legs beginning to collapse. "Papa, you're here, I can feel it," she whispered. "Just give me a little more strength so I can return to the family."

Batya ate, swallowed the pill next to the food, and decided to rest a little more. In the early afternoon she was awakened by the sounds of a new group of women entering the tent. Batya stood next to her bed, firm, strong. Misha, accompanying the new group, smiled at her. "You can leave your bed now. Please wait for me outside."

She did as asked. Some minutes later Misha joined her. "Come, let's go back to the camp. Rejoin your family. I've already told them that you've recovered and doing a great deal better."

Batya was now able to walk at Misha's brisk pace until they reached the gate, where he stopped. "Here's where I have to leave you but now you can walk on your own to the other side," he said, shaking her hand. "They're waiting for you."

Batya looked into his eyes. "Who are you, Misha? Who sent you to me?" she whispered. Light seemed to shine from his eyes when he smiled.

"I'm no one in particular," he said softly. "Do you think your father sent me to you? But we'll meet again."

THE LIFESAVER

Batya reunited at last with Miriam and Haiya. Her face showed she was still very tired, but Misha's dedicated care had brought the color back to her cheeks. She even smiled a little when she saw them. "The main thing is that we're together from now on," she said, embracing them.

"What happened over there?" Haiya asked, stroking Batya's cheek. "We were quite worried. And there's no one to ask… How'd you manage to get better? Did someone help you? Yesterday a man came over here, asked for us, and said you'd be all right. Who is that man? How did he know who we were?"

"I've also only just met him," Batya answered. "His name is Misha, and he saved my life. I don't know why, but he decided to help me. On the first day he literally spoon-fed me. Because of his care I started to recover and get stronger, otherwise I wouldn't have been able to come back here. They'd have sent me to Auschwitz instead. I have no idea who he is or why he chose me, but I owe him my life."

To Batya's surprise, a strange look came over Haiya's face. Batya couldn't decide: Was it astonishment? Dissatisfaction? "I have trouble understanding why he'd act that way. What's his purpose? Why was it important for him to save you? What does he want? Did he ask for anything? Batya, we must be very careful."

Both Batya and Miriam were taken aback, unable to follow her train of thought. But Haiya persisted. "He'll come and ask for payment for his help, wait and see. I'm sure he's got a hidden agenda. We need to be alert, especially you, Batya. Please. Don't get yourself mixed up with this Misha. If he comes here again, let me talk to him. In a camp like this there are no free meal tickets."

Batya didn't see eye to eye with her sister-in-law's opinion but decided not to say anything. Now wasn't the time for arguing or philosophizing.

***

Otmot Camp's women laborers worked in the shoe factory, as they'd done when they lived in the ghetto. The work was familiar, hard, but they all kept going. They worked long hours, from early morning to night, ending their day with two pieces of bread each. Anyone with a bit of money could enrich the meal from the camp's flourishing black markets: an occasional potato, or thick soup smuggled from the staff kitchen. Luckily for the three of them, they'd managed to conceal money in their clothes.

It was quickly clarified who Misha was: the most important food smuggling trader in the camp. At night he'd come to their barracks and wish the women good night. Then he'd look at Batya. "I've brought you something good. Hot soup with bits of pork. Come, eat it. You'll feel better."

Haiya, standing before him, adopted a distanced, business-like tone. "How much is that, Misha?"

His face showed he was insulted. "Free. I don't want to take money from you."

Haiya wasn't buying that. Her tone and face were serious when she spoke to him again. "Listen, Misha, I'm happy you're helping us but I don't want to be beholden to you. You've brought food? You'll receive payment. So tell us how much you want and we'll give it to you."

He had a good, warm smile, that Misha. Batya was already charmed; Miriam was sure he had no hidden intentions. But Haiya still wasn't buying it. "Misha? I'm asking again: how much do you want?"

Misha shook his head. "I really don't need the money. Food suppliers show up here every day, and I'm responsible for receiving the goods. I have everything I want; you could even say in abundance. I just want to help you, that's all."

Haiya was still unimpressed. Her tone became a tad more assertive. "We'll pay a few zlotys now for what you've brought. Each time you come, you'll get something. We don't want anything for free. Here, take these notes, and thank you, Misha. Thank you for your help and especially for taking good care of Batya."

Misha smiled again, took the notes, and without even counting them, shoved them into his pocket and left.

Batya was hurt. "Haiya, he really is a good person," she said. "Misha does want to help us. I believe him. Why are you so tough on him? What do you think about it all, Miriam?"

Miriam carefully worded her response. "He does indeed look like a good man. But I have to agree with Haiya. We need to be careful. We can never know what really hides behind a person's smile or where it could lead. We're in a war. As long as we're able and we have money, we'll pay Misha for what he brings, and we won't be obligated to him in any way."

Misha never ceased to surprise them. Every two to three days he came with vital foods, each time something different, and even though he never requested money, the three young women made sure to pay something. He always did exactly the same thing: didn't count how much, stuffed it in his pocket, smiled warmly and left.

Two months had passed since the three women had arrived at Otmot, working hard day after day, noticing that sometimes women disappeared from the camp, never to be seen again. One night Misha came to their barracks. His hands were empty, his face tense. "Don't go to work tomorrow," he instructed them.

Haiya jumped to her feet, surprised. "What on earth does that mean? How exactly do we get out of that?"

Misha took a deep breath, speaking in a soft rush. "Stay here. Inside. Do not put a foot outside. I'll come here right after everyone else has gone. Listen to me and don't go out." He spoke, and he left.

As usual, Haiya was skeptical. "Very odd. I'm not sure what he's cooking up here."

Batya and Miriam, though, were on board with his request. "I'm putting my trust in him," Batya said. "He hasn't disappointed us yet, so we should listen to him. I believe we should do as he says and stay inside." Miriam, looking at Batya, nodding her head in agreement.

Haiya gave the issue some more thought. "He really has helped us so far. All right, let's trust him."

Early the next morning, women headed out to work, emptying the barracks. Haiya, Miriam and Batya dressed quickly, along with everyone else, but managed to evade stepping outside. Peeking from the window, they watched their barracks mates marching off. Several trucks were parked adjacent to the camp gate.

"Schnell! Schnell!" came the order in German along with orders for the women to get into the trucks. Within a couple of minutes, they'd all boarded and were driven away.

Haiya and her sisters-in-law watched in terror. Had Misha not warned them, they too would now be on their way to who-knows-where, but almost certainly not to a better place than this camp. Misha quickly entered. "Follow me, hurry," he shooed them out and into a warehouse. "Wait here. I'll come and get you soon. Don't worry."

Shaking, they sat on the warehouse floor. Haiya's heart pounded. "What happened?" she wondered aloud. "Why were they taken away like that?" Batya tried to stay calm and hugged her. Miriam embraced the two of them together.

"Haiya, it'll be okay, don't be afraid," Miriam said. "Misha has always been here to help us. We have to trust him this time too."

An hour passed. Or perhaps it was an eternity, until Misha was back, his big warm smile creasing his face. "Come. Follow me." The three women walked behind him to a barracks that appeared to be a little more spacious. They sat down on a bed. "You'd do well to grab the best beds here," he suggested, "because another group of women will soon show up. From western Europe. Almost everyone who'd been with you so far was sent to Auschwitz this morning. I managed to save you and a few others. Only a few. Don't say a word to anyone about what happened. Tomorrow, go to work, like you did every day, with the new group. Everything will be fine, I promise."

Pale, stunned, they sat on the beds, one thought hammering in their minds: they were minutes away from being sent to Auschwitz. Even though Misha spoke calmly and reassured them, they felt the danger creeping ever closer. At any moment their fates could be sealed.

THE MAILMAN

Women from The Netherlands were Otmot's new recruits. They made every effort to fulfill the harsh commands and workload. It was clear to them that if they didn't work like the Polish women, they'd be on the short path to Auschwitz. Returning from their workday, the women were surprised to find Misha in their barracks. He brought them more or less fresh bread, some cheese, potatoes and even cooked beets; they paid in jewelry and diamonds. He was even more caring towards the Zaks women, bringing several sausages for each. Haiya paid him on behalf of the three of them.

Misha asked the three women to go outside with him. They stood flush to the barracks. He glanced around, checking to be sure no German guards were watching. He spoke fast. "Your brothers are in Blechhammer. Our food supplier brings supplies there too and can say that they're fine, all three of them. The fourth, who was a Polish soldier, was sent to a POW camp. I'm trying to make contact with him." Misha walked away quickly, leaving them stunned.

"That was more important than any food he could bring," Miriam burst into sobs. "It's filled my heart with joy. For the first time since we've arrived, I'm actually happy!"

Haiya hugged her. "We'll hold out," she whispered. "We'll survive this. News like that will help us get through another long period. Things will be okay, Miriam. We'll make it."

They returned to the barracks, smiling. The sameness of one day after the next saw several weeks more passing. Some of the Dutch women didn't last, perhaps too physically weak or perhaps because they lost hope or the will to live. Misha continued his efforts on the women's behalf, receiving his payment: cash from the Zaks family, gold and gems from the Netherlanders.

At the end of a very long workday, the women returned from the factory to their barracks. Several skipped the tasteless night meal and simply flopped onto their bunks, falling asleep right away. Misha showed up. Empty-handed. Batya couldn't understand why he was smiling. "What's this great mood of yours? We've had a tough day. We're starved and there's no food. So what's the smile for?"

Misha's smile broadened. "I've got something far more important than food for you," he said, holding a sealed envelope out to Haiya.

Her hands shook as she opened it, pulling out a letter. Instantly she identified Yisrael's wonderful handwriting, but couldn't connect letter to letter, word to word. She held the letter out to her sister-in-law. "Batya, read it. I'm crying too much to see clearly."

Batya glanced at the letter and burst into tears. "I can't see what's written there." She passed it to Miriam.

"We're in Blechhammer," Miriam read, the page crackling in her trembling hand. "We're together, me, Volf, and Avraham, and we're holding up okay. We miss you all a lot and think of you often. It's so tough here but we'll overcome it all. We were pleased to hear from our courier that you're all doing well. If you can, write to us about things at your end. With much love to you all. Yisrael, Volf, and Avraham."

Shoulders bobbed up and down as they silently wept, as they kissed the page, as they imagined their brothers excited about them receiving the letter. Misha handed them a pencil and paper. "Now write something back. The food supplier comes tomorrow. I'll send it with him and he'll hand it over in Blechhammer. But quickly. Write, write," he urged them.

Haiya took the page and wrote a few words on behalf of them all. "I don't think it matters much what we write. The main thing is that they know we're okay and together. Everything else is less important," she said to Miriam and Batya.

Misha took the pencil, folded the letter, shoved it quickly into his pocket and quickly disappeared back into the camp's darkness.

BREAD FOR BOMBS

The first spate of bombs dropped by the Allies took the brothers completely by surprise. Bombers attacked the camp ruthlessly, diving with ear-shattering whistles that raised fear in everyone. And again, and again. Explosions had the Germans hiding in bunkers. Jews were left to the mercy of fate: they sheltered in the barracks, hands over their heads; among them Yisrael, Volf, and Avraham. Others simply threw themselves onto the muddy, snow-melting ground and prayed they'd survive.

The mission came to an end, and silence filled the camp. The brothers stepped out, assessing the sight: destroyed barracks, flattened production halls, and synthetic fuel that had been blown up. Several installations were still whole and could be worked. Meanwhile, shocked Nazis exited the bunkers but quickly came to their senses and ordered the prisoners to wait for orders inside their barracks.

One prisoner, on his way to the shack, stopped next to an unidentified metal cylinder. He stooped to get a closer look, touching it with his hand. Boom! The prisoner evaporated. Only some blood stains marked where he'd stood. Several prisoners nearby were injured by the shrapnel and shockwave. Nazis came at a run, immediately realizing what had happened: the bomb that hadn't exploded on impact was triggered by the prisoner's touch.

An eerie silence fell on the camp. The brothers weren't familiar with the prisoner who'd just paid for his curiosity with his life. Death had become an inseparable part of camp existence but this was the first time they'd seen the effects of bombing up close. Volf broke the silence with the question playing in the minds of everyone in the barracks: "What if there are other unexploded bombs around? Who will handle them and prevent a catastrophe?" No answers were forthcoming.

Seated hunched on their bunks, each prisoner was lost in his thoughts. An hour or so later, they heard the command over the amplifiers. "Raus! Raus! Everyone out, now!" The men quickly formed groups of five in the yard. Anyone who couldn't stand up properly and fell was shot. Avraham, Volf, and Yisrael, locking hands with each other, kept each other physically and morally strong.

A further thirty minutes or so later, the camp commander arrived. Facing the silent prisoners, he began to talk loudly and in a tough tone. "The Reich's enemies have bombed us, and they will be punished for that. Several bombs did not explode, therefore we need to defuse them ourselves. I need volunteers. We will train them on how to disarm a bomb. In return, volunteering prisoners will receive several more slices of bread. If no volunteers step forward, we will choose the volunteers ourselves but they will not be entitled to any compensation." He paused for several seconds. "In five minutes from now, I want five volunteers to defuse the bombs."

A tremor of fear raced through the prisoners. "Quiet! Not a word!" the officer yelled. Volf glanced at his brothers. Before they could say a thing, he whispered to them. "I'll volunteer. It's extremely dangerous but I'm willing. The extra bread is worth it. But it has to be me. Avraham's too young. Yisrael's taking care of our family. Without you, Yisrael, the other two won't make it. Don't be afraid. You know I've got extremely precise hands and can learn quickly. The Germans will teach me how to defuse bombs and I'll do the task well, I have no doubt of that."

Yisrael opened his mouth to respond. A sharp look from Volf, and he shut it. Volf squeezed his brothers' hands and took a step forward. Moments later four more prisoners joined him. Holding a disarmed bomb, the German officer began to show them the parts.

"Pay attention. This is how it looks. The front is the fuse. You need to unscrew it. Inside is a small spring connected to the detonator. Dismantling the spring defuses the bomb. You must do this with extreme caution otherwise the spring releases itself and you will be vaporized. Now follow me."

Five men followed him. The officer pointed to a bomb lying in the snow. "This is yours. Undo the detonator," he ordered one of the volunteers. "The rest of you, follow me." They continued silently. Next to each of the blocks lay an unexploded bomb. The officer studied Volf. "That's yours. Get to work," he ordered. The officer and the remaining three volunteers walked him to the next one.

Volf shook with fear and cold. But very quickly only the fear remained. Sweat ran down his brow and froze instantly. For a moment he forgot the instructions and remembered only the outcome: one wrong move would cost him his life. A thought popped up in his mind: maybe he'd slip away, go back to the shack… but immediately he dismissed the idea. "Okay, just get a hold on yourself," he rebuked himself quietly. "Take a deep breath. You can do this. Dismantling a bomb is worth bread. It pays."

Touching the bomb, he identified the detonator immediately. Volf didn't lift the bomb but left it lying in the snow and began unscrewing the detonator slowly and very carefully. He was surprised at how easily the parts disconnected and the detonator could be removed. He took a deep breath. Now he was ready for the hard part: finding the screw and undoing it in a way that prevented it from touching the explosive. He waited for a few moments, wiped his forehead and touched the spring.

Boom! Volf flew backwards. He was sure he'd caused the bomb to detonate. He lay on the ground, eyes tightly shut, and felt his body. He was whole. Silence surrounded him. Volf opened his eyes. In the distance a plume of smoke was rising. Clearly one of the other volunteers had activated the explosive and was no more. Lying on the ground, shaking, he encouraged himself once again: I'm alive, I'm alive. Gazing at the bomb in the snow, he breathed in and out deeply a few times until his hands stopped shaking. Carefully, with a light touch, Volf released the spring. He'd defused the bomb! He stood, shook the snow off his clothes, and walked back to where the remaining men were assembled. He was the first of the volunteers to return.

Volf hugged his two brothers, who hugged him back firmly in relief. "C'mon Yisrael, it's all over for now," he whispered. A whiff of joy passed through them. Volf looked forward to the extra couple of slices of bread he'd get that evening, but to his surprise, one of the soldiers handed him half a loaf. Volf felt like a hero, saving his brothers.

But his happiness quickly turned to bitterness. "From now on that's your job. Neutralizing bombs," the German said. "For each one you dismantle, you'll get more bread. If you don't succeed," the German said, bursting into a cackle, "you won't get any bread that evening! Here, eat," the German said, stuffing the half loaf into Volf's hands.

Volf's throat went dry, as though the bread he'd earned for risking his life got stuck inside.

BLECHHAMMER'S HAMMERING

Defusing unexploded bombs became a daily job as the Allies bombed the area with growing frequency. Volf became highly proficient at quickly and efficiently dismantling them. Each bomb defused earned him extra bread, shared with his brothers. But every day, the bread became more costly. Food was becoming scarcer in the camp. Hunger was starting to take over. Yisrael studied his brothers: how skinny they were, bones poking out everywhere despite the extra bread rations. Not that other prisoners weren't getting thinner by the day. Rummaging in the garbage, hoping to find scraps of food, also became a daily activity, shamelessly carried out in front of whoever felt like watching. Hunger overcame shame. We have to get hold of food, he thought. We're losing weight, and we can't afford that. It's ruining our muscles, our strength.

Back from their hard day feeding the coal ovens, the brothers, hearing shouts coming from Block 14, went to see what was happening. His appearance far more wizened than his true age, a man was beseeching another block mate. "Give me my bread back. Why did you take it? I'll die. I can't do this any longer."

A young man answered rudely. "Better you die and we don't need to keep taking care of you. If you die, it'll be easier for all of us."

When he answered, the older man's voice carried deep pain and insult. "I'm your father. My whole life I took care of you. I made sure you had food to eat, and now you're taking my bread?"

But the son was adamant. "Yes, father," came his cruel response. "And that's how it is: either you, or us. Anyway, you're not going to last here but we have a chance of surviving. Maybe if you just don't get up in the morning, it'll be better for you and for us."

Silence. The father was silent. The block mates were silent. Some block mates had already fallen asleep in sheer exhaustion. Another piped up viciously. "Die already. We're sick of these arguments every night."

The three brothers exchanged glances, their stomachs churning in hunger and anger at the terrible scene they'd just witnessed: whatever happened to 'Honor your father and mother'?

The Allied Forces' bombing sorties continued. Nazis hid in protective bunkers as waves of bombs fell on the camp. Prisoners, unprotected, sat in their shacks praying. Some lay on the cold floor, thinking it may offer a little more protection. Each aerial bombardment lasted an hour or so. Each time, it was followed by an eerie silence. Someone would get up his courage, peek outside, and report. "No one's around. The Germans are still in their bunkers. Maybe we can go out."

Volf glanced at Yisrael and Avraham. "Looks like today's an extra bread day."

The men poured out of their blocks into the crisp air marred by smoke and devastation. The coal-melting facility was completely shattered, a large number of the ovens destroyed, and only the coal warehouse still stood. The brothers' hands flew to their mouths as they gasped in shock: Block 14 had been erased in its entirety. Dozens of men must be dead under the ruins!

Yisrael shook his head. "Yesterday the sons fought with their father over a slice of bread and now they're gone. None of them have made it. They're all trapped under the ruins."

"Destiny. Fate… At least we're still together," Volf said softly.

Block 12's men milled around giving vent to their anguish. "Why are they doing this to us? Why do they need to kill us? If the Germans aren't killing us, why would the Americans?"

Yisrael, in his considered manner, wanted them to see a larger perspective.

"Why blame the pilots? Yes, they hit us by mistake, but can't you see? They're trying to destroy the German war machine. They're targeting this camp because they know fuel's being produced here. It's really sad they missed their target but look at the ruins! Half the camp's wiped out. And that means the Americans are slowly winning this war. Eventually they'll release us! Wait and see!"

"May we all live to see it!" a prisoner sobbed, "but I'm not so sure. Let them blow Auschwitz up. That's where people are getting killed, burned to death. The American and Russian allies want to win, but if Jews get killed in order to win, what do they care? We're not even people to them. We're nothing but slaves to the Germans here, and cannon fodder to the Americans. That's what we are."

He paused, then roared with all his strength. "When the bombers come back, I'm going to go out there and direct them towards the ovens with a flag. I'm going to signal to them where to bomb. Those German cowards are anyway down in their bunkers hiding. So, if a bomb gets me, so what. Better to die in an instant with a bomb than languish here and die of slow starvation."

Shouts in German stopped the chatter. The prisoners were told to come out of the blocks and get back to work. The camp commander's voice boomed over the amplifiers. "Attention. Block 12 is going to rebuild the ovens. Block 13 will clear the ruins of Block 14 and bury the dead. Blocks 15 and 16 will continue working with the still viable ovens. From now on you will work two sequential shifts. That means double quantities of coal for each oven. Bomb defusers, start your work. If there's any bread, you'll get extra. And if there isn't, you won't get more. Schnell! Schnell! To work. Immediately."

Avraham's eyes lit up. He smiled. "Did you hear that? Rebuild. Building something new. How great, to build something!" Even the Germans had noted Avraham's technical skills: every type of building skill needed, he was able to handle, from welding to other metal skills needed in construction. Tough iron simply complied with his capable hands' wishes.

"Yisrael, stick close with me," Avraham asked his brother. "I trust you. You always help me get things right when necessary."

Yisrael smiled with gratitude, watching his younger brother, who'd matured well before his time. Avraham's metalworking abilities would stand him and his brothers in good stead now. Almost like a life insurance policy, Yisrael thought, each of us with our particular abilities. "Together, we will survive, we'll make it through anything," he grinned at Avraham.

Block 12's men gathered next to the shattered ovens. Yisrael spoke out. "From now on, Avraham is going to manage the work here and organize what needs to be done. Listen to him. He's the best welder and metalworker in the whole of Blechhammer. We'll do the absolute best we can, and that will go a long way to keeping us alive."

Avraham asked for welding equipment and metal saws. He surveyed the destroyed ovens carefully before speaking. "All right, first we need to separate the parts that are whole from those that need to be welded together, and put aside everything else that's so badly destroyed that it's beyond repair."

Secretly Yisrael feared that one of the men would try to undermine Avraham's authority; surprisingly, they showed excellent discipline. Work moved ahead in a quiet, orderly manner. The German engineers and technicians watched, amazed, as the ovens slowly took shape once again.

Later in the day, Volf showed up. Yisrael and Avraham hugged him quickly. "I managed to get five bombs defused today," Volf updated them. "One of them… I didn't, but fortunately it didn't explode." At that, the color drained from Yisrael's face but Volf just shrugged and smiled. "The main thing is, we've got some bread in our pocket. We'll have what to eat tonight."

It wasn't long before some of the ovens were restored and could be reactivated. The men returned to the block late that night. Most of them fell asleep right after eating their allocated single slice of bread. The brothers were glad of an additional slice each, earned for five defused bombs.

YOSSEF AT THE FENCE

Winter came in full force in November 1943. Early snowing made conditions even harsher for the cold, hungry women at Otmot Labor Camp. Luckily for the Zaks women, Misha continued to provide whatever he could, but money was running out. Despite seeing the cash situation deteriorate, Haiya insisted they pay for every slice of bread Misha managed to smuggle to them.

Misha surprised them yet again one night. "Tomorrow morning when you go to work, take all your belongings with you." Open-mouthed, they stared at him. "We're all going someplace else. Me too. The Germans won't tell the prisoners what's happening but instead of working here, they're taking you to a different camp. I'll try to help there, too, but it doesn't all depend on me. What's most important is to take everything. Money, any items you've got, anything you can use to trade with," he said before hurrying away. The three young women split the cash and jewelry among themselves.

Morning roll call was earlier than usual. "Raus, raus!" German guards ordered the women out. Several guards entered the shack, shoving the women with their rifle butts. "Schnell! Schnell!" again and again. A quick headcount, and the women were ordered to get on the waiting truck. Shoved shoulder against shoulder, many found it hard to breathe, and the cold air hit them mercilessly in open-sided trucks lacking a canvas cover or tarpaulin. They felt lucky that the journey ended no more than two hours later.

"Schnell! Schnell!" came the order to get off. Haiya, Miriam and Batya jumped down, their ears aching from the icy wind. German guards instructed them to enter a nearby block. Haiya, seeing that the crowding would be unbearable, quickly grabbed places for the three of them on the higher bunks, hoping they'd feel more comfortable there. They sat on the bunk's edge, staring at the filthy block and at each other.

"So, what now?" Batya asked as she sighed. "What do these bastards want of us now?" Of course the question was left unanswered, until shouts ordered them outside again. Their new job: inserting light explosives into rolls of paper that looked like cigarettes. What would they be used for? None of the women had a clue.

As surprising as every other time, Misha showed up one evening. He'd found a valuable job for himself dealing with suppliers once more and began occasionally bringing them extra food. Haiya, as usual, made sure to pay him and he, as usual, simply smiled, put the payment in his pocket, and disappeared into thin air.

One day, a woman who seemed familiar to Batya joined the workers. She looked around, came over and sat down next to Batya, but Batya didn't dare exchange a word with her, fearing the guards and the punishment of being beaten. The two glanced at each other in silence. Once in a while, the woman cast a surreptitious glance towards the guards. Noticing at some point that the guards had all gone away for a while, she quickly whispered to Batya.

"I'm Mrs. Beriski, from Strzemieszyce. I'm also working here."

Batya gasped. "But you're not even Jewish.... Why are you here in a concentration camp?"

Mrs. Beriski huffed lightly. "I wanted to earn some money. So, I come here like many other women from the city, working in the day, and going home at night."

Batya remembered where she knew the woman from: her father's shop. Hanokh had seen her suffering from the cold but unable to afford a blanket. He'd picked out a thick, woolen one and gifted it to her, making up an excuse about it being unsellable. Batya didn't remind the woman of Hanokh's generosity. Just then the guard passed by, checked their progress, and moved on.

Mrs. Beriski whispered to Batya again. "I'll never forget your father's kindness. He was like a saint. He saved me and my girls that winter before the war." As tears coursed down her cheeks, she placed her hand on Batya's with warmth and fondness.

Batya smiled: Papa sent her to me, she thought. When Mrs. Beriski needed help, he was there for her, and now we need help, Papa has sent her. Papa is always with us, when he was alive and even now after he's passed away.

As work came to a close for that day, Mrs. Beriski scanned the situation from the corners of her eyes, never moving her head. Satisfied that the guards weren't watching, she whispered again to Batya. "What do you, your sister, and sister-in-law need? Maybe I can bring something for you."

Her head down so the guards wouldn't see, Batya replied. "Some food. That would be wonderful. Thank you. And if possible, some medicine. That's always useful."

The next day, Mrs. Beriski sat next to Batya, took a small packet from her bag and slipped it unnoticed into Batya's pocket. Batya thanked her. They continued working in silence for the entire day. But that evening back in the block, Batya finally brought the packet out. It contained some sweets and chocolate. The three young women joyously shared the delights. "Papa sent her to us, I know it," Miriam sniffled. From then on, Mrs. Beriski brought small items almost every day.

Sundays were the only day that the prisoners were not taken to the factory. It gave them a chance to enjoy a few hours of rest or take a walk to the fence separating the men's shacks from the women's. They hoped to find familiar faces on the other side who could give them news of home and family. Haiya, Batya and Miriam joined many other women at the fence trying to find information about their loves ones.

"Is that Yossef there or am I hallucinating!" Haiya's words burst suddenly from her lips as she pointed to a group of scrawny men shivering in the cold.

Miriam almost fainted at the sight. "Yes! It's Yossef. No doubt about it. Look at him, he looks so sick, weak. Let's call him over. Maybe he can hear us if we shout."

"Yossef! Yossef! Come here! To the fence!" Batya shouted.

Was he dreaming? Yossef could hear Batya calling him. He blinked, and blinked again, then began walking as quickly as his legs could take him. They watched him: his body shrunken, his eyes sunken in their sockets. Their dear brother! Their dear brother-in-law! How he wanted to hug them! How they longed to embrace him! Fingers clutched at fingers through the fence. Warmth spread from one to another. Their touch overcame the air's dreadful frost.

Miriam's face was flush to the fence. "You're here, Yossef. Thank G-d! How did you get here?"

His mouth was dry, his lips parched and cracked from cold and hunger, but he managed to whisper to them through the fence. "I'm considered a POW. I got separated from our brothers at Blechhammer. All the men who served in the Polish army were sent here. I've been here six months and have managed to hold up so far even though I'm always hungry. There's hardly any food here."

Yossef's sisters were left speechless but Haiya, in her practical way, spoke up. "We'll take care of you. We have a friend with good connections inside the camp, and a Polish woman who's helping us from outside. Whenever you can, come to the fence and we'll try to pass food to you." Her tone was determined. "From now on, Misha will work harder for us. There's no choice. We have to save Yossef. Without us he doesn't stand a chance."

Batya looked up at the sky. "Papa, our dear Papa, thank you for helping us reunite. We'll save Yossef. I promise."

Back at work on Monday morning, Batya sat on Mrs. Beriski's right but Haiya changed her workstation, settling herself on Mrs. Beriski's left. The three women smiled at each other but didn't dare speak. They worked quietly, kept their faces focused on their worktables, and without moving their heads at all, whispered to each other only when the guard out of earshot.

"What have you got there?" Haiya asked, seeing the Polish woman slip her hand into her pocket.

Mrs. Beriski hesitated, swallowed, then whispered. "I've got something important for you but I'm afraid they'll catch us. I brought medicine. Pills.

Painkillers and pills for different illnesses. Remember the wonderful doctor who worked in the clinic with Batya? He sent them. He loves you all, and especially Batya."

"Mrs. Beriski," Batya said, "G-d sent you just on time. We truly need these. Not for ourselves but for our brother Yossef. He's on the other side of the fence, in the POW camp and in a dreadful state. Much worse than we are. Help us save him."

"Yossef, who sells in your shop? That lovely young man? Here?"

Batya nodded. The guard, having caught the sound of their whispering, moved closer. Immediately they resumed their silence, focusing on their work. The guard stood there, staring at them harshly. They tried to keep up their work but their hands shook. The guard continued standing there. He never said a word but kept his gaze focused on them. Mrs. Beriski smiled at him, then winked. He came closer and stroked her arm lightly. She responded, stroking his hand. Batya and Haiya looked down. The guard stopped staring at them: he was too busy with the Polish worker hinting that she liked him. Batya and Miriam were sure that in the German guard's mind, he was already meeting her after work.

The instant he moved away, Mrs. Beriski pulled the small packet of pills, gauzes, and bandages out and smoothly slipped it into Batya's pocket. An hour later, the workday was over. The Zakses went back to their shack but noticed Mrs. Beriski, head slightly cocked, smiling coyly at the German guard.

That night, Misha showed up loaded with goodies and smiling warmly as always. Haiya spoke in a very straightforward, businesslike manner. "Misha, we need a lot of help. My brother-in-law Yossef is also here, on the other side of the fence, and in a terrible state. We need you to bring more food as well as medicine to reduce his temperature. And we'll pay you. His life depends on our help. We have to save him. So, Misha, please, do everything you can for his sake."

"I understand," Misha said, before disappearing.

***

The following Sunday, four members of the Zaks family met at the fence. Haiya bent down and slipped everything she could hold in her hands through the gap under the fence and right into Yossef's hands. "Take these pills, Yossef. They'll help you a lot," she said gently. "I've got plenty of food. Vegetables. Potatoes. Bread. Eat, Yossef. We love you, and we want you to get well. Miriam will be here soon with hot soup for you."

Yossef's eyes shone with joy and tears, the first he'd cried in a very long time. Sitting on the muddy ground, he ate slowly and steadily. His stomach could barely take the food in, despite his extreme hunger. An hour later Miriam brought a cup of soup to him, courtesy of Misha. Yossef sipped the fatty liquid, feeling its goodness and heat spread through his shriveled stomach. He thanked her warmly when he'd finished drinking, handing the empty cup back.

"Girls, you've saved me. Without you here, I'd have probably died in a few days' time."

They smiled at him, love in their eyes. Slowly Yossef stood, putting the remaining food and the pills in his pockets. "We'll meet here again next week," were his parting words. "Just stay safe and watch out for yourselves."

"As long as we're here, Yossef," Haiya said, "we'll make sure you're okay. We promise you, Yossef. You'll live."

Darkness was descending on the camp. The women returned to their shack, and Yossef to his.

XMAS CAKE IN LUDWIGSDORF

Three weeks had passed since the women had first set eyes on Yossef at the camp fence. He grew stronger quickly, boosted by Misha's extra portions and Mrs. Beriski's medicines. His face filled out a little; his body seemed to regain its strength.

And it was winter, towards the end of December 1943.

And Xmas.

The women at Ludwigsdorf were delighted to learn they'd receive two days' vacation for Christmas, two days of rest, quiet, peace, a break from the Germans other than the guards. It was cold, snowy, and hunger was gnawing at everyone's stomachs. The Zaks women were hungrier here than in previous camps they'd worked in, and Misha's ability to help was decreasing.

One morning as they dressed and got ready for roll call and the workday, Mrs. Beriski entered the block in a rush. Ignoring the other women, she made a beeline for Batya. She positioned herself with her back to the others, preventing them from seeing what she was doing. Then she bent down, slid a large packet under Batya's bed, said "from home" and quickly left even though Batya was dying to ask her what she'd brought. Back in the block that night, Batya quickly pulled the package out from under the bed: fresh cake, made by the good Mrs. Beriski. It filled her mind with memories of home, memories of the days before threat, fear, and horror.

Inviting some of their friends from the block, the cake was shared around.

Most ate quickly. Not Batya. First, she lifted up her slice, breathing in its aroma. "C'mon, eat some too!" she said to one of her friends. The two nibbled slowly, savoring the flavor for as long as they could. Batya was clearly enjoying every crumb.

"Thank you, Papa," she said, looking up, "for sending Mrs. Beriski to help us. Thank you, dear Papa."

The door flew open: the block fell silent. A German guard stood in the doorway. Batya's friend went white and spat the rest of the cake out. Not Batya. She smiled in defiance at the German and just kept on chewing. He drew closer.

"You, the two of you, go to the camp commander's office. Now. Schnell! Schnell!" he barked.

Batya's friend started to cry. The guard slapped her hard. "Silence!" he screamed.

Batya wondered if these were her last moments here: any breach of discipline, even the slightest, could have a person sent to Auschwitz. Fearful, they walked to the office. Once again, Batya looked heavenward. "Papa, help me now. I need your help."

First to enter was Batya's friend. Batya waited outside. The minutes seemed like forever, especially with the guard keeping his gun at her back. "We're being sent to Auschwitz tonight!" the friend blurted when she came out, and instantly fainted. The soldier roughly stood her back on her feet and shoved her towards the shack.

"In, Jew," Batya heard the commander's roar. She kept herself tranquil, making sure her hands didn't tremble and tears didn't fall, even though her heart pounded wildly. *Papa, are you here?* she asked in her thoughts. *Papa, will you save me again?* Was that his reassuring voice he could hear? *Don't worry, my child. I'm here. I'll make sure nothing bad happens to you.*

Standing straight, Batya looked directly into the commander's eyes.

"What did you do in the shack, Jew?" he screeched.

Quietly she answered. "I ate cake, sir, commander."

"Hmmph. Who gave you permission to eat cake?"

Batya never flinched. “No one, sir, commander. I was just a bit hungry.”

The commander stared hard. “Do you not know this is prohibited, Jew?”

Eyes wide open, full of innocence, Batya answered. “No, sir, commander. I didn’t know it’s prohibited. But, sir, it was so tasty. I couldn’t stop myself.”

Amazed at the Jewish girl’s impudence, he actually smiled at her childlike answer. Guards in his room stared at her, surprised. They had no doubt she’d be sent to Auschwitz. The officer screeched again.

“You know that anyone not fulfilling the instructions and not acting in accordance with the camp’s discipline is sent to Auschwitz?”

Batya held his gaze. “I didn’t know it was prohibited, sir. If I had, I would have given the cake to you. It really was a very tasty cake.”

The officer’s face reddened in fury. “I want to know how the cake got to you!” he yelled.

Batya smiled her innocent smile. “I don’t know, sir, commander. Someone left it in the block. When I went in, I just saw it there and immediately had to try it. Please, sir, commander, may I go back to the block now and finish the cake? I promise to bring the commander whatever is left of it.”

“Get out!” the officer shouted, jumping to his feet. “Out, and I don’t want to see you here again.”

Batya breathed with relief. “Thank you, sir, commander.” She smiled again. “I promise, sir.”

With that, she walked away quickly, raising her head a little. “Thank you, Papa, for looking after me again!” she whispered.

Miriam and Haiya couldn’t believe their eyes when Batya returned without an armed guard accompanying her. She fell into their embrace; and they covered her face with kisses.

“I was sure it was the end of you,” Miriam said.

“Come, let’s finish the cake off. It really is very yummy,” Batya smiled.

MISHA'S JAR

The winter was over at last. 1944 was a blur of days. Day followed day; Ludwigsdorf Camp's women inmates worked on, though working with gunpowder was not easy. Exhaustion was rampant. The women now rolled the explosives standing up on legs that wobbled by the end of the day. A gaunt, pale woman worked opposite Miriam. The woman's eyelids were always half closed over eyes that had sunk into their sockets. She coughed and spluttered all day. Miriam was sure she was suffering from pneumonia. Mrs. Beriski couldn't help, either. So every time the woman coughed, Miriam turned her head, not wanting to catch any germs. Miriam hoped that the woman would overcome her cough and shortness of breath.

One day the woman had a coughing fit that wouldn't stop. She collapsed onto the work floor. Haiya hurried over to her, lifting her a little. Just then the woman coughed hard, spraying blood-spattered spittle everywhere. Haiya could feel it on her face. She laid the woman back down and wiped her face quickly, hoping she hadn't caught an infection. "I don't think she'll make it," Haiya said to Batya and Miriam.

Two German supervisors drew close. Haiya hurried away. Taking hold of the woman's armpits, they dragged her out. "Back to work!" they shouted. A single shot was heard outside. Not a word was heard in the hall. No one shed a tear; no one had any left. Death had become too common a visitor.

Coughing also became common among the prisoners. "Girls, we've got to stay strong. Thank goodness we've got Misha and Mrs. Beriski."

Misha continued bringing food, along with his smile, and every extra slice of bread fortified them. They always kept food and medicines aside for Yossef. Although he didn't look healthy, he was at least looking much better than he had.

That weekend the fence meeting with Yossef was strange. His hands and legs shook and he had trouble talking. Haiya moved closer to the fence. "Yossef? What's going on with you?" she asked gently.

Yossef muttered. "I'm afraid. I heard that they're going to erase the men's camp soon and we'll all be sent elsewhere. I'm afraid I won't make it without you."

"Have you heard any rumors about where and when?" Haiya wanted to know.

Yossef shook his head. "No idea. Maybe Misha knows something. Try to ask him. I hope we don't get sent to Auschwitz Birkenau. I heard that no one returns from there."

"Don't worry, Yossef," Haiya wanted to reassure him. "We'll get through that too. We'll ask Misha and let you know. But make sure you always stand straight and look like someone who can work. Do that and you'll be fine."

Yossef sighed. "Don't forget that for them, I'm a POW. My status is a bit different, and we'll just have to see what happens."

He looked up and his warm, wide smile lit his face. This visit with Batya, Miriam and Haiya had raised his despondent spirits a little. "Yes, we'll meet at our home when this war's done," he said. "I promise to be there. And you've got to promise to me, too." They grinned. Batya stroked his fingers through the fence. Yossef walked back to the men's barracks with an encouraged gait.

That night Misha slipped into the shack and gently shook Batya awake. Despite her fatigue, she managed to sit up. Misha held an envelope inside his coat. "Listen," he whispered, "the men's camp is going to be evacuated, and the women's camp after that. I've got something very precious here for you."

"What is it?" Haiya asked, always slightly suspicious.

Misha paused, then spoke in a rush. "I sold food to everyone, especially bread, and especially to the Dutch women who were very wealthy when they came here. For every slice of bread, I received a piece of jewelry and now I have amassed a valuable collection."

Misha paused again to catch his breath. They watched him, curious, not understanding why he was sharing his secret with them. "I'll also be transferred," he said, "and I have no idea when or where. But one thing I know is that I won't be able to take all this with me. It'll disappear in no time because I have no special privileges there as I do here. It'll all just be lost, gone to waste."

Haiya huffed. "Okay, Misha, so tell us what you want from us?"

Batya, on the other hand, spoke softly. "Where is your treasure, Misha? What do you have with you? Show us."

Misha pulled a very large jar out of his coat. It was filled to the brim: diamonds, gold, gems. Miriam and Batya gasped in disbelief. It would surely have been enough to buy a house, perhaps even an entire estate. The sisters' mouths fell open. Haiya, controlling herself, didn't react. She was no less shocked but as always stayed practical.

"We're not taking anything, Misha. We can't do anything with it. We can't guard this for you. You'll have to hide it in the camp. Bury it. But we can't take it with us."

Batya watched, listening, not believing her ears. She opened her mouth to protest, but Haiya stopped her with a sharp look. Miriam was also speechless. Misha wasn't giving up so easily. In a last ditch effort, he tried to convince Haiya. "Maybe we will bury it deep, this jar, and after the war we can come and dig it up and rebuild our lives."

Haiya was not about to change her mind. "Misha, I already told you: this is yours, not ours," she said again, firmly, although her eyes shone in astonishment at the jar's contents. "Do whatever you wish. We aren't your partners in this treasure."

Misha shook his head, not willing to accept Haiya's decision. He simply couldn't understand her refusal. He wrapped his coat around it and left silently.

An awkward silence fell on the three young women. Batya's heart pounded;

her head pounded, too. Some minutes later, she couldn't hold back any longer. Her tone was angry when she addressed her sister-in-law. "Haiya, why didn't we take the jar? Do you know how valuable all that is? It's a fortune!"

"Yes, Batya. But Misha wants one thing in particular. You. He's desperately in love with you. He wants to marry you. Are you willing to do that, out of gratitude?"

Batya scrunched her nose up. "No. No, of course not."

"So there's your answer," Haiya concluded. "What will we do with it all? The Germans will take it all and kill us for having it in our possession. If we survive all this, and Misha survives, he'll want it all back. More importantly, he'll want you. It's not worth arguing about. Now, let's get some sleep so we can work tomorrow."

But the incident shook them enough to prevent them from falling asleep. They'd never seen so many gems in their lives. Their money had already run out; gems could be used to pay for food and medicine. Misha had just offered them a fortune, and Haiya had rejected it. In the end, though, Miriam and Batya trusted their older sister-in-law. She always seemed to know the best thing to do.

The next day they never exchanged a single word about the incident. Mrs. Beriski didn't show up for work that day, and anyhow they lacked the energy to start explaining the entire situation. Nor did they really want to; they had no wish to endanger Misha. Or themselves, for that matter. That night, Misha was waiting for them in the shack when they returned from work.

"I'm being taken to Blechhammer. You should write a note to your brothers there and I'll hand it to them. As for the treasure, don't worry about it. I buried it deep in the ground, and I hope no one finds it until I can come back for it. Who knows? Maybe I won't even remember where it is."

He smiled but his eyes were sad. "I have some news for you, too. Your brother Yossef was transferred yesterday with the other POWs to a camp in Germany. I heard it's a decent enough place, they don't work there, and the conditions are better. After the war they'll want to swap your brother for their own soldiers taken as POWs. I'm sure he'll be all right."

A broad smile lit Batya's face. She shook his hand warmly. "Thank you, Misha, for everything you've done for us."

He shook his head. "No need to thank me, Batya. But I do hope we'll be able to meet after the war." Batya said nothing.

Haiya was busy writing briefly to Yisrael. "My beloved husband, Misha is a very special man, a precious man, who saved us and Yossef more than once. Please help him in any way you can. He'll find it hard in your camp, but I believe you'll know what to do. Much love and longing, my beloved. I look forward to seeing you after the war. Haiya."

She gave Misha the slip of paper. It went deep into his pocket. The women hugged him. He took a step away, gazing at Batya, then at the other two women. "Watch out for yourselves. We'll meet yet again," he said.

With a heavy step, he set off for the unknown. His status and connections, like his treasure, were now buried deep.

MISHA ARRIVES SAFELY

Misha's journey from Ludwigsdorf to Blechhammer was relatively short. For about half a day, he bumped along in a truck with several dozen other men. The disparity between his current status at Blechhammer's forced labor camp compared to the privileges he'd enjoyed in the previous camps was vast.

He sat in the truck, bent forward, head resting on his hands. In his pocket was Haiya's note to her husband, which he hoped to hand over quickly. He fingered his pants pocket: he'd sewn several hidden compartments into them, and slotted tiny diamonds inside. He had no clue whether they'd come in useful but it certainly didn't hurt to bring them.

The truck pulled up. Misha drew in a deep breath of the camp's suffocating smoke and nausea-inducing stink of burning human flesh. Never in his life had he encountered such a gut-churning stench.

"Off the truck. Schnell! Schnell!" came the shouted commands. "Now." The Germans yelled. The prisoners obeyed. Some fell on the ground. The guards never gave them time to straighten themselves up. Right away they set to beating them cruelly.

"Fives!" the Germans yelled. "Stand in fives. Schnell!"

The men Misha had arrived with were used to this requirement and moved into place without thinking much about it. They were prisoners, and as such had no rights. They were simply required to follow orders. Misha had no idea what "fives" meant but quickly caught on, moving to join a few men forming a line. A prisoner like everyone else, he thought, that's what I've become, and tonight I'll go to bed hungry.

The men stood in the yard waiting quietly for their orders. German guards wielding batons walked around them constantly. No one said a word. Misha felt his legs barely able to keep him up. He knew that if he fell, he'd be shot. He looked around, then whispered to the man on his left.

"Friend, help me, please. I have trouble standing on my legs."

The man ignored him, kept his eyes straight ahead, and his mouth shut. Other prisoners heard Misha but did nothing. The realization dawned: he was indeed completely alone in this world. Even the treasure sewn into his pockets wouldn't help now. He shut his eyes and repeatedly whispered encouragement to himself: don't fall, don't fall, don't fall...

He began to cry, silently at first, but slowly tears started to pour down, beyond his control. He trembled and cried. Prisoners more experienced than he glanced at him, some with pity, some with disdain.

"Look at him," one whispered to his friend. "He's got some good flesh on his bones. Clearly, he's been eating well. But what's all that fat going to help him now? He may not even survive the night."

And so, they stood for another hour at least until night fell. The German commander strode out towards them. Misha noticed all the men straightening up. Only he remained bent over. Other prisoners glanced at the helpless man. Misha didn't understand what they were implying, but the baton coming down with a loud thwack on his shoulder quickly brought him back to reality. He stood straight; instantly stopping to cry. How his shoulder ached, but he decided to ignore it. Still, he was having trouble understanding what was going on. Although a fluent German speaker, he couldn't understand what the orders he was hearing implied. Only one command echoed in his ears: three forty-five was the time they needed to leave in the morning for work. Never in his life had he woken so early.

"Prisoners, you are released," the commander ordered. With roll call complete, the prisoners dragged themselves to Block 15. Misha walked slowly, the pain in his shoulder pulsating, his legs aching. Inside, he was horrified to see that all the bunks were taken. No, there was one left on the upper third level. He wanted to climb up but fell onto the ground. He lay on the floor as though paralyzed. He thought about committing suicide but didn't have the strength to organize that action, so he just kept lying where he was, crying soundlessly.

Three men entered the block. "Someone here by the name of Misha?" one whispered. Misha raised his head but found himself unable to speak. Again he heard the whisper: "Misha?" A pause. "Misha?" This time he managed to raise his arm.

Someone came over to him. "It's you?" the three men asked in unison.

"Yes, I'm Misha."

The three men took hold of him, supported him, and helped walk him outside.

"Who are you?" Misha asked in a daze.

"We're the Zaks brothers. I'm Yisrael, and this is Volf and Avraham. We'll help you. We heard you'd arrived with the shipment of prisoners from Ludwigsdorf and look! We found you! We know about all your help to our sisters and my wife. Now you won't be alone here. Come, come and eat with us. The best we can do is a few slices of bread. Volf defused some bombs today so we're in luck. We've still got some of our extra bread."

With the last of his strength Misha pulled Haiya's letter out of his pocket and handed it to Yisrael. "For you. From your wife." Beyond exhaustion, he collapsed into Volf's and Avraham's arms. Yisrael read the letter under the labor camp's lighting. How is it that he had any tears left? But he cried, his heart bursting with relief and joy.

"Haiya and our sisters are well, they're fine," he relayed to his brothers. He glanced at Misha. "Thank you for bringing this, Misha, and thank you for looking after them. Now we'll do what we can to look after you."

Misha wept. I'm no longer alone, he thought. How good it was to have helped the women! Now their men will look after me.

Supporting him, the brothers began walking Misha towards their block. A few steps along, he started to feel better, more able to walk on his own, and followed them into Block 12. "Here's your spot," Yisrael pointed to a bunk prepared for him. Lying down, Misha fell asleep immediately.

THE MARCH OF DEATH

Blechhammer was bombarded so thoroughly that nothing much of it remained. It was January 1945, and the grapevine was saying that the Russians were moving fast towards southern Poland from the east, while German forces were withdrawing to Germany. But the Germans weren't about to leave witnesses behind. They ordered everyone to start walking.

And so began the march of death.

Twenty-four hours into their slow walk, every man could feel his strength fading. Volf, Avraham and Yisrael walked together. Behind them a shot was heard. Volf spun his head around for an instant, taking in the German soldier, gun still aimed at a man's body. The human convoy walked on. Shots rang out at intervals. Each shot meant another man would be left on the path exactly where he fell.

The brothers walked closely together, touching each other once in a while just to be sure they were not on the verge of collapse. Of the three, Avraham was doing reasonably well. Contrary to all expectations, he'd actually gotten stronger over the past several weeks. Welding and metalworking had built him up. Volf was the weakest, having lost more weight than his brothers. His body was scrawny: it was impossible to recognize him as the pleasant looking young guy from before the war. Yisrael, tallest of the three, was now hunched slightly forward, his back having borne the brunt of the horrid physical conditions. He, too, was fairly weak. But he wasn't giving in. If anything, he was the one keeping their spirits up with words of encouragement.

"We have to go on. We have to stick together. It's the only way we'll make it to our goal," he kept reminding the others even though, as he spoke the words, he had no idea what their goal actually was.

Volf halted. Immediately the two brothers on either side of him pushed him forward. "On, on," Yisrael whispered. "You must not stop. Can you hear me, Volf? Do not stop, not even for a second." Volf looked up at Yisrael. His eyes could no longer cry any tears but inwardly, he sobbed. He could barely walk alongside his brothers.

"I can't go on. I'm stopping. I wanted to say goodbye and thank you. After the war, tell Batya that it's such a shame we won't meet again," whispered Misha, approaching the brothers, and touching Yisrael's arm.

Yisrael wanted to prop Misha up but could barely keep Volf going. Misha purposely shuffled off to the roadside before Yisrael could say anything, disappearing slowly from the brothers' eyesight. He collapsed onto the path's edge. A German soldier approached.

Misha raised his arm slightly. "I want to die. Just do it fast, that's all I ask," Misha said to him. The soldier aimed his rifle at Misha's chest, looking Misha right in the eye and smiling as he pulled the trigger.

There it was, the shot, so much closer this time. The convoy stopped despite the prohibition and threat of death. "Misha! It's Misha!" someone shouted. Although he'd been in relatively fair physical condition when he arrived at the camp, his spirit had quickly broken. At Blechhammer he was a nobody, a prisoner, a tattooed number among tattooed numbers. The Zaks brothers had done all they could to lift his spirits but Misha seemed to withdraw with each passing day.

And now, the snow crimson with his blood, Misha lay dead.

Volf plodded on. "I want to die too, get finished with this. Nothing hurts Misha now. I want to sit down too. I don't want to hurt anymore. I've had enough," he said in an undertone. And stopped.

A German soldier approached the brothers. Avraham and Yisrael grabbed Volf and pushed him forward, dragging him through the snow as the soldier watched, patiently waiting for the moment that they'd lose their strength and Volf would drop to the ground. Volf almost lost consciousness. Avraham and Yisrael weren't going to let that happen. They pushed, dragged, coaxed, and urged him further. Avraham begged. "Volf, we're with you. We're not going to leave you. Don't stop. Please. We won't let you fall."

The German soldier hovered close to the brothers, waiting, waiting, waiting for that perfect moment. But the brothers kept on, dragging Volf with them. The soldier had this Jew in his sights and wasn't about to give up either.

To their horror, when Israel and Avraham looked back for a second at the soldier, Volf flopped out of their hands like a rag doll. Instantly they bent and pulled him up, ignoring his pleas. "Let me be. I prefer to die now."

A mean smile broke out on the German's face. Like a hound tracking a scent, the German knew the hunt would soon come to a close, the prey too tired to fight back. He cocked his rifle, moving closer to Volf while Avraham made every effort to pull Volf up and onto his feet.

"You want to die, Jewboy? Here, your turn has come!"

Volf smiled too. In his heart and mind, he'd already bid farewell to this world; death would surely be far better than this life. He closed his eyes and waited for the shot.

Bright, green…two eyes shone in the darkness no more than an arm's length away. White teeth bared. A long furious growl. The convoy halted. The soldier aiming for Volf was stupefied. Scared. He glanced towards the forest, saw the white wolf's eyes and teeth gleaming in the dark, and took a hasty step back, almost losing his balance. Quickly he took another step back to steady himself as he aimed for the wolf. The wolf never budged. It stood firm before the soldier, its teeth flashing, its lips curling back, its growl getting longer and louder. The prisoners stood in their places, mesmerized. The soldier aimed. His fingers would not obey: he was unable to shoot. A last howl before the wolf turned, its gleaming white fur a streak in the night's blackness. Only then was the soldier able to shoot. Bullet trails lit the night with bright sparks.

But the wolf's calls had roused Volf. Despair and apathy evaporated. He'd managed to see the wolf's eyes before the beast disappeared. And he knew:

the wolf had come to protect him. Together, the three brothers slowly moved on with the convoy into the unknown. The soldier was left behind, unable to fathom what had just happened.

He came again. For me. He's always there, for me, Volf thought, taking the fresh scenario in. The convoy inched forward but the brothers' minds were now seared with the image of the wolf coming from the forest, halting the soldier, keeping the soldier at bay, then returning, wild, noble, splendid…its fur a spotlight in the darkest of times.

GROSS-ROSEN, FEBRUARY 1945

How long had they been walking? No one had any idea. The convoy simply walked. To the prisoners, it seemed an eternity. Shots rang out every few minutes. Death marched with them: they couldn't have cared. They were too exhausted. Their bodies functioned somehow, but their hearts were apathetic. Time and hope had long since evaporated. The only goal now was to make it to the unknown end of this march.

They entered through a camp gate. "Halt! In fives. Schnell!"

Prisoners obeyed, darkness surrounding them, snow falling, threatening to freeze their ragged toes. Every time a prisoner collapsed, a shot rang out.

Arms wrapped tightly around each other's waists, the brothers made sure none of them fell. Guttman, Haiya's father, stood in the row behind them. The brothers had come across him for the first time in this march of death. Around Hanokh's age, he walked slowly, unable to keep up with the younger men, but nonetheless, he reached Gross-Rosen. Yisrael glanced behind him and whispered to his father-in-law. "Are you alright? Try to last it out. Just a bit longer."

Hearing whispers, a soldier approached. Yisrael faced front again. A shot, right behind them. Turning his head fractionally, Yisrael glimpsed his father-in-law from the corner of his eye. Haiya's father. Dead. Yisrael trembled. Tears came to his eyes. Volf and Avraham tightened their grip on their brother.

"Yisrael, hold us tight," Volf whispered.

"Don't fall. Grab my shoulders. Hold onto me," Avraham added.

Yisrael's body shook. "What will I tell Haiya… that I didn't save her father? I saw it happen but I couldn't do a thing," he muttered, to himself, to his brothers. "He was a good man. He survived this far, until the damn German murdered him for no reason at all."

The three fell silent, holding onto each other for dear life.

Another hour passed. The air got colder. The number of men surviving the march of death lessened minute by minute. Suddenly, headlamps shone on them all. A German officer in a crisp uniform, thick coat, and glossy boots stepped out of the car.

"You have reached Gross-Rosen Labor Camp," he announced. "Here you will continue to work. If you cannot work, you die." He paused for effect. "You will live in these two blocks and tomorrow at first light, you'll begin work. We do not have much bread to give you, so hope that as many of you as possible die and the rest will have more bread."

And that brief sentence, thought Volf, encapsulated the supposedly enlightened and glorious German nation's modus operandi, its perspective of life. Those words would stay with him his whole life.

Inside the block they fell on the bunks, falling asleep instantly. Yisrael did not mourn his father-in-law: exhaustion brought him to sleep before he could even raise Guttman's image in his mind. Volf could feel how frozen and numb his toes were, especially the right foot's big toe. He touched it with his finger: nothing. Yes, it was there, but with no sensation. Avraham quickly fell asleep too, a sleep with no dreams.

At daybreak, picks and instructions were handed out: to quarry the granite rock. Despite the weakness in their arms, they did what they could, knowing that if they didn't look like they were working, they'd be shot on the spot. Some minutes later they understood: the work had no purpose. Quarrying granite with picks was intended from the start to weaken them more and cause them to die slowly and painfully. Glancing around, they noticed how few guards there were, yet none of the prisoners dared sit, or even rest standing up.

Two slices of bread was the daily handout. As the end of their first week at Gross-Rosen approached, they were weaker and had lost a good deal of weight. Yisrael, studying his brothers, saw nothing but skin hanging on bone. Even Avraham's muscles had dwindled to nothing. To preserve their strength, they used only silence and glances as their language.

Until one day Avraham spoke: "We won't hold out much longer like this."

Yisrael noticed that Avraham didn't look at him when he spoke. He moved closer to Avraham. "Why aren't you looking at me?"

"I can't, Yisrael. You look like someone else."

"What do you mean, Avraham?"

"I don't know you. It's not our Yisrael," Avraham answered, stifling a sob. "That's not your face. I can't bear it."

"But you too, Avraham," Volf said, "you look different. It's as though our bodies aren't ours anymore. Because of the hunger."

"Look at me," Yisrael demanded, "and look at each other. They haven't changed our hearts, my brothers. They'll never manage to change our souls. We'll get through this only if we look into each other's eyes when we speak." He put his hands on each side of Avraham's face, turning it towards his own. "Look at my face, Avraham. It's still me. It's always me."

Yisrael stared into Avraham's eyes. Avraham looked back at him. "Don't look at the surface, at the skin, at the features. Look inside. Look into our hearts. That's where our strength lies. In our hearts, we're still brothers and we're still strong. So we're thin. So we're unkempt. The day will come when we'll have food to eat. This hunger is temporary, but the connection between us is forever. We are the sons of Yoheved and Hanokh Zaks, always."

Turning back to the granite quarry, they raised and swung their picks again and again, quarrying from dawn to dusk. Every day they succeeded less than the day before. Walking became increasingly difficult but they continued, from block to mountain, from mountain to block, with barely enough strength to chew their meager bread handout. And another day passed.

Aerial bombing could be heard not far off. Every day the explosions drew closer. Every time Warplanes shrieked over the camp, the bombing sorties gave rise to assumptions.

"This war will be over soon," Yisrael said to his brothers as they lay down for the night. Avraham and Volf looked at him, disbelieving.

"What are you talking about, Yisrael?" they said, doubting him.

But he was adamant. "Take note of what's happening around us. Fewer soldiers, hardly any officers. In my view, the officers are already fleeing back into Germany."

"So what are these explosions we're constantly hearing?" Avraham asked.

Yisrael's answer was delivered with a quiet certainty. "In my view, it's the Russians. The explosions sound like they're coming from the east. That's the direction the Russians are coming from. The Red Army is on its way to us, and the Germans are on the run. I'm pretty sure of that."

Volf raised his head a little. "So there's hope… Maybe it will be over soon. We have to keep looking out for each other. Let's get some sleep now."

For the first time in a very long while, they smiled. We'll help each other through this. Just a bit longer, they thought.

***

Some days later they were astonished to see a train on the tracks. Since their arrival at Gross-Rosen, not a single one had passed through.

"Stand!" the order came. "Put the picks down. Get on the train," the instructions continued.

Helping each other up, the brothers boarded. Bits of coal were scattered across the carriage floor. The smell reminded them of Blechhammer, where they'd breathed coal dust for many long months. Something in the smell reassured them. Harsh coughing grew increasingly frequent the longer everyone breathed the toxic dust.

Helpless, with not an ounce of strength left, the men lay down on the carriage floor. It was crowded and the air was filled with soot. The brothers had only one piece of bread left, so only once in a while would they take a bite. Their lives now depended on this single piece of bread. No one could know when the next bit of food would appear. It was their only possession in the world. Now their lives depended on it as the train began to drive to an unknown destination, moving, halting, moving, halting. No matter how many times the train stopped, the men were never allowed outside. They stayed exactly where they'd placed themselves on entering, not moving, as though sunk into a sea of black dust.

"Schnell! Schnell!" The train had stopped. "Raus, raus! Everyone out, Schnell!" a German ordered. As though waking from a dream, they raised their sooty heads and slowly made their way off the carriage, reeking of soot, of urine and excrement, having had nowhere to relieve themselves during the journey. Looking around, they realized they were in unfamiliar terrain. "You are now in Buchenwald," the Nazi officer's words answered the men's unasked question.

"Jedem Das Seine," the sign in the distance read: To Each Their Due.

BUCHENWALD'S "LITTLE CAMP"

A disorderly assortment of men moved slowly towards the roll call yard. Sooty-faced, and with their lungs battling toxic dust, the prisoners limped along. Their eyes nervously scanned the area, eventually settling on barrels emitting an acrid smell they couldn't place. Roll call again. Facing them, the German officer held a handkerchief to his nose, then moved it aside to speak, a look of utter disgust on his face.

"You have reached the Buchenwald Little Camp. You will all undress immediately. All your clothes. Throw them away."

The men obeyed. Some were sure they would now be executed. Some were too fatigued to care. Whatever happened would be fine with them.

Naked in the cold, the prisoners stood, shivering. They glanced at each other: skeletal legs, ribs poking out, genitals withered away, and limp arms as thin as matchsticks.

"Now you will wash in the barrels," the officer ordered. "Schnell! Schnell!"

Too surprised by this order, the men simply stood where they were. The stench coming from the barrels was gut-churning. One prisoner doubled over and vomited. He was shot. The officer repeated the order.

"Get into the barrels immediately. If you do not, you will die." With that, the officer nodded to a soldier who pulled an elderly man out of the lineup. He had survived until now. But no more. He was shot.

A number of barrels stood in the yard. The men were split into groups. The first was marched to the barrels. Blocking their noses, they lowered themselves in, finding themselves up to their necks in the unidentified liquid, their bodies shivering from cold and fear.

From one barrel, a shout: "It burns! Oh Lord, help!"

A soldier approached the man. This was the end of him, he was certain. But the soldier didn't shoot. "It may burn but it will clean you," the German said, smirking wickedly. "You Jewish mongrels, full of lice and fleas. This will kill them all. We can't have you contaminating us with your diseases. Anyone leaving the barrel before permission is granted will die."

Precisely then the man who'd screamed jumped out of the barrel and ran to the electric fence. The soldier watched with interest as the man placed both hands on the wires. Sparks flashed. The man's body shuddered. He collapsed on the ground. He never made a sound.

One after the other, the prisoners dunked in the disinfectant. When Yisrael, Volf, and Avraham were allowed to leave the barrels, their skin itched horribly. Folds of skin, empty of flesh and hanging over each other, burned. Red blotches spread across their bodies.

"Schnell! To the block!"

Naked, they walked into the dilapidated shack. Disinfected clothing waited for them on the bunks. The clothes stank, but at least they were clean and dry. The men dressed quickly, then tried warming themselves by blowing on their palms and rubbing them over their limbs. Absent an order to go back outside, they lay down on the wooden slats, scratching. Overcome by exhaustion, the men fell asleep. Astonishingly, the Germans left them alone. Nor did the Germans wake them the next morning. That day, none of them worked.

***

The sun was not shining in Buchenwald. Perhaps it never shone there, even in summer. Buchenwald Little Camp was Germany's most polluted location.

Waking at last, the men noticed how red their skin was, the chemicals so irritating that they'd scratched their arms and legs as they slept.

"I've never come across something like that disinfectant. What are they using it against?" Volf snorted.

"Look at it this way, Volf," Yisrael encouraged, "at least we aren't black now. We're out of the coal dust. It stings like hell, but it's a kind of pain we can overcome and maybe it did in fact eradicate the lice."

All day, the prisoners lay in their dry, clean clothes on the bunks, never leaving the block. If only there were some food! The last slice of bread had long since been eaten but no Germans threw any bread in, avoiding the block like the plague.

"We're lepers," Avraham said to his brothers. "They'll probably just let us lie here and die here from disease and hunger. They're just waiting for us to die in this little camp of death." Evening came, but no food was delivered. Hurting, and hungry, the men went back to sleep.

They did the same the next day: lay around and scratched. And the day after that, and the next. On occasion, a prisoner, his body fatigued to the extreme, would be seen weaving his way to the fence, throwing himself on it, and dying from electrocution, thus ending his torment. On occasion, a prisoner would die of starvation. The other men had no choice but to throw the corpse outside the block. Every two days, the Germans placed two loaves of bread on the steps: the prisoners shared it among themselves, two slices per man. And they continued to weaken by the day.

One morning instructions were heard outside. "Anyone able to leave the block should come out. If you can't come out, stay where you are."

Yisrael peeked outside. A group was slowly forming. No doubt they would be transferred elsewhere again. "Anywhere is better than Little Death Camp," he said to his brothers. "Let's join them."

Volf refused. He lay on the bunk with not enough strength to even lift his arm. "I can't," he said quietly. "You two go. It's all right. I'll just wait here. It can't take much longer. I'm sure I can survive here."

Yisrael wouldn't hear of it. "Papa said that no matter what, we don't leave any of us behind, so we're not leaving you, Volf. Either all of us go, or all of us stay. Whatever happens, we're in this together."

Volf shook his head. "No. I want you to leave me here. It's a pity for you two to stay in this dreadful place if there's a chance you could go somewhere better. I'm begging you. Leave me here and go. I promise we'll meet after the war. I can smell the end coming."

Understanding that Volf would not go with them, Yisrael and Avraham embraced him and left the block. Avraham turned around and waved. Volf, with tremendous effort, lifted himself on one elbow and smiled his wonderful smile. "Good luck," he wished them, "may G-d be with you, and may Papa look after you from heaven. We'll meet again, you can be sure."

Outside, both Yisrael and Avraham raised their heads, looking to the sky. "Papa, once again, we're forced to leave one of the brothers behind. Forgive us, and look after him until we reunite."

THE TUNNEL IN LANGENSTEIN MOUNTAIN

The weather was only fractionally better in March 1945. Having walked for two days, the prisoners reached the entrance of a tunnel carved into the mountainside. They had no idea where they were.

"Inside. Schnell!"

The prisoners obeyed, their legs barely carrying their exhausted bodies. Nothing but one slice of bread a day for a month now left Avraham and Yisrael emaciated; all the men were, and walking was close to impossible.

In the tunnel, bare electric globes barely lit the darkness. Several moments after all the men had entered, they heard a loud clang. The doors were shut behind them. They were trapped. Yet they were more worried about what the Germans would want them to do. Or were they planning to bury them alive?

Compressed air flowed from somewhere deep in the tunnel, encouraging the two Zaks brothers. If there was air, and if they're required to continue walking, perhaps the Germans weren't intending to kill them by slow suffocation. Among the prisoners were some so apathetic that when one fell, they weren't able to try and pick him up. Avraham and Yisrael were surprised: there was no gunshot behind them. The Jew who had fallen just lay where he was and the soldiers walked right over his face and body, advancing into the tunnel.

They followed a railroad track that was clearly meant for cargo transportation, not passenger carriages. No one spoke. Their fear had long since dissipated after seeing hundreds of fellow Jews murdered in the death march. They knew that at any moment, any of them could be the next victim.

"They must be taking us to an abyss," Avraham whispered, "to shoot us there."

"Perhaps not," Yisrael answered, trying to find a drop of encouragement.

And so they walked, without resting. To conserve their energy, Yisrael and Avraham didn't talk to each other. In almost complete darkness, they walked for some two hours more.

"Halt!" came the order. Several dozen men stopped in their tracks, in complete silence.

"You have reached a top-secret location," the German said. In the heavy darkness, no one could see his face, or even his body. "Here we produce the weapon of the future, the weapon that will determine the war. No one outside has any knowledge of what is produced here. You will not exit this place until we win the war with this weaponry, and only then will we allow you to leave. Anyone unable to work here will be buried here."

Once again, the order to walk was given. Seconds later, in sheer astonishment, they gasped. They had just entered a huge hall lit so strongly that the prisoners stood blinking hard as their eyes adjusted. Looking around, they saw two very tall cylindrical pipes, extremely wide at the base, narrowing along their length, eventually forming a point. Large swastikas were painted in black on the gray cylinders. One bore the letters "V1," the other was marked "V2." Uncomprehending, the men studied the tall cylinders.

THE SMALL SANDWICH

A week passed. Hungry and fatigued, the men were wasting away. In the morning, they woke up to shouts in German and set out for work. Late at night, they slept on the cold ground. Yisrael worked on wobbly scaffolding connected to the missile. He was sure that at any moment the whole thing would come down. The work was simple: he had to go around the missile tightening its screws. Who knows which city this missile is destined for, he wondered more than once, and how much damage it would cause.

Yisrael soon realized that the German commander's statements on their arrival were false: some outsiders definitely did know about this location and what was being produced. He was initially surprised to discover that working alongside him was a German who was neither a prisoner but a resident of a nearby town. Every morning he entered the tunnel. Every evening he returned home. A metalworker by profession, the man's job was to ensure that the screws were indeed tightened and would withstand the force. He stood next to Yisrael, double checking every screw. He never said a word, but seemed satisfied. Yisrael made sure to work as best he could: it was a way of ensuring that the German had no reason to hit him, push him off the scaffolding, or complain to the bosses.

Midway through the workday, the prisoners were allowed a break to eat and briefly rest. Yisrael brought the slice of bread he'd kept from the previous evening. It was dry; getting it moist enough with saliva was not easy.

He nibbled at it the entire fifteen minutes allocated as their break, until the German foreman gave the order: "Back to work." The civilian German metalworker, who did not eat together with the prisoners, also resumed his place next to Yisrael.

"You work well," he unexpectedly turned to Yisrael. "From now on you can continue without my constant supervision. I'll just come and check occasionally."

Stunned, Yisrael swallowed hard, speechless at first, then blurting his words. "Thank you, sir. You can rely on me."

The German turned back to continue work on his side of the missile. Yisrael wondered if he should thank him again but decided against it. Shortly afterwards the man spoke to Yisrael again in a pleasant tone, the likes of which Yisrael hadn't heard for a very long time. "By the way, my name's Schmidt. You don't have to call me 'sir'. When we're all the way up here and the other prisoners can't hear us, 'Schmidt' is sufficient."

Yisrael smiled at him. "Thank you, Schmidt," Yisrael said, as though testing the name. They looked at each other, then went back to work. At the end of the workday, they both made their way down the scaffolding. Schmidt adopted a severe expression and, without saying a word to Yisrael, went on his way. Yisrael rejoined Avraham. In seconds, they were asleep on the ground.

Yisrael was up on the scaffolding early the next morning. Some hours later, Schmidt joined him on the other side. As they finished tightening the screws on the row they were checking, they met up and smiled to each other. Down below the call for lunch break was heard.

"Stay up here with me, let's eat together," Schmidt invited Yisrael.

Yisrael took his dry slice of bread from his pocket, nibbling at its edges. Schmidt pulled out a thick sandwich stuffed with several slices of sausage. Yisrael, sniffing at the aromas wafting over him, swallowed hard. He suddenly felt so hungry. Schmidt was looking down below, his head moving almost imperceptibly from side to side. Once he felt certain no one was watching them, neither prisoner nor guard, he signaled to Yisrael.

"Here, what did you say your name was? Yisrael? Come, sit here next to me.

No, don't worry, I don't bite. I might just want to throw you off the scaffold," he smiled warmly.

Was he teasing? Yisrael wondered. He opted for silence but did sit next to Schmidt, munching on his dry slice of bread. Schmidt looked down again, as though double checking something. Seeing no soldiers around, he quickly pulled another sandwich from his bag and handed it to Yisrael.

"For you," was all he said.

A teardrop fell from Yisrael's eye. He devoured the sandwich in large bites, not caring that the meat was not kosher. He could feel some of his teeth, weakened by months of insufficient food, wobble in his gums but he didn't care about that either. In seconds the food was demolished. He collected every crumb that fell on his sleeve, and even those he ate heartily. "Schmidt. Thank you. It's been a very long time since I ate such good food."

Schmidt just smiled. "Let's get back to work," he said. And they worked at a good pace until the day's end. Yisrael felt his spirits uplifted.

Coming off the scaffolding later, the German first, followed by Yisrael, Schmidt once again said no parting words to Yisrael but left, with a stern expression on his face. Yisrael found Avraham working in a different section; quickly he described what had happened during the lunch break. "Enjoy it, my brother," Avraham said. "I hope he brings you a sandwich every day."

Yisrael sighed. "Who knows… maybe it was a once-off gesture. To be safe, I'll take the dry piece of bread up with me tomorrow."

The next day, Yisrael and Schmidt worked together as usual until the lunch break call was heard. Once again Schmidt invited Yisrael to stay there with him. And again, he took out sandwiches, one for each of them. This time the filling was a good quality cheese. Yisrael savored every mouthful.

"This stays between us, Yisrael?" Schmidt said softly.

Yisrael nodded. "You're saving my life. I have no words to thank you enough."

Schmidt squirmed, embarrassed. Standing, he resumed his place. "C'mon, back to work we go," he said by way of shrugging off Yisrael's gratitude.

For several weeks, Schmidt and Yisrael ate together high up on the scaffolding around the missile that was meant to wreak utter havoc on a fiercely bleeding Europe. Yisrael gave Avraham the other piece of bread. Every time Schmidt gave him a sandwich, Yisrael's thoughts reminded him that there are still good people in this world, and that this kindly man was risking his life for Yisrael's sake. He didn't need to do it, but he knew it was the right thing to do. These thoughts brought the station master to mind: how kind he'd been, helping Yisrael regain the bag of ghetto vouchers. Not all is lost, Yisrael concluded. There's still hope that the good will defeat the bad in this world.

UNDERGROUND OPERATIONS

Everything shook at the thunderous sound. Had the mountain burst open? Missiles they'd been working on swayed. Yisrael clutched the scaffolding as tightly as he could. Schmidt quickly came around from the other side. The faces of both were white. Their legs wobbled, trying to maintain balance until the rig settled back into place. Some parts were so damaged that they had come apart, dropping onto men below, killing some instantly, breaking others' bones and leaving them sprawled on the ground, paralyzed by pain and fear. Panic broke out: German soldiers and officers dashed around nervously shouting instructions.

Orders came for all the unharmed laborers still in their places on the scaffolding to get back to work, which they did, but at a much slower pace. Still in shock, Schmidt clearly wanted to get home and made his way down earlier than Yisrael with no more than a quick "See you tomorrow."

Yisrael went looking for Avraham: perhaps he'd caught some snippet of news about the explosion. And he had: the Germans were extremely fearful of the Americans, who clearly knew that the secret missile building location was in this mountain. He smiled in a pleased way as he related the conversations he'd overhead. "We're still virtually buried here for tonight, in this darkness, but tomorrow the Americans might show up and release us, and we'll get to see daylight at last," Avraham added. Smiling, they went to sleep next to each other.

The next day Schmidt didn't show up for work. Nor did most of the German soldiers. "Something's going on out there," Yisrael said to Avraham. Yisrael decided not to climb up the scaffolding but tried to look like someone with a job down on the ground. Barely a moment later, a German soldier came up behind Yisrael, slamming his rifle butt into Yisrael's leg. The pain was unbearable. Avraham shook himself out of his shocked reaction at seeing the open wound and quickly took off his shirt, ripping off the sleeve to use as bandaging.

"Stop. It doesn't matter," Yisrael whispered. "I can't go on anymore. Let me just die." Avraham was not about to let that happen. He kept his hands around the bandage to help stop the bleeding. They were both surprised that no German soldier came anywhere near, leaving Avraham to care for his brother. The Germans were too busy: they lay a cable along the track's length, connecting it to what looked like small packages which they'd attached to the missiles. The Jewish prisoners watched in silence. When the Germans were finished, they hurried out. Now only the Jews were left in the tunnel's darkness.

It was a tough night. Yisrael groaned with pain. Blood continued to seep from the wound. Strips of Avraham's shirt lay soaked in blood. Feeling around with his hands in the dark, Avraham collected papers and unwrapped work tools from protective pieces of cloth, using them to bandage Yisrael's leg, pressing and pulling as tight as he could despite Yisrael's cries of pain. Avraham wanted to prevent the infection from spreading through Yisrael's leg, which was already starting to smell very bad. But Avraham wasn't giving up yet: he kept finding pieces of cloth and papers to mop up the blood.

The next morning, only a small number of Germans arrived, ignoring the prisoners, not even shouting out orders to them about work. Their attention was wholly focused on checking the cables and little packets attached to the missiles. Two Germans passed Yisrael, who was groaning in agony.

"Ha! Let's shoot this Jewish mongrel," one said.

"Why bother?" the other answered. "He'll die anyhow in the next few hours."

They laughed heartily and stepped over Yisrael.

The mountain trembled again so hard that the Germans feared the tunnel would collapse. Bits of earth and plaster showered down on the prisoners. Avraham wasn't paying attention to the hubbub around him: he was wholly focused on saving his brother.

"Anyone here with medical knowledge?" he called out.

A prisoner raised his head. "I was a hospital surgeon but I'm not sure I can help you at this point."

For the first time since Yisrael was injured, Avraham felt that perhaps something could be done after all. He grabbed the man's hand and begged. "Please, come with me, quickly. Help my brother. There's a fresh wound on his leg from yesterday that won't stop bleeding. The flesh is turning black. Save him. Please. I'm begging you."

"I'm not going to lie," the surgeon said after checking Yisrael's leg. "Basically, the leg already has septicemia and is rotting. We could say it's dead. If you want to live," he said, looking gently at Yisrael, "I need to remove it, or at least cut out all the rotten flesh, and quickly, before it spreads through your entire body and kills you."

Yisrael went pale and gasped. He weighed his chances and quickly understood that he had no choice. "Do what you have to," he said, gripping the surgeon's hand.

"I'll need a knife. Who's got one?" the surgeon stood, addressing the prisoners. A prisoner came over with a knife he'd stolen and kept hidden all this time. But the knife was black with filth.

"I have to sterilize it," the surgeon said. "I need fire, and fast. Let's get a small fire together. Quickly."

Someone lit a match, putting it to the papers and bits of wood the men had collected. In no time the fire took hold. The surgeon passed one side of the blade through the flame, then the other, repeating his actions until satisfied the knife was ready to use, working quietly and uninterrupted because the Germans had fled, locking the tunnel from the outside. Although now free of orders and cruel punishments, the Jewish prisoners had no way to escape.

"We need to check what this 'gift' is that the Germans left us. I don't like the look of those cables and packets," one of the prisoners said to his friend.

"Fellow Jews," he shouted after checking, "they're going to blow us up inside this tunnel! Those black cables are time delay fuses. The Germans will light the fuses outside. We've got to neutralize them otherwise we don't stand a chance."

But Avraham and Yisrael were not paying attention to the remarks; they were focused on the surgeon readying for the difficult job ahead. Yisrael shook with fear and pain when the surgeon bent over him, bringing the knife close to his leg. "It'll be all right," the surgeon said gently to Avraham, "and I'll do everything I can to save your brother," he added, beginning to cut the flesh away. To Yisrael it felt like his leg had been fed to a meat grinder. Unbearably painful, he shouted, cried, slipping in and out of consciousness.

As Yisrael's operation progressed, the prisoners were looking for places to hide before the inevitable explosion. There were none.

"It's no good!" one shouted in desperation. "When this tunnel collapses, we'll all be buried alive under the rubble."

"We have to cut the cable," another suggested. "At least that will prevent the missile from exploding. Anyone got a knife?"

"I gave it to the surgeon. He's doing an operation…"

"All right," the man answered, quickly making his way to the surgeon working at some distance from everyone else. "Doctor, give me the knife. We need to cut the delay fuses quickly. Please."

Without raising his head, the surgeon answered softly but firmly. "I need it to complete the operation, otherwise this young man will die."

"Better one of us die than all of us. Give me the knife!" he demanded.

"I'm a doctor. I swore an oath to save lives, and that is what I will do," the surgeon answered without stopping his work for even a moment. "It won't take much longer. If you let me concentrate without interruption and allow me to finish, you'll have the knife in no time."

But another man lost his temper, trying to shove the surgeon aside and snatch the knife from his hand. Noticing the man lurching towards the doctor, Avraham kicked the man as hard as he could, flinging him against the wall. Breathless and hurting, the man didn't try interrupting again. Yisrael's screams came one after the other. He bit down on his sleeve, trying to muffle the sound. And then he passed out again.

"That's it. I've finished," the surgeon said, raising his head at least. "Avraham, you need to bandage that wound now, and you," he added, handing the knife over, "can have this. I've saved his life. Now you go and save all of ours." The man snatched it from the surgeon's hand and dashed off.

Regaining consciousness and overcoming the pain, Yisrael began to whisper. "Thank you for saving me, doctor."

"Thank me when you've gotten through this night, assuming we all make it through this night," the surgeon smiled at Yisrael, taking his hand, squeezing it lightly in encouragement.

Avraham hugged the doctor. "I'll never forget what you did for Yisrael. You gave him his life back," he wept in relief and joy.

Closely examining the tunnel's doorway, the two prisoners set to work. One raised the cable a little and held it taut. The other sawed with the knife. Minutes went by tensely. At last, the cable was severed. "We did it!" they called out. The men breathed with relief.

"Now we've got to find a way out of here," one said.

Before anyone could come up with suggestions, there was a massive boom. The tunnel's doors flew inwards; several prisoners were blown back in the blast. The men blinked furiously. Daylight filled the space. The light was so strong to their unaccustomed eyes that no one could face it; they shielded their eyes with their arms, turning partly away. But darker shadows began moving in the light: soldiers, entering the tunnel, slowly, warily, in uniforms unfamiliar to the prisoners. The sleeves and helmets bore the American flag.

ALONE IN BUCHENWALD

Lengthening days marked spring of 1945 but they brought no pleasure to Volf, who was lying alone in the block. For some days now he hadn't eaten. The Germans were no longer bringing food to prisoners left behind. Every day, another corpse was removed from the block. "That's their plan. Just to let us slowly die here," Volf muttered.

Lying prone on the wooden slats, his muscles had atrophied badly and he was slipping in and out of consciousness. He hardly had the strength to care whether he lived or died. Every time Hanokh or Yoheved seemed to appear before him, he would mutter "I've reached heaven at last. My days of suffering are over." But every time he snapped back into consciousness, he found himself still on the filthy bunk, overrun by lice. He no longer had enough strength for that to even disturb him. Nor did he disturb them: he no longer had the strength to scratch or pick them off.

Volf had lost all sense of time. He couldn't remember when Yisrael and Avraham had left. When he fell asleep, he would dream of them walking in the forest, arms around each other, walking towards him… and then they'd disappear.

Something was glaring at him, blinding him. He closed his eyes. Darkness was more hospitable. Darkness made him feel tranquil; at ease. Volf wasn't keen on returning from the darkness back to his life's reality. Eyes closed, and fully conscious, he muttered. "This isn't a good world to be in. I prefer the world to come. I don't want to open my eyes and wake to the block, the camp, surrounded by the dying and the dead. Maybe if I keep my eyes shut, I'll eventually wake up in paradise."

But then another thought would worry him. "I do want to live." He tried opening his eyes, but the blinding light forced him to shut them again immediately. Around him were voices he didn't recognize; not German, not Polish, nor Russian. "What are they saying to me?" he wondered. "Are they angels? I must be hallucinating."

He felt his body raised from the bunk. He didn't dare open his eyes: why disturb this journey to heaven? His heart overflowed with joy: "At last it's over, I'm being taken to a better world," he thought.

A hand touched his forehead: it felt good, so gentle, just like his father's hand, like his mother's, stroking his head. He reached for the hand, touching it, its tough but gentle skin, and he feared opening his eyes. "I want to dream on," he muttered, "I want to hold this hand, which moves me so much." He heard the unfamiliar language again, and was still fearful of opening his eyes to see the words' speaker.

He was no longer moving through the air. He was set down carefully on something soft. A cloud, perhaps? "I'm on my way to heaven," Volf thought, "and this is so good, this soft cloud. The angels speaking in the language of angels is so kind. I don't know what they're saying, but their voices are so calming."

"Can you open your eyes?" he heard a gentle voice say in a familiar language: Polish.

"I can, yes," Volf whispered, "but I don't want to. I'm more comfortable like this."

The pleasant voice was insistent. "Please, open your eyes. We want to help you, give you medical care."

It took Volf a huge effort to open his eyes, but the beam of light was so strong that he immediately shut them again. He blinked, opening his eyes once more. He was lying on a bed. On a mattress... When was the last time he'd lain on a mattress? He couldn't remember and it felt so wonderful. Tears flowed from the corners of his eyes.

Slowly Volf began looking around. He was in a large room filled with mattressed beds, one person on each. One person, on one bed! When was the last time he'd seen that? A man in uniform came over, speaking in the unfamiliar language. He was joined by a soldier speaking Polish in a gentle, calm tone the likes of which Volf hadn't heard for a very long time.

"We're American soldiers," the soldier said in Polish, gently touching Volf's hand. "You are liberated now. No more Germans. For you, this war is over."

The American spoke and the soldier translated. "Please don't be afraid anymore. Now we're taking care of you all. Soon we'll give you medication and food. You'll get better slowly, you'll see."

Volf heard. His heart was filled with joy and pain. "I'm alive!" he wept, the two soldiers' eyes moistening at this acknowledgment. "The war's over and I'm alive!" More than that he was unable to say. He closed his eyes again, but this time did not fear opening them only to discover it was all a dream and he'd find himself still in the accursed camp. Tremendously grateful, he committed himself into the American soldiers' capable, compassionate hands.

GÖRLITZ, JANUARY 1945

Work at Ludwigsdorf wasn't physically difficult, but months of breathing gunpowder was taking its toll on the women in the camp. Coughing was almost incessant and became an inseparable part of their lives. Once a woman was considered too weak, she was sent to Auschwitz. As if that wasn't enough, the Zaks women began suffering from hunger. Misha had gone, Mrs. Beriski was no longer coming to work, and fear of death hung around like mist in the air.

Miriam's job was to weigh the amount of gunpowder for each packet on a very sensitive scale. The weaker she grew and the more her stomach growled in hunger, the more frequently her hands trembled. She was forced to stop for short rests, letting her hands stabilize. Errors in weighing the powder were forbidden.

One day Batya noticed Miriam's discomfort and wanted to help. Haiya stopped her. "I'll go," she said between almost closed lips. "I'm not scared of the Germans." Stopping her work, she went over to Miriam without hesitation.

"How do you feel?" she asked. But before Miriam could answer, the German supervisor was at her workstation.

"Talking is forbidden!" he said to the two women. "Get back to your place."

Looking straight at his eyes, Haiya's tone was authoritative. "She needs water. Bring her some." The German was stunned, unused to that tone of voice from a prisoner. He was so shocked that he complied. He swung on his heels and returned shortly afterwards with a glass of water which he held out to Miriam. She took it but was afraid to drink. Thirst got the better of her, though, and the pain was conquered. She took slow sips. Haiya squeezed Miriam's hand, then turned again to the German. "In an hour I'll come over and check how she's doing again."

Without further delay, she returned to her own workstation as the amazed German watched. Batya, closely and fearfully watching the scene play out, smiled. "It pays to be impudent," she whispered. Haiya smiled too. Feeling a lot better, Miriam's work quickly picked up pace. Every day the number of women in the block lessened. Anyone not sent to Auschwitz or who did not die, lost weight at an increasing rate. As hunger became more widespread, women would steal bread from each other, but not from the Zaks women. The other prisoners knew: do not meddle with the Zaks women.

Work at Ludwigsdorf continued through the winter as 1944 became 1945. The women were tired and hungry. Boom. Another boom! Explosions could be heard and they seemed to be fairly close. The Germans ordered work to continue although they themselves hurried away and disappeared from view. Another thundering boom, and smoke rose in pillars from a camp structure. The women stopped to watch what was happening. Hesitantly, they exited the labor hall, mesmerized by the burning building. Another boom, massive. A bright tongue of flame rose to the sky. The blast pushed them all down onto the ground.

"Get away from the burning building now," Haiya instructed. "Run, follow me, hurry, hurry!" She raced back to the labor hall with Miriam, Batya, and several other women in tow. "Lie down on the floor and put your hands over your heads," she called out. The women obeyed. And then a massive blast made the entire hall shudder. Its ceiling blew off. Walls started caving in. When the noise seemed to be over, the women stood, shaking the dust and debris off them, checking each other. Some were bleeding.

"That was the explosives storage," a woman said. "All the gunpowder just blew up!"

The women watched as the Germans surfaced from their protective bunkers, racing about trying to douse the flames. It took an hour before things were sufficiently under control. Soldiers ordered the women back to work.

Evacuation orders came the next day. In the morning, the women were awaken by loud shouts. "Raus, raus, Schnell! Every prisoner will take only what she can carry with her. Schnell! Out, and stand for roll call." Obediently the women stood in the yard, their bones aching from the harsh cold. Everything they possessed was with them: the clothes on their backs, a small bag with a few items, bread, if anyone was lucky enough still to have any. Nothing more.

"Forward march!" came the order. Obediently the women exited the camp gate and walked, not knowing where they were headed. Hundreds of women walked in exhaustion, hungry, shivering from the cold. Haiya, Miriam and Batya walked with their arms around each other's waists to try and keep themselves warmer.

"Hmm," Haiya said unexpectedly, "I know why the camp's being cleared. The Germans are about to lose the war. They're retreating and taking us with them." Miriam and Batya, used to trusting their sister-in-law's hunches and advice, admired her deduction.

"Are you sure?" Miriam asked, barely moving her lips.

"Absolutely sure," Haiya answered. "Simple logic. The Russians are approaching. Those explosions were from the Red Army. The Russians probably bombed the daylights out of that camp because it held the store of explosives. No explosives, no war. The war will soon be over."

On they walked, given no breaks to rest. Some hours later, they reached another camp. The convoy of walkers stopped at a gate marked by a simple sign: Görlitz.

"On, on, keep going," a smartly outfitted German ordered. The women went through the gate into a small roll call yard. "Halt! In fives! Schnell!" The officer, in his crisp uniform, walked between the rows, touching several women with his baton before walking to the front to address them.

"You must work if you wish to live here. We will stop the enemy here. You will stop the enemy with your own hands. Tomorrow morning, you will begin digging anti-tank canals. You will be given spades. Anyone without a spade will dig with her hands. You must dig very deep so that enemy tanks cannot pass across the canals. So dig properly or those tanks will flatten you."

This was where it would all come to an end, the women realized. From here, there'd be no escape. But some women made an additional realization: liberation was near. The tanks would liberate them. Despite sighing with relief, no sound could be heard: the women's breaths instantly turning to fog in the cold air.

Eventually the commander's final order for the day was barked at them: "To the shacks."

Haiya, Miriam and Batya found bunks on the second level and instantly fell asleep.

THE RUSSIANS ARE COMING

Three paces wide, five paces deep: for two months the women dug pits meant to stop the approaching Russian tanks. It was March 1945, and every day the thud of explosions grew closer. The women's hands were sore and raw, but Haiya's grin never left her face.

"They're done for, I'm telling you. The Germans have lost. The Russians are moving fast. Watch those Germans' faces. They're in complete panic."

Nonetheless the Nazis forced them to keep digging from morning to night. Every day another woman or two died, their strength having been exhausted. "They didn't manage to hold out," Haiya said to her sisters-in-law, "but we're going to. We have to, no matter what happens. Tomorrow morning, we'll check who died overnight and take the bread from their pockets. We have to eat as much as we can. We'll hide the bread in our clothes."

"What? Steal a dead woman's bread…?" Batya and Miriam were horrified.

"Do you want to live? Anyone who's no longer breathing can no longer eat. Every extra slice we find gives us the chance of surviving another day, and every day we get through brings us closer to our liberation. They know that. You can see it in those bastards' eyes. They don't have much time left and they're scared to death of how they'll be treated when the Russians get hold of them."

Once again Batya and Miriam nodded, accepting Haiya's view. The next day, waking earlier than everyone else, the three of them checked who hadn't survived the night, collecting extra food. Another slice every night before sleeping would help them get through another day, until salvation came.

The next morning, they walked to the newly dug pits to continue their work. As they were about to kneel and start work, the thunder of a nearby explosion sent up a thick plume of smoke. Fleeing, the Germans headed for their bunkers, leaving the women unsupervised. "Stay inside the pits!" Haiya shouted over the noise. "They'll keep us protected. May G-d watch over us and make sure none of us are killed now, so close to the end."

For an hour, the bombing went on. Then there was a thick silence. Women began climbing out of the pits they'd dug. Some canals had been destroyed. Nazis left their bunkers to find the women. "Back to work! Schnell! If you don't work, you die," the soldiers ordered.

Looking around, Haiya noticed that only low-ranking soldiers remained on the grounds. Not a single commander was anywhere in sight. Right away she understood what that meant, smiling to herself. "Miriam? See that? Haiya's smiling again. Where does she get all those smiles from?"

"If Haiya's smiling," Miriam answered, glancing at her sister-in-law, "she's come to a smart conclusion. We're winning, and we need to just keep going a bit longer. The Russians will be here any moment."

The afternoon saw another heavy round of Russian bombing, this time even closer than before. Into the pits, the women dove. Another hour of explosions. When it was all over, everyone was still alive. They went back to work although there was very little supervision. At night, they all made their way back to their bunks.

Silently, they nibbled on what was left of their bread. Not a sound could be heard outside. Not a single word in German.

"It's too quiet. I'm going out to see what's happening."

"Don't, Batya, it's too risky," Miriam tried dissuading her.

Batya just waved the concern away and smiled. Stepping outside their shack, the first thing she noticed was that she couldn't see a German anywhere. No soldiers. No guards. Quickly she went back inside the shack.

"No one is in sight! I think they've all run off."

Again, Haiya smiled. “It was obvious that they would. I’ve been waiting for this for some days now. Nonetheless, we mustn’t become careless. We’re on the verge of liberation, but the Germans could suddenly decide to return. A bit longer, girls. A bit longer. Let’s wait for the Russians to arrive.”

The other women were sleeping. A fierce smell of kerosene filled the air. Haiya, Miriam, and Batya looked at each other, wondering, uncertain, when a German soldier stormed into the shack and went directly to Haiya.

“You’re their leader, yes?” He spoke firmly but not loudly. To Haiya that was odd. She decided not to respond but he wasn’t waiting for an answer. “Wake them all up. Schnell!”

Haiya signaled to Miriam and Batya, who helped her wake the women up.

The soldier spoke quietly, his voice tinged with urgency. “I’m the only one left here. My orders were to wait until you all fell asleep, lock you all in, pour kerosene around the block, and set it alight.” He fell silent. One woman let out a cry and fainted.

Speechless, Miriam and Batya stared dumbfounded at the soldier. Is this how it would end? By burning them all alive?“

Haiya whispered to Miriam. “He’s not getting out of here alive. I’m going to smash his head in with the spade. We’ll kill him with our bare hands if we have to.”

But the soldier continued speaking in his deliberate manner. “I decided not to do that. I’m saving your lives by giving you warning. Remember that. The Russians are on their way, the Americans are very close, coming from the opposite direction.” He paused, swallowing hard. “I have one request. Please tell whoever enters first and liberates you that I saved your lives. I do hope it’s the Americans rather than the Russians. I prefer to be a POW under the Americans. As far as I’m concerned, this war is over. I am helping you and I ask you to help me in return.”

In no time, he disappeared into the darkness, leaving only the smell of kerosene behind him.

Outside, voices were shouting in Russian. Engines of vehicles were revving. Some scattered shots were fired. Suddenly the lights went out and the voices stopped. The camp was surrounded by Russians but none were entering in the darkness. They were going to wait until sunrise.

"Haiya? What do you think... should we all go outside?"

"No, Miriam. Just look at these women. They don't have the strength to stand, let alone walk. I'm also afraid that the Russians might confuse us for German soldiers and start shooting. We've waited this long, let's wait a few more hours."

That night, hardly any of the women slept, and those that did, dozed and woke fitfully, on tenterhooks over what dawn was about to bring. And dawn brought Russian soldiers on foot and in trucks to the camp. "Now we should go out," Haiya said.

The three of them slowly made their way out, arms about each other's waists. Other women shuffled out. Those who couldn't stand simply crawled. The women gazed at the Russian soldiers. Some were silent. Some sobbed quietly. Staring, dumbfounded, many soldiers wiped a tear away. Most were not surprised at how emaciated the women were; after all, they'd been among the liberators at Auschwitz just two months earlier.

A Russian officer addressed them in Polish. "Ladies, we have liberated you. We have work still to do, to conquer Berlin, but for you this war is over. No one will harm you anymore. No one will starve you anymore. We'll prepare hot porridge for you soon. I need to say this: and it's important. Please, for your own sakes, don't gulp your food down. Eat a little at a time, and very slowly. We will increase your portions with each meal. Sadly, we've seen too many prisoners die after being liberated because they ate too quickly. Your stomachs can't handle so much food at once. We know it's difficult, we know how hungry you all are, but we want you to heal and get strong. So please, do as I ask. Be restrained, it is beneficial to your recuperation."

For the first time in years the women could smile warmly. Batya and Miriam burst into tears. Haiya, among the stronger prisoners, walked towards the Russian officer, her hand outstretched to shake his. Only then did she burst into uncontrollable sobs.

"Thank you, sir. Thank you. This is the happiest day of our lives. Today we begin new lives because of you, because of your men. We will never forget this day, this moment. We will always be grateful to the Red Army."

Her legs buckled. No longer needing to be brave and encourage others, her strength evaporated. She sat on the ground, pale, her eyes raised to the sky as she repeated one word over and over. "Dziękuję." Thank you.

CONVERGING PATHS

Yisrael woke up, blinking, slowly getting used to the light. He lay on a bed, not a filthy, lice-infested bunk. He touched the pillow in disbelief. He couldn't remember the last time he'd slept on a bed with sheets and a pillow. Yisrael tried moving his legs but they felt lifeless. He tried rising into a sitting position on the bed, but lacked the strength and flopped back, sighing. His racing heart only calmed down when he saw Avraham standing next to him, smiling.

"Yisrael! You're awake at last! Don't move. It's okay, we're safe now," Avraham said softly, stroking his brother's forehead.

"Where are we, Avraham?" Yisrael was confused.

Avraham laughed warmly. "It's the American hospital and if you haven't figured it out yet, the war's over!"

Hearing Avraham's words, Yisrael tried to smile, but after being a Nazi prisoner in forced labor for so long, they didn't fully make sense. "Good you haven't lost your sense of humor, Avraham," he grimaced.

Avraham grasped his brother's hand. "I'm not kidding, Yisrael. This isn't a dream. The American army liberated us and we're now in the field hospital at Halberstadt near Langenstein. It's a really large hospital, and they're treating us excellently. We get fed like infants, slowly, a bit at a time. They told us that our bodies need to relearn how to eat and digest food."

Yisrael wasn't sure yet if Avraham was still teasing. He tried raising himself on his elbows but once again, fell back. "Yisrael, please, just lie there quietly and don't move at all. Your leg's in bad shape. The doctors were about to amputate but decided to give you a bit more of a chance to heal. That surgeon in the tunnel saved your leg and your life, otherwise you'd have died from the spreading infection."

But Yisrael was insistent. "I need to see my leg. Why can't I stand up yet?"

"Yisrael, please, listen to me. Trust me. I'm your brother. Your leg's completely bandaged. Every day the bandages are changed and you receive painkiller injections. That's also why you've slept for so long. Let the leg heal. It's for your own sake."

"I do trust you, Avraham," Yisrael finally smiled, nodding. "Are you also hospitalized here?"

"Yes, I'm in the bed next to you. I'm listed as having stomach poisoning and severe fatigue, but I'm getting stronger by the day. Unbelievable, but I've put on almost three kilos in the past few days. Yisrael, the war is over! No more Germans around. Now they're fighting over Berlin, but I heard that the Russians are already there and within days Germany will surrender."

Slowly Yisrael was getting his thoughts in order. Hearing this, more questions started arising in his mind. "Avraham, how long have we been here?"

"Almost a week. Most of the time you were unconscious. The doctors are most pleased with your progress. They said that your leg would heal faster that way. They certainly know what they're doing."

Yisrael studied his brother and shuddered, realizing that only the two of them were there. "But Avraham, what about Volf? Have you heard anything about Buchenwald?"

"Nothing yet," Avraham said softly, lowering his eyes. "And nobody seems to know anything. I'm pretty sure he's still in Buchenwald."

"We have to find him and bring him here, Avraham. We must not leave him there alone. Tell the doctors to bring him here, to us. Don't waste even a moment. He must be in a terrible state, in need of emergency care. I'm praying we're not too late...."

Nodding, Avraham left the tent immediately, heading for the clinic office. He started out hesitantly but slowly his voice grew stronger and more assertive. "Hello, sir. My brother and I have a third brother who was left in Buchenwald some weeks ago. I'd appreciate if he could be brought here to be with us. Please help us."

"And your brother's name is…?" the man asked pleasantly.

"Volf Zaks. Please, send me to Buchenwald to find him. I need to find out if he's alive…"

"Ambulances are constantly going to Buchenwald and returning with the ill," the clerk explained. "We're slowly bringing them all here. But if you do want to go and search for your brother, you can ask one of the ambulance drivers for a ride."

Avraham shook the clerk's hand as he thanked him. From the clinic office he went straight to the yard where the ambulances were parked. "Anyone driving to Buchenwald now?" he called out loudly. One driver nodded. "I'm coming with you," Avraham said. Once again, the driver nodded. "Do you mind waiting two minutes? I need to go to the tent and I'll be right back." And again, the driver nodded.

Avraham hurried to Yisrael's bedside. "Yisrael, I'm going on one of the ambulances to Buchenwald to look for Volf."

"Go. Be sure to bring him back with you," Yisrael said softly.

Avraham walked back to the ambulance and took a seat in the back. A minute later, the driver and a doctor took their places in the front, together with an armed guard. Ninety minutes later, the ambulance drove into the camp. Glancing at the sign he remembered so well, "Jedem das Seine," made his heart pump harder; he remembered the feeling of entering as a prisoner, momentarily forgetting he was now a free man. "Jedem das Seine," he shouted, "I hope you Germans get what you deserve, harsh deaths, and all the evil the world can come up with!" But instantly he calmed down as the Americans glanced at him.

"Don't worry," said the doctor, speaking in German, and placing a hand on Avraham's shoulder, "they'll all be brought to justice, these criminals. Not a single one will get away with what they've done. You'll see the law on your side quite soon."

Avraham smiled. "Thank you, doctor. I'm truly looking forward to that moment." Avraham leaned forward, tapping the driver gently. "Would you mind taking me to Little Camp? That's where my brother got left behind."

Gently the doctor replied. "That camp doesn't exist anymore. Everyone we found there has been transferred to a field clinic, each in his own bed, and we're checking them one by one. We'll find your brother. Don't worry, young man."

The ambulance slowed near the field clinic but Avraham jumped out before it came to a full halt. He was still weak and had a pronounced limp as he entered the tent. Going bed to bed, he checked the men, until his patience ran out. Standing where he was, he yelled at the top of his voice.

"Volf! Volf!' Silence. From the furthest wall, a hand rose. Then a head. Then an upper body. There was no doubt in Avraham's mind: here was Volf. Despite the limp, he raced over. Yes, his brother Volf! They hugged and kissed, Avraham leaning over Volf, too overwhelmed to say a word.

"Are we all alive?" Volf whispered.

"Yes, Volf, all of us boys are," Avraham's tears rolled down his cheeks. "Yisrael's in the field hospital not far from here. In Halberstadt. I've come to take you there."

Volf rose from the bed, infused with new energy, as though he hadn't been lying there just a hair's breadth from death only a few days earlier. He stood, leaning on Avraham, as the two embraced and wept. "Let's go, brother," Volf said.

There was nothing to take. All Volf had was the clean, hospital-green gown he was wearing, an appreciated change from the filthy, striped prison clothes they'd worn for so long.

Slowly but determinedly, one step at a time, the two skinny brothers made their way back to the ambulance. "Right. Heading back now?" the driver asked.

Avraham laughed with joy. "As fast as you can before I start roaring again like I did before!"

As the ambulance left Buchenwald, the brothers turned to catch a last glimpse of the gate that had marked such horror in their lives. Sitting with their arms around each other, Volf was the first to speak.

"I didn't do a thing after you left. I just lay there waiting for death. And just when I was sure I was taking my last breath, the Americans burst into the camp and saved me." Volf smiled at last. "And you two? What happened to you?"

"Oh, not a whole lot," Avraham said, not wanting to sap his strength, "but let's wait until we're together with Yisrael and you'll hear it all. He's in a bed in the field hospital and can't move around right now. They almost amputated his leg but a brilliant surgeon, one of the prisoners, saved it. The main thing is, we're all alive."

The ambulance pulled in to Halberstadt. Avraham was raring to go but restrained himself when Volf asked for help with walking. "Wait for me, Avraham. I'm not strong enough to walk any faster yet."

Slowly they reached Yisrael's bed. Volf sat heavily on the bed's edge and took Yisrael's hand in his own. That woke Yisrael.

"Volf? It's you?"

"Yes. Not in full health, but alive and happy to see you both."

"Wow, Volf. Wow," Yisrael kept muttering, gripping his brother's hand before closing his eyes and falling asleep again under the influence of painkillers. But suddenly he raised his head and spoke in a rush. "I dreamt such a nice dream. I dreamt it was over. I saw American flags waving, British, Russian flags. Other flags I can't identify. But there was one I couldn't see anywhere: the German flag. The war's over, the Germans are defeated, we're alive, and we're together! Yes, we still have to find out about the girls and Yossef, but I have a good feeling about them. I'm sure we'll all reunite very soon. I'm sure of it."

Outside, the loudspeakers crackled before an announcement was made, first in English, then in German and lastly in Polish.

"Tonight, 8th May 1945, Germany has signed a Document of Surrender to the Allied Forces, being the USA, Britain, France and other countries. The war is over."

FIRST STEPS

The Görlitz camp was partly opened. The Russians were very generous, caring for the liberated women prisoners with devotion, but did not allow them to leave the campgrounds. After their first modest meal, carefully measured out by the medical staff, a Russian soldier sat down next to the sisters and began to talk to them in Yiddish, smiling and holding his hand out to shake theirs.

"I'm Grisha. I'm Jewish, as you no doubt realize, and I'm a soldier in the Red Army," he said with pride. "The commanders got all of us Jewish soldiers from the brigade together and asked us to take care of the liberated camps. So from now on, all the soldiers here will be Jewish and you can completely put your trust in us. We'll do everything we can to help you."

Miriam's jaw dropped in amazement. "I don't believe what my ears are hearing. Jewish soldiers in the Red Army? You fought with the Russians against the Germans?"

"Of course, yes," the soldier nodded. "I'm originally from Ukraine. I was in the underground and with the partisans. About a year ago, I joined my friends in the Red Army to fight and defeat the Germans. There are literally hundreds of us in the Red Army.

Slowly Miriam put her hand out. He shook it gently, not wanting to hurt her. "We have no words to express our gratitude, dear soldier, and Red Army," she said quietly as tears welled in the corners of her eyes. "It's been two weeks since we were initially liberated and we still have no idea what's happening."

"As of tomorrow, we're opening the camp gates. You'll be able to walk around the city. There are Russian soldiers everywhere, but nonetheless be careful, because after so much time at war, the non-Jewish soldiers are keen on finding themselves some girls. If you wish to take a bit of a walk in the city, feel free, enjoy the change of scenery, but don't be out too long, and always walk together in a group. Never walk around alone."

Batya wanted to go out right away. Regina and Marsha, two other young women from the block who'd become her friends, were happy to join. They showered, put on clean dresses provided by the Russians, and smiled at each other as Miriam clapped her hands. "Just look at us, how pretty we are, real women and not prisoners in rags!"

The camp gates were open, manned by Russian soldiers. As the women walked through, the guard wished them a pleasant time… in Yiddish! They smiled, waved, and arm in arm, stepped out. They'd forgotten what the real world looked like for having been behind fences for so long. Slowly they made their way down the street adjacent to the camp. Batya's heart was pounding in excitement.

"Where to, ladies? You realize we're taking our first steps into freedom?"

They gazed at her. But Batya wasn't waiting for their answer. "Doesn't matter. The main thing is, let's just walk. Do you know what the main thing actually is? That we get to decide where to walk, and when, without being shot. We can stop to rest if we want, without being shot. We don't have to line up in fives or else be shot. We're our own bosses again!"

The city had a sorry, abandoned look. Here and there, they noticed a grocery store stocking the very simplest of basics. Some thirty minutes later, Batya sat down on a bench. "I can't walk anymore. I don't know what to do with myself. This freedom… it's no good for me. I want to go back to the camp."

"Are you crazy, Batya?" her friends protested. "What kinds of thoughts are these? We're free, so we can do what we want, see what we want, watch the world around us. C'mon, Batya."

"Sorry, girls, but I'm not feeling so great about this. I think I went too far and too quickly. Maybe tomorrow I'll go out again for a bit longer and go a bit further."

"But why, Batya? What's bothering you?"

Batya signaled to her two friends to sit next to her. "What's bothering me?" Her voice was so loud that she was almost shouting. "Look around and you tell me. What can you see? How far is it from the city to the camp? About three hundred steps, four hundred at most? Do you see what I'm saying?"

The friends were silent, gazing at her expectantly. "They lived here in peace and knew what was happening. They ate and drank and dressed like people. They sat with their families. So tell me: is it possible they didn't know what was going on in the camp? They didn't hear the shooting? The screaming? They didn't know what was going on inside the camp? They had no idea we were digging pits against Russian tanks? They had no clue we were being starved in here, being killed for no reason?"

Batya's friends were silent, pondering. They'd never thought about that until Batya said it aloud. She took a deep breath before continuing. "I don't see a city here. I see death here. Up until two weeks ago, we were in a sea of death, and now, look around: do you see any life? The city is dead. The Germans have fled. Cowards, they were scared to be trapped inside the camp. For years, people living here ignored the camp, as though there were no people behind its fences. But as soon as the Russians showed up, they picked themselves up and left. We were saved, we're still alive, but what kind of life do we have? I still don't really feel that I'm alive. I see this ghost town, and it stinks of death. The only folks walking around here are like ghosts. Enough. I can't be here a moment longer. Let's go back." She paused. "Maybe tomorrow we'll try again."

Silently the women turned and headed back to the camp.

STROLLING THROUGH THE CITY

The next morning, Regina and Marsha urged Batya to join them. "We want to take another walk in the city. Will you come with us?"

Batya hesitated, then turned to Haiya and Miriam. "Will you come too? Yesterday, being out there made me feel terrible, but if you come, it'll be easier for me"

"I'm not going out yet," Haiya said. "I just don't feel strong enough yet. I don't want to see that much of the world outside anyhow. I need more time."

Batya looked questioningly at her sister but Miriam shook her head. "I'm too tired, Batya. Sorry. I don't think I'm ready for so much exertion. Maybe tomorrow I'll feel a bit better. But if you want to go, you should. Join your girlfriends. I'll be happy to hear your descriptions later on."

The three young women reached the camp gates. Again the Jewish guard smiled at them. "Be careful, ladies. Stick together. There's a lot of no good out there."

Batya was feeling more at ease when they set out this time for the same streets. "I'm strong," she kept repeating under her breath, "and I can handle this world."

From a distance they saw a group of Russian soldiers. Remembering the Jewish soldier's warnings, they stopped. Using an abundance of hand gestures, the Russians tried chatting in awkward German with a bunch of girls further up the street, and bent to hug them, stroking their cheeks and shoulders and backs. One playfully pinched the young, plump woman's butt, drawing rolling laughter from her. "Davay, davay," the soldier urged the German lass, "c'mon," as he tugged her into a building's entrance. He was followed by the other soldiers and the rest of the women. The street fell silent.

Very quickly Batya felt as distressed as she had the day before. "I need to rest a bit," she said softly, before unexpectedly loudly announcing: "I want to rest in one of these houses. This isn't as ghostly a city as it seems. There are people here, afraid to come out. Miserable cowards! I want to go into these Germans' homes, I want to see how they lived: well, comfortably, while we worked to death in the camp, starved, and humiliated. I want to see any filthy German dare oppose me. We'll shout 'Now we're the masters here! Now you're going to suffer as we did!' That's what we'll shout at them!"

Regina and Marsha were shocked at Batya's outburst. They stroked her arm, shushing her. "What do you think about this house?" Regina asked, pointing to one nearby. "I'm not afraid of the Germans. May they be forever erased from the face of the earth! What can they do to us now? Call the Russians? Let's go in!"

On the door a small sign read "Miller Family." Batya knocked and immediately stomped her foot. Why did she have to knock? Just go in, she told herself, you have every right to walk in here as you please!

"I think the door is open," Batya said, turning the knob.

"Anyone home?" Regina called out in German. Silence. They walked in. Despite their outward self-confidence, they were shaking inside, their legs trembling, their breath coming in short gasps. The house was clean, and empty of people for now.

"Anyone home?" Regina asked again as she walked down the corridor past doors and into the dining room. No answer.

An armchair stood in a corner. In the room's center, a framed photo of an SS soldier in uniform was set on the heavy wood dining table. The photo infuriated Regina who picked it up and smashed it on the sparkling, clean floor.

Batya and Marsha were taken aback. "What happened? Who shot…?" Marsha shouted.

Regina called back. "I was just destroying the photo of this stinking bastard. I wish I could kill him. What's he looking at me like that, in his fancy frame? Does he think I'm his prisoner? Look at his spotless black uniform. What's he smirking about, the filthy Nazi? You won't be smiling anymore, you miserable murderer."

Regina was stomping on the photo, the glass, the frame, until the smile on the face of the man in the photo was shredded. Bending down, Regina picked up any pieces of the photo still large enough to hold and ripped them into tiny pieces, her face a mix of fury and disgust. Her friends simply watched in silence until the pent-up anger dissipated. She then broke into sobs. For many minutes her friends stood hugging her, calming her, until she spoke again.

"I want to kill them all. Every. Single. One. Of. Them!"

"Let's see what's in the other rooms," Batya said, getting up. She opened a door and looked around. "Don't you also get the feeling there are people here but we just can't see them?" she said softly. "Maybe they're hiding?"

Finding the spacious living room, they sat down for a few moments. Paintings by renowned German artists hung on the walls. The furniture had an expensive air to it. One armchair, its back to the room's entrance, faced the window. "I think someone's sitting in there looking out," Batya whispered.

Regina laughed. "Sure. They're waiting for the Russians to come and take them to POW camps."

Together they went to the armchair and swiveled it around to face them. The faces went ashen. They screamed. "Who is this? Who are you?" they screeched.

Marsha lost her balance and fell. Batya and Regina held each other's hand and stared at the pale figure with its hollow blue eyes. The woman's arms hung limply at her sides. She never said a thing. Nor did she move. Marsha stood up again and joined the others as they leaned forward a little, checking the woman.

"Do you think she's alive?" Regina asked.

"Doesn't look like it," Batya said. "She looks totally dead."

Regina let vent to her anger and fear. "So why's she looking at me, what did

I ever do to her?" She lightly kicked the woman's foot. There was no reaction. "She really is dead. I can't look at those eyes of hers."

Something caught Batya's attention. Bending down, she pulled a small box from under the armchair, opened it, and found it empty, nothing left but a little powder in the bottom. "These are sleeping tablets," Batya said. "She simply took her own life. I can't see any other reason for why her eyes are still open."

"Nazi coward, mother of a Nazi, Kurwa that you are," Regina blurted, using the Polish word for whore. "She committed suicide so she wouldn't have to accept their defeat and the terrible things they did." She spat on the floor, expressing her hatred. But as she looked down, her eyes caught sight of another small box. "That's a jewelry box like I used to have," she said, opening it. "It's empty. I want this filthy Nazi's jewels."

Batya lifted the dead woman's hand. Diamonds dripped from her fingers. Every finger held one, sometimes two, and even three diamond rings. Not giving it a second thought, Regina slipped the rings off. Only one wouldn't come loose, a wedding ring.

"I'm not giving up on this," Regina said. "I'm not going to leave this Nazi scum a single thing of value." Regina paused, then walked to the dresser where a large sewing box stood. Rummaging among its contents, she came back with scissors.

"Regina! No!" Marsha screamed.

Regina ignored her. As the other two watched, too stunned to move, Regina slipped the finger between the scissor's blades. They turned their faced away as they heard the sickening crunch of bone and cartilage being crushed. Regina removed the gold ring, tossing the cut finger on the floor. Picking up the jewelry box, she stashed all her findings inside. "Let's go," she said, shrugging. "We're done here."

Sighing with relief, Batya and Marsha went towards the door, Regina following until unexpectedly she turned, and returned to the living room. "Wait a second, I forgot something!" she called out. The other two spun around, in time to see Regina slip her palm under a large gold necklace bearing a bright green centerpiece around the woman's neck, and yank it so hard that it came off in one move. "Oh, I love emeralds," was all Regina said, signaling with her hand for them all to go back into the street.

Her friends said nothing at first. As they walked back to the camp, Marsha whispered. "Can you believe she did that?"

Batya was quiet before quietly answering. "I want to go back to the camp. I have so much trouble with this kind of theft. I can't be in this city for a moment longer."

Regina fumed. "Theft? You call this theft, Batya? And what did the Germans do, if not steal our very lives? Our businesses, our jobs, our homes, our jewels, our gold, our silver, sure, but our lives too, our youth, our joy, our families. So, I think that because we managed to survive, we deserve to take anything we want from them and even that isn't enough payment."

Silently they strode back, passing the church on their way. "Stop, girls," Regina asked softly. "Let's go in. Maybe someone's in the church and will ask us for forgiveness. If people are praying there, I'll ask what the church did for our sakes. I know you really want to get back, but just a bit longer, please. We won't take very long. I promise," Regina said, her steely gaze locked on Batya's eyes.

They went inside. It, too, was empty. The entire city is empty, Batya thought. Church figurines looked down on them from their places high on the walls. "See how patronizing they are?" Batya raised her voice. "Where were you, holy ones, during the war? What did you do when they abused us, starved us and killed us? Looking down on us, saying nothing, even smirking a bit, you holy cheats and hypocrites."

Approaching the altar, they noticed that no candle was lit in the gold candlestick. It seemed like the place hadn't been cleaned for quite some time. Old wax melted in piled-up drips held a visible layer of dust. Of highly buffed, white marble, pretty Holy Maria looked down on them, her head adorned in a diamond encrusted tiara. Her eyes were downcast, as though ashamed of the abandoned altar's forlornness.

Regina was the one to speak up first. "Good that you're ashamed. You've got nothing to be proud of. You don't deserve that crown. You're not holy to me in any shape or form. Just a figure that will always be shameful." Reaching up, Regina pulled the tiara off.

"What are you doing?" Marsha was again taken aback by her friend's audacity.

"What do you care? What does she care? She's nothing but a statue," Regina laughed raucously, ripping the diamonds out and stuffing them into her already tightly-packed little jewel box. "Here, take your decrepit crown," she hissed at the statue, putting it back on the statue's head as she hurried out. Without another word, the three hurried back to the camp.

PASSENGERS

Regina didn't offer to share her spoils with Batya and Marsha, and they weren't about to ask for anything. Instead, Regina was already trading with her stash. "Let her enjoy it," Batya said quietly to Haiya and Miriam.

Some days after Regina's looting spree, Haiya and Miriam agreed to Batya's cajoling and joined her on a walk into the city. In these early days of May 1945, right after Germany's surrender, the city was already beginning to get back to routine. More and more Germans were seen in the streets although they did their best to avoid any interaction with the Russian soldiers, who were strutting about like lords.

On one such clear spring day, as the trees on the main thoroughfare began to blossom and nature's hues were coloring the world once again, the three young women walked down the main road, breathing in the heady, floral scent. "I miss home so much," Miriam said. "I want to go back and see the trees blossoming next to our house. I miss walking there, the way we used to."

Batya hugged her sister. "Enjoy what's here for now. It's so very pretty. The world, no doubt, will go back to being beautiful again once this dreadful catastrophe is behind us. We'll get back there, for sure."

Noise in the street made them turn their heads. Russian soldiers, already drunk at this midday hour, were furiously beating a young German man. One drew his pistol, waving it threateningly in the air. "Tell the truth now. Were you a Nazi soldier? Did you fight against us?" the soldier challenged in broken German.

In seconds, the street had emptied. People hurried to close themselves inside their houses. The soldiers kicked the young man about, batting at him with their rifle butts as he pleaded and cried. "No, no, please, I'm not a soldier. Stop, please." The Russians kicked at him until their anger dissipated and left him, bleeding, on the pavement.

"Enough. Enough for today. I don't want to go on walking anywhere," Batya's voice was firm. She glanced at Haiya, who looked down at the street and sighed.

"Tomorrow, we're leaving the camp and going home," she said in her determined tone. "We have to get out of this place. This isn't where we should be in any case. We can't rely on the Russians to ensure law and order. They could end up harming us, too."

Back in the camp they gathered their possessions together: the dresses they wore, an overly thin jacket, and one small bag containing a few slices of bread and some apples for their journey. They left the next day early in the morning, walking to the main road east to Breslow. For three hours they walked, and they weren't the only ones: the road was filled with people going both ways, people bereft of all just wanting to get back home, back to better days.

Very few cars passed, and those that did had to navigate massive potholes and craters left by aerial bombing. For the most part, they noticed that the vehicles were mainly Russian military vans. "Let's just sit on the roadside. Maybe someone will pity us and let us drive with them for a while," Haiya suggested. "I can't walk anymore, I'm exhausted. We can eat a bit, rest a bit, to get our energy up for the next leg of the journey."

Sitting beneath a thick-trunked tree at the roadside, they bit into the juicy apples, which helped ease their thirst as well. For some minutes, they slowly munched until Batya broke the silence.

"Do you miss home? The house there reminds me of horrific things. I'm not sure I miss it."

Miriam was surprised. "I'm curious to know if our house is still standing, and what happened to our neighbors, our friends." She paused. "But mostly, I want to know what happened to our brothers in Blechhammer and where

Yossef ended up after he was sent away from Ludwigsdorf. I keep wondering where they are, and how we'll find them."

In a clear and confident tone, Haiya answered. "We'll find them, don't worry. If they stayed together, I'm sure they would have survived just as we did. We didn't split up. We stayed together as Papa constantly insisted. It might take some time but we'll find them. The one I'm most worried about is Yossef because he was forced to separate from the others."

They ate and rested for a few minutes more. "I don't miss home. Not at all. I don't even really want to see the place again. I don't really care if I never see it again. It reminds me of too many unpleasant events. What I miss is all of us. I want my husband, I want him to be with his brothers, with his sisters. In all honesty, the house doesn't interest me."

While Miriam and Batya were still pondering Haiya's remarks, two military vans stopped alongside them. Several Russian soldiers hopped off and walked over. "Where are you going?" one asked. By his insignia, he was an officer. The three women, trained to respond instantly to authoritative men in uniform, stood at once, were frightened, and looked down. Batya trembled and grabbed Miriam.

"You two be quiet and let me talk," Haiya said to them in Polish between almost closed lips.

She straightened her back and looked the officer right in the eye. "We're heading east to our home. If you could let us travel with you, we'd be very grateful." She paused, and then added, "All we want is a ride. Please don't entertain any other thoughts." The sisters were stunned at Haiya's forthrightness but as so often in the past, trusted her to handle the situation best.

Neither of the vans were large. One seat was available in the first, and two in the second. "We're heading to Breslau, about 200 kilometers from here. We're actually hoping to get there by evening. We'll be happy to let you travel with us. There's no room for all three in one van but if you're all right with splitting up, you'll all get there. And please, don't worry. I'll be responsible for your safety."

"Thank you," Haiya said, shaking her head, "but we never split up, we can only go with you if we sit together. We don't mind squishing into one van."

The officer refused. "Sorry, I can't do that, and you'll have to decide on the spot if you're coming with us or staying here."

Haiya was weighing the options and was on the verge of agreeing to split as the officer began walking away. Miriam called out first. "It's all right, we'll split up."

Batya and Haiya stared at her. "Are you crazy?" Haiya shot at her.

"Don't worry. You two go together, and I'll go in the other van. I know how to look after myself and you, Haiya, will look after Batya. Come on, this is too good a ride to miss."

Her gumption left them speechless.

Miriam joined the officer in the first van, and waved Haiya and Batya towards the other. None of them wanted to show that their hearts were pounding furiously: the crowdedness was very uncomfortable. Squashed together, Batya and Haiya were jiggled about in the van, not knowing if the terrible roads made the soldiers' legs touch their own, or whether the men were taking some advantage of the situation.

"We have to ask them to stop and let us off. I'm scared," Batya whispered to Haiya.

"I'm scared too, but let's keep going a bit longer and hope for the best," came the answer.

Miriam, on the other hand, sat comfortably in the officer's van, chatting with him. "Firstly, thank you for being so kind," she said. "We have suffered so much in the camps, more than two years of terror and we really deserve to be back home at last. We're immensely grateful to the Red Army for defeating the Germans."

Glancing at Miriam, the officer smiled. "It wasn't at all easy. We had to fight hard. We lost many, many of our friends, our unit mates. We haven't seen our own homes for two and a half years. You and your sisters aren't the only ones dying to get home. We all are. That's why I stopped to take you. I hope you get back quickly, but who knows what you'll find there after this terrible war."

They drove on. Once in a while, Miriam turned her head to make sure the other van was close behind. An hour had passed when she realized, shocked, that she couldn't see the other van. "Sir, officer," she asked, panic in her voice, "can we please stop and wait for the other van? I'm worried about my sisters."

"Please," the officer answered, "don't worry. They'll be here quite soon. My soldiers were given orders to make sure the girls are okay, and they carry out my orders. They'll be all right."

Glancing behind her again some minutes later, Miriam still couldn't see the second van. She was not feeling good about the situation. They drove on for another thirty minutes or so. Still no van. She made a decision: as the officer was driving, she opened the door and screamed. "Stop, now. Stop, or I'll jump."

Horrified at the scenario playing out in his mind, the driver slammed on the brakes, losing control of the vehicle. It zigzagged across the road before sliding into a ditch. "We're turning over!" soldiers in the back shouted. The van careened down the ditch until it stopped at last, one of its wheels in the air over a large crater.

Soldiers in the back slowly climbed down, stunned. "Are you out of your mind? You almost got all of us killed!" the officer shouted furiously.

Miriam held his gaze. "You left me no choice. I asked. You ignored me. Now we'll wait for them here as I asked you. I'm not willing to travel apart from my sisters."

Gritting his teeth, the officer was on the verge of slapping her but held himself back. His soldiers were stretching their legs and craning to see if the other van was coming. Some minutes later it did roll up, stopping next to them. Surprised, the soldiers in the second van got out to look at the damage: three wheels stuck in the mud, the fourth hanging in the air.

Batya and Haiya also stepped out. "What's going on here?" Haiya asked.

"I asked them to stop and wait for you but they kept ignoring me so I stopped them myself," Miriam answered softly.

Ordering the men to push the van out of the ditch, they heaved and tugged until it eventually righted itself back on the road. The officer studied the three women, his eyes flashing with anger. "Right, I don't have time to waste, otherwise I'd punish you for the damage you caused," he leveled at Miriam. Glancing from one to the other, hands on his hips, he delivered his verdict. "We've had enough of you. You can all stay here."

He spat, got back in the van, revved the engine and began to move away. The women did not argue with them.

"So. What now?" Batya asked once they'd disappeared from view.

"Don't worry. We've already gone much further than we could have without the ride," Haiya smiled. "I was also getting worried when I couldn't see you in front of us. Your van was going much faster. But come on, let's sit on the roadside and get our breath back. I'm sure there are other good people along the way."

THE VAN AND THE LAUGHING MAN

"It's not that bad," Batya said. "It's not like we have any reason to hurry. Is anyone waiting for us there?"

They walked at an easy pace. The sound of brakes made their heads turn. A van pulled up next to them even though they hadn't signaled for a ride. "Where are you headed, young women?" a man, sticking his head out of the window, said in Polish. They didn't answer. They just kept a close watch on his movements. But he smiled, his thick mustache covering much of his mouth. Perhaps he wanted to hide the few teeth he had left. Still ignoring him, the women walked on.

He drove slowly alongside them. "You don't need to fear," he laughed. "I'm just a lazy little trader traveling to Breslow to bring folks some of this and some of that. I've got cigarettes, chickens, and two cats. I've got a sack of potatoes, and a few eggs that my hens laid this morning. So, if you like, you can be in Breslow in an hour. You're invited to ride up in the back of the van. I can fix some space to sit. The ride's safer back there."

They were having a hard time not bursting into giggles. Trying to keep a straight face, they stopped walking, assessing the rickety van. "Are you sure this can get to Breslow?" Haiya asked. "It looks like it can barely make it anywhere!"

The driver pulled a face, pretending to be insulted. "It'll get there, and how! I do this trip to Breslow and back almost every day. That city's filled with refugees and they all need everything. Thank heavens I have a way of earning a livelihood," he said, shrugging and throwing his hands up to the sky.

They couldn't help but laugh. "He's funny. I'm not afraid of him," Miriam whispered. "Let's ride with him. What have we got to lose?"

Turning to the driver, Haiya thanked him and agreed to his offer. "It's very kind of you. We'll be happy to ride with you!"

Hopping out of his seat behind the wheel, the driver lifted the cage holding the chickens and several eggs smashed on the ground. He tried to shove them aside but when that didn't work well, he tossed a couple of cushions over them. "No worries," he said, "anyhow I'll be offering these cushions for sale only on their good side," he laughed. "Come, ladies, up you go and enjoy the drive."

They snuggled down on the cushions as the driver chuckled. "If you behave nicely, maybe I'll sell you to the Russian soldiers too, but I'd recommend the American soldiers more. I wouldn't trust those Russians, you know. And anyhow, the Americans have tons more money and you deserve the best there is. And they're also more cultured, the Americans. And more polite."

That rattled them. Haiya leapt from her place. "I'm not going with him. Are you both nuts?"

But Batya gave a warm, rolling laugh. "Haiya, can't you see he's teasing? He's basically a decent fellow."

Slipping back behind the wheel, the driver swiveled his head around towards the back. "An hour, ladies. Hold on tight. I learned that the best way to get past these holes in the road is to go faster. So hold on, because we're going to fly!"

Revving the engine, the driver put the van into gear. They were off. He drove fast, as he said he would. Haiya, Batya and Miriam bumped up and down back in the goods cabin. Hens cackled. A goose wriggled out from a corner and nipped Miriam's butt, making Miriam shout in pain. Potatoes rolled from one side of the van to the other like waves, each time the van lurched to the left or to the right. The broken eggs dribbled across the floor, no longer held down by cushions that had also been tossed off their places.

Miriam felt a sharp pang of pain in her stomach: In shock, she watched cabbages the size of footballs roll out of an unraveling sack. They seemed to be attacking her repeatedly. Cloth fell from shelves above their heads. Somehow, they managed to stand and kick the cabbages back into a corner.

And then the van stopped moving.

"Are we there?" Miriam asked.

The driver shook his head. "Soon. But I stopped because I think I see a good bit of business coming up."

Their hearts skipped a beat when they saw an American military vehicle parked at the roadside. "Ladies, keep an eye on the van for me. I'm going to talk to those guys."

"About what?" Haiya asked, getting concerned.

"Maybe I'll sell you. Let's see," the Pole said, laughing raucously at the sight of their anguished faces.

"Let's run away from him," Haiya said. "He's mad."

But this time Miriam laughed out loud. "C'mon, Haiya, can't you see he's kidding? Don't worry."

They watched as he approached the soldiers. He slipped his hand into his pocket and pulled out a handful of something, which he handed over to the soldiers, receiving a large stuffed bag in return. Quickly he walked back to the van and got behind the wheel, offering no explanations. They were flying over potholes again.

"What's in the bag?" Batya asked the driver.

"American cigarettes." His voice was pleased, even proud. "And not just any cigarettes, but Camels! The Russians are crazy about those cigarettes. I buy Camels from the Americans, sell them to the Russians, and everyone's happy."

"All right," Haiya said, "and how did you pay for them?"

"Ah, in diamonds," he grinned. "Bright, shiny diamonds that I found in the village."

That surprised her. "Diamonds in the villages? What kind of village folk have diamonds?"

He laughed. "Calm down, ladies. It's all fake. Everything here's fake," he shrugged and winked. "Diamonds? Well, really, they're sparkly miserable beads I took down from lampshades. The main thing is that the stupid Americans believe they're getting diamonds for cigarettes."

He gave a sudden laugh, as though remembering a good old joke. "Ha! Did you really think I'd try to sell you?" They all laughed. "Truth is," he said, wiggling his mustache, "it's not that I didn't try but the Americans weren't interested. He said you aren't nearly pretty enough. So that's it. Diamonds for cigarettes." For a moment, he became more serious. "It's all bluff. Lying. Everything here's one big fat lie," he sighed. "Believe me, ladies, the Russians are not nice folks. As soon as they can, they'd stick a knife in your back. Did they save us? Maybe they did. Do you think you'll be free now? Independent? Believe me, you won't. When Russians move in, they don't move out. The Americans, the first opportunity they get, they'll sell you to the Russians. All one huge lie. Everything."

He fell silent as did his passengers, thinking about his comments. Not more than a couple of minutes passed before he spoke again, quietly. "I also steal, like everyone else. I lie, just like the rest of them. But the thing is, I steal cigarettes, a bit of food, and sell it so that I can live. Them? They steal entire countries. They steal and sell countries and millions of those countries' citizens." He drew a deep breath. "I'm a Pole from Katowice, not far from here. So you're probably asking yourselves what a Pole like me's doing in Germany?"

"All right," Haiya spoke again, "then what is a Pole like you doing in Germany?"

"So, it's like this," he continued. "I drive to wherever there's something I can steal and sell. There is no more Germany, and there's no more Poland. Nothing. Europe has no clear borders. Once it was Poland. Then it was Germany. Now it's who-even-knows-what; I have no clue. Am I in Germany? Am I in Poland? That's the end of all the countries. They swallow up whole countries. Now, after this war's done, they're planning to steal some country or another for sure."

He gave another cynical laugh. "Germany sold us to the Russians first. The Russians fought the Germans in order to steal us back. The Americans and the Brits are selling us to the Russians. The Russians will take our coal and our water and our farm produce. They'll take everything they can lay their hands on. They're the biggest thieves of all. I'm just a pipsqueak thief. If I get caught, what will they do: toss me in jail for a bit? But they... they'll keep stealing one country after another."

He fell silent again for several minutes before announcing, with obvious joy in his voice: "We're here, ladies. This is the Breslow train station. Here's where you hop off. And they'll give you somewhere to live, and some food, and even some cigarettes. And if you can bring me some, I'll be really happy. Breslow's packed with refugees. Coming. Going. People will help you here, ladies. And I wish you the very, very best. See you!"

They barely had time to thank this odd, precious man, who waved at them and quickly steered the van back onto the potholed road, his merchandise flying about inside the goods cabin.

SIGHTS SET ON STRZEMIESZYCE

Thousands of people swirled around them at the train stations. Dozens seemed not to know where they were actually heading. Near a side wall hung a sign: "Refugee Information." Haiya noticed it.

"Let's try over there," she suggested. She, Miriam, and Batya joined the long line. Like everyone else there, they had nothing but the small bundles in their hands. Some people were chatting with each other. Mostly, the conversations began with questions: Where to? Where from?

"Polish or German?" the man behind the desk asked in German, his voice warm and gentle, his eyes calm and filled with hope as though saying: don't worry, from now on things will only get better.

"Polish is easier for us," Haiya answered, "but if it's easier for you, we're fine with German."

"We're a voluntary organization," the man answered in Polish, "comprised of Poles and Germans and we try to help everyone reach their homes. What are your names, please?"

"I'm Haiya Zaks, and Miriam and Batya Zaks."

"Sisters?"

"Miriam and Batya are. I'm their sister-in-law."

"Good," the man said, writing the information down. "Let's see how we can help. Where are you headed, and how long do you think you'll stay in Breslow?"

"We want to get back to Strzemieszyce in Poland," Miriam added. "A small town between Krakow and Katowice. Our home is there. We want to wait there for the rest of the family."

"Please write down your family members' names. All of them. It may be that one or another will also pass through here and we'll try to connect you."

"Sorry," Miriam said when a tear fell onto the man's ledger as she bent to write.

"It's all right, miss," he said gently, "I completely understand. There are plenty of empty apartments in Breslow. The Poles are congregating in one area. It helps make connections. We'll give you a room in one of the apartments already containing several other women. Here's the address," he slipped them a note. "Join them. They're standing over there," he gestured, "and you can walk to the apartment together. Here's a key. The apartment is yours for two to three weeks. At the next booth you'll find food. Please take whatever you need: bread, cheese, potatoes, vegetables. And the best of luck, ladies. I truly hope you reunite with your family very soon."

They thanked him and joined the other women, introduced themselves, and reached the address on the note. They had come to an abandoned apartment: two rooms, very little furniture, but plenty of beds, clean bed linen, and running water not only in the kitchen but in the shower, too. They claimed one of the rooms for the three of them; the other women took the second room.

Although the shower lacked hot water, they didn't mind. They washed, enjoying the stream of water and clean towels. Then they lay down. And looked around: mold outlined the joints between the walls and the ceiling. "Doesn't bother me," Batya said. "For me, this is a palace. I haven't been in a proper bed for so long. They're beds, not camp bunks. This is a palace, I'm telling you. A palace!"

Haiya and Miriam said nothing. The women in the other room were holding a lively conversation. "This is much too noisy for me," Miriam shot, raising herself up a little on her arm. "I want a bit of quiet, to be alone with myself, to sleep. In silence."

Batya and Haiya simply gazed at her. Some minutes passed. “I’m not in a hurry to get back,” Haiya said. “No rush. Let’s stay here as long as we can, until we find the boys. I don’t want to go to Strzemieszyce on our own.”

Batya sat up. Her tone was angry when she spoke. “Haiya? Are you nuts? What’s gotten into you? You promised Yossef you’d go there. Maybe all the boys are already in Strzemieszyce? We can’t not go home. We have to go, all of us, and you’re coming with us.”

“I know I won’t be able to bear looking at the destruction there,” Haiya said softly, trying to explain. “I can sense that the whole town’s dead and I don’t want to see that. I want to remember the place the way it was before the war. I want to keep the good memories.”

Miriam sighed. “We’ve got plenty of time, Haiya,” she said in a tired voice. “We’ll wait here for some days and then start making our decision. The most important thing for now is to get used to living again. Just living. As simple as that. Breslow is good for us in that respect. Please. Please give me some quiet and let me sleep.” Closing her eyes, her breathing gently slowing as she fell into a deep sleep.

All three slept a dreamless sleep that night, waking some hours later and deciding on a walk through the city. Batya suggested asking the other women to join them but their room was empty. What wonderful silence, Miriam kept thinking. Outside, the street was not excessively busy. Most of the people there were refugees, like them, wandering around without any specific purpose. They were looking for their pasts, seeking their futures: they were people without a present. “I want to go back to the apartment,” Haiya suddenly said. “I’m not happy watching all these refugees.”

Over the coming days, they frequently checked whether any of their family had reached Breslow. Day after day, they experienced only disappointment. “Enough,” Batya said after yet another check with the clerk, “we need to get back home. Tomorrow we’re going to Strzemieszyce.”

Miriam sighed. Haiya said nothing. But the next day, all three rose early and set out eastwards to Poland. Home.

***

An empty road except for a rare military vehicle distanced them further and further from Breslow. But the roadsides carried heavy pedestrian traffic: countless refugees, like them, coming and going.

Haiya spoke quietly. "There are no more borders in Europe, as our jolly thief said. I haven't a clue about anything." She stopped walking. Batya and Miriam gave her a questioning look.

Haiya's voice rose a little. "I can't. I just can't walk back home. You go on without me. I'm going back to the place in Breslow. I'll wait for you there until you come back. I'm sorry. I just can't go on."

Her shoulders shook as she wept silently. Batya and Miriam hugged her. Haiya pushed them gently away, wiping her cheeks. "Go, my beloved sisters-in-law. And take care of yourselves." Spinning on her heel, she quickly headed back towards the apartment they'd just left. She halted again, turned, waved, blew Miriam and Batya kisses, and strode on, back into the city of refugees.

Not long afterwards a wagoner pulled up next to them. "Ladies?" the man reined the horse in. "I'm heading to Katowice. I'd be happy to take you if you're going that way." Silently they climbed into the wagon, both lost in thoughts of what they might find at home.

"Polska!" the wagoner broke their silence as he pointed. Looking up, they saw the old rusty sign, pocked by bullet holes. The wagoner spoke so softly that they weren't sure if he was talking to them or himself.

"Here's where the border used to be," he muttered. "From here on, this was Poland. How I loved Poland. And now I have nothing." A minute later he turned around. "That's what Poland is. Like that sign you saw. No legs. Nothing but holes, and skew, and it will never rise again."

Unexpectedly, he brought the whip down on the horse, encouraging it into a canter. Miriam and Batya gripped the wagon's rim as tightly as they could, trying not to fall off. Again he whipped the horse. "Faster, horse. Faster! We need to get away from here!"

Once the sign was out of sight, the wagoner calmed down, folded the whip, set it down at his feet, and they moved forward at an easy pace. "I'm sorry, dear horse," the wagoner said, tears rolling down his cheeks. "Forgive me, please. For whipping you. For forcing you to gallop. We'll stop soon and you can rest, dear friend. You're all I have left in this world."

The sisters' hearts were broken by the wagoner's compassion.

Sunset marked their entry into Katowice. The wagoner halted, gesturing with his hand for the sisters to climb down. "Thank you, sir," Miriam said. They walked to the well-lit train station. Like all train stations of those days, it buzzed with refugees, some lying on the ground dozing, many on their way to, or on their way from, some other town or city or country. They, too, lay down on the platform, their fingers tightly linked with each other, and fell asleep.

Waking with the first light, the sisters set out once more. Where a sign stating "Strzemieszyce" once stood, there was nothing at all. Standing at the town's border, they wondered, "Are we here, and if so, what now?"

THE OLD STONE HOUSE

"I don't feel anything," Miriam said. "I don't feel like I've come back to the place I grew up in, the house we…" Her voice trembled.

"Yes, I understand you completely," Batya said, nodding. "Who's waiting for us here? I'm also feeling nothing but a vast emptiness. I'm not happy. I'm not sad. I'm simply empty inside. My heart couldn't care less about…." she gestured with her hand at the destruction, "all this. I think we need to get home, see what the damage is, and see what we can do. Maybe with some kind of purpose, we'll feel a lot better."

They set off for their home, slowly, arms linked, eyes flashing from one side of the street to the other, taking everything in, stepping gingerly as though fearful of meeting haters and snitches. They didn't have far to walk, but they couldn't see the big old house, so large that it had carried two numbers: 76 – 78.

"Why can't we see it yet? Do you think they blew it up?" Batya whispered in horror.

"Our house was the strongest in the whole town," Miriam tried to reassure her. "I can't imagine anything could have harmed it. C'mon, let's keep going."

They walked on, but Batya shook and trembled the whole time, despite her older sister's arm around her.

"Batya! Miriam? You're alive?" a stunned Mrs. Beriski, hands at her cheeks in shocked astonishment as she walked quickly towards them, called out. "Oh, let me hug you!" she spread her arms, enveloping her former neighbors. In no time they were all crying together. "I'm thrilled, just thrilled, to see you alive, and back here at last. I prayed the whole time that you'd survive the horrors safely."

Mrs. Beriski stroked first one and then the other's cheeks. Batya kissed her gently: this good Polish woman had taken risks on their behalf. "We'll never forget your help," Batya said, her voice quavering, "we'll always remember how you brought us food and medicine and helped us survive. What an angel you were to us, Mrs. Beriski."

"And that's thanks to your father. In my hardest days, he helped me. He was always ready to help. So of course I wanted to repay in kind and help his girls." She fell silent, gazing at them, before smiling warmly. "But what am I standing here for, chatting away in the street? Come, let's go inside. I will host you and you can stay here for as long as you need to."

"Thank you, thank you so much, our dear Mrs. Beriski, but not now," Batya deferred the offer gently. "Now we want to go and see our house. We'll come back to visit you later on. Thank you for everything."

They hugged again before leaving Mrs. Beriski and walking on. She went back inside, crossing herself and gazing up at the statue in her living room. "Thank you, our Holy Lord Jesus, for saving those girls."

***

And there it was. Their house. Home! The roof was the first thing that caught their eye, rising high above the other roofs, as it always had, its shingles a rich dark shade of burgundy. Batya gasped and stopped in her tracks, disbelief etched on her face.

"Why'd you stop?" Miriam asked. "I want to run home. Come on, I'll race you!"

As though waking from a dream, Batya smiled. "Sorry, Miriam. But I need to do this at my own pace. Slowly." She gasped and sobbed. "It's there. It's really there, our home. Let me just stand here a bit longer and take that in. I need to convince myself I'm not dreaming, that we've really come back."

Miriam hugged her. "It's okay, Batya. We'll go as slowly as you like."

The upper floor came into full view. "Look!" Miriam cried out, relief and excitement mingling. "All the windows! They're all whole, all the glass panes are in place. Our home is whole." Miriam grinned. Slowly, Batya broke into a smile.

"Race you!" Batya challenged, setting off right away, a new surge of life filling her body and heart.

They stopped to catch their breath, then ran on. And stopped again, puffing. And ran on, until they reached the front door.

They peeked into the shop's dark interior. It was empty. Not a single bolt of cloth lay on any of the shelves. In fact, the shelves were very dusty. "It looks as though no one's been in here since we left," Batya said quizzically. "How I would love to clean the shop and stand at the till again."

Miriam glanced at her with uncertainty. "Well, you realize that would be extremely difficult," she said in a comforting tone.

"Look how filthy the yard is!" Batya gestured to objects strewn around. Her tone was angry. "Miriam, what do you think? Is it still our house? Or is someone living here? And why all this rubbish…?"

Gently, Miriam placed a hand on her sister's shoulder. "Of course it's our house and always will be. Let's go inside. If it's empty and no one's there, we'll just start living here ourselves. After all, it is our house.

"It stinks in here!" Batya exclaimed as they stepped over accumulated garbage and filth in the stairwell. But then Miriam burst into tears.

"Look, Batya, the mezuzah, it's still in its place. Proof that the house is still ours." Batya touched it, remembering how her father would always put his fingers to it every time he entered and went out. A deep longing welled inside her.

Both stood next to the door, fingers pressed to the mezuzah. Finding a bit of rag, Miriam began wiping the dirty doorpost. Suddenly the door flew open, the wood scraping against the floor. A heavily-bodied Polish woman stood there leaning on a cane.

"What do you want, uh? Come here to steal? There's nothing here. Get out. Now."

That raised Batya's ire instantly. "This is our house, do you hear?" she screamed at the top of her lungs. "This is ours, always has been, and always will be our house. You've stolen our house but we're not going to let you get away with it." She began to weep.

"When we lived here, it was spotless," Miriam's tone was just as furious.

The Polish woman brandished her cane at them. "What do I care? Maybe it was your house once, but now it isn't, you scum." Her tone and her words were vulgar. "There was a war, and now this house belongs to the person living here. The rules have changed, young misses. We're renting rooms out. There's one left at the end of the corridor if that's what you want. But you need to decide fast because plenty of people are looking for places to live."

"This is our house, you piece of garbage!" Batya screeched. The Polish woman took a step forward. The sisters moved backwards, onto the step. "What was, no longer is," the woman said. "I don't know you, and all I know is that Jews lived here and all the Jews died. Scat, now, before I hit you." With that, she turned, walked back inside, and slammed the door loudly.

Miriam and Batya stood on the step, astounded. "Let's go," Miriam said.

"It's all empty as far as I'm concerned," Batya blurted. "Now I understand why I felt such emptiness from the moment we reached Strzemieszyce. This isn't our town anymore, this isn't our country, this isn't our house, and we'll never get it back. Papa's soul isn't in this place. I could always feel Papa, like a cloud floating in here. But not now. Everything here is empty."

"Nor can I sense Mama here," Miriam nodded. "There's none of Mama's cooking aromas in the kitchen. It's all dead."

Batya grabbed her sister's hand. "Miriam, are you listening? I swear that I will never, ever come back to this house. Let the gentiles take it and choke to death on it."

"Let them choke, with it or without. But what about the treasure? Remember, Papa hid a treasure box in the safe under the floor. We have to find a way in somehow and get that safe."

Batya shook her head. "Forget it, Miriam. That safe will stay under the floorboards forever. It won't help us now. We can't dig under the floor when people are living there. I made a vow and I intend to keep it. I'll never come back to this house."

Batya touched the mezuzah and began making her way quickly down the stairs, Miriam following. "We still have a few things to do here, before we leave this town forever," she said quietly to Miriam. "We need to visit Marek. He's always helped us, those nights when we crept out of the ghetto to sleep in his house, remember? Papa gave him cloth from our shop. Maybe there's some left. But if he's sold it all, maybe he'll give us some of the money. Let's go to his house now."

THE MASS GRAVE

"How I hate this town now," Batya blurted once they were down in the street. "All the more so because Papa died because of me."

Someone in the distance was waving to them. Mrs. Beriski. An elderly man gripping her arm walked with her. Mrs. Beriski pointed to them and whispered in his ear.

"There's something familiar about him," Miriam said softly to Batya, "but I can't quite place who it is."

A few strides later there were face to face with each other. Mrs. Beriski introduced the elderly gentleman. "Do you remember the doctor? Batya, you worked in his clinic in the ghetto." The doctor bowed slightly and smiled. Batya felt a little ashamed: how could she possibly forget him. Mrs. Beriski spoke excitedly. "He saved you. The medicines I brought you in the camp which saved Yossef were from him. He wasn't afraid of helping. The Germans didn't scare him at all!"

Batya's arms flew around the elderly doctor as she hugged him at length and kissed his hand. "Do you remember me, Doctor?" she smiled through her tears. "You were such an angel, and we have no words to thank you. Because of you and Mrs. Beriski we know that there were nonetheless some good people in Strzemieszyce. You helped Yossef survive the camp. We have no idea where he is now, but I'm sure he's still alive, and a lot of that is thanks to you."

The doctor sniffled tears away. "My dear girl, yes, I remember all of you.

Your brothers… where are they? Did they survive?"

Batya wrung her hands. "We don't know, Doctor. But we have every intention to keep searching for them. If they're alive, we'll find them.

"Yes, of course you must. A family needs to watch out for each other," he nodded his approval, "and now that this terrible war is over, what is your next step?"

"We'd like to meet with Marek," Batya answered. "Before the war he had a lot of business with Papa and helped us in the war's early days too. He helped all of us. So now we wish to thank him for all his efforts."

"Of course, of course. I know Marek well. I'll walk you over there," the doctor said.

Mrs. Beriski said her goodbyes and continued on to her own house. A few minutes later Marek's home came into view: the sisters remembered it at once even though it had lost much of its elegance. Batya knocked lightly on the door. A moment later, it opened slightly and someone peeped out.

"Oh my. Batya? Miriam? Is it really you?" Marek cried out, taken by surprise. "Come in, come in. Please. I can't believe my eyes. Thank goodness I've lived to see you come through this!"

Thinking about the nights she and Miriam had snuck out of the ghetto to the safety of Marek's home brought tears to Batya's eyes. Miriam turned to her. "Batya, don't cry anymore, please."

"It's so good to see you," Marek repeated over and over. Then a silence fell over them. They stood together awkwardly until the doctor asked to sit down. "Yes, yes, of course, and thank you for accompanying the sisters here," Marek said, gesturing to the armchairs and sofa.

The doctor sat but Miriam and Batya continued to stand facing Marek, searching for words of thanks to this non-Jew who risked his life on their behalf and helped their father throughout the earlier years of German occupation. Marek slowly broke into sobs, finding himself unable to talk.

"Let's sit together," he said at last. "Thank you for coming. The doctor and I have something to tell you. It's a harsh story that we've kept secret for two years, since that accursed 23rd of June in 1943. I could never reveal the secret that the doctor and I shared to anyone. But now I will tell you. First, though, my wife will make us some tea and we'll drink, and then we'll go out for a bit. We'll tell you on our way there because you must see this with your own eyes."

***

Marek's wife brought out tea, cake, and a little fruit. Around the table the conversation mostly detailed how the sisters' and brothers' paths disconnected and reconnected over the war years.

"Well, now that we've had some refreshment, let us go… it's not very far," Marek said at last. First he walked over to a dresser, opened a drawer and took a slip of paper from it, which he folded and placed in his pocket. Out in the street, they walked in silence, passing the train station again. Batya couldn't bear to look at it. Miriam peeked but immediately turned her face back towards their little group.

Marek could feel the tension growing. "We'll be there soon. Patience," he reassured.

A few minutes later he stopped at a small hill covered in mounds of earth and glanced at the doctor. "It's here, yes," the doctor confirmed. A pang of pain knifed through the girls' hearts and minds: they realized why these two good men had brought them here. Silently, heads bowed, they stood, hurting inside.

Embracing them, Marek spoke. "This is where your father is buried. Not just him, but seventeen more Jews from our town. This isn't a Jewish cemetery but the doctor and I did the best we could." He fell silent and brought his feet together, standing at attention. The doctor stood silently at his side. Batya and Miriam stood in silence, too, and only the tears of all four fell silently onto the mound of earth covering Hanokh Zaks and his fellow Jews. The girls collapsed onto the ground, weeping. Batya buried her head in Miriam's arms.

"I can't anymore. I just can't. I want to be close to Papa, as close as possible."

Marek and the doctor hugged them tight.

It was some minutes later before Marek spoke again, emphasizing every word. "After the terrible massacre, I came here at night with a spade. The Germans had already gone, having expelled or exterminated all the Jews. That left them with nothing more to do here." He paused, taking a deep breath as Miriam and Batya turned their faces to him, waiting to hear the rest of his testimony.

"I saw it all," Marek continued. "I saw the corpses. I wanted to bury them all. But how could I bury eighteen people on my own? And then I thought that perhaps someone could help me. I wondered about the doctor, went to his home, described the situation and what I planned to do for these innocent people, and he agreed at once to help. We came back here, to the pile of bodies."

"I wanted to start digging but the doctor held me back. 'Marek, wait. We must first identify them before burying them. We must keep a list of the murdered people's names otherwise their families will never know where they're buried.' So the doctor pulled a page from his prescription booklet and we began writing down the names of everyone we could identify. Sadly, your father was instantly recognizable. He was so tall, so proud, and such a good friend, Hanokh was, and surely G-d gave him a place in heaven. Then we went from body to body and listed them. All of them. There wasn't a single person there that we didn't know. We spent two hours just separating the bodies and naming them. They were covered in blood but that didn't deter us. We had to do this, out of respect. We would never leave them out in the field to rot or become fodder for wild animals and hawks."

Marek sighed before continuing. "And then, once we'd finished identifying them, we began to dig in the dark of night. We placed the bodies next to each other. Eighteen lie here. We worked until midnight." His voice broke, and the girls wrapped their arms around him.

"We have no words," Miriam said. "Thanks to you and the doctor… There are still some angels in this vile town. Some righteous in the city of Sodom."

Marek pulled the piece of paper from his pocket and held it out to the sisters. "Here are the names. It will help you in the future."

Collecting planks of wood and flat stones from nearby, Batya and Miriam built a makeshift fence around the mound of soft earth. Marek and the doctor watched, letting them do what they felt appropriate, stepping back, not wishing to interfere with the sisters' actions. These Jewish girls would know best how to mark the gravesite of their father and his fellow Jews.

When they were done, Batya raised her head. "This will mark the grave. And sadly, how easy it was to mark. Clearly the earth is still moist with the blood of the innocent."

"Let us go back now, and be my guests, please," Marek now suggested. "This time you can sleep in my home without the fear of neighbors handing you over to the Germans. My wife has already prepared the beds for you."

They nodded in agreement. "Thank you, Marek. We'd be happy to stay with you," Miriam said.

On the way back, the doctor bid them goodbye, kissing each sister's hands. "My wish is for you all to reunite as soon as possible. You deserve a little happiness after all you've been through."

Almost before their heads hit the pillows, the sisters were asleep. Sunlight streaming in through the window woke them the next morning. Miriam stretched in bed. "How long it's been since I slept so well!"

"Good morning, sis," Batya greeted her. "The sheets and blankets are so comfy and smell so nice, almost like Mama's laundry. Remember?"

Miriam nodded as someone knocked on the door, which was then gently pushed open. "Good morning, young ladies! Please come down for breakfast." Marek's wife invited them. Downstairs the table was set with fresh bread, boiled eggs, and tea.

"It's so wonderful to feel that we're in a home," Batya said as they tucked heartily in.

Breakfast over, Marek suggested they visit the refugees office. "Everyone coming into town registers there, and also writes down the names of people they're looking for. You should too, and check the lists. Maybe someone you know has registered. Or maybe someone will arrive and be able to find your names and make contact. I think it's very important to get that done as soon as we can," Marek explained, pausing before continuing.

"I need to tell you something more, of importance. Your father was very dear to me, and gave me all the cloth from the store. I promised to take care of it as far as possible, but we did speak also of a situation where I may need to sell it for survival. Sadly that's what happened, and there's nothing left. I had no choice… But your father's cloth kept my wife and I alive during the war. Every time I sold a bolt of cloth, I thought of him, of your Mama, of all of you. When I saw him among the town's murdered Jews, my heart ached. I promised Hanokh my friend to guard the merchandise, but couldn't keep that promise. No one had any idea at the time how long the war would last. But perhaps one day I'll be able to repay that debt. I can't at the moment. I… we… have nothing. But I'm acknowledging that debt to you and will pay it back when I can."

Batya nodded. "Dear Marek," she said softly, "you preserved our Papa's dignity in his death, and we will never forget that. You did whatever you could, for him, for us. The cloth you sold we consider as fair payment. There are no outstanding accounts between us. Cloth, compared to your devotion and risking your life over burying him… no, there's no comparison at all."

***

At the local offices, Miriam and Batya listed themselves as located in Breslow, giving the exact address, then listed the names of everyone else in the family. On their way out of the building, they passed a man who seemed familiar. They studied his face. He stopped for a moment and studied theirs before entering the refugees office.

"Who was that?" Miriam asked.

"I'm sure we know him but I can't remember the name," Batya answered, her eyebrows raised as she puzzled over the memory.

I know them, but from where? How silly of me not to have just asked outright, the man's puzzled thoughts spun. He went over to the clerk, registered his name, and an idea came to mind. He could check the lists, too. Immediately he came across the newly registered names of the sisters. Running his finger down the list, he saw they were looking for, among others, their brother Yossef Zaks. He spun on his heel, racing out into the street, shouting: "Batya! Miriam" But the street was already empty. Now he was angry with himself: why hadn't he simply asked? They'd disappeared and he had no idea where.

"Oh, oh," he muttered, "what will I tell Yossef? He's waiting for me in Breslow. How can I tell him I saw his sisters but didn't speak to them?" Still berating himself, he went back into the office and checked the lists again. His face broke into a smile. "Well, well," he muttered, "look, look, look. They're in Breslow too. Thank G-d they left an address and I can give that to Yossef." Relieved, he made his way back to the apartment in which he and Yossef were staying.

***

"Did you see that the photographer reopened his place?" Batya remarked. "I was thinking, Miriam, that maybe we should go and see if he has any old photos of the family. After all, he took shots of us all before the war."

"What an amazing idea. You always have great ideas, Batya," Miriam smiled.

The photographer instantly remembered them, exclaiming, "Oh yes, of course I know who you are." Batya then explained to him what she was seeking. "Since we have no possessions left in this town, and both our parents died, it would be wonderful to have some mementos. At least some family photos... would be a good thing to have."

The photographer was deeply moved, inviting them to wait while he checked in a back room. Miriam broke the tension in the air. "I do hope he finds something. It would be the most precious thing we could take with us." Batya squeezed her hand.

Minutes later he was back. "I do have something here, and I'm sure it's your family, but let me just check the film under the light." Switching the desk lamp on, he held the negative up at a slight angle, slowly unrolling the film, glanced at the sisters, and went back to unrolling more of the film. The corners of his lips began to curl upwards, slowly broadening into a big smile.

"I think there's a family photo here. It's a bit faded but I'm pretty sure it's the Zakses. Take a look. Tell me what you think."

"I can't see a thing," Batya said, blinking back tears. "You look, Miriam."

Silently, Miriam studied the images: suntanned faces of young men and girls, standing together. Were these really her brothers? She wasn't sure. Years had passed, and no one looked like that anymore. But then she saw the older couple seated in front. Her heart skipped a beat. Here was Papa Hanokh, and Mama Yoheved. No mistaking them, even though she was looking at them in the negative's reverse black and white. She closed her eyes, imagining the words they seemed to be saying: Please, take us with you and away from here.

"Yes, this is our family," Miriam confirmed, her pulse pounding wildly. "All of us are here. Yitzhak, too. How wonderful it will be to have this visual memory of Yitzhak, our dear younger brother."

Walking over to Miriam, Batya peered at the little square of film. Everyone was smiling. "Yes, this is our big, happy, lovely family," Batya said. "And it will become that once again," she quickly added.

"Would you be able to make a copy of it by tomorrow?" Miriam asked, "because we're leaving tomorrow and this photo would be the only thing we have left of our past, of life before the war. Everything we remember is captured in this single photo. It's the most important thing we could have."

"Of course," the photographer agreed. "I'll do my best. Come back tomorrow morning and hopefully I'll have produced a larger copy for you. I'll also give you the film."

The next day, with the photo and Marek's list of eighteen buried Jews from Strzemieszyce in their bag, they caught rides back to Breslow. "You know," Miriam said in a contemplative tone, "that photo is more important to me than all the treasure hidden in the house. That photo is our greatest treasure. The house is dead, but the photo will keep living."

PASSING NOTES

Three Zaks brothers lay in the Halberstadt field hospital's beds, registered as survivors of Langenstein and other camps. It had been some weeks since the camp's liberation and they were slowly recovering although their weight was still no more than an alarmingly low forty-five kilos, barely a little more than half of what it should be for young men of their height and age. Their appetites were improving by the day, and their health was shaping up well under the American doctors' constant, devoted care.

"We should start looking for our sisters and Haiya," Yisrael said as they sat together one evening. "I think about them constantly. Where could they be? What's happened to them?"

"We're not exactly in good enough shape to go looking physically, but yes, we should at least start looking for information," Volf added.

The brothers sat silently pondering for several minutes. "Maybe we could ask the soldiers here for exercise books so we can write some notes, give them to people to read, to pass around, to hand out as they travel, and so on. Eventually one of the notes could actually find them. We have to start somewhere. And some time. So why not right now?"

Avraham went in search of the hospital offices to ask for notebooks. The American staff, hearing his idea, were happy to oblige. Not long after he returned to his brothers, the doctors entered with a commander and important news.

"So, listen up, guys," the commander said. "This is a field hospital and as such, it gets moved from one location to another as needed. We've just been told we need to pack up and head for the Pacific and the Japanese front. The Germans did surrender to us here but the war with the Japanese is continuing and we're needed urgently on the other side of the world. This means you'll be evacuated to a proper hospital quite soon, the well-equipped hospital at Bergen-Belsen, where a city's been set up for camp survivors."

"All right," Yisrael said, once the commander and the medical staff had left, "so now we've also got a specific address for anyone reading our notes. Let's write as many as possible, and make sure you write in clear lettering. Here's what we should each write. 'We, the brothers Yisrael, Volf, and Avraham Zaks, are together, and at the Bergen-Belsen Hospital. Please make contact."

Ripping page after page out of the notebooks, they wrote the message over and over. It didn't take long before they were feeling tired. "We need to sleep. Get our strength up," Volf said, yawning. "We can do more tomorrow."

The next morning they kept writing, producing hundreds of notes until the very last page of the last notebook was pulled out. During morning rounds, the doctors looked at the pile of notes, amazed. "Do you think this will help?" one asked.

"Yes. But even if it doesn't," Yisrael answered, "it certainly can't do any harm."

Meanwhile, more soldiers were entering their tent. Seeing the notes, one remarked that they'd be traveling the next day to southern Germany and Poland. "Please, if you don't mind," Yisrael asked, "could you take some of these notes with you and hang them in every railway station you go through and any other central places in every city your pass? If you spread these around, all across your European travels, we might find our family. We have no other way of letting them know where we are and this seems like the best option."

The Americans grinned and chuckled. "Well, look at you!" they laughed. But their thoughts wondered how survivors of hell could be so focused on coming up with crazy ideas like these and actually believing in them. "We've got to admire your solutions!" one said, taking a bunch of notes and promising to pin them up to noticeboards wherever they go. The soldiers were very surprised to discover that other patients had quickly adopted the Zaks brothers' idea and were asking for the same assistance. Hundreds of notes bearing the names of people seeking family members were handed to the American soldiers.

The next morning, the brothers were already on their way to Bergen-Belsen.

***

Back in Breslow, Batya and Miriam told Haiya of their visit to their house in Strzemieszyce and the horrid Polish woman who'd taken it for herself. They described the visit with Marek, the doctor, and Mrs. Beriski. Once she'd asked several questions, they told her about the mass grave where Marek had buried their father, showing her the names of the deceased on Marek's list. For some minutes, Haiya's sobbing was the only sound in the room. "It's good I didn't come with you," she said at last, wiping her eyes. "I wouldn't have held up."

"But we also have a wonderful surprise," Batya added. "Actually, it's the most precious thing we brought from there." Pulling the photo out of the bag, she placed it on Haiya's lap. Haiya's eyes few open; in her mind they became flesh and blood.

"What do you think's happened to Yisrael and the boys? Yossef too?" she asked, studying the photo. "He was sent to central Germany when Ludwigsdorf was evacuated. I wonder where he is."

There was a knock on the door. They hardly had any time to answer before the door was dramatically shoved open. In strode Yossef. "Here I am!" he laughed and shouted at the same time, jumping onto his sisters, hugging them and Haiya. They stood in a tight circle, embracing, for some minutes. "But Yossef," Batya eventually asked, "our beloved Yossef, how'd you know we were here?"

"Because of Horowitz," he laughed. "He was in Strzemieszyce and saw your names on the refugees list. We came to Breslow together and we're sharing the same place." Yossef breathed in deeply. "And... he also saw you both. He was looking and looking at you, he knew you were familiar, but he couldn't quite place the name. So he checked the lists and realized he must have seen you two. He went racing back out into the street but you'd disappeared from view."

"Horowitz. Yes, that was the man we also thought was familiar," Batya said to Miriam. "What incredible luck that he checked."

Yossef took Batya's hand in one of his, and Miriam's in the other. "The main thing is that we've found each other. So, now, where are Yisrael, Volf, and Avraham? Have you heard anything?" he asked, breathless and impatient.

That evening Yossef moved into their apartment, wishing Horowitz well and thanking him for the amazing information that brought some of the Zaks family together again. The four Zakses slowly began acclimating to life in the city. At the refugees assistance center, they received food allocations and other kinds of help.

As for his time as a captive, Yossef kept his description brief. "In Ludwigsdorf I was on the verge of death. If not for those medicines and food, I wouldn't have made it. They also helped after we split up. And I came out of it all much stronger. Things in the POW camp weren't so terrible, actually. We didn't have to work. We were told we'd be released when the war ended. One day, they just opened the gates and shooed us out. We weren't even good enough for prisoner swaps," Yossef laughed. "So we set out, a few of us, and eventually Horowitz and I ended up here."

Yossef fell silent, but no one insisted he say anything more. Looking down after several minutes, he spoke softly. "Don't be angry with me, but please, don't tell me what happened to you. Not yet. It's all too difficult for me right now. I prefer to ignore as much as I can, to know less rather than more. The main thing is that you're alive. And if we can find our brothers, things will be all right."

Very quickly, Breslow's train station filled with notes on small bits of paper, or large sheets, this one going here, that one seen there. Thousands of notes filled every spare space in railway stations in those post-war days. It infused Haiya with hope. "Look how many notes there are. I know Yisrael. He'll be trying to find us using this system, too. Keep your eyes open. The number of notes grows day by day and we need to check every day."

At first light every morning, Haiya came to check the new notes, knowing that trains loaded with soldiers were passing through the city during the night. Soldiers stretching their legs briefly at these stations hung new notices every day along their journey. For days, Haiya kept her sunrise vigil going. "I'll never give up," she encouraged herself, "because we will find each other this way."

Early one bright August morning in 1945, Haiya stood at the Breslow station, as she had done for months, waiting to check the noticeboard. Blocking her was an American soldier busy tacking a notice up. When he saw her, he smiled, and quickly went back onto the carriage as the train hooted, getting ready to pull out.

Haiya felt her mouth fall open. Right there in the center of the board, on a page ripped out of a notebook, was handwriting she'd recognize anywhere. Yisrael! No mistaking it. No one's handwriting was quite like his, rounded, each letter perfectly shaped, clear. She could identify it from a distance but now she was reading the words. Yes, it was Yisrael! She cried. She ran to the board. She stood in front of the page. She shouted with all her might: "He's alive, he's alive, Yisrael's alive!" No one heard her, alone on the platform at that hour.

She then swiped the tears away, yanked the page down, and started to read. "We're together at the Bergen-Belsen hospital. Yisrael, Volf, and Avraham. Please make contact."

Seeing the words "Bergen-Belsen" brought on another round of tears. "But they're alive," she whispered repeatedly. She dropped down onto the platform bench, trying to catch her breath. And cried again, but this time in joy. Leaping up, she raced home, pushed the door open, and blew in like a storm.

"Look, look! It's them! They're alive. Yisrael, Volf, and Avraham. They're alive and they're together! Tomorrow we have to start traveling."

HIMMLER'S MERCEDES

Immediately at the war's end, the German military camp was redesignated as a center for displaced persons, survivors of Bergen-Belsen, and of other camps in Germany and Poland. The camp hospital, restaffed with Allied forces, took in people needing rehabilitation, among them survivors of Buchenwald and Langenstein. Among those survivors were Yisrael, Volf, and Avraham.

Yisrael was recuperating from the emergency operation on his leg. Volf was still fighting a severe bout of pneumonia that almost killed him before he was liberated. Both weighed a fraction more than thirty-five kilos each. Avraham was a little healthier than his older brothers, making him able to assist them at the Bergen-Belsen Hospital which administered almost exclusively to Jewish patients.

The brothers were given a room to themselves and new clothing. The devoted care they received, and generous dollops of their own sheer willpower, kept them improving by the day. Within weeks, Volf and Yisrael were standing on their own legs. "We've returned to the living," Yisrael laughed, "and now we have to find the rest of the family."

"I think we should get as healthy as we can first," Volf answered thoughtfully. "We've been taken care of well by the Americans and the British. Our weight has gone up. But we're not strong enough to start traveling around yet. I have this feeling, though, that we'll all be getting together quite soon."

Avraham, not needing direct medical intervention, had gone for a couple of walks in the nearby town, constantly thinking how he could earn some money. "Countless old bits of garbage hanging around here," he mumbled to himself. "I need to find a way of using them as trading materials. They're the most needed raw materials in Europe right now."

Avraham loved poking around the recast Bergen-Belsen camp where Himmler's castle was located. It was an opulent structure, its floor was made of marble, pillars graced the entrance and its interior, and the furnishings were made of mahogany. The temptation was too strong: he decided to try going in. A heavy lock on the gate didn't stop him. Avraham was determined to see what was inside. He wandered undisturbed from room to room, then went downstairs into the basement and underground parking space. To his surprise, parked there was a perfect, whole, sparkling Mercedes. Grinning, Avraham ran his palms over the sleek car's length, opened the door, and sat down behind the steering wheel.

He was even more amazed when he noticed the key in the ignition. Without a second thought, he turned it. The engine revved immediately. He turned the car off and decided on the spot that this would be his car.

The carport door swung up smoothly. Avraham closed it. I'm coming back tonight, he promised himself, and driving out in this car. He chuckled. On his way out of the parking space, he took off the two small flags above the headlights: one was the German flag, the other the swastika. Tossing them into a corner, he wondered if anyone else knew about the vehicle but concluded that it was unlikely, otherwise it would have already been in use. It has probably just been forgotten about, he nodded to himself, and no one knows about it except me.

Thrilled, Avraham made his way back to the brothers' room. Yisrael and Volf sat on their beds. "I've found a car," he said excitedly, his eyes shining, his voice low to prevent anyone overhearing.

"Yeah, right," Yisrael rolled his eyes.

"No, really, I have. It's a Mercedes, in excellent condition. I just turned the key and the engine was purring right away. I'm taking it out of there tonight."

"Out of where?" Volf wanted to know.

"Nowhere special. Just Himmler's palatial abode." And how he loved watching his brothers' eyes fly wide open.

Yisrael laughed. "Okay, right. Enough with the joking. Let's get to bed, we're exhausted."

But Avraham could feel his adrenalin pumping. Waiting until his brothers slept deeply, he snuck back out to the castle, now in utter darkness. Avraham's excellent memory quickly took him to the underground parking space, where he swung the garage door up and looked inside. No one was around. He sat down behind the wheel, stroking the leather cover before turning the ignition on. Instantly the engine responded. He grinned, slowly drove out of the garage, stopped to close the garage door behind him, and steered to the palace gate.

On the way he waved to two British soldiers absently gazing at him at the roadblock. His heart pounded. He did his best to stay calm and look confident. Nonchalantly, the soldiers opened the gate. "Go, go," they waved him on. It never occurred to them that the car had just been stolen from Himmler's palace. Swallowing hard, he drove on slowly towards the junkyard, one of many owned by Jews good at finding ways to do business with almost anything, including the junk left from the war, which to them was a treasure.

The trader, a friend of Avraham's, almost fainted when he saw the shiny Mercedes roll in. "Help me dirty the car a bit with mud so it won't be identified," Avraham said.

In no time they also removed the military license plate from the car's front. "Better that there's no easily traceable number," Avraham's friend agreed.

"If anyone finds it, we can now say it was lying in the junkyard here," Avraham smiled slyly. To be safe, he opened the hood and twisted a few wires out of place. "Now, even if anyone does find it, they will believe it's from the junkyard," he added, clapping his friend on the shoulder.

British soldiers and a commander were in the junkyard the next morning following rumors that someone drove out in a luxury Merc towards the yard. Avraham and the trader stood next to the dirtied car and pretended to be busy with their work.

"Whose is this? How'd it get here?" the commander asked, slamming his stick down on the hood.

"Ah, we found it some weeks ago, abandoned on the roadside," Avraham said, straightening up and looking the officer in the eye.

But the commander wasn't convinced. "Where's the ignition key?" he asked angrily.

"Inside," Avraham said.

Slipping into the driver's seat, he turned the key in the switch. Nothing. He tried again, furious. Nothing. He got out. "Right. I don't know whether I should believe you but you can keep this thing. Let's move," he added as he turned to the soldiers and they drove off.

Barely able to keep themselves in check, the two burst into peals of laughter once the soldiers were out of earshot. "Good that you disconnected those wires! But tell me, Avraham, what do you need the car for? It's not for you. You need something smaller, less ostentatious. How about I buy the Merc from you at a fair price."

Avraham rejected the offer. The trader upped the price. Avraham was determined. "It's my car and I'm not selling it," he insisted. "I can do plenty of business with that car."

Reconnecting the wires to the engine, Avraham revved the car up and waved to the trader as he drove out of the junk yard. He cleaned it up only enough to avoid rousing anyone's suspicion that it was Himmler's, and stolen, and went for a ride in town. Yisrael and Volf realized with a shock that he'd been telling them the truth the whole time.

The soldiers weren't giving up so easily, though. They returned repeatedly to question Avraham about the car's source and how it got into Avraham's hands. He stuck with his version of the story: finding it in the junk yard, fixing it up, and therefore it's his. In the end, the soldiers showed up with a confiscation order. Avraham was beside himself with sorrow.

"That car's mine," he kept telling his brothers angrily, angered more when they shook their heads in doubt. How could their brother possibly think he'd take on the Allied Forces?

A week later Avraham was back at the military base, asking to speak to the commander who signed the confiscation order. He knocked loudly on the door. Without waiting, he barged right in. "Sir, officer, I'm willing to buy the car from you."

The officer smirked. "Well. And for how much?"

"Not in money. Right now, you can find a Mercedes in just about every junk yard but I'm just connected to this one emotionally. It was a pile of junk, which I managed to fix and get working again. It's like what my brothers and I went through under the Nazis, you know? Surely you get my drift, officer, sir? I'm willing to give you an almost new car instead of this one."

Surprised, the officer studied the lad. "Find me one like that and if I'm pleased, we'll make a swap."

Avraham raced back to the junk yard and hugged the trader. Both had golden hands when it came to mechanical objects, they were both resourceful, and within a short amount of time they found the chassis of an old Mercedes and enough spare parts to put an entire vehicle together. When they were done, they painted it to perfection.

A week later Avraham entered the military base in a gorgeous Mercedes. Coming out to look, the officer couldn't believe his eyes. "Officer, sir. I made a promise. And I've kept my promise," Avraham said, pointing to the car. "So, let's do the swap," Avraham added.

Strolling over to the car, the officer touched the steering wheel, circled the car, and asked to have the hood opened. He checked engine parts until, satisfied, he stepped back.

"Here, this is yours," the officer said, holding the keys to Himmler's Mercedes. "Just one moment," Avraham added calmly, "I want all this to be formal. Please give me a written confirmation that I've just legally purchased the car from the British army."

"No problem at all," the officer smiled and winked. "I'll get the clerk to type that up right away."

Thanking him, Avraham waited for the formal document on letterhead carrying the emblem of His Majesty's Royal Armed Forces. Back in the car, he drove off feeling a glow in his heart.

For four years, Avraham drove evil Himmler's car. As for the vehicle given to the officer, it ended its life two weeks later when its engine caught fire but by that point, the British officer couldn't blame Avraham who was keeping safely out of eyesight the entire time.

HANNAH AND VOLF

Having almost completely recuperated in what was now known as the Bergen-Belsen Displaced Persons Center, the Zaks brothers found work in Jewish organizations established to assist the displaced. Among them was the Jewish Joint Distribution Committee where Volf served as head accountant.

Twice a week, he devoted some time to his great love: the game of bridge. It wasn't the only thing attracting his attention. A pretty young woman had caught his eye, making waves with her bridge game skills. Hannah wasn't altogether unfamiliar: he knew her also from her job in the Joint's offices and frequently wondered about the flurry she always seemed to stir up. All it took was for Volf to gaze into her blue eyes, and he was hooked. Perhaps it was the complete contrast between them: he was quiet, moderate, cautious; she was opinioned and sharp-witted.

One evening he stood next to her while she was playing in another foursome and watched her actions closely. She plays excellently, she'd be really suited to my foursome, he thought. Excited at the idea, he touched her shoulder. She turned, her face questioning. "I play in another foursome, but I'm looking for the best partner I can find and I think we could play fabulously together. Shall we try?" Not waiting for an answer but not wanting to give her a chance to refuse, he rushed on. "I think my foursome plays at a fairly high level and would match your skills. You really should try us out."

"Oh, yes, I'd love to, but it's taken you so long to ask me," Hannah laughed. "And anyhow, you're my boss at work, so how could I possibly refuse?"

Holding his hand out, he led her to another table where a couple already sat ready to begin. Instantly there was wonderful rapport between Volf and Hannah. She didn't need more than a glance to figure out the cards he had. "Bridge is great for connecting people," he said and she nodded in agreement. By evening's end, the two had won all their games. As the last game of the evening came to an end, Volf stood, pulling her chair gently back and taking her hand. This time, he thought, I won't let her hand go, either.

"Walk you home?" he offered.

She laughed. "Sure. I'd be happy if you did, bridge champ."

Hand in hand they left the bridge club. "Well, Volf," she began to tell him as they walked, "I'm here with my mother. We were both in Auschwitz and from there, brought to Bergen-Belsen. This is where we were liberated. What happened to my father is anyone's guess. I'm afraid he's died. There's no reliable news yet. And what about you?"

It was too distressing to talk about his experiences. "It's a bit difficult for me to talk about all that just yet," he said after a pause. "I was liberated in Buchenwald and arrived here with my two brothers, Yisrael who's the firstborn, and Avraham, who's the family's youngest."

He paused again, feeling somehow released: for the first time in a long while, he could disclose some of what he'd been through. Talking to Hannah had a very natural air to it, and he longed to shed off some of the heavy burden of memories he was carrying. Hannah buoyed him with a sense of safety and security he'd never before experienced.

"Yisrael and I were in a terrible state," he felt comfortable continuing, "and needed several weeks of recuperation and intensive medical care. We have another brother, Yossef, and two sisters, Batya and Miriam. We still don't know about their fate, or that of Haiya, Yisrael's wife."

They chatted as they walked, until Hannah said that they were just houses away.

"If you don't mind, Hannah, I'd be happy to meet your mother."

"Of course," she smiled up at him immediately, "I'll introduce you."

Reaching the apartment, Hannah opened the door. "Mama?" she called out in the most natural way, "this is Volf. He's the greatest bridge player ever.

He's also my boss at the JJDC office." Then she gestured with her hand. "And this is my mother, Esther."

Esther stood up, smiling. Looking at her demeanor, Volf kept thinking: what a noble woman she is, her face still beams with love, gentleness. Bending slightly, he kissed her hand. Esther looked deeply into his eyes.

"You have lovely eyes," she said.

Back in their apartment, Volf's brothers noticed his good mood. "So? So…? Spill the beans?" they prodded him.

"I think I've just fallen in love," he said. Avraham and Yisrael gazed at each other with open mouths, then hugged him.

"Tell us, tell us everything, who is she, what's her name, how'd you meet?" So Volf told them everything. "Well," Yisrael concluded, "may this reach joyful fulfillment and let's hope that quite soon you can establish a fine Jewish home together," Avraham added, chuckling.

As the love between the two young people grew, Volf began to feel more at ease with the world. Her sensitive soul saw the sorrow in his eyes at not yet being able to find his siblings, but when they were together, his eyes lit up. He loved every moment of their time together, and the way she made his heart leap. Every evening after bridge, he walked her home, and every time before turning back to his apartment, he kissed her. I can't imagine my life without her, he thought, smiling as he walked home.

One morning, Volf noticed Hannah standing near his desk, intently focused on him. "Hannah? Yes?" he asked, raising his head.

"Tell me," she whispered, "are we a couple?"

He blushed and smiled shyly. "If you think so, then of course, we are, yes."

Hannah laughed. "And if I think we aren't?" she teased.

Gazing back at her with his compassionate eyes, he answered. "Even if you think we aren't, we definitely are a couple." In his eyes she saw only a sparkle. "But I think you should get back to work now, otherwise I'll be forced to rebuke you!" he said in jest.

"As though you possibly could!" she laughed, quickly walking to her desk with a grin on her face.

The whole office knew: those two were madly in love.

MEETING

Incredulous, Yisrael was staring at the small postcard. "Volf, come here, quick!" He held the postcard out. In an instant Volf recognized Haiya's handwriting.

"My beloved Yisrael, we found one of the notes you sent with messengers. A soldier hung it on the Breslow railway station noticeboard. Yossef, Miriam, and Batya are with me. We're in Prague on our way to Bergen-Belsen. I'll send another postcard when we know our precise arrival. The main thing is that everyone's alive!"

"Yisrael! Yisrael!" Volf shouted for joy. Yisrael burst into sobs. Since the brief note Misha had managed to bring to Blechhammer, he hadn't heard a word. This endless period of uncertainty and anxiety had come to an end with one postcard. Volf hugged Yisrael. "Our family's made it!" he kept repeating.

This was a moment Volf wanted Hannah to share. He asked her to come over right away. She rushed over but seeing the brothers' happy faces, realized that there must be a sign of life from their family after having sent hundreds of notices out across Europe. Just then Avraham walked in and caught the excitement. "What's going on here?" he asked, seeing his brothers crying. But in an instant, he realized these were tears of joy.

"Signs of life! Your family's survived!" Hannah pointed to the postcard.

Yisrael threw his arms up in the air. One small postcard, one unbelievable message: the promise of a family about to reunite.

Questions hung in the air. How did they survive? Where did they come across Yossef? "Brothers, let's go," Yisrael said.

Not a word of explanation was needed. They strode to the synagogue, passing the postcard from hand to hand, kissing the words "We're all alive." Standing before the Holy Ark, they pronounced one of the most unique blessings in the Jewish liturgy together: *Blessed are you, Lord our G-d, King of the Universe, who keeps us alive, and keeps us sustained, and has brought us to this occasion.*

"And what an occasion it is," Volf said. "We're healthy, and all of us are alive. For years we've been waiting for this moment. Nothing could be greater."

Yisrael stood silently but inside, his emotions were running wild. They sat for a while in the synagogue, slowly calming down, until Yisrael spoke at last. "On June 23rd, 1943, my world was crushed. I lost both my parents, and decided that I had no G-d. He abandoned me. But today some of my faith has been restored." His brothers nodded.

"I'll wait to hear their stories and then decide if there is a G-d, or not," Volf said softly before smiling. "The truth is, I don't really care if there's a G-d or not. The main thing is that I have my brothers and sisters. I have my family again. G-d can wait his turn. C'mon, let's go eat at Hannah's."

Three days later, a second postcard arrived. "We're on our way. Everywhere we go, we're helped, and the trains are running fine. On Thursday, 30 August at 5.20 p.m., we will reach the Celle station from Hanover. We all miss you so much and are dying to hug you all." Yisrael's hands shook. "Two days from now! We'll reunite at last."

That Thursday, the brothers woke early. Avraham buffed his Mercedes with care until it shone more than it had ever done before. Shortly before the time they had planned on setting out, another vehicle which they'd ordered drove up. Avraham drove the Mercedes, Yisrael sat in the front passenger seat, with Volf and Hannah seated in the back. The second vehicle, for the rest of the family, followed. The journey passed in silence; each brother lost in his own thoughts.

Avraham was thinking about their family home. He remembered kissing the mezuzah when they'd snuck out of the ghetto. He wondered if Yossef would continue being silent. Gazing at the heavens as the car sped on, Yisrael was thinking about his wife and how he'd try to make it up to her for the terrible events she'd experienced.

Volf sobbed, wondering what his sisters had been through, whether they were whole and healthy, or had been compromised in some way. Then he thought about Yossef and where he'd been the whole time, alone, without siblings for support – knowing that he himself would never have stayed alive without his brothers nearby. He sobbed, stopped, and then sobbed again. Hannah placed her arm around him, wiping the tears off his cheeks.

At 5 p.m., they drove into the station. Avraham wiped the seats once again. He wasn't about to let a single speck of dust cling to them. They deserve the same honor that a king deserves, he thought.

Built of gray stone blocks blackened by soot and fires, the railway station was engulfed by the chime of bells from the nearby church. They waited outside on a stone bench. "Did they ring four months ago, too?" Volf asked cynically.

The clickety-clack of a train's approach grew louder; the brakes beginning to squeal and the engine chuffing as the train slowed and came into view. As though signaled to do so, all of them checked their watches. No, too early. Not the train they were expecting. Hannah was gripped by fear, unable to utter a word, as she remembered that just such a train had brought her from Auschwitz to Bergen-Belsen. She'd stood, crushed among hundreds of fellow Jews in a cattle car. That train, too, had passed through Celle and ended its journey in hell. She shuddered and slipped her arm through Volf's, grasping him tightly.

"It's okay, Hannah," he said softly, understanding her, "the war's over and from now on, things will only be good. There's nothing evil in those trains now." But Hannah tightly cupped her hands over her ears until the very last carriage had passed and the wheels' vibrations on the tracks had dissipated. Only then did she begin to breathe easily again.

Volf, Avraham, and Yisrael were immersed in their own thoughts. Although this train would bring them only good, it reminded them of their journey to Buchenwald on the cattle trains, lying on the carriage floor, exhausted, starving, watching death slowly overcome them. Now they stared at the tracks, glancing frequently at the station clock. Only when the stationmaster announced over the loudspeaker that the Hanover train would be thirty minutes late, did they relax a little. Yisrael's fingers were tapping his knee; Volf was gazing intently at the clock and silently counting the seconds ticking by; Avraham was standing, pacing, sitting, and then pacing again. For the thousandth time Yisrael re-read the postcard to be sure he hadn't gotten the day or time wrong.

The instant that the train could be heard approaching, everyone stood, moving closer to the platform's edge to catch a first glimpse. The train's horn sounded, growing stronger as it rolled slowly into the station.

"The Hanover train has arrived," the stationmaster announced.

"How will we know which carriage they're in?" Avraham suddenly asked. "Don't worry," Yisrael soothed, "it's a small train, it's a small platform, we'll see them right away, I'm sure of it."

Slowly the train drew to a halt. Doors opened. People stepped tiredly down. The three brothers stood midway along the platform, glancing constantly in both directions. What if.... They were all thinking. What if the girls hadn't made it to the train?

Batya was the first to jump down from a nearby carriage, followed by Miriam and Haiya. Avraham was the first to spot them. "There, look, over there!" Six people raced towards each other. Dozens of travelers stopped, watching the three young men roaring at the top of their voice towards three young women who'd frozen in their places. The Zaks men shouted, giving vent to their pent-up emotions; the Zaks women sobbed and smiled as they kept their arms up, waving. Always the chatty ones, this time the Zaks women were utterly silent as their brothers, usually the silent ones, shouted and cried, cried and shouted.

How they hugged, with their knuckles turning white under the pressure as they came together in a tight group. They sobbed out loud, they laughed, they sobbed, they stood and hugged each other, making up for two lost years. The train was not moving on yet: people inside and others on the platform watched the family reunion. Germans on the train watched, too, and not a word came from their lips. How well they understood the meaning of this scene, their gaze glued to siblings lovingly holding on to each other.

"But where's Yossef?" Avraham suddenly shouted. The Zaks women looked around. Indeed, Yossef was nowhere to be seen. A moment of sheer panic clutched at six hearts. And a moment later, dissipated, as Yossef jumped down from the carriage, smiling.

"I'm here too," he said.

Having given them some time together, Hannah now came at a sprint and joined the family embrace. No one asked who this young woman joining them was; they simply included her with the same warmth and love. The church bells rang out again. And this time, the bells' melody was pleasant. Looking up at the bell tower, they saw the bells swing back and forth, tolling harmoniously. Pigeons swarmed up into the sky as though announcing a welcome.

Arms around each other, the family began making its way through the station. Only once they'd left the gray stone building, could the slow clatter of wheels on the rails be heard as the train began rolling on to its next stop.

THE HOWL OF FAREWELL

Before piling into the cars, Hannah was introduced to the rest of the family. Haiya, Batya, and Miriam secretly hoped that "the girls" would include her too as soon as possible. "If only Papa and Mama were here, to see us together, be together with us..."Batya's voice trailed off as she spoke the words that her siblings were thinking.

Driving back to Bergen-Belsen, each of them had the same thought: later we'll tell each other everything, but for now, we'll just be happy over reuniting at last.

Not long into the ride, Hannah asked if they could stop for a minute at the gates of Bergen-Belsen, the concentration camp purposely burned to the ground mere days after liberation to halt the severe spread of typhus. Hannah wanted to show them where she'd been, where she was liberated. The motors were switched off. A murky silence filled the air. They stood, eight in all: brothers, sisters, a wife, and a steady girlfriend, gazing at the dark, gloomy place where so many had needlessly died, where so many had gone up in the hell of flame and smoke, and evaporated.

"This is where they almost succeeded in exterminating us. But here we are, alive, because of our sheer willpower," Hannah said. Just a few months ago, they might have ended in one of the many hells too: Blechhammer, Buchenwald, Gross-Rosen, Ludwigsdorf, Görlitz, Langenstein. And yet their pledge to stay strong for each other had gotten them through one horror after another. Gazing at the burnt concentration camp, they noted how it contrasted so sharply with the forest surrounding it, with the soft, bright green grass covering those horrors.

Orange and pink hues cast a regal glow as the sun was about to set, its last rays of light glimmering through the treetops on the place that had buzzed with murderous terror. In the distance, a short howl was heard. They spun around towards the sound's direction as the howling, not harsh but low and pleasantly toned, grew closer.

Out of the forest came a large white wolf, walking slowly towards them. Mesmerized, they watched it confidently approach, lifting its head, and opening its mouth in what was clearly a sign of friendship. Step by step, it came closer – almost to within touching distance. It howled briefly, its eyes sparkling. But inside the shining green eyes were rays of orange-red light, as though reflecting the sunset. The wolf stood before them. They gazed at it, never moving from their places. It raised its tail high and growled gently. Suddenly they heard more howls coming from the forest. They grew stronger but were not menacing. Was this a pack of wolves?

Volf couldn't resist. Placing his hands around his mouth like a megaphone, he let out a long howl. His family watched, startled at first, and then one by one, they did the same, joining him. There the eight of them stood, howling all their joy, their sorrow, and their gratitude for being reunited, their devastation at having lost their parents. Their hearts released pent-up emotions into the forest.

Was the great, white wolf with green eyes smiling at them again? Slowly it turned and accompanied by their howls, stood at the edge of the forest as the sun slid behind the trees, darkness fell, and the moon began to rise in an orange halo as the pack's howls from the forest grew louder and louder. Stopping at the first line of trees, the white wolf was joined by six wolf cubs flanking it like bodyguards protecting their leader.

The pack moved slowly together into the forest: the white wolf, a proud leader, escorted by the younger, livelier wolves with lives still to live.

Eight young adults stood in stunned silence, watching the scene unfold.

Even after they could no longer see the wolves, all eight of them continued to stand, without moving, for several minutes. At last, they turned, walking back to the cars. Far in the distance, they could hear howls growing fainter until, slowly, silence settled on the region.

In silence they drove back to their destination.

CATCHING UP

The cars pulled up outside Esther and Hannah's Bergen-Belsen home. Barely able to contain her excitement, Esther waited for them, her delicate biscuits in bowls on the table, and pots of tea ready. "Come in, come in, welcome," she greeted them, gesturing with her arms. "Come, sit down." Looking around the table, the Zakses smiled at each other with great love but Yoheved and Hanokh's absence was blatant and still too difficult to mention.

Batya was the first to speak, her heart bursting. "I need to get something off my chest," she began. "I left Papa when I went to find medication because he was dying there, in the yard, and that image hasn't left me throughout the whole war. I let our father down. When Volf didn't return, I realized he must've been caught. So I went to the clinic, and I slapped the evil woman in the clinic who wouldn't give me Papa's pills. I was so mad at her that I think I could have killed her with my bare hands. I was thinking of Papa. I took the pills and ran as quickly as I could to where I'd left him but he'd disappeared. I looked everywhere but couldn't find him. Papa died there in the yard because of me. Then I saw a truck with corpses and realized he was probably among them. He died because of me. I needed to tell you that."

Overcoming the tears filling his eyes, Avraham reached out and took her hand gently. *He's matured so much since we were all separated*, Batya thought, *just two years, and look how he's become an adult.* Then he stood and went to hug her.

"Batya, you're not guilty at all," he said softly. "You didn't find him in the yard because I took him from there." He turned to glance at his brothers, who already knew the details. They nodded.

"You took him?" Batya exclaimed, her eyes open wide in surprise.

"Slowly. This is very hard for me to talk about," Avraham continued. "I hid Mama in the apartment upstairs and went to look for Papa. I found him in the yard, alive. Are you listening, Batya? He was still alive."

A storm of emotions battled inside her. "But how is that possible?"

"I carried him upstairs. I barely made it, but in the end, I did, I put Papa down next to Mama and went to look for you and Volf. I think that is when you came looking for him, I was partway up the stairs with him in my arms." Avraham's hand went to his heart; it was beating hard. "When I went downstairs, Gestapo soldiers were patrolling the streets looking for Jews who were hiding. So I turned back, wanting to get home, and Papa came out into the yard, walking slowly on his own two legs."

In shock, Miriam called out. "What happened, Avraham? Tell us."

He swallowed hard as he remembered that terrible day. "I hid in the bushes, fearing that the Gestapo would find me." His tone had dropped almost to a whisper. "And then I heard shots. I couldn't see exactly what happened but the shots came from the Gestapo. I couldn't do anything. If I'd have come out of hiding, they would have shot me too. And Mama was upstairs. So I stayed hidden until the shots stopped. There was a lot of shooting…."

Avraham paused for several seconds but no one spoke, waiting for him to compose himself. "Then I heard the Germans moving away, and then everything went quiet, so I came out of hiding. Papa lay there, blood everywhere. He was dead. The German's shot him dead."

Silently, the family watched Avraham, who trembled as he remembered the events. Volf hugged him close. "I realized," Avraham continued, "that the Germans had gone into our house. I hugged Papa, I cried. His blood was all over my clothes."

"And Mama? What happened to Mama?" Miriam couldn't contain herself.

Avraham fell silent. "I waited until the Germans had gone," his voice was cracking as he sobbed and spoke. "I left Papa where he was and went back into the apartment. Mama wasn't in the room where I'd left her, nor in any of the rooms. The Germans had taken her to the Auschwitz train." He drew a deep breath: if only he could erase that day from his memory. "So I went to the train, telling myself that now I was an orphan and what was the point of living. It's only because of Limping Henshil that I didn't get sent to Auschwitz but managed to join the second group. That's where I found our three brothers."

Batya raised her arms, feeling the distress ease out of her heart. "I'm not guilty then," she wept. "I didn't kill Papa. He came to me in a dream and told me that; he said, 'Daughter, you're not to blame. I'm with you and I'll help you.' He promised and kept his promise."

To Batya it felt that not just a single stone had been lifted from her heart but a whole mountain of guilt. "Miriam and I went back to our home in Strzemieszyce after we were liberated. The house is filthy. Nothing of us remains there, except the mezuzah, a reminder that we once lived there." She paused, gathering her thoughts. "A rude Polish woman opened the door, a real beast. She tried to get rid of us. Can you believe that? We get back home and she's doing her best not to let us in. Criminal." A look of disgust came across her face. "That revolting creature wasn't at all ashamed to offer us the room at the end of the corridor for rent. She was renting all the rooms out. 'But only if you really want it,' she said to us," Batya mimicked the woman's tone.

"And you won't believe," Miriam took over, "what a horrible smell the house had." Nausea swept over her as she remembered. "Instead of Mama's chicken soup and Shabbat cholent, the place smelled like rot. A pigsty is more pleasant than there!"

Emphatically, Batya nodded. "We swore we wouldn't go back there, ever!" she brought her palm firmly down on the table. "The house belongs to us, but it's no longer ours." She paused after that short outburst. "But there are also good Poles. We met Marek and the doctor, whose medicines saved us in the camp. They took us to Papa's burial place. He's buried along with other Jews from our town that the Nazis killed that day. Miriam and I marked the grave clearly. When the time comes, we will bring him for burial in Israel, but until then, we can all be comforted that at least he is buried."

This news moved them deeply. But Batya had more to tell them. "Marek and the doctor acted like saints. They not only buried Papa and the others to prevent them from being dismembered by wild animals, hawks and eagles, but identified all the others murdered that day. All of them! Here's the list they gave us, with all the names, and Papa's first. Can you imagine that? Two Poles digging a grave and placing the bloodied, shot bodies inside, and making sure that the names won't be erased from peoples' hearts. Wonderful people, Marek and the doctor."

Batya passed the list to Avraham, who read the familiar names. Batya waited until the list eventually made its way back to her. "And now I have a special surprise," she smiled broadly, "a memory of our lives from before the war. Look…" and she placed the enlarged family photo in the table's center. Yisrael picked it up, gazed at it, sighed and smiled, and passed it on. It went from one to the next, bringing smiles and chatter and laughter to the room.

"This is how we looked before the start of September 1939. Mama, Papa, and even Yitzhak's here too. Isn't that wonderful?"

"You couldn't have brought a better or more important item if you'd tried," Yisrael grinned. "This is so much more valuable than the house."

"Thank you," Volf whispered. "Miriam, Batya, I have no words. This is unbelievable."

And once again the Zaks family fell silent but this time there was no tension. The war was over, they were alive, and they were together, just as Papa Hanokh had always wanted.

SAYING KADDISH

"What will we do tomorrow?" Miriam asked.

"Haiya will move into my room," Yisrael laughed. "In case you've forgotten, we are a married couple!" He never took his eyes off her the whole time, and she blushed. "Batya and Miriam, you can share one room for now."

"And tomorrow morning," Yisrael said, "we will go to the synagogue." He spoke softly but with authority. "It has a Holy Ark with Torah scrolls, and there's always a quorum of people praying. We will go to recite Kaddish over Papa and Mama and the worshippers will answer 'Amen.'" The others around the table were taken by surprise. "The truth is," Yisrael added, "we never really conducted the mourning rituals in any meaningful way. For two years, yes, we ached inside, but we were constantly focused on fighting to stay alive. We never consciously devoted any time to honor our parents' passing. We owe this to them."

Volf shook his head. "I think that we shouldn't only recite the Kaddish. We should actually conduct the proper seven-day mourning period. We're all here now because of them, because they taught us how to stay together. We saved each other from various situations. But they taught us how to do that. We will spend the seven days of mourning in Hannah's home. We will give our parents the utmost respect. We will sit on low stools, together, as the Jewish custom holds, and talk about our family, our parents, and honor them through the education they instilled in us."

Miriam yawned, which made Batya and Haiya yawn. They were so tired: from traveling, from the excitement, from sitting up late talking together. Miriam and Batya thanked Esther and Hannah and went to lie down on freshly laundered sheets, falling asleep right away. Batya dreamed that Papa was watching her, the love pouring from his eyes. 'I told you you're not to blame,' he bent low to whisper in her ear, 'and now you've heard it for yourself. I'll continue watching over you, over all of you.' Batya's sleep was deeper than it had been for many months. Her dream meant that wherever she and her siblings would go, Papa Hanokh would be with them in spirit.

***

Quietly, they filed into the synagogue early the next morning. It was a modest space, with several benches allocated for the women. The rabbi faced the Holy Ark. Yisrael had already contacted him earlier the previous day, seeking his guidance.

"I would be honored to stand here with you and pray for your parents, of blessed memory. Any Jew would be glad of such a privilege, of the opportunity to show respect and fulfill this important commandment."

The synagogue doors opened. Dozens of men wrapped in prayer shawls entered, friends and acquaintances of the Zaks brothers. Miriam and Batya hugged Haiya, Hannah, and Esther as the synagogue slowly filled up. The worshippers stood in complete silence as the four brothers took their places before the Holy Ark, overwhelmed by the sanctity of the moment, reciting the Kaddish prayer clearly and together.

"Exalted and sanctified is G-d's great name throughout the world... glorified and celebrated, lauded and praised... far beyond all hymn of glory which mortals may offer... May He who brings peace to the universe bring peace to us all and to all the people of Israel. And let us say: Amen."

The worshippers responded with a rousing "Amen," and silence filled the synagogue. The generation that survived saw their parents in their imagination, just as everyone there saw loved ones they'd lost in their minds' eyes.

Turning to face the community, Yisrael spoke, his voice wavering with emotion. "Thank you, my friends. Yoheved, our late mother, died in Auschwitz and has neither a burial place nor a gravestone. There is only the memory of who she was, and we will never forget her. We do know where Hanokh, our Papa, is buried, because two good Polish men who cared about him buried him themselves. Before this community as our witnesses, we commit to reburying him in the Land of Israel. My sisters Batya and Miriam were at the burial site, saw it, and marked it. So now I have sworn: when it becomes possible, we will give him the burial he deserves."

Moved by Yisrael's words, people sobbed silently for their own murdered family members.

"We will carry out the seven days of mourning together and honor our deceased and yours. We will remember them all."

Fulfilling the seven-day mourning ritual led the usually silent Zakses to talking, and none more so than Yossef. "I was as skinny as a skeleton. I hadn't seen food for days," he told the family. "In the camp, when I was weak and hungry, I'd go towards the fence separating the camps to look at girls. There was no food, but at least I could look at young women. And then one day I hear shouts. 'Yossef? Yossef?' I looked up and who did I see if not Haiya, Batya, and Miriam."

"I kept telling myself, 'Yossef, you're hallucinating. Either you're dead and they are too and so they've come to heaven to receive you, or…' I couldn't get my mind around the idea that they were really there. I pinched myself and actually said 'ouch'. I needed to know this wasn't a dream."

Guests visiting to comfort and console the family, as is the Jewish custom during the mourning period, smiled. "I walked towards the fence and what did I see? My family. I was so sure I'd left hell behind and gone to heaven because it wasn't possible that our girls were in hell. But they saved me. They brought me food, a bit of soup, and medicine. It's to their credit that I'm alive."

Avraham grinned. "Well, and we at Blechhammer, we kept praying that the Allies would keep bombing it, because Volf had turned into the camp's bomb defusing expert," he said, pointing at Volf. "A simple equation: every bomb defused equaled one more slice of bread. The Americans eventually did bomb the place up, the Germans kept diving into their bunkers, some bombs exploded, and the unexploded ones kept us fed with bread."

"A man came up to us in our camp," Miriam said, talking softly, "and offered us a jar full of diamonds. We could have bought Himmler's Bergen-Belsen palace three times over. But Haiya refused the offer. 'We're not taking anything from anyone,' she insisted. We could've been millionaires," she sighed as everyone shook their heads in disbelief. "Ah, well," Miriam's voice carried resignation, "Haiya always knew what she was talking about. She saved us quite a few times."

Day after day for seven days, the siblings talked, sharing their stories and experiences, and bringing up memories of times before the war. Every morning began with the sorrow of the mourning of their parents, but as friends began to join them, sit with them, and talk, their moods improved greatly. Now they could talk more freely without getting as choked up as they had. Sometimes they even laughed, lightening the load they carried in their hearts and souls. Hannah and Esther fed the mourners and their guests, glad to be involved. As the last day reached its end, the Zakses felt they'd been through a powerful experience together, increasing their pain yet easing their minds simultaneously, as though being reborn into new lives.

"Thank you, all of you," Batya said when visitors were leaving. "We've met so many wonderful people." To Yisrael, she acknowledged the mourning period with simple words that spoke for them all. "It was a wonderful idea for us to keep the traditions of mourning. It's been amazing, enlightening, we've cried and laughed together, we've remembered together. But most of all, we've been infused with new strength to go into the future as a family."

THE SHABBAT MEAL

"This coming Shabbat there'll be an evening meal on Friday in the tradition of the Zaks family, and for Shabbat's lunch the next day, there'll be cholent," Miriam stated. "I'm trusting my brothers to get everything I need, right? Yossef, Avraham, it's your responsibility to get hold of the food and wine. I'm relying on you," Miriam laughed.

Yossef winked and flicked his sister's cheek playfully.

"One hundred percent!" Avraham said. "Don't worry, Miriam. We'll find everything so that this meal will be just like what we're used to!"

That Friday, after Shabbat began at sundown, the family gathered in the home where Esther, Hannah, and Volf were living. From a distance, Yossef could smell the soup. Avraham caught whiffs of the cholent's aromas slowly wafting through the air. One thought kept running through everyone's minds: at last, the family is together again. Or, almost all the family. Volf showed Hannah how they used to set the table, and how their chairs should be positioned, each with their fixed place. "And at one end of the table, an empty chair, for Papa; opposite him, a chair for Mama. We'll set it up exactly the way it used to be," he explained.

Hannah was more than a little surprised. Clearly the Zakses had their own family customs.

"Hannah, Volf, thank you so much!" Yisrael said, nodding with approval. "I wanted to check that there were chairs for our parents." Hot on his heels were Haiya, Miriam, Avraham, and Yossef, each of them bearing pots of food. Yossef and Avraham had put all their energy into making sure nothing was missing for this first Shabbat meal together, from the goose fat and fried gizzards to the pâté made from grilled chicken livers.

Miriam had baked fresh challah; its scent and the aroma of fresh chicken soup made Avraham tear up. He sat in his permanent place. "Just like home," he whispered.

The smell of goose baking in the oven had Yossef wiping a tear away. "Only Mama and Papa are missing," he sighed.

Each Zaks family member gravitated to his or her place around the table so naturally that an outsider would have been excused for thinking the tradition had never endured a hiatus. Now the table held extra place settings and chairs, one on each side of Volf, for Esther and Hannah.

Yisrael stood. "Let's drink a glass of wine in memory of our beloved parents. Their chairs may seem empty, but we know that they're here with us."

Yossef and Volf filled everyone's glasses, including those of the absent parents. Then Yisrael began to recite the traditional Shabbat blessings over the wine. *"Blessed are you, Lord our G-d, King of the Universe, who created the fruit of the vine."*

'L'Chaim!' they called out. To life, to life! Yisrael broke the challah into chunks, scattering salt on each piece and passing them down both sides of the table from one person to the next. The challah's aroma had a profound effect on them all.

"I'm home at last," Batya whispered. "It's the challah, all of us sitting around the table together, plus the flavors of home. I'd love some more challah please." Avraham passed her a chunk.

"Me, I'm waiting for the soup. To me, that's the smell of home," Yossef chimed in.

Brought to the table in its large pot, the lid was taken off as they sat and watched, steam filling the room, which gave the ambience of warmth and love. Yossef began to eat his soup, but his siblings spent a long time gazing at the soup, lost in their thoughts.

Volf pushed his bowl away a little. “I don’t want to eat it too quickly,” he said. “I want to feel it…smell it. I don’t care if the house smells of soup all night!” he laughed.

Avraham, on the other hand, drank each spoonful slowly, relishing every drop. “This soup’s amazing,” he said, looking around at his siblings, “but I’m already looking forward to tomorrow’s cholent. For me, *that’s* the smell of home.”

There they sat, alternating between laughing and the occasional crying, chatting, or occasionally keeping quiet, enjoying their renewed Shabbat tradition together. “This, I believe,” Volf said, “is our true liberation meal.”

LOVE IS IN THE AIR, EVERYWHERE WE LOOK AROUND

It was the start of 1946, and Haiya was so excited. Not only had she and her brother Shalom found each other at last, but Shalom and his wife Aviva were anxiously awaiting the birth of their first child. Taking Batya's care-giving experience into account, Haiya asked if she'd be willing to travel to Munich to help Aviva and the baby. Of course Batya agreed. Taking the train, she was scheduled to stay with Lazar Levy and his wife Lilly, long-time friends from Strzemieszyce. Reaching the Levy's home that evening, she was surprised to find a young, handsome, muscular, young man there who was nonetheless modest and even a touch bashful. She gazed at him. A bit disconcerted, he looked down.

"If I may ask," Batya spoke to him using the formal, polite, and somewhat distanced phrasing, "who are you?"

He stood, walked over to her, and bowed slightly. Struck by her beauty, he kissed the back of her hand, following the customs of the times.

"Yossef Mondry," he answered.

"And are you indeed wise?" Batya played on his family name and its Polish meaning.

He blushed, tongue-tied and unable to answer for a moment. "Not really, but yes," he said before returning to the sofa. Batya laughed.

"Ah, but he's not for you, Batya. He's for Miriam," Lilly said. "I've got someone else up my sleeve for you." Batya's face registered surprise. "You'll get to meet him later," Lilly added.

Shortly before dinner, Leib walked in. He was flabbergasted to see Batya, love of his childhood and youth, standing there. She studied him. "It's you?? This is who you've got set up for me, Lilly? He was after me for years when we were kids." Turning to Leib, she hugged him warmly. "But you've remained short as you always were, haven't you, Leib Levy! Couldn't you steal a bit more height after all these years that we haven't seen each other? Ah well. But aren't you anyhow the cutest."

When Leib looked at her, his eyes were filled with love. He never skipped a beat when he spoke. "I always loved you, Batya, and always will. You won't slip away this time."

"But I managed to slip away every day on the train to high school, didn't I?"

"You certainly did, but now I've got more experience," he smiled, speaking with confidence.

Aviva wondered what they were talking about. Lazar, Leib's brother, turned to her. "I have to tell Mondry and Aviva what happened."

"Tell, tell," Batya said, "and I promise to add my two cents' worth as well."

"Every morning, Leib waited for the train. He wanted to catch the same train that Batya, and her brothers Yossef and Avraham caught, to high school. He always arrived in a rush and hopped on at the last second and then he'd start looking for the Zaks boys and even more especially, for the Zaks girls."

"And he always found them. You should have seen his face when I hid once behind the seat. He wanted to get off and not go to school that day." They smiled when they noticed Batya's big smiles. "Oy, how I pitied him, so I suddenly jumped up and his white face got its color back immediately."

"Every day," Lazar continued the tale, "I said to him, 'Why don't you invite her over to us?'"

Without skipping a beat, Leib continued. "I did, but she always turned me down."

"Of course. You were too short. How can I go to someone who's so short?"

Leib's eyes were filled with joy when he looked at her. "Oh sure. So, tell me why you never wanted to sit next to me on the train?"

"You're still asking that? You always vomited. You and your vomit bag were the best of buddies, and Yossef and Avraham had to give you their bags too. We even knew the exact moment when you'd start."

Leib wasn't at all embarrassed. "It was all worth it, Batya. Every minute with you in the train to school was a minute of sheer joy for me. It's actually the only reason I went to school. Just know this, Miss Batya: throughout the war, those memories of our train rides kept me strong, they gave me the will to live, my dear."

Walking over to him, Batya embraced and kissed him. "We always knew you were a wonderful guy but we Zaks girls are used to tall…"

They sat with their arms around each other the whole evening. In fact, they spent their entire lives with their arms around each other.

Batya noticed Yossel Mondry sitting quietly. "Mondry, tell us about yourself, where you were in the war, because if you're going to meet my sister, you first need to pass my test," she laughed. "And in our family, if all goes well, you'll be 'Mondry' because my brother's name is Yossef and we'd want to avoid confusion."

"Mondry was a partisan and an officer in the Red Army," Lilly explained. "He fought the Germans from the forests throughout the war. He's strong, muscular, and I doubt there's anyone who could knock him down. The Russian officers were all very afraid of him."

"Strong, tough," Batya repeated, "and wise?"

"You'll discover his wisdom as time goes by," Lilly said.

Two weeks later, Lazar and Lilly felt that there was great value in both Leib and Mondry returning to Bergen-Belsen. Batya wrote a letter to the rest of the Zakses, informing them that two young men would be joining her: Leib, who they knew well, and Mondry, whose journey was for a very worthwhile purpose.

Miriam and Avraham waited in the Mercedes for the three travelers to step out of the Celle station, load their bags in the boot, and set off for Bergen-Belsen. Quickly taking in the muscular young man's appearance, Miriam immediately understood 'very worthwhile' and grinned at her sister.

Back in the apartment, the family was waiting. Leib was warmly received: he'd grown up with them all, and they knew he'd not only be a wonderful match for Batya but a great asset to their activities. Batya, for her part, had begun to show some hesitation over accepting him as her beau. "He needs to make a little more of an effort," she said.

Miriam looked straight at Mondry. Every so often he'd look up, their gazes connecting. She smiled. Batya stood, raising a toast. "So, we've got Leib back, but don't be too joyous yet. He still isn't in the inner circle of Zakses." She smiled at him. "He's got some work to do to earn that privilege. And I've brought Mondry with me, a war hero. While we were suffering in the camps, he was fighting in forests. A brave man. It seems that the other officers in his unit in the Red Army who absorbed partisans into their tanks were dead scared of him. As his name suggests, he is truly 'mondry.' And you, Miriam, I think you really should get to know him a bit better. You're the bravest woman I know, and you deserve a war hero just like yourself."

A few glasses of wine later, Mondry suddenly stood up. "Dear friends," he began, "this is the first time I've felt that I truly do have friends. I've known you for such a brief time, I've known Batya a little longer, but after the war I had no family, and you make me feel wonderful. Thank you."

Removing his jacket, he sat down, leaning back more relaxedly in his short-sleeved shirt. Miriam was mesmerized, charmed by the muscular arms fit for a wrestler. To her, he epitomized Samson, the legendary, strong man in the Bible.

Watching her sister closely, Batya laughed. "Miriam? Is your imagination going into overdrive?" Miriam blushed.

Batya turned to Mondry. "Listen, despite being a bit skinny, she's no push-over. She stood up to the Gestapo at our house and wouldn't let the Nazis take our parents' bed. She stood up to them in the ghetto, too. She steps up, faces them and they back off. Her eyes are tougher than your biceps. On the way to Strzemieszyce, when she felt endangered, she wasn't afraid of opening the door of the military vehicle she was riding in while the Russian officer was driving. She stepped out but the officer and his men got tossed into the ditch. She's as gutsy as a partisan."

Miriam went over and sat next to Mondry: "Prove you are indeed 'mondry.'"

"Speech is silver, silence is golden," he answered. "I learned that from my rabbi."

From that moment on, he was no longer shy. Mondry and Miriam's love grew, remaining steadfast until their dying day.

THE IRON CROSS

Life in Bergen-Belsen took on an increasingly routine structure. Avraham and Yossef continued doing what they knew best: buying cheap, selling for more. Experience gained in the shop under their father's guidance was proving its value: they were slowly building up a business that bought and sold cloth, and their work was beginning to turn a profit.

Avraham was taking advantage of his good connections with the American soldiers to find out in advance about every shipment of cloth designated for the army. Soldiers in charge of military supplies would always cream off something for private business. The brothers purchased cheaply from the soldiers, who could never figure out why the army needed cloth at all. The soldiers were pleased with Avraham and Yossef buying from them. Avraham and Yossef were even more pleased, selling the cloth to sewing factories at much higher sums.

Back from a visit to Hanover, Yossef called Avraham over. "Listen. Jewelry, diamonds, gems… they're small and valuable. We can hide them anywhere. The Germans have got so much, and the soldiers will soon start going home and what will they bring their girlfriends and wives? Anything that sparkles. Let's start working with jewels."

It took Avraham no more than a few seconds to think the idea over. "Where do we begin?"

"Money, we've got. A respectable Mercedes, we've got. How to make an impression, we know. We'll dress elegantly and I'll do the talking."

The next morning, they were off for Hanover. Avraham drove the buffed and polished Mercedes, his left arm hanging out of the window. From the American cigarette between his fingers, he'd draw in a long breath, releasing it slowly in smoky swirls.

"They sure knew how to build roads, those despicable Germans. Bombing barely damaged them. These concrete roads are so tough they'll last forever."

Yossef glanced at his brother. What an expert driver he'd become without ever learning how to drive, unlike Yossef who'd been trained professionally in the Polish army.

"Let's go to the elite neighborhoods. Lots of war widows there, and I'm sure they don't need all their jewelry. They need money for food."

Driving into an area that had an air of pre-war prestige now supplanted by rampant negligence, Yossef guided Avraham. "Find the largest house in the neighborhood. That's where we'll stop and knock on the door."

Avraham pulled up next to a home surrounded by a wall. A great iron gate showing specks of rust was open. The wall had been breached, stones scattered about on the ground. They halted at the front door, smoothed their suits down, glanced at each other and smiled. Each knew what the other was thinking: Who could ever have imagined where we were just six months ago!

"Yossef," Avraham stopped Yossef's hand before he knocked, "what do we even understand about all of this? We've never dealt in gems before."

"We're about to learn, Avraham, and we'll learn fast. By the end of today, we'll be experts. If we think the way Papa did, everything will work out fine."

Yossef knocked. They could hear footsteps approaching. The door was opened no more than a sliver, and an elderly woman peeped out. "Yes? I don't give donations, I have no money, so please go away."

The tip of Yossef's shoe was already in the doorway as she leaned forward to push the door shut.

"Madam, we're not beggars. Look at our car there, in the driveway."

Slipping her glasses on and peering at the Mercedes, she looked the two well-dressed young men up and down, her face registering surprise. "Well, in that case, why are you here?"

"May we come in and explain how we can indeed help, Madam?"

She hesitated a bit, but eventually opened the door and gestured them to come in. They glanced at the armchairs but would not sit down until she invited them to do so. "Madam," Yossef began, "we can see that you're a very respectable woman. We are jewelry merchants. We appreciate that now, with the war over, people are in need of cash. We'd be happy to pay cash for any nice jewelry you may have."

She stared at them. "Do you want my jewelry?"

"Not at all, not at all, madam. We don't want your jewelry. We want to give you cash and would be happy to help you at the same time dispose of some of your jewelry."

"And you say you have money? I want to see it first."

Pulling a wad of notes bound in a rubber band from his inner suit pocket, Avraham placed it on the table. Her eyes flew open in amazement. "Feel free to count it," Yossef said. "These are real banknotes. You may touch them, count them, and they could be yours, serving you well over the coming months for food and other basics."

Yossef's speech was quiet, deliberate, but he discerned how the appeal of that wad of notes was seeping into her thoughts. He held them out to her, inviting her to take a whiff. She held the packet and began counting. After reaching three hundred Reichsmark, she placed them back on the table, her eyes glimmering.

"Wait here."

When she left the room, Yossef whispered. "She's ours." Some minutes later, she was back holding a carved oak chest with a delicate key in its aperture. The lid was engraved with an eagle, beneath which long intertwining deer horns featured. She twisted the key and lifted the lid. Avraham and Yossef were blinded.

Diamonds sparkled in the box. There was a necklace with an oval amber stone that shone so beautifully it put the diamonds to shame. Next to it lay several emeralds. Turning to look at them, the woman's face was a question mark. The brothers made sure to keep poker faces.

"Is that all there is? Does Madam not have anything more?" Yossef asked.

Her gaze went straight to the bundle of cash on the table. She removed a panel of wood from the jewelry box, drawing out an amethyst that shone even more brightly than the other gems.

"May I?" Yossef asked.

She nodded. Yossef picked the amethyst up and lifted it towards the electric light. He clucked his tongue once, then walked to the window and held the gem up to the natural light. Turning it from one angle to another, he examined it with confidence, as though this were an everyday occurrence.

"Madam. Sadly, the stone is scratched and its value is less than you think." Feigning disinterest, he placed it back in the box but winked at Avraham while he was bent forward.

"And what is this?" Avraham asked, lifting an iron cross from the chest. Its center was adorned by a swastika, and through a loop at the top ran a short red and white ribbon. The woman took the cross from Avraham, kissed it, and placed it on the table. "It's the only memento I have of my husband, a general in the German Army, and this is his decoration of excellence. It's called the Knights Cross of the Iron Cross." Tears fell from her eyes but she continued to speak. "He was a war hero at the battle of Stalingrad. This is a mark of heroism given to very few. Only 7,300 soldiers and officers received it for outstanding service and he was among them."

Avraham shot a questioning glance at Yossef.

"We have no interest in this, Madam. We certainly wouldn't want to take your memory of your husband." Turning to Avraham, Yossef spoke in Polish. "I'd strangle the murderer. We'll leave her only the damn cross." He smiled at her. "Madam, we will take the jewelry chest with us, with the gold chains and gems for five hundred Reichsmark. We're happy to let you keep the cross which is so understandably dear to you, and that's because of our compassion and your noble self, and because you're a war widow."

Yossef turned to Avraham, blurting in Polish: Niech Cie szlag trafi. May he go to hell.

The woman caressed the gems, clearly finding it hard to part with them.

Yossef and Avraham sat apathetically, their eyes gazing at the ceiling. Some minutes later, Yossef stood up, turning his face only partially towards Avraham. "Well, let's be going because clearly Madam does not want to sell." Avraham stood up as well. "Have a good day, Madam."

"Count to five," Yossef quietly said to Avraham, "and she'll stop us."

They began moving slowly towards the door, Avraham counting in his mind. One. Two. Three. Four. Five. Silence. She locked the door behind them. Yossef smiled as they left the house. They reached the gate and the front door was still shut. Yossef turned back. "Follow me," he told Avraham.

They walked right into the house. "Didn't we leave something here, Madam?"

Caught by surprise, she screamed, the notes falling from her hand.

"Did you think they would stay here?" Calmly picking up the jewelry chest, he checked that the contents were still inside, making a point of setting the iron cross down on the table.

"The deal is done. After all, you took the money, is that not so? And before we call for the military police at your attempt to steal, we are leaving with the jewelry. Goodbye, Madam, and remember to kiss the cross and keep your husband always in your thoughts."

Heads high, they walked with a firm step out, leaving the front door open, and slipped into the Mercedes, leaving the woman open-mouthed on her front doorstep.

BUSINESS AND COURTING

The entire way back to Bergen-Belsen, Yossef and Avraham rejoiced over their anticipated profits. "We bought in marks, and now we'll sell to the Americans and Brits for dollars and pounds sterling. I'm sure we'll make a hundred times more than we spent," Yossef hooted. "Avraham, I think we just got a whole lot richer. Tomorrow we'll go back to another house and find some more bargains. There'll be enough left to gift to our sisters too. What do you say?"

"Batya and Miriam will love something, and so would Haiya. She's included, of course. And they deserve it," Avraham grinned.

By evening's end, they'd already sold the diamonds for a handsome profit. The next day, they went back to the same street, with Reichsmarks in their pockets. The Mercedes had barely rolled into the street when a young woman clutching a luxury leather handbag quickly entered one of the homes, disappearing from view. Avraham and Yossef paid no attention to the incident, focusing entirely on their next mission. Knocking confidently on the door of a nice-looking home, it was opened by the young woman they'd just seen, elegantly attired, her makeup perfect.

"Yes?" she asked, suspicion in her voice. "Who are you and what do you want, sirs?"

"Guten Tag, Madam," Yossef greeted her. "Good day to you. We've come to offer you a business deal you'll find worthwhile. If you'd just let us in, we'd be happy to tell you more."

The woman laughed. "You want to buy jewelry, right? You're too late, boys. I've just sold everything to a lovely young woman."

Yossef went pale. "And who is this lovely woman?" he asked, trying to control the tremor in his voice.

"Her name is Tzilla, and she's very nice. I couldn't believe she was a Jew from Bergen-Belsen. She's pretty and knows how to talk. I sold her all my jewels. Sorry, boys," she said, shutting the door.

"Well, there are plenty more houses which means plenty more jewels," Avraham consoled his brother. He pointed to the next house in the street. "Let's check here."

It was a smaller house. They knocked at the door. Moments later, a pretty young woman opened the door, took one look at them, and before they could open their mouths, blurted. "I've sold everything."

Yossef's head was spinning. "To Tzilla?" was all he could say.

"Yes, sir. To Tzilla."

They walked to the car in silence and drove off. "Let's go back to Bergen-Belsen," Yossef eventually said. "I need to think. And who is this Tzilla, anyhow? Harming our business! I need to find her."

Back at the military section, Avraham asked to speak to the commander but was coldly received. "You again, Avraham? What's up? Got another car to sell me? Another pretty heap of junk?"

Avraham chuckled. "No, I just need some information. I heard there's a jewelry merchant here, a woman named Tzilla. Can you help me find her?"

"Sure, my dear friend."

Avraham wondered whether the commander had forgiven him for the car incident. "Everyone knows her. Tzilla is the fastest person at math anyone's ever seen. A true trader."

"My dear General, I need an address," Avraham was impatient.

"Here you go," the commander said, handing him a note. "Just yesterday she was here with gems and gold chains."

"That's great," Avraham made a point of smiling warmly. "Thanks so much. Oh, we also have gems and jewelry, if you're interested."

"I think not," the commander laughed. "I've already done one brilliant deal with you. And that makes it once too many for me."

Back in the car, Avraham shared the information with Yossef, who was thinking hard.

"All right," Avraham eventually said, wanting to cheer Yossef up, "let's go to the military stock officer and see if he's got any cloth to sell cheap."

"Not a terrible idea. They took jewels so maybe they'll give us some cloth."

But the supply officer disappointed them this time. "Sorry guys, you're too late. Tzilla was here and took everything, and here it's first come first served. I guess you'll have to try harder from now on. You've got yourselves some competition."

As they left, Yossef vented his anger. "Tzilla," he tossed at Avraham, "will be hearing from us!"

Back home, Yossef slowly calmed down. "Avraham, I need your Mercedes this evening," he said. "I'm cooking up a plan."

"I'll get it all cleaned up," Avraham readily agreed. "Anyhow I'm going to the dance this evening. The car's yours until tomorrow morning."

Yossef drove to the address given to him earlier. He knocked on the door. A young woman with long black hair opened it. Yossef's plan was to immediately take a line of attack. His eyes locked onto her deep warm eyes, his heart skipped more than a beat, and there he was, his intended stern face melting into a broad smile, his attack evaporated.

"So do you plan on coming in or shall we talk here outside?" she said, her smile making his heart go haywire.

Hesitantly he stepped inside. "I'm Yossef…" he began.

"Enough, Yossef. I know who you are. You're one of the famous Zakses. I've been waiting several days for you to show up and couldn't understand what was taking you so long. Did you need to lose out on a few deals to force you here?"

Yossef's confidence returned. "I wasn't out to cause you any harm," he said slyly. "I was waiting to see who I was dealing with. And now that I know, don't expect any consideration from me! We're strong, and you're meddling in our territory, Tzilla."

She folded her arms over chest, a smile playing at the corners of her mouth. "And what were you about to propose to me, Yossef?"

She was teasing him, so he answered in the same vein. "If you play nice, perhaps I'll offer you a partnership in the future."

She laughed. Oh, his heart… Yossef loved her fresh warm laugh. "Not interested in partnerships. I can manage on my own. Got any other good ideas?"

Yossef grinned. "Let's go out and I'll show you."

They walked to the Mercedes. Yossef ran his hand over its glossy roof. "I'm offering you a spin in this gorgeous toy, which once belonged to a senior German official."

Standing next to the car, Tzilla had a hard time hiding her astonishment. She stroked the hood and then the door handle with a mix of amusement and awe. Yossef's smile widened from ear to ear. She's mine, he thought.

"Please, Madam, all yours," he said, opening the door and bowing gallantly. Sliding into the passenger seat, Tzilla lifted her hem. Yossef didn't miss the brief view of her shapely legs. He walked to the driver's side, sat down, flicked the glove box open and pulled out a pair of light-tan deerskin gloves. A wonderful ploy for lightly touching her bare knee. She didn't flinch. She simply smiled.

Reaching out a little, he eased each finger of the glove onto his right hand. Slowly and purposefully, he did the same with the left, eyeing Tzilla with an air of importance. "It's far more pleasant to drive with the gloves on." he said. "Shall we be off?"

"How long," she grinned, leaning comfortably into the seat, "do you think I'm going to wait? Shouldn't we have been off long ago?"

"Wind your window down. It's a lot more fun that way," Yossef suggested. The Mercedes' engine roared into action. Yossef released the clutch quickly and the beast lurched forward into an unbridled sprint. Tzilla hunkered down into the seat, her mouth open in shock. Yossef raced down the road, each pothole and bump in the road greeted with her "whoa, wow!"

All the way to Celle, Yossef handled the Mercedes like a racing car. He took every left curve or turn more slowly so Tzilla wouldn't find herself thrust against the door. But on curves to the right he accelerated hard, forcing her upper body to sway onto his. And every time he did this she called out "O mój Boże!" Oh my God! Slowly he increased the speed on the turns until on one right-hand turn, he drove so fast that she reached out to grip his hand on the steering wheel so hard that her knuckles turned white.

"I can't see a thing!" she screamed," her hair blowing into her eyes.

"No need to see, just feel! Feel me and the car. Feel how we're like one body."

He slowed when they reached the Celle train station. Tzilla was still clutching his gloved hand. Leaning over, he kissed her cheek lightly. She smiled at him.

"Home?"

"Yes, but please, a little slower this time."

Looking deeply into her eyes, all he said was, "It depends on what my car wants to do."

But Yossef did drive back at a pleasant, comfortable speed. Stopping at her home, he slid out of his seat, went around the car, and opened the door on her side. Tzilla stepped out. She stood facing him. She was silent. So was he. Eventually she spoke first.

"People always told me that the Zakses don't talk a whole lot." She giggled. "Well, perhaps we will become partners, and perhaps more than that. Would you like to come in and have something to drink?"

He nodded in silence, his heart overflowing. Yossef, at last, was filled with joy.

TWO TO TANGO

Avraham noted Yossef's good mood when he drove away in the Mercedes. Clearly Yossef had cooked up a winning plan. Avraham lit a cigarette and made his way to the dance club. He loved dancing. His body and soul connected deeply to music, which cast its magic on him even when he wasn't on the dance floor, making him move sensually. Catching the sounds in the distance, he danced his way to the club.

He spied her the instant he stepped inside. The previous evening he'd noticed her high, full cheeks and blond hair. A tango was playing in the background. Avraham remembered how she'd danced last night, her movements infused with happiness, her laughter generous, her pleasure in dancing wholesome. Avraham was planning on dancing with her tonight, but before he could make a move, she rose, accepting an invitation from another young man who swept her into the dance.

Disappointed, Avraham approached another young woman, holding his hand out and bowing ever so slightly. He enjoyed the dance but couldn't wait for it to be over; he wanted to bring his current partner back to her place and try his luck again. Every time it was feasible, he glanced over at the young woman that made his heart flutter. Towards the end of the dance, both couples were fairly close to each other. Avraham looked at the other man's partner. She winked and smiled. He smiled back, knowing that they would, indeed, dance together tonight.

The dance over, Avraham took his partner back to her seat. He waited to hear what the next dance would be. A Viennese waltz. He waltzed over to the woman he fancied, holding his hand out in invitation. Did she leap into his arms? So it felt. And it took his breath away. Within three steps they were holding each other close, swirling to the rhythm.

"Tonia," she said softly.

Leaning forward a little, he whispered into her ear: "Avraham."

Was he dreaming or did she just answer: "Yes, I know."

Surprised, he held her closer, his body moving faultlessly to the music. As did Tonia's. She pulled away, drew closer, pulled away, moving into his hold as smoothly as the waltz required. Its quick beat was perfect for them both: they took the center of the dance floor and never stopped smiling at each other, moving as one. Slowly, others stopped to watch them with admiration.

Light on their feet, their bodies spoke the melody, their hands locking throughout. Avraham knew: he wouldn't let her go, ever, not after this dance, not after the dances that would follow. Silence. The waltz had ended. They stood, their arms enveloping each other. A moment later, an English waltz began playing, quieter, and familiar to them both. Avraham and Tonia ignored the other couples. They were swept up into the music, their eyes for no one but themselves.

The other dancers moved slowly away from this young couple, whose movements were beautiful, compelling. The dance floor was all theirs. Only Avraham and Tonia remained, splendid, their connection electrifying the atmosphere. Again the music ended. Again they stood, alone, in the center of the dance club, surrounded by warm applause. The sound of clapping broke the spell momentarily: they turned and bowed to the crowd, smiling, as though thanking the other dancers for giving them the room to speak their souls.

Elegant, precise, a foxtrot caught them by surprise. Avraham and Tonia were still in each other's arms. She leaned back a little; his hand gently caressing her back as they changed tempo. Each time they turned their heads in time to the rhythm, they smiled warmly at each other. His grip felt so safe and secure. She knew, in those moments, that he'd never leave her, not tonight, not ever. Music and dance would always connect them.

Late that night, they walked through quiet streets, arms around each other. They walked and talked until dawn, not wanting the night to end. At Tonia's door, they whispered on.

"I have three brothers and two sisters and I'm the youngest. I'd love you to meet our large and wonderful family. We managed to stay together almost throughout the whole war, keeping watch over each other. And now that it's finished, we'll never separate."

Taking his hand in hers, she looked into his eyes. "Of course, Avraham. I'd love to meet them."

He kissed her lightly on her cheek before she entered her home. She was excited, moved, not at all tired. Avraham danced all the way back to his place. As he arrived, he heard the Mercedes' engine humming behind him. Turning around, he saw Yossef behind the wheel looking happier than he ever had.

"Only now you're back?" Avraham asked.

"And what do you think? Business wasn't the only business I had with Tzilla," he laughed, mischief playing in his eyes. "Let's go in. We deserve a bit of rest after a night like that. But what about you, Avraham? I could ask the same: only now you're back? You look like you're dancing on a cloud."

Avraham smiled broadly. "For sure," he said, spontaneously hugging Yossef and drawing him into their apartment with dance steps. "I danced almost until the morning and boy, have I got something to tell you!"

HANNAH & VOLF

Honest, simple, the two-word proposal was written on a small note in Volf's beautiful, rounded handwriting and lying on Hannah's desk before the workday began. "Marry me?" She could barely read it for the tears of joy that blurred her vision. She gazed on and on at the wonderful, special note, then added two words of her own: "Of course!" She folded it over and asked one of the other office staff members to take it to Volf's desk. The silence in the office was thunderous. Hannah waited. The office staff waited. They were used to seeing her excitable nature but today was different. Some seconds later, she raised her head, noticing the entire staff focused on her: what could have made her go quiet, and even shed a tear?

Despite their very different personalities, Volf unobtrusive, Hannah bubbly as a gurgling spring, they were perfectly harmonized when they played bridge, making them win regularly. He was also an excellent mathematician who never erred in the figures he calculated in his mind for the accounts ledgers, doing his work quietly and confidently, always available to answer other office staff's questions. But now, seated at his desk, Volf felt as though everyone could hear his heart, which beat hard when he opened the note to read the response that brought him boundless joy. Looking up, he saw the entire staff waiting tensely. Volf walked over to Hannah, grinning from ear to ear. She stood to greet him, tears of joy coursing her cheeks. They hugged and kissed wordlessly. Then Volf returned to his desk and continued his work.

"Well, everyone," Hannah said, gesturing to the office staff, "you could say we just got engaged."

First to hug her was her aunt Eva. "In the past, all your notes back and forth made noise, laughter, and exclamations. Today, however, your notes went back and forth in complete silence..." With that, the whole office became a jumble of well-wishers, of hugs and kisses. Volf smiled throughout. Some minutes later, he stood to address the staff in his quiet way. "Thank you, everyone, but now we need to get back to work."

Hannah loved Volf's handwriting, the way each letter was rounded, each given the space it needed as though worthy of due respect, and every letter that had a longer upward or downward stroke ended at the exact same point along the line. For Hannah, reading his handwriting was like being allowed to see into his soul, the soul of a person who was not about lip service but meant what he said, and thought about what he said carefully before saying it.

A wedding! It gave Esther no end of joy organizing the event, and she volunteered to sew her daughter's dress. Poring over journals, Hannah finally found something she liked. It was time to hunt down fabric. Yossef remembered seeing white cloth at the camp's British section. Avraham and Yossef went to ask if the soldiers would be so kind as to donate some curtain cloth as a gift to the bride. Letting them choose, the brothers went back with several pieces. Hannah chose a soft, white fabric.

Two days later, Esther had the work done, and never had such a pretty bride been seen in the displaced persons camp. Now the only thing left to do was to find matching shoes. Since the closest shoe store was in Hanover, the Zaks women decided to rummage through the JDC clothing storage, piled high with donations from Jews from the USA. Finding a pair of sandals made of silver-dyed leather, Hannah tried them on. "Cinderella!" Batya clapped her hands in joy. A perfect fit.

25th February 1947. One rabbi. Sixteen weddings. All in Bergen-Belsen. Hannah wanted to be the last. "Let all the others go first and then, when he gets to us, there'll be no need to rush through things and meanwhile our guests can dance and be happy," Hannah explained. Hannah was a pretty, elegant bride. Lace adorned her shoulders, matching the edging of her veil. Guests were amazed at the dress, which reached a little above her ankles. She wanted to be sure everyone could see those glittery sandals.

At the festive meal, Esther stood and tapped her knife against the wine glass to catch the guests' attention. All eyes turned to her. She was a quiet woman, but when she did speak, it was always words of wisdom. The hall fell silent. Hannah was especially surprised; her mother had never taken a public role before. With sincerity and calmness, Esther gave her speech.

"Dear friends, thank you. Here we are, at a particularly emotional moment. Who would have thought, two years ago, when we weighed thirty-five kilos and looked like we wouldn't see the next day, that we'd instead see days of such happiness. We never dared dream of life beyond the fences, or that we would conduct normal lives again, that we'd live as humans rather than as the numbers tattooed on our arms. This wedding is testimony to our strength, our ability to overcome all evil. Your wedding, my dearest daughter Hannah, is the best memorial we ever could have established for those of our family who did not manage to survive.

"Establishing a new family in this of all places is the greatest victory we could wish for. Our dear Papa Kuba, like so many others, is not with us, but he's here in our hearts, like Volf's parents and like so many others of our beloved families who are not here. Hannah, my daughter, it's no secret that I'm here because of you, your encouragement, your resourcefulness. You are one tough young woman, and only one who has experienced what you have, can say that with all honesty. If not for your courage, obstinacy, and your inner strength, I simply would not be here today.

"You carried me on your back during the harshest of times, when we were sure there was no hope left. You always had a sparkle in your eye. Your eyes are so much stronger than Mengele, than Himmler and Eichmann put together. Let those wonderful eyes lead you and your husband to a new era. That sparkle in your blue eyes is the light at the end of the tunnel. New families will rise on the remains of the old; we will never forget the old, and honor them with the new. Set out now onto good new lives, and rebuild our families, and may I enjoy seeing the gift of life with grandchildren in the very near future! L'chaim! To life!"

Captivated by Esther's words, the guests were left speechless, some crying openly, some crying inside, all thinking of who they had lost and what their futures might contain. In their minds, they could see their murdered family members in the hall celebrating together. Each survivor was a testimony to their names being remembered.

Still under the influence of Esther's speech, no one noticed that the rabbi was standing quietly at the hall's entrance, listening and deeply moved. He waited a minute more before making his way to the bridal canopy, inviting the young couple to do the same. Hannah didn't understand the blessings that were recited in a mixture of Hebrew and Yiddish. She was caught up in her emotions; she was sure her father was standing beside her, head slightly bowed, smiling in satisfaction, his spirit uplifting her as she began her new life. Volf slipped a simple band onto her finger, raised the veil, his lips lightly brushing hers. Verses from Psalm 137 were recited before his foot came down on the well-wrapped glass, an act symbolizing that Jewish people everywhere would never forget Jerusalem. At that, the crowd roared "Mazel Tov! Congratulations!" bringing Hannah out of her reverie.

"I promise," Volf whispered into her ear, "that we'll have a wonderful life together, Hannah." And his promise, made in Bergen-Belsen, was kept throughout their lives.

THE FIRST ALIYAH

At last, in March 1947, following two years in which the Zaks family's businesses flourished in Bergen-Belsen, their visas arrived. Not long beforehand, the family had sat around the table and deliberated together over a simple question: Where to? They had two choices: America, or British Mandate Palestine, as the area was commonly known.

"So far," Yisrael began, "we've done just about everything together. I believe we should continue that way."

Volf asked to express his views first. "I want to go to the Land of Israel. Palestine, to the Brits. But Palestina to us, as our Jewish Agency people call it. It's where I think I should build my life."

The others looked at him with surprise and some uncertainty. As the serious and reserved sibling, he'd often agreed with others or simply pointed out glitches. Now he was setting the tone.

Yisrael's eyes were full of gratitude when he glanced at Volf. Haiya's sister Gitta had gone there before the war and written to them. "Make Aliyah, 'ascension,' which is what coming to the Land of Israel is called because it is considered not only a bodily ascension but, particularly, a spiritual one. And indeed it is. Aliyah connects us to the deepest source of our Jewishness. Build your new lives in the Jewish state which will soon assert itself."

Yisrael's heart was also set on Palestina, but hearing Volf's remark moved him. He himself had yet to speak, and so had the others. Yossef and Avraham gazed at each other.

"Palestina? Everyone there's Jewish, right?" Yossef asked.

"No, there are also Arabs there, and British, and a war to boot," Yisrael answered.

"The Brits will leave this year," Volf intervened, "and that will leave only Jews and Arabs. It's the only place in the world where we can establish a Jewish country."

"If everyone's Jewish, how will we do business?" Yossef pondered aloud.

The family burst into laughter. "Don't worry, we will. And how!" Avraham said.

"All right," Yossef agreed, "so Avraham and I are for Palestina too."

"We'll be marrying soon too and then we'll all go to Palestina and build new lives together there," Batya piped up.

Yisrael stood, pulling out a letter from Gitta, which he read to them. "My dear loved ones. I live in a beautiful country, a land of sun, a land where we have a future. We are building this land for us and for you. My husband Srulik is an agronomist and farmer himself, and is helping to replant the Jezreel Valley. We have green fields here, and orange orchards where I can just go out and pick what I want. Winter here is fairly easy, with almost no snow ever. The summer's pretty hot but you get used to it. The most important thing is that we have hope, this land gives us hope, the hope of a Jewish country, a Jewish homeland. This is the place for us, and we're looking forward to your arrival. With much love, Gitta."

What else needed to be said? A decision was reached within minutes. They'd make Aliyah; they'd continue living together, just as Papa Hanokh had requested.

***

The first two visas were given to the two married couples. Esther and the other Zakses were still awaiting theirs. "We'll be the forerunners," Yisrael said without pause. "True, they're still fighting over there, but we'll join Gitta and Srulik and wait for the rest of you."

"I think we need to make a small change," Volf said. "We can't go and leave Esther behind. We'll stay here with Hannah's mother. I'll forego the visa until we can make Aliyah together."

Just a month later, Haiya and Yisrael were ready to leave Bergen-Belsen behind and make their way with two hundred additional visa holders, issued by the British Mandate authorities.

Batya was excited. "Look at you, Haiya," she said, lovingly caressing her sister-in-law's growing belly. "The ninth month. That's no laughing matter! You're carrying the grandchild that marks the first generation of revival! Mama and Papa must surely be looking down on you and are so proud. We're the generation who'll raise the first truly free generation of Jews in a Jewish homeland." She paused. "And that is our mark of victory. As soon as there's a new generation, we've won."

Avraham buffed the Mercedes. No one had a clue how Yossef, master of all trades, had managed to find two small Israeli flags, their white backgrounds emblazoned with two bright-blue stripes and a bright-blue Star of David between them. Just two years earlier, the nickel posts on the hood's outer corners held very different symbols. Now they bore the flags of the Jewish people.

PASSOVER ON THE PROVIDENCE

Almost one thousand Olim, as people making Aliyah were known, boarded the Providence on April 5th, 1947. The Hebrew date was 15 Nissan, in the Jewish year 5707. In fact, the 15th of Nissan was the first day of Passover. On April 6th, as dawn began to light the sky, the boat set sail eastwards from Marseille, crossing the Mediterranean Sea.

Things weren't easy on board. Overcrowding caused uncomfortable conditions in the cabins. The deck was the more pleasant place to be, and once Haiya and Yisrael arranged their bags in the tiny, cramped cabin, he suggested they go back upstairs. "It'd be best for you to rest in bed, but I'm pretty sure the air up on deck will be better than down here." Slowly, they made their way up, Yisrael holding her hand to steady her.

Yisrael was drawn to the boat's prow, his gaze following the wake it cut in the waves, his eyes looking to the future, his soul drawn ahead. But he knew it would all take time.

On deck he heard the lively chatter of teenagers in Polish.

"Where are you from?" he asked.

"Bergen-Belsen," they answered. A young woman stood next to them. "I'm also from there, Ma'am. Who are these young lads?" he asked them.

"I'm Ilana, their teacher. As soon as I was liberated from Bergen-Belsen, I gathered all the youngsters and set up one class after another until a small school was operating. For more than a year we've been battling to receive the visas, and a few weeks ago the certificates arrived. So here we are, our hearts brimming with joy as we make Aliyah."

"I'm Yisrael," he said, feeling tears welling in his eyes. "I was also liberated from the camps. My wife and I are also making Aliyah now. We spent the last two years since the liberation in Bergen-Belsen. I'm so thrilled to meet you."

Haiya, Yisrael, Ilana and the youth stood on deck, all eyes turned eastwards, dreaming of the moment they'd see the shores of the Land of Israel. An idea came to Yisrael's mind and he turned to Ilana. "Last night was the first night of Passover, the Seder night, but we didn't celebrate it. Outside of Israel, it's celebrated for two nights. How about we do that with these youth on the deck here tonight? It doesn't matter that we don't have a festive meal. If we can find a single matzah," he said, referring to the unleavened bread eaten on Passover, "that would be sufficient, and then we can recite the Haggadah service. After all, haven't we all been released from slavery to freedom, like our Hebrew ancestors who left ancient Egypt behind?"

Ilana's eyes sparkled. "Yisrael, you couldn't have come up with a better idea! In an hour it will be nightfall. Let's meet up here on deck and celebrate Passover!" And with that, she asked the youth to go down into the ship's kitchen to bring whatever they could for a festive Passover meal. One came back with a bottle of wine. Another walked into the kitchen and saw the chef about to slice a matzah in two. In a flash he'd slipped it off the board before the knife could break it, and was back upstairs like a bolt of lightning.

As night fell, the youth sat in a circle on deck. Ilana placed the wine and the single matzah in front of her. Yisrael and Haiya joined them. His voice trembling, Yisrael spoke. "Admittedly we don't have all the items needed to fully celebrate Passover according to our tradition, we don't have candles, but we do have our memories, and we will always remember reciting this Haggadah service."

"Ah, one second," Ilana intervened, "but actually I do have candles. I always do, because you never know when they could be needed," she said, bringing two slim candles out of her bag. She lit them and recited the prayer: "*Blessed are you, Lord our G-d, King of the Universe, who keeps us alive, and keeps us sustained, and has brought us to this occasion,*" she recited softly.

No sound could be heard except the breeze blowing against the waves. The moon began to rise. Yisrael continued. "We have no traditional Seder night plate, but perhaps someone knows how to draw the items we need?"

Standing up, a short girl asked Ilana for chalk. The girl drew a large, traditional Seder plate, then drew the six items that would have been set on it, assisted by Yisrael's guidance. "On the lower right, draw the *charoset*, made of nuts, apples and wine chopped together and symbolizing the mortar between the bricks of structures our ancestors were forced to build. Above that, the charred wing bone, representing the mighty arm of G-d who liberated us." Item after item he guided her: the bitter herbs, the leafy herbs, the hard-boiled egg, and in the center she drew a hefty chunk of horseradish.

"Don't you think you exaggerated a bit with the horseradish root?" he chuckled.

"Not at all," she answered in all seriousness. "We had to live through so much bitterness these past years that this drawing can't even begin to encompass it all."

Yisrael stroked her head gently and nodded.

"Now that our table is set," Yisrael addressed the youth, "I want to say a few words. We are indeed just like the ancient Children of Israel. We, too, are leaving our Egypt. Now we are on our way to the Land of Israel, the land of our forefathers. Each of us is one of the Children of Israel, and so tonight we will tell the story of our Exodus, and one day you will all tell your children of this, your personal exodus. My wife," Yisrael pointed to Haiya, "is carrying our first child and he, or she, can already hear what I'm saying."

The youngsters were completely taken in by his words. "The second thing is that we're leaving slavery behind and entering our freedom. For years we were subjugated, humiliated. For centuries. Remember this forever so that you are never subjugated again: we are now a free people." The wind blew more strongly and the boat rocked but everyone stayed in their places, their bodies swaying lightly in unison. They looked just like worshippers at prayer in a synagogue.

"Now, let's drink the wine." Opening the bottle, he poured a little into a cup, recited the blessing and passed it to Haiya, who took a sip, then passed it to Ilana, and so on around the circle.

"Who's the youngest here?" Yisrael asked. A lad raised his hand, dropping his eyes to the floor. "Come, sit next to me," Yisrael invited him. "What's your name?"

"Moshe," the boy answered softly.

Yisrael stroked his head. "A lovely name, and so appropriate to Passover, since Moshe fought with Pharaoh for the Hebrews' freedom and then guided them out of ancient Egypt. Moshe, I'm going to break our matzah into two and hide one half, and you'll find it and ask me for something. I can't promise that I'll fulfill your wish, but I'll try. Meanwhile, let's start singing 'Mah Nishtanah,' *Why is this night different from all other nights?*"

Moshe began, and the other youth joined in until they were all singing loudly. At last, they reached the stage where the hidden piece of Matzah, known as the Afikoman, needed to be found. Moshe slipped his hand beneath Yisrael's rolled up jacket and pulled it out. "And what would you like, Moshe?"

Moshe's eyes were glued to the floor. "I have two requests if you don't mind. Is that all right?"

"Let's hear them," Yisrael answered.

"My first request," Moshe began, then fell silent. Yisrael stroked his cheek gently. "Say what's on your mind, Moshe. It's all right."

"I want to see Mama and Papa one last time."

Only the wind and the rush of waves could be heard. Slowly, the sounds of sobbing joined them. Yisrael hugged him tightly. "Yes, I'd like to as well, dear child. If only that were possible..." Yisrael waited for the boy to quieten down a little. "And what's your second request?"

"I want to go to the Land of Israel, to my new home," Moshe said, gazing intently at Yisrael.

Grasping the boy's chin warmly in his hand, Yisrael answered. "That request is one I can certainly help you with." He hugged the boy again. "And now I want to say a few closing words. You are the new generation. You are the generation of freedom. Never forego that freedom. Your children, your grand-children and the generations that come must preserve it. Tell all of them about your personal exodus from Egypt, and they will tell it to the next generation."

***

On their seventh day of sailing, as Shabbat drew to a close on 12th April 1947, most of the passengers were crowded on deck, gazing intently east. Haiya, despite the difficulty, joined Yisrael.

"Look! Look, Haifa's lights! We're home!" a roar suddenly went up.

Jumping up and down for joy, hugging each other, kissing each other's cheeks, the passengers gave vent to their emotions as the sun set behind them. The lights twinkled as though saying, "Welcome, dear brethren. We've been looking forward to your arrival."

There wasn't a dry eye on board. Haiya clasped her hands under her belly, wondering if so much happiness would hasten the birth. Yisrael wiped his eyes, imagining his parents, whom he'd last seen four years ago almost to the day, on June 23rd, 1943, standing there with him. Four years ago, his world had blackened beyond belief; now, at last, bit by bit, it was lighting up again. Could he see Hanokh and Yoheved there among the sparkling lights of Haifa? He hugged Haiya. "I've only now realized," he said, "that this ship's name is Providence. Do you know what that means? It's like divine guidance. This is our divine providence, which has rescued us, reunited us, and will now help us build both a new home and a new family. I'm so sorry our parents aren't here to see this new start in the Land of Israel."

With one arm around Haiya, Yisrael felt a tug on his free hand. Looking down, he saw Moshe. "Thank you, Yisrael, for helping make my second wish come true." Pulling him close, Yisrael stroked his head as Providence slowly pulled into the port and was fastened to the dock.

"We have arrived in the Land of Israel. Please collect your belongings from your cabins and prepare for disembarking. Tomorrow morning, you will be leaving the ship," the captain's voice came over the loudspeaker.

Never had Yisrael and Haiya seen a sight prettier than the lights of Haifa climbing from the shore to the tip of Mount Carmel, promising that now life would be good.

THE FIRST LETTER

Yisrael's handwriting. How well Volf knew it.

"Hannah! Can you call the family together right away? We've got a letter! I want everyone here when we open this first letter from Yisrael."

In no time they were all around the table, bursting with excitement. Slitting the envelope open, he pulled several pages of finest onion-skin paper out.

"Dearest brothers and sisters, you've got a nephew! Haiya gave birth to a healthy boy on May 2nd."

Miriam and Batya immediately burst into tears.

"Sshh, sshh, girls. Calm down. Let's read the rest."

"Oh, but we need a moment, Volf. We need a minute to take that in. What lovely news. A new generation at last! Yisrael and Haiya have taken the first step and we'll all follow suit. It's the start of our wonderful victory!" Batya said.

Hand to her fluttering heart, Miriam chimed in. "We're all right now. Let's hear what else they have to say."

"His name is Tuvia," Volf continued reading. "I couldn't help but recall that dreadful day in Gross Rosen when my father-in-law Guttman fell, exhausted, and we couldn't help him. He died, alone, in the snow. We heard the shot ring out and stood frozen in our places. So, we feel this is the right thing to do, as though we've brought him to life again. 'Gutt' means good in German. 'Tov' means good in Hebrew. Could there be any more perfect way of honoring him than naming our sweet son for him? I am the happiest I could ever be."

Volf swallowed hard, stifling a sob of joy and recollection. Hannah gently stroked his back. "I'm thrilled. Just thrilled," Batya laughed. The Zakses wiped tears from their eyes but signaled to Volf to read on. "Patience," Volf smiled, "we've got four pages of news here!"

"Now, after giving you the stunningly great news, I want to describe our experiences so far. The journey by boat wasn't simple. The vessel was dirty and Haiya had a hard time, but knowing that it was taking us to our new home helped us overcome that aspect. On the first night we held an improvised Passover Seder service with children from Bergen-Belsen. I described our forefathers' exodus from ancient Egypt and felt as though I was already telling my own child about his past, present and future. '*And you shall tell your children*,' just at it says in the Passover service.

"The instant we saw Haifa's lights is one we will never forget all our lives. You see them glinting from the shoreline all the way up to the tip of Mount Carmel and your heart just floods with joy. You feel: I'm home! It's the strangest thing, coming to an entirely new place and yet feeling immediately that you've come home. But believe me, when Haifa's lights will sparkle for you too, you'll understand."

"At the port, nothing was clear. Comings, goings, and we had no idea what to do. We saw a long line of people so we joined that. Some hours later, there we were standing in front of a clerk who gave us a certificate in Hebrew and English. It isn't a formal identity document yet but nonetheless something official. We looked around, still not knowing what to do next. I asked someone nearby; he pointed to a gate and said that if we go through it, we'll find cars and cabs which can take us wherever we need to go. And then, a miracle!"

"Miracle?" Miriam wondered, "that's simultaneously exciting and scary."

Volf looked up for a moment and grinned before continuing. "Suddenly we saw Gitta and Srulik! Haiya clutched her belly and broke into a run. Nine years, can you believe it? Nine years since they'd last seen each other and here they were together at the port's exit, quietly waiting with arms outstretched. The sisters just hugged and wept, and wept and hugged, joy, relief, sorrow, all bundled into those tears. Srulik and I also hugged and wiped a tear from our cheeks. What a reunion! 'Well,' I said to Srulik, 'Srulik is the diminutive for Yisrael and I'm also Yisrael and here we both are in the Land of Israel. Together!

"They drove us back to their home, which I'd hardly call a smooth, pleasant drive, and it took some hours before we reached Afula, which is about the size of Strzemieszyce. But here's the difference: everything's in Hebrew! Afula is a pretty place, with small homes, and the town's surrounded by green fields. Remember when Srulik studied agronomy in Krakow? So like a true pioneer, he has also worked on paving roads, and that means clearing rocks too! Here in the Land of Israel, everyone knows how to do a bit of everything and they work together to build the country up. Yes, they're building it for your sakes. Afula's residents all speak Hebrew. Luckily for us, we learned Hebrew back home!

"Every evening when Srulik and Gitta came back from their work, we talked and talked. They wanted to know every detail of the horrors there. It wasn't easy but Gitta and Srulik insisted. What luck they had, I kept thinking to myself, for coming to the Land of Israel in 1938, right before the Germans began conquering Europe. And they've also begun a family: Udi, their son, is five. They called him Udi and here's why. Take a look at chapter three in the book of Zecharia the Prophet. Read verse two: 'Is this not a burning stick plucked free from the fire.' They gave their son that name in our family's honor!

"Now, a secret: Gitta's pregnant again, and is convinced she's carrying a girl this time. She also said that if she indeed gives birth to a girl, they'll call her Raya, which means 'closest friend.' For Gitta and Srulik, the name honors the close connection between our two families.

"And another bit of lovely news. Remember our cousin from Katowice, Dr. Leon Zaks? He's a physician here, in a place called Kibbutz Geva and he's known as the best doctor in the entire Jezreel Valley, which is why the Zaks name here already holds a good reputation. Leon is also happy to help us as needed. And so I've come home: not to Strzemieszyce, not to Poland, but here, in the Land of Israel. This truly feels like home. I've seen the local synagogue, and there's a school here. There's even a fabric store, a shoe store… There's plenty of room for us in this country, and plenty for us to do."

Volf halted, looking up at the eager Zaks family faces. "It won't be long now," he said, "and we'll all be there." He slipped the page he'd just read behind the others and continued.

"I've already found work as the accountant for a flour mill, can you believe that? There are plenty of fields, some growing wheat, and there's no shortage of bread in our new country. It's one of the things that encourages me the most. Volf, my dear brother, you'll also do fine here, without a doubt. They're constantly on the lookout for accountants. It's not that they don't know math. But they're not so good at organizing the paperwork the way it should be! You'll have tons of work.

"Yossef and Avraham, you're the niftiest merchants ever, having studied under the best, our dear Papa. Our new home is just waiting for excellent merchants like yourselves. We'll all have plenty to keep us busy."

Volf stopped reading, took a deep breath and sipped from his glass of water as the family chattered about the news so far but very quickly they fell silent, all eyes on him, the message clear: please go on.

"Last but not least," his voice was firm, "the war is still going on here. No, it's nothing like we had in Europe but it is a war nonetheless. The Germans didn't manage to erase us there, and certainly no one will succeed here, not the Brits, not the Arabs, no one! Jewish soldiers, fighting for a Jewish homeland. Can you believe such a thing? I'm considering joining them, because fighting for your own home is a privilege. It's so very different to how we lived in Europe. Here, I'm not afraid of what may happen. I'm hoping you'll receive your Certificates of Entry very quickly and we really will be united at last. We've got the nicest home, not as large as Papa and Mama's was in Strzemieszyce, but it's ready and waiting for you."

"I love you all very much, my dear brothers and sisters, and our dearest in-laws. Baby Tuvi (as we're calling him), Haiya, and I are looking forward to meeting you here. Write to us, please. Lots!"

A long silence followed. A silence marked by broad smiles and the occasional sigh. "May I have the letter to read too?" Miriam asked. When she'd finished, Batya held her hand out. And so it passed around the circle, to Yossef, to Avraham, to each of them, the words leaving a deep impression on the listeners and readers' minds.

THE CHILD BORN ON THE REBIRTH OF HIS COUNTRY

In the Bergen-Belsen Displaced Persons Camp, on 14th May 1948, corresponding to 5th Iyar 5708 according to the Hebrew calendar, Hannah, having patiently waited out a full day's labor pains, gave birth to a healthy baby boy. As always, Volf was calm throughout. The entire previous day he'd insisted, "You'll give birth tomorrow to our son, no matter what."

Hannah laughed. "And how on earth do you know it's a boy?"

"Ah, simple," he answered without hesitation. "It's a boy because in our family, the Zakses, boys are always born first. In any event, he'll hang on until tomorrow."

"And if the labor pains get stronger and more frequent today?" Hannah asked.

"It won't happen, my love. You'll give birth tomorrow and let's not argue about it."

"But why's tomorrow so important to you?"

"Why tomorrow?" Volf was shocked. "Because tomorrow, David ben-Gurion is announcing the establishment of the modern State of Israel. Our son will be born tomorrow at the same time as our country is reborn, and there could be no greater gift. It will be the happiest day of my life. Think about that: just three years since Auschwitz, Blechhammer, Buchenwald, Bergen-Belsen, extermination camps, forced labor camps, and suddenly tomorrow we'll truly be a family, and we'll have our own country. Could you have imagined such a thing a mere three years ago, during those days of horror and hell?"

Hannah's labor pains were now coming every hour. "Volf? Can you call Mama please? I'm sure she'll know what to do."

"No need, Hannah," he waved his hand dismissively. "Just lie and rest, and everything will be fine. A pang every hour or so isn't so terrible. Nothing will really happen until tomorrow."

Hannah slapped the sheet in anger. "Go and get my mother, and this isn't funny. You and your country!" she huffed.

Volf gave in. "Okay, I'm on my way. But really, nothing will happen until tomorrow…"

Lying in bed, Hannah was terribly excited and nervous. Her husband's words echoed in her mind. Just three years earlier they'd all been in hell. Her will, and that of her mother, to beat the Nazis drove them to overcome the Germans' evil. In the end, determination beat the Nazis' murderous intentions. Any moment now, she'd be bringing new life into the world.

That pang again. Never mind, Hannah whispered to herself. I'll get over this too, because what's a bit of pain for the baby's sake compared to all the pain we coped with in the past? Hannah was thinking through names again. Volf predicted a son. He was most probably right, she thought. Probably Hanokh, after Volf's late father. My own father's fate is still unknown and it isn't our custom to name a child after someone who's still living. What a strange name Hanokh is. I never even knew it existed, let alone how to pronounce it, until I met Volf. But it's much more important to perpetuate the deceased than wonder about how the name sounds. I'll gladly name the child after my wonderful husband's father, she decided.

Esther burst into the room like a hurricane just as Hannah gripped her belly again in pain. Right behind Esther was the midwife, who asked everyone to leave the room so she could check Hannah.

"Volf asked me not to give birth today. Is there any way to make sure it's tomorrow?"

The nurse laughed. "Men! What would they know! Let's take a look and see." Reaching the end of her examination, the midwife laughed again. "Well, you've still got plenty of time, it seems, so your husband's one lucky guy. It really does look like it'll be tomorrow. Meanwhile, try to get as much rest as possible. You'll need your strength later on."

Hannah couldn't fall asleep, and Volf and Esther stayed awake with her most of the night. Early the next morning, the labor pains were stronger and more frequent, enough for Esther to send him out for the midwife again. A quick check and she directed them to the hospital. Morning slowly turned into midday and Hannah still hadn't given birth. Volf decided to go home: he didn't want to miss the radio announcement of the State of Israel's Independence Day. "Promise I'll be back soon, but I need to hear that we've got our own country with my own ears," he said, bending to kiss her.

She smiled, tired from lack of sleep and the increasingly stronger labor pain. "All right, Volf. Go listen. Mama will stay with me. But please come back as soon as the broadcast is over."

The hospital was filled only with Jewish patients, and they were all bundles of excited nerves over the upcoming declaration. The Brits in the medical team knew very well why. Meanwhile, the midwife stood at the ready next to Hannah. And where was Volf? At home with his new country, Hannah thought, upset, and doesn't he always say everything in its good time, so the child's time will come too....

The birth began. The doctor, the midwife, Esther, were all ready to help. There were no complications. Hannah shouted with each wave of pain, she laughed with joy and immediately cried at the ache of the next contraction. All she wanted was to see the baby, safe and sound, to hold her child, to kiss her newborn.

At two that afternoon, the baby's cry pulled Hannah out of her hazy consciousness. She was fine. The baby was fine. But Hannah cried uncontrollably. Where was her mother? Where was her husband? She thought of her father. None of her family was with her in that instant, only she and her baby and a happiness so vast that she could not contain it. The idea of a Jewish country for her people was not on her mind right then. All she could think of was this new life that had come into the world, this new beginning, and she was so grateful.

At the midwife's beckoning, Esther entered the room, embracing her daughter. Volf was still nowhere to be seen. That infuriated Hannah: after all, isn't there a radio in the hospital? Couldn't he have listened together with the other patients? An hour passed; the faint murmuring of a radio could be heard in the background, and the occasional whimpers of the newborn lying in her arms. Another moment passed. Thunderous applause came from the radio. Not everyone understood what was being said in that broadcast, but everyone understood one thing well: this was a momentous occasion like none other in all their families' histories.

"We've got a country!" a man roared.

"And I've got a son," Hannah tepidly answered, still fuming.

But her anger evaporated the instant Volf stepped into the room. He was choking with excitement. "I told you we'd have a son and that he'd be born today. I was convinced of it!" He wrapped Hannah in his arms, kissed their baby, and couldn't stop grinning. "What could be better than this?" he chuckled with pride. "At the same time, on the same day, my country and my son. Twins! I've got twins!"

He was silent and thoughtful as he stroked the baby's cheek and held his hand. "Let's call him Yisrael." Hannah's eyes opened wide in a question: Yisrael? Volf kissed her hand. "Yes. What could be more beautiful than that? Born together, and they'll live together – how symbolic is that!"

Hannah gently shook her head. "Volf, isn't it more important to perpetuate your parents? We can call him Hanokh after your late father, but if you want Yisrael for the commemorative value, let that be his middle name. Hanokh Yisrael." Very firmly she concluded: "That will be his name among the People of Israel, his people." Volf knew that this was not a point to be argued over.

Early in the evening, the family began arriving to congratulate the new mother and see the baby. "This is no place for men," Batya instructed firmly to the Zaks males. "Only women are allowed into the room. You'll wait outside," she said, giving a wave of dismissal. On tiptoes, Batya and Miriam entered the room, where Hannah lay, tired but thrilled. Batya kissed her sister-in-law. "Another Zaks boy! One in our new country of Israel, and one here in this place where another nation tried to eradicate the us. We'll win, again and again."

"May I hold him?" Miriam asked when the baby began to cry. Hannah passed him into Miriam's loving hands. He cuddled down into the crook of her arm, sensing her maternal nature.

"Hannah," Batya quizzed softly, "did you decide on a name yet?"

"Of course, Batya. His name will be Hanokh," she answered gently. Batya could feel the tears about to overflow; Miriam was so moved that she almost dropped the baby.

"I knew it, Hannah. I knew it," she said, almost whispering. "Thank you, Hannah. I know you're the one who thought about this and decided. After all, what do men understand? Hey, I want him a bit too!" Batya laughed, reaching out towards her sister. Miriam passed the baby to her; tiny teardrops fell on his plump cheeks. "You realize who I'm hugging here… Papa. It's as though Papa's been born again. I can feel it. I can feel Papa coming back," she said, kissing the baby gently. "Just as he was Papa to us all, little Hanokh will be a son to us all. He is our perfect victory, him and all the girls and boys who will follow."

Volf stepped back in. Miriam and Batya smothered him with hugs, kisses and congratulatory wishes. "Mazel tov, mazel tov!"

"Thanks, my dearest sisters," he said. "And do you know that today, our country was also born? Reborn?"

"The country. That's what's in your thoughts the whole time. You've just received this amazing baby boy as a gift, and the country..." She shook her head but smiled nonetheless.

MIRIAM MAKES AN ANNOUNCEMENT

"Batya," Miriam began explaining after calling her sister to a secret meeting, "if we don't force them to marry, they won't initiate anything. Nothing's a rush for them, but for us things are moving, and fast. We've got the immigration certificates for America filled out and filed, and we've got Aliyah certificates for Israel registered too. Thank G-d we've got a country of our own. Yisrael keeps writing how wonderful it will be for us there. We have to marry and get things rolling."

"You're right. Let's talk to Hannah. She's already a true-blue Zaks. She'll probably have a good idea or two."

Hannah opened the door, took one look at her sisters-in-law, and understood right away. "Volf, I need you to find some other place to be, if you don't mind. Your sisters and I need to have a women-only *tête-à-tête*."

"Yes, boss," he laughed, kissing Hannah on the nose and going outside to smoke, shutting the door behind him.

The women settled themselves around the table, Hannah started pouring tea and passing around freshly baked butter pastries. "You don't need to explain yourselves. I get it. The time's come for wedding canopies. We need to set dates and simply let the men know. That's the only way. We'll set the time and place, and they'll show up. And we also need to dish up some real-life facts to Avraham and Yossef. They also need to marry. We'll arrange the whole thing."

Batya and Miriam grinned. They were right for choosing to speak to

Hannah. She was down to earth, decisive, and would have things wrapped up fast.

"Word has it that all Jews will receive entry permits by around the coming April, which means that by March 1949 we all need to be married. Let's do it by order and age: first the girls, then the boys. I'll marry first, then Batya, then Yossef, and last but not least, Avraham."

By the look on Batya's face, Hannah and Miriam knew Batya was brewing an idea. "What is it, Batya?" Hannah asked.

"How about if we all get married together? Two canopies on the same day at the same place?"

"No, Batya, that's not such a good idea," Hannah cut in, practical as always. "Each one of you deserves that special moment, your own special day." Batya nodded in agreement. "There'll be four marriages, and we'll celebrate four times, all the Zakses."

"So, if we make Aliyah in April," Hannah flipped through the calendar, let's set one for each month. December 1948 will be Miriam and Mondry. January 1949 will be Batya and Leib. February will be Yossef and Tzilla, and March will close the festivities with Avraham and Tonia's wedding."

Without skipping a beat, Hannah continued. "Miriam, at Shabbat dinner on Friday night, you'll simply advise everyone round the table what we've just decided. I want to see any of them," she said, wiggling her forefinger, "mess with our united front!" The three women roared with laughter.

Shabbat dinner saw everyone in their set places. Hannah had half-prepared Volf, only instructing him that after the blessing on the wine, he would announce that Miriam had something important to tell them. Couple by couple, they sat around the table, the aroma of chicken soup filling the room as harbingers of good tidings to come. The freshly-baked challah's scent wafted into their nostrils, another harbinger of the wonderful. Yossef casually mentioned some of the week's trading adventures with Tzilla. Avraham was waiting for the meal to end, even though he loved being with everyone, but he loved taking Tonia to the dance hall even more. No one was expecting any change to their Shabbat evening norms.

Blessed are you, Lord our G-d, King of the Universe, who created the fruit of the vine, Volf proclaimed. "Amen, l'chaim," all the Zakses heartily responded. And then Volf surprised them. "So, hang on, don't start with the challah yet. Our sister Miriam has something to say. Please," he said, facing her and gesturing with his hand for her to start.

Miriam stood, glanced at each person, and spoke. "It's simple: the time's come to get married!" Several mouths dropped into an 'Oh' of surprise. She was dying to giggle at their reactions, but confidently carried on. "All the couples here have been dating for many months. We're all sure we want to be with our partners. So it's time to marry. And don't ask any questions." She avoided her accomplices' eyes to help her stifle the chuckles she could feel percolating inside of her, but the ploy was working!

"The dates have been set, so mark them down please. First, us girls by seniority. Mondry and I will marry on 19 December 1948. Batya and Leib, on 1 January 1949. Now the boys: Yossef and Tzilla on 15 February; and Avraham and Tonia on 17 March. No one will change the dates. We, the girls, have already booked the rabbi for all the weddings."

Tonia and Tzilla glanced at each other, grinning from ear to ear. At last! At long last!

"Is this for real? Are we getting married?" Yossef asked Avraham.

"Looks like it. Everything's not only been decided but arranged for us," Avraham laughed.

"Well, well, and who'd dare contradict them!" Yossef added, laughing too.

As Miriam sat down, Volf stood, refilling the wine glass. "L'Chaim, congratulations, mazel tov, and may you all be blessed with the very best!"

Mondry hugged Miriam tight. Leib took Batya's hand in his, raised it to his lips and kissed her fingertips. Yossef was still taken aback, trying to digest the idea that in a few short months he'd be married, but Tzilla patted his arm and smiled so broadly that his heart melted. Tonia stayed silent, her head slightly cocked, smiling shyly at Avraham.

"A toast," Avraham said, raising his glass. "Thank you, my big sister Miriam. Congratulations. We'll be the biggest, happiest family in the whole wide world!" And that's precisely when baby Hanokhi, as everyone called him, decided to remind them all that he, too, was part of this big, happy family, and that Papa Hanokh and Mama Yoheved were there in spirit with them.

The meal over, Batya and Miriam had a hard time falling asleep. "Miriam," Batya whispered, "it's so exciting. I need to tell Papa I'm getting married."

"So tell him, Batya. You're used to talking to Papa. Tell him because he listens to you and of course he'll be beside himself with delight. You talk to Papa while I talk to Mama." They fell asleep as soon as they stopped whispering to each other.

Waking early the next morning, they saw clouds filling the sky. "Miriam? Are you awake?" Batya paused. "You know, I spoke with Papa the second I fell asleep. He smiled, he was so thrilled, I felt so calm, as though a veil of tranquility came down and covered me. I heard him say, 'May you be successful, my child. I've always loved Leib. Yossef told me he was courting you, and I know that the day will come when you'll establish a family together." Batya felt so sure of her love for Leib and his for her. "I told Papa that I'm incredibly happy and I could see his eyes, how happy they were, and I promised him we'd continue building our lives for his sake, that he didn't die for nothing, and we'll go on forever."

"And I spoke with Mama," Miriam added after a while. "She was quiet, as she so often was, and only smiled. I told her about Mondry, what a good, strong person he is, and she never stopped smiling. Mama had already turned, as though leaving, when she suddenly spun her head back to face me. 'Miriam, it's all right, you don't need my permission. Of course I agree. I know Mondry will bring you nothing but gladness,' and then she faded away and I woke up and cried quietly, but at the same time felt flooded with gratitude and contentment for having received her blessing."

Miriam and Batya hugged each other, sitting on the edge of the bed together, gazing out at the brightening sky.

FOUR WEDDINGS

Arms linked with Hannah on the left, and Batya on her right, Miriam was led to the wedding canopy. Mondry, a grin never leaving his face, stood with his head held high. Volf, Avraham, Yossef, and Leib each held one of the four posts to which the four corners of a large prayer shawl were tied, forming a traditional Jewish wedding canopy. This December 19th, Miriam walked slowly, her dress as white as snow, the three young women teary-eyed and smiling: tears of joy at escorting Miriam to her marriage, tears of sorrow that Miriam's parents could not be fulfilling.

"Dear guests," the rabbi addressed the people attending the celebration, "Here we are, celebrating the marriage of Miriam, of the Zaks family, and Jozef Mondry, two very precious young people. This is a unique occasion marked by an absence of parents. But it is additionally unique for the fact that the large Zaks family and the Mondry family already have buds blossoming in Israel, and all are rebuilding their lives. Encompassed by brothers and sisters, brothers-in-law and sisters-in-law, all have adopted something of a parenting role to our dear Miriam and Jozef, embracing the young couple heartily.

"We all know how strong and courageous Miriam has been and continues to be. As a teen in the ghetto, she banished Nazi soldiers from her parents' home. After liberation, she prevented Russian soldiers from harming her sister and sister-in-law. Miriam, fearless, is marrying a man well matched to her, our dear Mondry, partisan and war hero in forest and snow. With almost nothing of value as a weapon, he fought the oppressive Nazi war machine with courage and bravery. These two forces of strength, Miriam and Jozef, together with the embrace of their extended families, will shape an invincible unit."

Mondry passed the wine to his bride, slipped a ring on her finger, and each time he caught her gaze, his eyes filled with love for his bride. *"If I forget thee, O Jerusalem, let my right hand forget its skill,"* he repeated the rabbi's recitation before bringing his foot down on the wrapped glass.

"Mazel tov!" the guests called out.

Mondry, lifting his bride in his muscular arms, whispered in her ear. "Never, ever will I leave you, my beloved wife, not even for a day!"

Three brothers and a sister hugged and jumped up and down for joy, quickly joined by Hannah, and the in-laws-to-be, Leib, Tzilla and Tonia. "May we wish mazel tov to you soon, too," they said, blessing each other with good fortune.

Two weeks later, on January 1st, 1949, Batya was led to her marriage canopy, her right arm linked with Hannah's, her left with Miriam. Leib, under the canopy, was watching them slowly walking towards him. For long tough years he'd waited for his love, ever since their school days. How proud he felt now. Patience pays, he thought, smiling. Just thinking about her during the war kept me going and got me through the Holocaust. My dream that she'd be my wife drove me forward, day by day, and here we are, about to marry. But why has Batya stopped? Dear G-d, I hope she's not regretting our decision! Patience, Leib. Give her a bit of time, he quickly rebuked himself: You've waited until now. You'll wait a few seconds more.

Hannah and Miriam stopped too, turning their heads to glance questioningly at Batya, who was gazing at her Leib. Slowly she looked upwards as though towards the heavens. "Slowly, slowly, I can't do this so quickly." Miriam and Hannah waited. All eyes were on Batya. She longed to see her father. "It's not how I imagined this moment, Papa," she muttered, barely moving her lips. "How I wish you could have walked me to the canopy. Mama, how I wished you could have stood next to me right now. A wedding without the two of you is not complete. I have the white dress, I have a bouquet, and I have a wonderful groom who you knew well, ever since he was a boy. I have almost everything. But a wedding without both of you is hard for me to accept."

Hannah understood only too well what Batya was feeling. "Batya, now you need to look ahead. See him there? He's the man who loves you, and your entire large family is waiting for you. They can never replace your Papa and Mama, but they'll always make sure you're safe and looked after. Always look forward and you'll know, by looking at your wonderful family, that Papa and Mama are present in them and looking down on you with love, joy, and pride." She paused, giving Batya another moment. "Now, come, Batya dearest, and let us walk you to your marriage."

Leib visibly relaxed once Batya, escorted by Miriam and Hannah, began to move towards him. His eyes, speaking of love and welcoming her, reassured Batya. Once again, the rabbi referred to family lore.

"Our dear Batya and Leib, you met in childhood, traveling to school together on the train. Leib has loved you ever since, and it's that love which brought him through the harsh events. It's a love that no German could extinguish. And it's that love which, having overcome the war, will help you both not only survive but flourish in your future."

Leib's and Batya's cheeks were moist when he slipped the ring on her finger and recited the blessing. "*By this ring you are consecrated to me as my wife, in accordance with the laws of Moses and the people of Israel.*" As though awakened from a dream, and for the first time since joining her beloved under the canopy, Batya broke into a huge smile when Leib kissed her. Avraham and Tonia broke into a wild happy dance, drawing everyone into the swirling melodies with them.

A repeat of these joyous events was held on February 15th. Yossef and Tzilla stood under the canopy, now surrounded by three married couples. "Who knows what might have happened," he said to Tzilla on several occasions, "if Miriam, Hannah, and Batya hadn't decided for me!"

"Do you think I would have given up on you?" Tzilla always answered.

"Yossef," she said one day as their wedding date drew nearer, her tone jovial but simultaneously serious, "I'd just like you to know that on our wedding day, I want the red-carpet treatment! Like the one they rolled out for David Ben-Gurion when he came to visit. All the way up to our canopy! So please, make sure there is one!"

Stunned, Yossef's eyes opened wide. "Tzilla, your wish is my command! You'll have a carpet like the one Kaiser Franz Jozef I of the Hapsburg Dynasty walked on," he whispered, his lips brushing her ear as he hugged her close.

"I know," was all she said.

Yossef's excellent contacts with supplies commanders in the Allied Forces stood him in good stead. Having done business with so many of them, his efforts eventually located the red carpet, intended for VIP guests, in the British military supplies storage. Promising the carpet's return after the ceremony, he thanked the officer, certain that once Tzilla had used it to reach the canopy, it would forever stay in the Zaks family. And so it was.

To guests gasping at what they saw, Tzilla proudly walked the red carpet marking the way from the hall's front door to the canopy on its raised platform. Accompanying her were Miriam, standing in for Yoheved, and Batya, standing in for Tzilla's deceased mother, as others had stood in for their own. Like the other brides, Tzilla shed a silent tear of sorrow for her absent parents and a tear of gratitude for being able to join such a large, wonderful family. With a bounce in her step, she walked towards her groom. Flanked by his brothers, Yossef couldn't stop smiling. Watching every step she took, Yossef's heart was filled with joy. Like an empress, he thought, just as I promised her.

As pretty as a ball-roomed Cinderella, Tzilla stepped out proudly in her high-heeled, white shoes. Those were another of Yossef's finds at a store where he did business. She'd simply accepted them, sight unseen. "I know her foot as well as I know her hand," Yossef had said to his brothers before heading out to buy them, "so there's no need for her to try them on. I'll bring her the very best surprise there is!" Volf and Avraham never doubted that for a moment. Yossef was the savviest merchant of them all back in their shop in Strzemieszyce, perfectly picking coats, hats, gloves, and shoes out for their customers. One glance at a client's foot and he would know in a fraction of a second what size she needed, and what she'd like. When he brought Tzilla this little wedding surprise, they fitted her to perfection.

Standing together under the wedding canopy, surrounded by siblings who had survived the Holocaust, their love for each other helped alleviate their parents' absence. "I promise you, Tzilla," Yossef addressed his new wife, "that you will always be my empress, and we will spend our lives walking the red carpet together. You are a skilled merchant too. Together, we will be an unstoppable force. Soon we'll be in Israel, where we'll establish our successful company. No one will stand in our way." It was the longest speech that Yossef, the most silent one of them all, had ever made. Nor did he wait for the rabbi to finish the blessings but impatiently brought his foot down on the wrapped glass and kissed his bride. The red carpet blushed at the amount of wine flowing at their wedding.

Avraham and Tonia decided that their wedding should reflect their love of dancing. On March 17th, they joyfully headed for the wedding dais to the background music of a Chopin Mazurka. A long, wide ribbon was attached to Tonia's dress. The groom held the end of the lace-covered satin, and the couple danced elegantly, as the familiar Polish melody required. In Tonia's footsteps came Miriam and Batya, Hannah and Tzilla; following Avraham came Volf and Yossef, Mondry and Leib. Guests clapped to the rhythm, accompanying the young couple to their marriage. Standing at the ready, the rabbi's face was a picture of amazement: never before had he seen a Jewish couple dance the path to their own canopy.

Good naturedly, the rabbi smiled broadly. "I hope you dance as light-footedly throughout your entire lives," he wished them before beginning the ceremony. "Here before us is a very special family," he addressed the guests. "Although not present today in full count, they have already reunited. During the war, the brothers kept each other going, as did the sisters. How well they value the essence of togetherness. They left no one behind. And with commitment like that to each other, there's no need to explain to the Zakses the importance and the blessing of commitment in marriage. It flows in their veins."

Looking at Tonia and Avraham, the rabbi paused. Avraham looked down:

In his mind, he once again saw that terrible day when he carried his beloved father and mother to their room, and only minutes later, his father was murdered. Gritting his teeth and balling his fists, Avraham kept his arms tightly by his sides as he trembled, never hearing the rabbi's closing sentence. "This family will never be forgotten. That's why they'll succeed in reestablishing their lives and new generations of the extended Zaks family."

Avraham shuddered, then suddenly whispered to Tonia. "Are we married yet? Did I break the glass?"

Stunned, Tonia quickly answered. "Not yet, Avraham. A bit more and we'll be married."

"Take a sip of this wine and pass it to your bride," the rabbi instructed, holding the cup out to Avraham before guiding Avraham through the blessing that would sanctify the marriage: "*By this ring you are consecrated to me as my wife, in accordance with the laws of Moses and the people of Israel.*"

Avraham slipped the ring on Tonia's forefinger, according to Jewish custom, but instead of precisely repeating the rabbi's next verse, he took everyone by surprise. "*If I forget thee, O Jerusalem, let my right hand lose its skill, and if I forget you, dear Mama and Papa, may my tongue cleave to my palate.*"

Silence spread through the guests, absorbing his words, before they all broke out into lively calls of congratulations. "Mazel tov!" Glancing down, Avraham noticed that he had now broken the glass, even though he didn't remember actually doing it. Brothers, sisters, and in-laws all clapped him on the back, hugged Tonia, and in no time a circle of four recently married couples enveloped the newest couple with the tremendous love and relief they felt for their youngest brother and the lovely young woman who'd just joined the Zaks family.

With the Mazurka still playing in the background, Avraham led Tonia to the center of the hall where they danced gracefully, the music slowly speeding up, their rhythms always perfectly matched, guests clapping and enjoying the beautiful sight of these two lovely young people so light on their feet. Batya squeezed Leib's hand, and they joined the dance floor. Yossef took Tzilla's hand in his, Miriam winked at Mondry, Hannah gave Volf a little shove. All of them on the dance floor together. They circled round and round before guests began to pair off and join them as the music flowed into a polka, and then into waltzes. Avraham and Tonia danced until the early hours of the morning, eyes glued to each other, never tiring.

INDEPENDENCE DOCKS

Certificates of immigration arrived at last for all the Zakses except Leib but he had no doubt that his big, new family's resourcefulness would fix that too. While all of them also had visas for America, it was abundantly clear to them all where they'd go as a family. The unanimous decision on making Aliyah was already two years old; that's how long Israel and Haiya had already been there. As married couples, they began organizing for the journey. Meanwhile Lazar, Leib's brother, came to visit. He was concerned. "Lilly and I have decided to go to America, but although she has a visa, I don't, and I have no idea what to do."

Leib needed no more than a few seconds to come up with the solution. "No problem, Lazar! You can have mine!" he laughed warmly. "From now on you'll be Leib Levi. After all, there's no need to change your family name, so take my papers, no one will have any inkling and go in peace with Lilly."

Lazar's face lit up with surprise. "Hang on, but if I'm going to be you, what will you be?"

Leib laughed again. "Don't worry about that. I'm with the Zakses and they've always got some solution up their sleeve!"

But Lazar wasn't feeling reassured. "Well, what if you don't do so okay there, in those deserts in the Land of Israel," he persisted. "What then?"

"Don't worry, Lazar," Leib answered firmly. "True, everyone in that family's got visas for the USA, but nonetheless they're crazy about going to Israel. And I'm going with Batya. All the way."

Lazar embraced his brother. "All right," he smiled broadly, his eyes moist. "From now on I'm Yehuda-Leib. I'll never forget your help on this." And Lazar returned to Munich, his brother's papers in hand.

"Batya," Leib was now relating the events to his wife, "I gave Lazar my visa for America, and he's going to go under my name. So now I have no name, no visa for America, and no immigration permit for Israel. What are we going to do?" he said, shaking with laughter at the very odd situation.

Batya huffed to show her momentary annoyance but right away got practical. "All right, let's go talk to Volf and Hannah. I'm sure they'll have something up their sleeve."

Leib laughed even more loudly. "You took the words out of my mouth! That's what I told Lazar!"

Volf listened closely to his brother-in-law. "The emissary from Israel is a friend of mine. I'm very active in the General Zionist Movement. Let's go over there but let me do the talking. Maybe we can fix this easily."

Over in the office, the Israel representative came up with a suggestion. "I can produce another permit for a Zaks but not for some other name." He glanced up at Leib. "Is your name Zaks? And what's your first name?"

Leib fell silent. Volf didn't hesitate. "Yitzhak, that's his name. He's another of our brothers. Can you make the permit out to Yitzhak Zaks, please?"

And in no time Leib received his immigration permit under the name of the young brother who'd drowned so long before the war. On the way back, Leib couldn't contain his glee. "I must be the only guy who married his own sister!"

The immigration permit glitch solved, Himmler's palace, used by the community for a variety of purposes, now filled with busy pre-departure activity. In the large hall, Mondry set up a carpentry workshop and with his golden hands, built five massive, wooden luggage crates for the family's belongings and equipment purchased for the lives they were planning in Israel. Three 'factories' were packed to ship to Israel: one was the carpentry workshop, outfitted with professional electric saws and tools. Mondry would need to no more than find a location and set it all up. In the second lift, as the crates were called, was all the equipment needed for an ice factory. The third was to produce nails and screws using the latest in German technology.

The other two lifts were packed with household goods, including prestigious German dinner services. Mondry supervised: he was far more than a talented carpenter. In fact, he was an excellent engineer, everything packed so that nothing would break either in the ship's hold or when loaded and offloaded by the cranes. He anchored the lifts to prevent them from flipping over. Standing and waiting for his instructions, the Zakses filled with admiration as they watched him calmly go about his work.

Despite the Israeli weather, the women purchased expensive furs, not only to look as good as classy Polish ladies but because the pockets had been lined with diamonds, gems, and jewelry. Almost all the money left after buying the items needed for the three factories had been invested in valuables that could easily be carried on the body. Some of the leftover funds had been exchanged for dollars and pounds sterling. The family was extremely well organized.

Avraham decided to sell the Mercedes back to the British officer. The purring vehicle drove smoothly into the camp. A knowing smile came across the officer's face. "Oh yes, Avraham? And what have you got this time? Another Mercedes?"

"Oho!" Avraham laughed. "This time, I'm returning your lost car. We're all heading for Israel now, and I came to offer the car you fell in love with back then, but this time really for a price you won't want to pass up."

A spark lit in the officer's eyes. "How much?"

"Make me an offer," Avraham answered, "and whatever you say, that's the price."

The Brit tested his luck. "Three hundred marks and it's mine?" he asked, playing the nonchalant.

Avraham held his hand out. "Deal. The car's yours."

The officer almost snatched the keys out of Avraham's hand, as though unsure if Avraham might yet change his mind. "Well, well, well!" he said. "In the end, it is a pleasure to do business with you!"

"Just one request, my friend," Avraham said. The officer's very vocal sigh said, '*What now?*' But he said nothing, merely gesturing with an open palm for Avraham to continue.

"I'd like you to lead our convoy to the Celle train station when it's time for us to go, which will be in a few days from now," Avraham asked.

The officer agreed right away. "It would be my privilege."

Documents and keys changed hands. Before turning to leave, Avraham had one more thing to add. "A last lone request, if I may, my dear friend the General."

The officer laughed. "My dear good Avraham, you could squeeze water from stone if you tried hard enough! Yes? What is it?"

Avraham pointed to the two flags of Israel flying on the Mercedes' front fender. "When you accompany us to the station, please leave those flags in place. I want them to be the last thing I see when the train pulls out."

Shaking Avraham's hand, the officer nodded his agreement.

***

With Avraham's beloved Mercedes in the lead, the convoy rolled out proudly flying Israeli flags. Avraham and Tonia sat in the back seat as the officer drove on the last time they'd ever make this journey. Behind them, four more married couples followed. No one turned their heads around to take a last look.

Although Bergen-Belsen had slowly come back to life as a small bustling city of displaced persons, increasingly flourishing after the liberation, not a single Zaks would ever forget the long days of Nazi terror there. The Zaks family left Germany forever.

Aboard "Independence," the Zakses set sail from Marseille on March 31st, 1949. It would be the Independent's last journey, ten Zakses among the 3,000 Jewish immigrants sailing to their new home, and five crates stuffed to their brims in the ship's hold.

On that first night of sailing, Volf and Hannah, Miriam and Mondry, Batya and Leib, Yossef and Tzilla, and Avraham and Tonia sat together in a circle, ten-month-old Hanokhi cradled in his mother Hannah's arms. But that never lasted long: In no time he was being passed from one pair of loving arms to the next. Hugging Hanokhi close, Batya spoke up.

"I have something to say," she began, as she had done so many times in the past. "Do you all realize we are making Aliyah to our country? I mean, all of us, literally, without exception," she said, excitement tingeing her voice. "Look, even Yitzhak's here! Our sweet little brother, his name carried by Leib. I'm holding little Hanokhi, Hannah and Volf's baby, but who also represents Papa," she said, wiping a tear away. "He disappeared from the yard in Strzemieszyce and here he is now again with us all and I'm hugging him, and he's living, breathing, smiling, and he'll be with us forever."

Batya swallowed and paused. "But not only Papa is with us," she continued, smiling. "Mama is with us too." All eyes were now turned questioningly towards her. She laughed. "My dear Zakses, I'm pregnant and I'm carrying a little girl. And how do I know that? Because Papa appeared in my dream and told me! 'Batya', he said, 'I'm already with you all, embodied in little Hanokhi, and in your womb you carry the embodiment of Mama.' So that's how I know without a doubt that we'll have a little girl, and we'll call her Yoheved."

The Zakses stood, embracing Batya. As so often, laughter and tears intermingled, but there were no whoops of joy: the Zakses were a quiet clan. And so, with Batya's announcement, they choked on their tears as they smiled and embraced the joy.

"Well," Miriam stood after they'd all calmed down, "I've also got something to say."

All eyes now turned to her as Hannah clapped her hands and almost shouted for joy. "You're also pregnant!" she gasped.

Miriam smiled. "You don't miss a beat! Like a real Zaks, you catch every detail," Miriam laughed, winking at her sister-in-law. "Yes, I'm also pregnant, but I have no idea if it's a boy or girl."

Mondry stroked her belly. "It's a boy, Miriam. I keep telling you, it's a boy!"

***

Early on Monday morning of April 4th, 1949, Volf went on deck, the boat surrounded by fog, and Hanokhi cradled in his arms. Volf smiled at the thought of Hanokhi being simultaneously the infant and the father for the entire family. Several other passengers were on deck; they and Volf exchanged nods of acknowledgment. But everyone was looking east: they'd been told that six days after setting sail, they'd see Haifa in the distance. Today was the sixth day. Where is Haifa, and its lights? they asked themselves, and where is Mount Carmel?

Volf wondered if he wasn't hallucinating. "Is that a mountain opposite us? Am I seeing right?" he asked the others. "Can you see it too?"

"Oh, yes!" they laughed. "It is! It's Mount Carmel."

Slowly the shapes grew more visible despite the fog, and there it was, the mountain that rose from the shore. The sky grew lighter and clearer. Volf looked around: the whole family had meanwhile come on deck too. Unlike other passengers, who chattered excitedly away with each other, the Zakses stood quietly, in awe, taking in this moment as the Land of Israel revealed itself. Here was the mountain renowned because of Elijah the Prophet. The Zakses huddled together, hugging each other, taking in this sight, the sight of their new home, where they would raise their children and grandchildren and live forever more.

Raising Hanokhi a little, Volf showed him the mountain. "See, Hanokhi? We've come home, my dear son. We've come to the best, most beautiful place there is in the world," he whispered in the baby's ear, kissing his forehead softly. "Just three years ago, we were sure it was the end for us all and look, we've bounced back, bigger and stronger than ever. Look, Papa, look over there, look how we're getting closer and closer. I couldn't save you then, Papa, but now I've brought you with me to our own land, to Israel." He hugged the baby, his mind superimposing Hanokh and Hanokhi, the blue eyes of the former looking out through the blue eyes of the latter, sparkling, vibrant with life.

Haifa Port appeared some hours later, framed by the mountain decked out in springtime greenery and wildflowers, the small houses of the city nestling among the forest trees. Hooting loudly, the boat seemed to be laughing warmly as its last mission drew to a close.

The Independent moored. Watching the heavy, iron anchor drop down into the water, every Zaks there shared the same thought: We've also set down our anchor. We've docked at last in our new home.

THE LITTLE HOUSE IN AFULA

Volf, Hannah, and Hanokhi, together with Hannah's mother Esther, joined Yisrael and Haiya in Afula. It was a small place, with just two rooms and a balcony. But the house was overflowing with the warmth of two mothers and one grandmother devotedly caring for two tiny tots: two-year-old Tuvi and one-year-old Hanokhi. Volf found work right away as an accountant at the city's flour mill. As Yisrael's younger brother, Volf was warmly received, especially since Yisrael had accrued seniority in the same role in a different mill. Every so often, a small sigh would escape one or the other: who would have thought that flour would be the focus of their livelihoods. Flour, so readily available for making different kinds of breads and cakes, which didn't need to be earned as the salaried pittance for defusing bombs.

The other families settled into Tel Aviv, the equipment and items they'd brought in the shipped lifts helping them through their first months. Two babies were born in Tel Aviv. First was Batya's little Yoheved. Now both of the Zaks parents' names were perpetuated by young new lives. Three weeks later, Miriam gave birth to a son who she and Mondry named Hayim after Mondry's late father. Not only was Mondry's father now perpetuated, but the very name itself, meaning 'life', held great significance for them.

Sadly, Yoheved struggled with health, weakening and losing weight. Doctors were perplexed, not finding any obvious reason. Batya was crazy with worry. After another appointment, and no improvement, the order came from

Afula: "Come to us, immediately," the telegram said. Haiya then sent Miriam an urgent message: "Come to us with Hayim." Although he was a large, smiling child with a good appetite, Haiya wasn't taking no for an answer.

"Papa told us to stay together. That's what we're going to do," she insisted in a letter urgently sent to her two sisters-in-law, "so Yisrael and I want you all here, where I'm sure Yoheved will get healthy again, nursed by four mothers and a grandmother. Together, with Esther's help too, we'll take care of little Yoheved. We, the Zakses, never leave each other behind!"

Two rooms, one balcony, four fathers, four babies, and five mothers (after all, Esther was also an experienced mother). The men went out to work. Mondry began setting up his carpentry workshop. Yoheved was still weak but slowly began showing improvement, her weight increasing bit by bit. As in Strzemieszyce, the Zaks family was a steadfast united bloc, sharing good and bad. Batya wondered aloud whether she shouldn't hospitalize Yoheved. Afula was a small city but the Emek Medical Center was known to be one of the best the country had to offer. The family sought their cousin's opinion.

"There's no need," Dr. Leon Zaks explained when he visited. "Just give her plenty of love and she'll get well. Watch her carefully, and she'll be fine. She's got the Zaks's genes: tough, obstinate. She'll get over this," he added. Leon visited on an almost weekly basis to check little Yoheved's progress.

Cramped as the home was, everyone enjoyed lavishing love on Yoheved, and on each other. At night the entire house turned into one huge bedroom. Mattresses were spread on the balcony floor for the men. Freshly laundered cloth diapers were hung anywhere a line could be put up. The house filled with the gurgles, laughter, and cries of four little ones. There was never a shortage of food. Haiya would say that a little more water added to the soup never hurt anyone. But Miriam, handling the cooking most of the time, kept everyone satisfied.

Behind the house was a small municipal garden and a kiosk which sold sweets and drinks. Afula enjoys wonderful valley breezes and fresh air, making it a joy for the families to spend early evenings in the garden. The little Zaks boys ran around, the babies were still breastfeeding, and the good, clean air was not only a refreshing break but a boost to everyone's health. Yoheved was soon being called the shortened "Yohi" by her little cousins and the adult Zakses alike. Yohi grew to be as strong and resilient as her namesake grandmother had been.

On one of their adored cousins' visits to the tiny home in Afula, Batya had a question. "You're a fantastic physician, Leon. And I'm curious: what healed our Yohi? After all, we haven't given her any medicine."

Without skipping a beat, Leon answered. "A home isn't just rooms and walls. A home is the people in it. When that translates into a loving family, closeness, warmth, and concern, it gives everyone the power to not only survive but to overcome. You know that from the Holocaust. When any of you were weak or ill, the others propped that one up emotionally and physically. Modern medicine doesn't have all the answers," he smiled, "but it's abundantly clear to me that no medicine can compete with the love and embrace that the Zakses know how to share, supporting each other and not giving in."

A FINAL RESTING PLACE

In the summer of 1968, twenty-five years after the massacre of June 23rd, 1943, two IDF soldiers in uniform, red berets on their heads, stood in the Kiryat Shaul cemetery. They were the cousins Tuvi and Hanokhi Zaks. They looked out at the silent crowd gathered around a headstone. The drape was drawn away to reveal a large black basalt headstone bearing eighteen names engraved in gold lettering. They were the innocent victims of Holocaust murders, hastily buried by Marek and the town's doctor after listing the victims' names. Their bones had been located and brought for reburial in Israel's land because long ago, Miriam and Batya had marked the mass grave where their own Papa was also buried.

The cantor recited the prayers; and the attendees recited Kaddish, the mourner's prayer, together. Participating, too, were all the members of six proudly Israeli Zaks families.

How those red berets contrasted with the brown and green colors of the surroundings. Batya closed her eyes, seeing Papa in the face of her nephew Hanokhi. The kind and special man from Strzemieszyce was now epitomized by the young, robust soldier protecting their country. In her imagination, Hanokh's and Hanokhi's visages interchanged repeatedly. Helpless to defend himself, Hanokh had been murdered in the yard and was now, at last, being reburied in the sacred land of Israel; but not really, because here he was, ramrod straight and proud, his uniform declaring 'Never Again!'

"Never again!" Batya suddenly spoke aloud. "I see it in our soldiers' eyes, I know they will make sure of that. Throughout the war, Papa kept watch over me. Now his grandchildren will take up the guard. I feel so protected, and so much the stronger for knowing that."

Volf hugged his sister. "Yes, our young Hanokhi will guard us. Papa's spirit is with him in that uniform."

Yisrael's eyes were moist with pride as he looked at Tuvi. In the young man, he could see his father-in-law Guttman, who died towards the end of the March of Death. There was Haiya's father, standing tall and proud in the image of their son Tuvi, pledged to ensure no one could ever inflict such harm on his family again.

Miriam and Avraham thought about their mother, never buried as Jewish custom requires, her spirit seeming to radiate from little Yohi, whose good-heartedness was a perfect reflection of their late mother.

Yossef's thoughts were of dark days which he had chosen to bury under a mantle of silence. Choosing to remain silent at the cemetery, he did allow himself a slight smile when he thought about how his brothers and sisters had brought him back to life, and how his father taught him the art of commerce in the Strzemieszyce shop. "Thank you, Papa," he whispered. "At last, you've reached eternal rest even as your legacy continues vibrantly into the future."

Moist-eyed as they remembered the worst, the Zaks siblings broke into smiles as they spoke of their gratitude for how good their lives were now in their ancestral home, and how their children represented hope and pride. As always, sorrow and happiness mingled. "Rest, Papa. You deserve to," Yisrael said. "Strzemieszyce, which you loved so much, murdered you but Israel, which you never merited experiencing, has received you honorably. Papa, you're here at last, in our true home, safe and sound. Rest in peace, our dearest Papa, and keep watching over us."

Although the ceremony was formally over, the Zaks family stayed at the fresh gravesite. Whistling through the tops of cypress trees growing nearby, the breeze was the only sound that could be heard. A large shepherd dog suddenly appeared, its fur shining white, its stride firm. Slowly, deliberately it made its way towards the group of people. All eyes turned to follow it: the stunning creature raised it head, walking with purpose towards the two soldiers. Hanokhi got down onto one knee, holding his hand out, inviting the dog to approach. It walked up to the young soldier, licking his hand, leaning against Hanokhi's leg, growling softly with pleasure. Silently, the older Zakses watched, mesmerized, smiling to each other. Raising its head again, it gazed at everyone before turning and regally walking out of the cemetery, barking softly once at the gate before disappearing from view.

A SILKEN THREAD

June 23, 1943, marks the date that Yoheved and Hanokh were murdered by the Nazi criminals. Hanokh was murdered in the yard of their ghetto home; Yoheved in Auschwitz where she was sent that same day.

At the ripe age of 94, Batya passed away on June 23, 2017. Her daughters Yohi and Shuli brought her for burial at the Kiryat Shaul cemetery. Passing the gravestone marking the eighteen Jews of Strzemieszyce, they paused, paying their respects to Hanokh Hendel Zaks, his name clearly visible in the Hebrew letters of his ancestral heritage.

Meeting with the cemetery director, the family described the events leading to Papa Hanokh's reburial in Israel. Not a dry eye was left in the room. "There is an empty space beneath the headstone," Yohi told the director, which he confirmed. "We wish to bury our mother Batya there, beneath the headstone marking her father, our grandfather."

Softly, the director spoke. "There is no more worthy place for your late mother. I can feel the deep love you have for her. There she will be reunited with her father."

Yohi and Shuli set about preparing the necessary documents. Yohi shuddered when she checked the dates. Their mother had passed away on 23rd June 2017, the same date on which their grandfather had been murdered seventy-four years earlier. The corresponding Jewish calendar date was 29 Sivan 5777.

"Indeed, our mother was taken as though by an unseen hand to ensure she reunited with her Papa," Shuli said.

"Yes, Papa cared for her so much and she for him that he appointed the same date of passing, it seems. She always spoke about how much he watched over her," Yohi added, "and he continued, right up to the last second."

The gravestone bore a telling inscription: Batya's name, her date of birth and death, and a simple sentence: "He always kept watch over me" and in the next line, "A pure soul who returned to her beloved father's embrace."

But the unseen hand had more in store. Precisely a year later, on the Jewish date of 29 Sivan 5778, Avraham, last of the Zaks's earlier generation, was brought to burial. The young lad who had tried to protect his mother and was helpless to save his father, rose to heaven to reunite with his family seventy-five years after his parents died. How telling that the two Zaks siblings who had tried to save their parents by risking their own lives, but had not succeeded through no fault of their own, returned their souls on the same date that their parents had died.

A Personal Afterword

I never enjoyed the experience of a grandfather, and I'd love to be my grandfather.

Hanokh, or Chanochi in its current Anglicized spelling, is the name I was given, in honor of my grandfather of the same name, murdered in the Holocaust. Through his name, I carry him into the future, but he was never mine. I had aunts and uncles, I have cousins, I did have a grandmother, but never a grandfather.

When I tell that to my grandchildren, they simply can't comprehend the idea. "Saba," they ask, using the Hebrew word for grandfather so naturally, "how is it you didn't have one? How is it that we have four grandparents but you didn't even have one? Did you play only with your Abba but never with your Saba?" Did I only have a father to play with, but no grandfather, my grandchildren ask.

"That's right," I say, and see in their puzzled eyes that they can't fathom the concept.

I grew up without a grandfather but how I wanted one, a grandfather who'd tell me tales, listen, be there, someone of whom I could say "My Saba came with me, my Saba is there, he's doing this, he did that…"

We were new immigrants who came from "there," as the vast swathe of Europe devastated by the Holocaust was referred to in hushed tones. We came from "there" because it was hard to say, "Our parents came from the Holocaust."

How I envied the Israeli-born and bred kids I came across, whose parents spoke Hebrew with a natural Israeli accent, the gutturals and inflections enunciated perfectly, who could pronounce my name correctly, unlike my mother who never got the 'kh' combination quite right, always mixing up the guttural "kh" for the softer "h."

And so, if I could be my own Saba, I'd grow a beard, a long white one that I could stroke as an older man, gaze into my grandchild's eyes as I tell a story, and as that grandchild, reach out and connect. I'd prepare lots of stories, keeping them in a back drawer in my mind, always ready to pull them out and tell. I'd sit with me, embrace me, and let me choose which story I'd like to hear.

I'd give my stories free rein. As a child, I'd close my eyes and imagine journeys to deserts and jungles; and as the Saba I'd find ways to make those stories come to life. And I'd also make time to help explain math problems. Yes, my father was a mathematical genius, it all came so easily to him and to me much less so, but perhaps, as a Saba, I could explain the problem to my 'grandchild-self' through a story, patiently, without ever hearing, as my father would say, 'How is it you don't get it?' As a Saba I'd have plenty of time, which I could invest in my grandchild-self.

I'd explain to my grandchild-self that the older generation has a lot of wisdom, not the kind that's taught in school but the kind that comes from living, year after year, linking one experience to the next. I'd explain that experience can't be taught, it has to be lived. As a Saba, I'd tell my grand-self about the days when there were no cars, no TV, not even a telephone. I'd try to describe what it's like to live without these, how we'd have fun outdoors making up games, making friends, how we'd play together, bumping into each other, and how 'tag' means touching your friend as part of the game. That's what I'd like to explain about how my Saba lived.

As I grew up, I imagined myself as a grandfather, my body heavier, my thoughts a little more scattered, my movements a little slower, and my grand-child-self coming to help me, returning in kind what I gave as the grandfather.

And here I am as the child wanting to tell Saba things. I want to run into my Saba's arms, never mind that I'm all sticky and sweaty, and tell him about the fantastic goals I scored, or the amazing way my basketball sailed through the hoop in the final game. I want to tell him about the Scouts camp and the fun things we see and do on treks. I want to tell Saba everything: what's going on in the world, about my first love, who's in my army enlistment unit, the battles I fought as an Israel Defense Forces soldier to make sure my Saba would always be safe, unlike me, whose Saba was murdered in the Holocaust. I want to tell him how, as a young man, I perceive the world. I set out on long journeys and see the countless tales that my Saba-self told me. I see it all, experience it all, and want to give back to my Saba. The story I told as a Saba comes back to me as a mature experience, but as the Saba I'm already a little hard of hearing, find some things harder to understand, and can't be fully involved in my grandchild-self's experiences as he grows up.

I am my Saba. We share the name: Hanokh and Hanokhi. I could be the last in our line to carry this name. It's looking like it would be that way. Can I dare say I'm curious about hearing my own eulogy, what I, as the grandchild-self, would say over my Saba-self's grave? I wouldn't read it all out here, but I would just like to note something about my name.

Of Hanokh, the book of Genesis 5:24 states: "*And Hanokh walked with G-d, and he was not, for G-d took him.*" Hanokh never actually died in the sense we understand dying. For me, my grandfather Hanokh simply 'was not' but I so wished him to be. Here, now, is the first time I've chatted with him, something I've never done before.

Knowing

My grandson shall know
the name
of his grandfather's grandfather
but I shall not
know the name
of my grandfather's grandfather

by Itzik Reicher

The lineage

Hanokh and Yoheved had 6 children, who together represent the great generations of this family that survived the Holocaust
10 grandchildren (9 still living)
27 great-grandchildren
41 great-great-grandchildren
38 wives and husbands
In the Jewish year 5780, corresponding to 2020, the Zaks clan numbered 115. This is the Zaks family's manifestation of victory.

***

Backstories of survival

We found it interesting that Miriam and Volf shared the same date of birth: July 28th. Batya and Avraham shared a date of birth, too: October 13th.

Initially we wondered if the dates were simply erroneously registered in Polish towns back then. Perhaps they didn't really know the correct dates and so simply registered children with the same date. But in a conversation with my dear aunt Batya, I asked how she and Avraham shared a date of birth, as did Volf and Miriam. A glitch?

Batya laughed heartily. "Oh, no, not at all. Very simply, twins weren't called up for military service in the Polish army, so Papa registered Volf and Miriam as twins, and Avraham and me as twins, which kept the two boys free of obligatory recruitment. Unfortunately, Mama didn't give birth to additional children close to the times Yisrael and Yossef were born, and so both served, and even more unfortunately, Yossef actually served active duty during that horrid war."

Avraham and Batya continued to celebrate the birthday that Papa Hanokh officially registered for them even though Batya was older by a year. What we couldn't ascertain was whether the birth years were 1922 and 1923, or

1923 and 1924; we all continued celebrating their registered dates out of respect. Volf and Miriam restored their original birth years, 1915 and 1918 respectively.

ACKNOWLEDGMENTS

Books don't get written by the magical wave of a wand. Books come about through cooperation. I wouldn't have been able to produce this one without our family having a complex tale to tell.

First and foremost, my gratitude to our parents, from whom we drew the family's history, and for their fortitude in retelling the details and events of the harshest of times. They are deeply loved. May their memories be a blessing.

Boundless thanks to their parents, the grandparents we never knew, Hanokh and Yoheved, brutally murdered by Nazis on 23 June 1943. None of the grandchild generation met them, yet we felt their presence with us as a source of inspiration in life and the spirit behind the family's history.

Special thanks to everyone who provided the backbone and details: our beloved aunt Batya, whose dozens of hours of recorded sessions were listened to with fascination and love by so many of us. Without these taped recordings, I would have found it tremendously difficult to produce the book.

Thanks to everyone who helped along the way: my dear teacher Ilan Scheinfeld for guiding me, chapter by chapter, through the wonderful writing classes he gives, and for his constant encouragement. Without a doubt, Ilan, you're my greatest ally as I continue to write books. I'll never forget your support.

My deepest thanks and appreciation to my literary editors Amira and Aharon Morag. Your ability to dig deep, alter and correct, finding the most appropriate way to present the material while preserving the tone of my writing, is superbly impressive.

Special thanks to Mati Alma Elhanati, editor, proofreader, stylist, producer, publisher, and everything else in between as the book took shape. Most of all, thanks for your big heart: for always being there for me.

My heart holds a warm spot for the wolves in America's Lakota Wolf Preserve in New Jersey. There I learned a smidgen about their lives and social conduct, heard their goose-bump inducing howls for the first time, and saw with my own eyes the unbelievable emotional and deep link that can form between this stunning creature and humans. Visiting the reserve was the inspiration for the white wolf resurfacing throughout this book.

Last, but hardly least, thank you to my wonderful family for understanding my need to step aside a little in order to write this family history, which had to be written. Your support and your reactions to chapters I occasionally sent out infused me with the energy to keep going and bring you, at last, the family's legacy in its entirety.

Chanochi Zaks (named for Grandfather Hanokh)

Printed in Great Britain
by Amazon

46627817R00219